SLOUCHING
TOWARDS
INNOCENCE

Happy
Birthday
Cory!

Ron
Thomas

SLOUCHING
TOWARDS
INNOCENCE

A Novel

RON NORMAN

[N₁ [O₂ [N₁
CANADA

Library and Archives Canada Cataloguing in Publication

Norman, Ron, 1953–, author
Slouching towards innocence : a novel / Ron Norman.

ISBN 978–1–988098–37–1 (softcover)

I. Title.

PS8627.O7637S56 2017   C813'.6   C2017–904636–5

Printed and bound in Canada on 100% recycled paper.

Now Or Never Publishing
#313, 1255 Seymour Street
Vancouver, British Columbia
Canada V6B 0H1

nonpublishing.com
Fighting Words.

We gratefully acknowledge the support of the Canada Council for the Arts
and the British Columbia Arts Council for our publishing program.

For Joan, Lauren and Julia

"But I don't want to go among mad people," Alice remarked.

"Oh, you can't help that," said the Cat: "we're all mad here. I'm mad. You're mad."

"How do you know I'm mad?" said Alice.

"You must be," said the Cat, "or you wouldn't have come here."

~ *Alice's Adventures in Wonderland*,
Lewis Carroll, 1865

Prologue

TITLE SEQUENCE:

The Bryan Adams song *Can't Stop This Thing We Started* PLAYS OVER a series of election posters with the photos and names of candidates.

1st POSTER: Elect Jeffrey Watling, photo of a wide-eyed man in glasses, late 40s. He looks both surprised and guilty, as if the camera has caught him doing something he shouldn't.

2nd POSTER: Re-elect Mike Visser, photo of a 35-year-old man with a distinct cowlick. The picture of innocence, it could almost be a school photo from Grade 5 that has been photoshopped.

CLOSE ON 3rd Poster: Elect Steven Davis Premier, photo of confident, lightly tanned man in his late 40s, his eyes locked on the camera.

INT. HOTEL ROOM—NIGHT

GRACE DAVIS
47, sits in a chair flipping absent-mindedly through a magazine. She is model-thin, impeccably dressed in a Dior suit, her bronze skin matching her bronze hair. Her son Michael, 17, and daughter Jennifer, 15, sit on the edge of the bed immersed in their smart-phones. The TV is on in the background, tuned to the election coverage. The news anchor is seated at a desk with two doughy, middle-aged political pundits, one on either side of him. In the background is a hotel ballroom, which is decorated with political posters and banners. The Bryan Adams song plays over the loud-speakers. The anchor says they have been told that Premier-elect Davis will take the stage shortly. The anchor adds that this is a

historic night for the United Party as they sweep to power for the
first time and decimate the ranks of the governing Liberals. There
is a sharp knock at the hotel room door and MAURICE LLOYD
enters without waiting for a response. He is about 50, short and
thin with wiry brown hair and gold wire frame glasses.

> LLOYD
> We're just waiting on the Boss before
> we go down. (Pause). He hasn't called
> you, has he?

Grace doesn't look up from flipping the pages of her magazine.

> GRACE
> Lost him again?

> LLOYD
> (nervous smile)
> No, nothing like that. If I know him
> he's probably still campaigning.

INT. HOTEL STORAGE ROOM

SHOT—CLOSEUP of plastic bottles of cleaning supplies on
the top shelf. The Bryan Adams song can be heard in the distance. The shelving is noticeably jarred and one of the bottles
tilts and falls over. A hand abruptly clamps onto the shelf and
the fallen cleaning bottle rolls to the edge, past the hand, and
over. It can be heard crashing onto the floor. SOUND of a
woman MOANING with pleasure.

The CAMERA moves slowly down the shelving to reveal two
people having sex. The male is pressing the female against the
shelving. He is wearing a dark pinstriped suit. A bright blue tie is
flipped over his shoulder. We can't make out who they are. The
moaning gets louder and more rhythmic. The shelf rocks in time

with the moaning. CAMERA PULLS BACK to show PRE-MIER-ELECT STEVEN DAVIS gripping the shelving.

SHOT—FROM BEHIND
Premier-elect's pants are down, his shirt tail covers part of his bare bum. He is having sex with a young woman whose face we glimpse over his shoulder.

INT. HOTEL BALLROOM—UNITED PARTY CELEBRA-TION—NIGHT

(BRYAN ADAMS SONG PLAYS):

SHOT—FROM BEHIND
Premier-elect Davis in his dark pinstriped suit makes a TRIUMPHANT entrance into the hotel ballroom surrounded by a crush of TV cameras and supporters. He wades through the crowd smiling and shaking hands as he goes. Camera follows him closely through the crowd giving sense of claustrophobia, pande-monium and excitement.

CUT TO:
Close-up of Davis from the side. A TV cameraman elbows sup-porters out of the way to get a clear shot of Davis. Davis is in no rush to reach the stage.

CUT TO:
SHOT—ON DAVIS FROM THE FLOOR
Davis is shown through a SMARTPHONE video from the per-spective of a person in the crowd. Davis is partially obscured by the crowd as he moves toward the stage.

CUT TO:
SHOT—ON DAVIS FROM STAGE
Davis finally climbs the stairs to the stage. Camera tracks him from the side as he reaches down with both hands to touch the

outstretched hands of adoring supporters pushed against the front of the stage.

CUT TO:
SHOT showing his family looking out from off stage. Grace Davis looks bored.

SHOT—ON DAVIS FROM IN FRONT OF STAGE
Davis gradually makes his way to the podium. He's smiling, face beaming. The crowd chants, "Dav-is, Dav-is". He waves with one hand. He grabs the podium firmly with both hands and looks out over the crowd, letting the adulation wash over him. Finally he raises his both arms and motions for the chanting to end. The chanting turns to cheering and grows even louder. Again he raises his arms and motions for the applause to end. He does this several times while mouthing the words "Thank you". Eventually it subsides enough for him to speak.

DAVIS

    We did it!

THUNDEROUS applause and shouting. More chants of "Davis, Davis". Davis is forced to wait for the noise to subside.

CUT TO:
SHOT of young woman who was having sex with Davis standing in the crowd in front of him. She is wearing a *Davis for Premier* button. She straightens her blouse.

DAVIS (CONT'D)

    You did it!

MORE APPLAUSE

CUT TO:
MID-SHOT of DAVIS at podium. Camera begins slow movement around Davis in clockwise circle when he starts speaking.

DAVIS

First, I want to thank each and every one of you who worked so hard to make this happen. It is a victory that we all share in . . . a victory made all the sweeter by the fact we have reduced the Liberals to just a handful of seats.

CROWD erupts in APPLAUSE, forcing Davis to stop speaking.

DAVIS (CONT'D)

Over the last decade—the decade of despair—we have seen this magnificent province reduced to a shell of what it once was. Now we have an opportunity to make BC great again. And we will!

CROWD shouts their support, which forces Davis to stop speaking. Camera stops directly behind Davis and shows crowd cheering. Camera begins again when Davis begins speaking.

DAVIS (CONT'D)

We have an opportunity to bring integrity and honesty back into BC government. And we will!

EXTENDED APPLAUSE stops Davis from speaking.

DAVIS (CONT'D)

We have an opportunity to be the most open and transparent government in the world. And we will!

WILD cheering. Davis waits for the cheering to subside before speaking.

> DAVIS (CONT'D)
> We will start by focusing on families,
> because families are the foundation of
> our great province. I want to thank my
> own family . . .

CAMERA stops in front of Davis (where it started).

CROWD again cheers wildly.

CUT TO:
WIDE SHOT of DAVIS from the side and his family in the
background offstage. He motions for them to join him onstage
and they walk out to join him.

> DAVIS (CONT'D)
> I especially want to thank my wife,
> Grace.

CUT TO:
CLOSEUP OF GRACE
She raises her slender hand in acknowledgment and offers an
equally thin smile.

> DAVIS (CONT'D)
> She is my rock and I wouldn't be here
> without her. Can you believe that we
> have been married 24 wonderful years
> today? Yes, tonight is our anniversary!

THUNDEROUS APPLAUSE

CUT TO:
CLOSEUP OF GIRL IN BLOUSE

> DAVIS (CONT'D)
> Honey, Happy Anniversary.

Everyone around the girl is madly cheering except the girl, who is checking her smartphone.

> DAVIS (CONT'D)
> I also want to thank my children . . .

CUT TO:
CLOSEUP OF CHILDREN SMILING AND WAVING

> DAVIS (CONT'D)
> Michael and Jennifer. They were two
> of my best campaign workers. Kids, all
> your hard work paid off!

APPLAUSE

CUT TO:
CLOSEUP of chief of staff MAURICE LLOYD standing with press secretary MATT MCDONAUGH offstage left looking out to DAVIS.

> DAVIS (CONT'D)
> As I said, we will start by focusing on
> families because too many BC fami-
> lies are struggling to get by . . . strug-
> gling just to make their mortgage
> payments . . . and send their kids to
> university. That's because for the last
> 10 years families have been ignored. I
> say no more!

APPLAUSE

> LLOYD
> (staring straight ahead while he talks)
> Is the avail teed up?

MCDONAUGH
(also staring straight ahead)
Yup. Media have all been told. They'll head next door as soon as he's done here.

CUT TO:
SHOT over McDonaugh's shoulder at LLOYD.

LLOYD
How are you going to manage Bev? We shouldn't even let that bitch ask a question, the way she's treated us.

DAVIS (CONT'D)
And we will put an end to the favouritism given to special interest groups, friends and insiders. I say no more!

MCDONAUGH
(laughs)
Freeze her out, you mean?

LLOYD
Yeah. Show her what happens to reporters who fuck us over.

MCDONAUGH
(checks his smartphone, then turns to look at Lloyd with a frown)
You think that's wise?

LLOYD
Sure. It'll set a tone. Make the rest of those assholes think twice.

MCDONAUGH
(turning back to look at Davis)
I don't see how we can ignore her.
The gallery will just defer to her. Then
it'll be worse because we'll look like
we've lost control.

DAVIS continues his speech to his supporters in the background:
Make no mistake—we have our work
cut out for us. But we have a plan. Our
Fresh Start for British Columbia. It's a plan
we laid out for British Columbians over
the last 28 days. A plan that tonight
British Columbians overwhelmingly
endorsed. From Prince George to Port
Alberni . . . from Cranbrook to
Chilliwack . . . from Valemount to
Vancouver . . . British Columbians have
said it's time for a Fresh Start.
And they're right!

LLOYD
Okay. But just make sure you don't
start with her or the whole avail will go
for shit.

MCDONAUGH
Don't worry, White's getting the first
question. I've already talked to him.
He's going to ask if we were surprised
by the margin of victory.

LLOYD
Good. Let Steven know that when you
walk him over. Make sure he says he's
always surprised because he never takes

the voters for granted. Or some shit
like that. And have someone sheepdog
White so he doesn't wander off. Just
like him to decide to take a piss and
miss the start of the avail . . . the lazy
asshole. How does he keep his job?

MCDONAUGH
I swear he's fucking the publisher's
wife.

LLOYD
Be a change from fucking the dog.

MCDONAUGH laughs, steps back and motions to a young
woman standing nearby. He whispers instructions in her ear and
she leaves the backstage area. DAVIS continues in the background:

We will begin delivering that Fresh Start
tomorrow. I will meet with our newly
elected Members of the Legislative
Assembly and ask them to roll up their
sleeves and get right to work. It's what
British Columbians expect. It's why
British Columbians elected us.

MCDONAUGH
(staring at Davis and his family at the podium)
How's Grace?

LLOYD
Better, now the campaign's over.

MCDONAUGH
I still can't believe you kept it together.
I thought the whole election was going

into the ditch after what happened in
Kamloops.

LLOYD

Four years in opposition will make you
do anything. And she didn't put up
with him this long to not be at his side
now that he's finally premier. Okay,
he's almost done. Make sure he doesn't
take any questions on his way to the
avail. I don't want him on Global
tonight pinned down by reporters in a
hotel hallway. He's the next premier of
British Columbia; I want him to fucking well look like it.

MCDONAUGH

Got it.

CUT TO:
CLOSEUP of television screen showing PREMIER–ELECT
DAVIS.

DAVIS

We have an ambitious agenda over the
next 100 days . . . an agenda that will
once again make British Columbia a
land of opportunity for everyone—and
not just for Liberal friends and insiders;
that will once again make British
Columbia a place where our sons and
daughters can live and work and raise a
family; and that will once again make
British Columbia a leader in Canada
and in the world. Thank you!

TITLES END

PART ONE

(MAY 2013)

CHAPTER 1

"WHO YOU PICKING?"

Malcolm was in the staff kitchen studying a sheet of names tacked to the bulletin board with the heading "EDUCATION MINISTER POOL $5" when Gerald Morris ambushed him. They'd met on Malcolm's first day. "I can do your job," Gerald had said. Malcolm immediately disliked him. He disliked him even more when he found out that Gerald was right.

"He used to be in communications," explained Don Henderson, Malcolm's boss. "Light years ago, during the early days of the Liberals' first issues management team—the Policy, Initiatives and Special Services Office, affectionately dubbed "PISSOFF" by the press gallery. Didn't last long."

"PISSOFF or Gerald?"

"Both. His performance review found that his work habits weren't aligned with PISSOFF's goals and objectives. Government-speak for he was lazy," said Don, who like everyone in communications devoured gossip like candy. It was one of the many ways government was a lot like high school—only with politicians instead of teachers.

Gerald was transferred to Municipal Affairs—a ministry backwater—where he planned to keep his head down and do as little as possible for as long as possible.

"Unfortunately for him, Kay Thomas had other ideas," said Don.

Kay was Gerald's com director. Bought out in one of the never-ending rounds of cost-cutting at CanWest before it finally went bankrupt, she landed on her feet in government.

"You would have thought she'd have been happy," Don said. "But Kay is one of those people who's only happy when everyone else is unhappy."

After hearing him whistling cheerily in his cubicle, Kay took a special interest in 'Gerbil', as she took to calling him. At first he resisted, even when she yelled from her office to "shut the fuck up" and later still when she stormed down to his cubicle and threatened to duct tape his balls to his mouth if he even so much as thought about puckering his lips.

"In the end he was no match for Kay," said Don.

Before long he was as grim-faced as the rest, which made Kay smile.

Then, as suddenly as he had come, he was gone. Parachuted out of communications and into a highly prized ministry job in community relations.

"No one knew how he managed it," Don said. "One of the mysteries of the government hiring process."

From there, Gerald drifted through several ministries, never staying long enough for a performance review to catch up with him until he landed in the Ministry of Education, where apparently he figured it was as good a place in government as any to lay up.

When he wasn't outside smoking, Gerald spent a lot of time in the staff room, where he now found Malcolm.

"So?" asked Gerald.

"I haven't decided," Malcolm said.

"Well I have," said Gerald. He waited for Malcolm to ask him who. When it was clear Malcolm wouldn't, he continued: "Ginny Jones will get it. They owe her for co-chairing the campaign. I'd prefer Visser. Nicest politician you'll ever meet."

Malcolm wasn't sure Visser would even be in cabinet. He had lost to Davis in an acrimonious leadership race that was less a campaign than a street fight. On the other hand, they say you should keep your friends close and your enemies closer, so it wasn't implausible that Davis would find a spot for Visser around the cabinet table—where he could keep an eye on him.

"So you've met Visser?" Malcolm couldn't resist tweaking Gerald.

Gerald ignored him: "Whoever gets it, big changes are coming."

Malcolm had to give Gerald that: big changes were coming. The United Party had made it clear it was going to do things differently—and with a lot fewer government workers. With their commanding majority they could do whatever they wanted for the next four years.

"What about your shop?" Gerald asked. "There's been quite an exodus already, so I'm guessing whoever's left is taking their chances."

"I haven't asked," Malcolm said. He hadn't been there long, though long enough to know not to ask. It was a sensitive time: every day a new rumour. The latest was that the UP were going to fire half the communications staff and replace the other half with people who had worked for the party during the election.

"I'm surprised Don's stayed," Gerald said.

Malcolm wasn't. Don was what? 55? 60? What else would he do at his age? Malcolm felt a loyalty to Don because Don had hired him. When Malcolm lost his job at the News Daily, his editor, Tim Matheson, offered to put in a word with Don.

"He owes me," Tim said. "The least he can do is give you an interview."

As it turned out, Tim was doing Don a favour: com shops were desperate for bodies. The UP had been 30 points ahead in the polls for so long that any communications staff who could had already jumped. Those who had remained behind were left to anxiously await their fate, like deckhands on a sinking ship without a lifeboat.

"Every new government guts communications to make room for their own stamp lickers," Don said during the interview. "It's always been that way. So there's no guarantee you'll still be here after the election. Ironic huh? A government job without any security. Still interested?"

Malcolm started two weeks before the writ was dropped, one of the last positions filled before the government hiring freeze snapped into place for the duration of the election. He was assigned to write news releases, and he churned them out at a furious pace. Liberal desperation had soared as their hopes for re-election plummeted, and with each disastrous poll they dumped a truckload of money to try to win back voters: the worse the poll, the bigger the truck. Soon the media wouldn't report on any announcement less than $100 million. By the end, the Liberals could have announced a cure for cancer and the media wouldn't have given it anything more than a sniff.

It seemed like a lifetime ago. Malcolm had been so new he hadn't known that he should feel the uncertainty that others felt. Now he did. The change they'd all been waiting for was here, and though no one knew what it meant, everyone expected the worst.

"The UP won't get rid of him," Malcolm said, feeling a duty to defend Don.

Gerald just smirked.

"Why would they?" Malcolm demanded. "The UP are Liberals in everything but name."

"Don's attached to the old regime. Think Russia in the 1930s—but without the show trials. And he's a com director. That's why I've always kept my head down. Less likely to get it shot off. You'd be wise to do the same."

For the first time in his seven weeks in government Malcolm felt vulnerable.

"Don't look so worried," Gerald said, reading his face. "You'll be fine. You're so new you haven't got any political baggage. Besides, the UP can't get rid of everyone; it would be impossible to fill 200 government communications positions— even if they cut half the jobs."

When Malcolm got back to his cubicle a phone message blinked at him impatiently. It was from a Jordan Leopold in Premier-elect Steven Davis's office. He wanted Malcolm to call him right away. Malcolm thought it must be a mistake. He listened to the message again. It wasn't. He took a deep breath and dialled. Jordan picked up the phone on the first ring.

"Malcolm," he said with the warmth of an old friend. "Thanks for getting back to me. I'm wondering if we can get together? Say this afternoon? One o'clock?"

"Sure," Malcolm said. "Can you tell what it's about?"

"Ahh . . . I'll save it for when we meet. So one o'clock. Oh, we're on the third floor of the Sussex building on Douglas. Room 340. Oh, and don't say anything to anyone, okay? See you at one."

Leopold hung up so abruptly Malcolm thought the phone had gone dead. It was several seconds before he carefully placed the receiver back in its cradle. In the cubicle behind him he could hear Mackin on the phone arguing. Likely his wife. Mackin was going through a messy divorce. The house was up for sale, but nothing was moving. With the fragile economy, and now public workers uncertain about their future, no one was in any mood to buy. Neither Mackin nor his wife could afford to move out, so his wife had started inviting her boyfriend to stay the night. Talk about uncomfortable.

Malcolm got up and went to Don's office. The door was open and Don was on the phone. He was facing the door, his feet on the edge of the desk, his chair propped against the wall behind him. He signalled for Malcolm to sit in one of the chairs by his desk.

On the wall behind Don was a photo gallery; Don called it his "wall of shame". Don was in every photo. The photo at the centre was Don with former Premier Gene Pritchitt. Taken on a golf course. It was sunny, and they both wore short-sleeve polo shirts and squinted into the glare. Pritchitt will have lots of time to golf now. Beside that was Don with Education Minister Jim Beebe—or former education minister. He'll have more time for golfing, too. Don hadn't bothered to remove them. Like he was daring the UP to fire him. There were also a few with local sports celebrities: Don with Rich Harden, in his first stint with the As. Don with Trevor Linden, both dressed in a shirt and tie. Linden, his playing days over, looked trim in his hand-tailored suit and designer glasses. Don looking like a former reporter: a crumpled sports coat one size too big and baggy pleated pants that bunched around the ankles. Other photos Malcolm didn't recognize. On the desk near the phone sat two framed photos of a boy and a girl and a smaller framed photo, the colours washed out, of Don looking much younger and slimmer, his arm around a woman.

Don hung up the phone, put his feet down.

"What's up?"

"I just got a call from Steven Davis's office. Somebody named Jordan Leopold wants to meet with me. Do you know him?"

"Never heard of him. He's probably part of the transition team. What's he want?"

"He didn't say. I thought you might know."

Don leaned back in this chair and slowly shook his head. "Nope." He shrugged: "But then I'm probably the last one they'd tell."

"So you don't know if anyone else is meeting with him?"

"No, but you could ask around."

"He told me not to tell anyone."

"Then don't ask around."

"Is that usual? To ask me to keep it quiet?"

"There's no 'usual' right now Malcolm. Everything is new. They're making it up as they go along. When the Liberals got in, it took them nearly a year to put together their communications structure. I wasn't here, but I was told people pretty much downed tools and waited. The UP don't have that luxury because they've committed to a hundred-day action plan. They'll need communications support for that."

"So why would they want to see *me*?"

"Who knows? But don't worry—they're not going to fire you. Not today anyway. It's too early. The election was only last week. Tomorrow maybe. I'm joking, I'm joking. They'll fire me long before they get to you—not that I think they'll get to you. And if they do, there's a whole process they have to follow. There'll be a Public Service Agency counsellor on hand to make sure you don't steal any paper clips on your way out. One thing's for certain: they won't invite you to meet with the premier's staff at their office."

All you could say about the office in the Sussex building was that it was clean and bright. Very bright. The door entered into a reception area where a young woman sat behind an oversized wood-grain laminate desk with shiny silver metal legs. On the desk were a telephone and computer—nothing else. Two worn black office chairs were pushed against one wall. Above the chairs, someone had tacked the front pages of newspapers from the morning after the election. The Vancouver Sun showed a grinning Steven Davis with the headline: UP SWEEPS TO HISTORIC VICTORY. The tabloid Province paper shouted: UP WINS! with a photo of Davis, arms raised, standing with his wife, while the more sedate Victoria News Daily mused: UP WIN BRINGS FRESH START.

At the back of the room two doors presumably led to offices. Both doors were closed. The reception area was spartan and appeared even more so because the covers from the fluorescent ceiling lights were missing.

The receptionist told Malcolm that Leopold would be with him shortly and asked him to take a seat. A few minutes later one of the doors at the back of the room opened and a man about 25 years old came out. He was tall and thin with freshly styled, close-cropped black hair and wearing a tight-fitting Armani suit, white shirt and tie. He could have stepped straight out of an Esquire ad. He moved easily around the reception desk and reached out his hand to Malcolm.

"Malcolm. Thanks for coming. Jordan Leopold."

Leopold's office was even more barren than the reception area, with only a desk, chair, computer and printer.

"Let me get a chair for you," Leopold said, and he disappeared out the door and returned with one of the black office chairs from the reception area. "Here you go," he said. He then rolled his chair around to the front of the desk and sat in it so his knees were nearly touching Malcolm's.

"I'm short on time so I'll get right to why I asked to meet with you. I'm responsible for filling some of the staff positions in the premier's office. We think you're a perfect fit for an opening we have and we want you to join our team."

Outwardly, Malcolm's expression remained unchanged; inwardly he felt like he had been hit by a truck. He was still trying to clear his head when Leopold continued.

"The position is with our communications team, reporting to the communications director. I don't have a formal job description yet, but I do have an org chart and a list of some of the responsibilities."

He got up and went around to his desk where he leaned over and stared at the computer screen. At the same time he placed his hand over the computer mouse, lifting it gently then slapping it noisily on the desktop surface, as if it were mildly misbehaving. After several clicks, the printer whirred to life and spat out a single, thin sheet of paper. Leopold leaned across his desk and offered it to Malcolm.

"These duties might change once the team is in place. You'll see that the salary is generous and certainly an improvement over what you are getting at the Ministry of Education. Mind you, you will still be part of the public service but as an order-in-council appointment."

Leopold remained standing behind his desk.

"I know all this seems rushed, but we've actually been working on this transition for a while. I've personally been working eighteen-hour days, seven days a week for months now. And there was that little thing called an election thrown in that had us all scrambling."

Malcolm didn't know what to say, which Leopold seemed to take as a positive sign.

"I know you'll want to think about this, but I have to fill this position as soon as possible so I need you to let me know your decision by the end of today. Give me a call back at this number."

He came around the desk and handed Malcolm a card.

"We won't have government offices until after the swearing in. This"—he waved his hand around the room—"is really just somewhere to hire staff. I'm handling everything on my cell, so if I don't answer, leave a message. I'm very good about returning calls. Any questions?"

"How did you get my name?" Malcolm asked weakly.

Leopold smiled, his teeth gleaming white, his pink gums exposed. "Let me just say that you came highly recommended." Then he leaned forward confidingly so that Malcolm could smell his cologne, which reminded him of the mango and ginger scented organic cleaner that Rachel used in their bathroom: "If you know what I mean."

Malcolm had no idea what he meant, but was reluctant to admit as much. An electronic beep sounded and Leopold glanced at his watch—a great glittering glob of glass, dials, and metal—and pressed one of the many knobs protruding from it, then stuck out his hand.

"I've got to be somewhere else at 1:45. I don't want to rush you, but if you don't have any other questions . . ."

"No, no. No more questions," Malcolm said, rising and clumsily shaking the outstretched hand. "Uh, thanks. Thanks very much."

Leopold walked Malcolm through the reception area. "It must feel good to be back."

Like much of the interview, Malcolm didn't know what to make of this statement so he gave a single silent nod, more an acknowledgement than an affirmation.

At the door, Leopold put his hand on Malcolm's shoulder. "Really looking forward to you joining us."

The end of the day didn't leave Malcolm much time. It was already 1:30. He felt flattered that the newly elected premier wanted to hire him, but he had one glaring concern: Rachel. He needed to talk to her. Then again why should he talk to her? He knew what she would say: you can do better. Besides, was she in any position to offer advice? She didn't have any idea about government or what he did. And it was his career. His decision. Did she ask him when she started working at that NGO? Making next to nothing? He thought about what he would do if he wasn't living with Rachel. The answer was easy: he'd take the job.

The more he thought about it, the more Malcolm realized he would be crazy not to accept. He would be turning his back on a full-time permanent job, and for what? He couldn't even be sure about his job in Education. For all he knew, he could be gone tomorrow. Then again Leopold had said he had come highly recommended. Surely, they wouldn't fire him if he said no. Would they? He knew what Adam would tell him: take the money. Adam was all about the money. It was more money—a lot more money. He thought about what Gerald had said. Keep your head down and you won't get it shot off. But he was never one to play it safe. No risk, no reward. He'd never liked Gerald.

CHAPTER 2

"SO YOU'RE NOT from the Island, then?" asked Beth in a tone that suggested there were only two kinds of people: those who were from Vancouver Island and those who weren't. "Originally, I mean," as if she needed to be perfectly clear.

Malcolm had forgotten they had invited Beth and Rob for dinner until he walked in the door from work and found the table set for four and Rachel busy in the kitchen tearing lettuce. Malcolm and Rachel had met Beth just once before, at the News Daily Christmas party—his first and last. She had arrived late and left early, and was in a foul mood the whole time. Rob had spent most of the following week apologizing for her.

"Vancouver," Malcolm said.

"I'm from the Cariboo . . . originally," Rachel said. The archness of the comment was lost on Beth.

"I was born and raised in Victoria," Beth said proudly, leaving Malcolm to suspect that she had only posed the question as an excuse to talk about herself.

"One of those Vancouver Islanders who've never left the Island," Rob added.

"Why go anywhere else when you're already living in paradise?" Beth asked. "Besides, my family and friends are all on the Island."

She spent the next ten minutes telling them about summers at the cottage on Shawnigan Lake with all of the other Islanders who never left, and winters skiing Mount Washington. By the time Beth had moved on to telling them about growing up in Mount Doug, Malcolm was sure she was one of those who loved to make wry comments about her Island-centric life on Facebook and Instagram: 'Ferries cancelled due to high winds; mainland cut off from island'. Not the island cut off from the mainland. And though she had lived in Victoria all her life, and Victoria had been the capital and seat of the provincial government for more than 150 years, she had no idea how government actually worked.

"So, Malcolm, Rob says you got laid off at the paper," Beth said when she finally took a break from talking about herself. "Have you got another job yet?"

"I told you," Rob said, sounding mildly exasperated. "Malcolm's working for the provincial government."

"What do you do?" Beth asked.

"Not much right now," Malcolm said. "We're just waiting for the cabinet to be sworn in."

"He's in the Education Ministry," Rachel explained, as if Malcolm had misunderstood the question.

"Education?" Beth asked. "Don't you have to be a teacher for that?"

"Nope," Malcolm said. "In fact, they say it's best if I don't know anything about what I'm writing about. That way I'll come at it with fresh eyes and won't get caught up with all the technical jargon. Kinda like reporting."

"Ha, ha," Rob said.

"But what do you actually do?"

"Well, before the election they had me writing news releases—"

"He was the one responsible for flooding my inbox," laughed Rob.

"—but I'm supposed to do a bit of everything: think up questions the media might ask the minister and then get the answers to those questions from ministry staff, post Facebook items, write speeches, newsletters, blogs. Track down information for media—"

"He's a spin doctor," interjected Rob, with a grin that slashed menacingly across his face.

"It's not spin," Malcolm said. Then turning to Beth: "It's communications. I present facts that the public or media might not know. You'd be surprised at all of the things the Ministry of Education does. I know I was."

"But you don't put out any bad news," said Rob. "Right?" It really wasn't a question and Rob wasn't looking for an answer. "So you only give part of the story. Not the whole story."

"Absolutely right; it is only part of the story. But it's the part of the story that people often don't hear. We're just trying to provide some balance, let people know about government programs and services that are available."

"We?" asked Rob. "You've only worked there two months and you're already spouting the party line."

This was new for Malcolm. He was used to sparring with Rob, but had been secure in knowing that while they didn't always agree, they were on the same side; now he felt squarely in the other corner—and he didn't like it, so he decided it was time to move the conversation on.

"Yeah, yeah. But I do have a funny story for you," he said.

He got up and went over to the stereo, turned it on and flicked easily through the playlist until he came to Great Lake Swimmers' Ongiara album. 'Your Rocky Spine' started playing.

"I never told you about the time I wrote my first news release."

"Is this going to be as dull as it sounds?" asked Rob, only half-teasing.

Malcolm ignored the jibe.

"Guess how many people had to approve it?"

Rob shrugged.

"Six!"

"No way!" Rob laughed.

"Six!" Malcolm repeated. "And that didn't count the minister and his staff."

"Well at least someone reads your stuff," said Rob. "I've had my stories go right into print without anyone looking at them."

Malcolm met Rob Ryland a year ago when he was an intern at the News Daily. His first assignment was doing "streeters". He hated it. He had to stand on a busy sidewalk and ask people the question of the day. "Do you support amalgamating Greater Victoria's thirteen municipalities?" "Should the NHL ban fighting? "Are ferry fares too high?" People never wanted to stop and those who did were more than likely certifiable. Like "George G. Gooey" who wouldn't quit talking and followed him back to the paper and waited outside for him until he finally had to call security. Even worse was doing streeters in the rain. With his notebook turning to a soggy pulp and his waterlogged pen refusing to write, he would stand slump-shouldered, rain dripping from his nose, sure that this wasn't how Anderson Cooper got his start.

Then his fortunes changed. The legislature hadn't been sitting for months, so the paper pulled Rob back from the press gallery to do a series on First Nations politics. Rob wasn't happy about it and asked for some research help. He got Malcolm. Malcolm and Rob hit it off immediately. Malcolm supposed that Rob saw him as a younger version of himself.

Before long, Rob was sharing his byline with Malcolm. Their series was so successful that when Malcolm's internship ended the News Daily hired him fulltime. Malcolm quickly earned a reputation for being calm under pressure. No matter how tight the deadline or how manic the situation, he kept his cool and remained clear-headed—"delivering the goods," as his editor said with satisfaction. Though in the end it didn't help him keep his job during the next round of cutbacks. Union seniority trumped talent and hard work every time.

Rob had a habit of reminiscing about "the golden age" of newspapers, "when there were copy editors, and reporters could write 100 inches and get it in print." No longer. Copy editors were made redundant in one of the previous rounds of bargaining and in-depth stories had been swapped for top 10 lists in a cynical bid to boost online page views.

"Blame the Internet," Rob said. "It started with Craigslist. Craigslist killed the classifieds. When I first came to the News Daily, classifieds alone could support all of the operating costs of the paper. Now they're lucky to cover the pencils."

It wasn't just classifieds that evaporated. As more readers started to get their news online, ad revenue shrank—and with it the news hole. Papers were smaller. The News Daily eliminated the Monday edition to cut costs; now carriers complained the Tuesday paper was so light they couldn't throw it onto porches.

It was made worse by the revolving door of owners, each of whom issued a prepared statement pledging to restore the paper to its former glory and then promptly introduced tough "restructuring" measures that pitched the paper into a further spiral downward.

Employee buyouts were the favourite form of restructuring. Rob, like many of the long-time reporters, talked about taking a buyout and writing "The Great Canadian Novel". He even went so far as to make an informal inquiry by going directly to the newly appointed publisher.

"No can do," said the publisher, a former executive from Netscape that reporters were all calling The Mad Hatter. "The editorial side is so skeletal we can't afford to lose anyone."

In fact, with the imminent launch of another strategic plan that was again guaranteed to turn things around—this one called "Digital Now"—they would need all the reporters they had, and need all of them "giving 120 per cent".

"I wonder if this is what he did at Netscape?" Rob joked with Malcolm later over a beer. "I can see how all that hands-on experience with an obsolete product makes him the perfect fit as a newspaper publisher. Fucking shoot me now. I get depressed talking about it."

But Malcolm knew that Rob never really wanted to leave; he loved being a political reporter too much, though it hadn't always been that way. He had started out on the police beat.

"I was paid to write about gangs and murder," he said, "because I couldn't write well enough to do anything else." Self-deprecating and untrue, but a good set-up line. "The legislature was a good fit," he continued, "because everyone knows politicians get away with murder." Ta-dum. That always got a chuckle.

Still, as Rob was fond of repeating, he was better off than Bev Hayden: "She went from being a fashion reporter one day to covering the leg the next . . . from the catwalk to catcalling."

Truth was, Rob was a natural reporter and a great writer, and too good to leave on the police beat, so they shifted him first to the city desk and then to the press gallery where he'd been for twenty years.

"Being a political reporter is no different than being a baseball reporter," he told Malcolm one day in the car as they drove down an unpaved road pitted with potholes on the north Island trying to find a remote First Nations village. "Baseball is all about strategy and timing . . . knowing when to pinch hit . . . when to go for the extra base . . . when to pull a pitcher. Hell, the strategy in baseball changes from pitch to pitch—that's why most managers are calling pitches from the dugout rather than letting catchers do it. Politics is the same: strategy and timing. It's just played out over four years instead of nine innings."

"But don't you just get superficial stories that way?" asked Malcolm, fresh out of journalism school where such debates were daily grist. "You focus too much on polling and winning, instead of on policy and governing . . . on the battles instead of on what they are fighting about."

"Politics is all about winning and losing—just like baseball," said Rob. "You can have the best coaching philosophy in the world, but if you don't win you won't be coaching for long. And you can have the best policies in the world, but if you don't win the election and form government, they will never see the light of day."

"So are you two going to get married?" Beth asked during a lull in the conversation.

"Nice one, Beth," said Rob.

"Well, it's a natural question. How long have you been together?"

Malcolm looked at Rachel.

"Twenty-six months," said Rachel.

"But who's counting?" laughed Rob.

Rachel frowned.

"We haven't actually talked about it," said Malcolm, hoping to put an end to the conversation.

"You haven't?" Beth asked.

"We like living together," said Rachel, "so what's to talk about? We don't need to be married to have a committed relationship. In fact, sometimes marriage just changes everything."

"You mean things get worse?" asked Beth in a feisty tone. "What do you think Rob? Did things get worse for us after we got married?"

Rob had the look of a man who wished he was someplace else.

"Gee, who can remember that far back?" he laughed while his thumb dug into the label on his beer bottle. Malcolm wondered if Beth was always this combative.

"I'm not saying marriage changes everyone," said Rachel, her voice rising. "I'm just saying that marriage isn't for everyone."

"Malcolm, what do you think?" asked Beth.

"I don't know," said Malcolm slowly and hesitantly.

"You're putting him on the spot," said Rob who was obviously voicing his own feelings. "Be nice."

"It's alright," said Malcolm. "I guess I always thought I'd get married, but I hadn't really thought about when."

"Well," said Beth, "Two-and-a-half years—"

"Twenty-six months," Rachel corrected.

"Twenty-six months," repeated Beth, "is plenty of time to decide if you want to spend the rest of your lives together."

"What makes you think we're not going to spend the rest of our lives together?" asked Rachel.

"But you've never talked about it," said Beth.

"Beth, I'm only twenty-four and Malcolm just turned twenty-five."

"I'd already had Matthew and Sarah when I was your age."

"You make it sound like there's a deadline."

"Can I give you a hand with anything?" asked Rob, laughing nervously. "Malcolm?" He turned to look directly at Malcolm.

Malcolm was standing by the stereo, as if enlisting support from the Swimmers's Tony Dekker, who in his floating falsetto was extolling the virtues of being part of a large family. He felt he had to say something to change the conversation.

"I got a new job today," he said.

This wasn't how he had planned to tell Rachel. He had wanted to tell her as soon as he got home, but she'd been preoccupied with dinner. He thought he would tell her after Rob and

Beth left, but with Rachel and Beth disagreeing, now seemed as good a time as any.

"What?" said Rachel a little too loudly. "You never told me."

"No," said Malcolm defensively. "It came up kind of quickly."

"I'll say," said Rachel, still feeling quarrelsome.

"So what's the job?" asked Beth.

"It's in the premier's office. With his communications team."

"What?" It was Rob's turn to be surprised. "How did that happen?"

"I don't know exactly. I got a call at work and a guy on the premier's transition team asked to meet with me and he offered me a job. I report to the premier's director of communications."

"You took it?" asked Rachel.

"He needed to know by the end of the work day," Malcolm said apologetically. He'd known this wasn't going to be easy—that's why he had wanted to tell Rachel on his own.

"You could have called me," Rachel said, sounding more hurt than angry.

"Rob never tells me anything," said Beth with a hint of sympathy and feeling a newfound kinship with Rachel. "I'm used to it."

"I don't want to get used to it," Rachel said, and she got up and went into the kitchen where she banged cupboards in noisy preparation for dinner, though Malcolm was sure there wasn't anything more to do.

"I'll be right back," said Malcolm and he moved quickly toward the kitchen.

"Smart boy," said Rob with a supportive smile. "Take it from someone who knows." Now it was Beth's turn to frown.

"Hey," Malcolm said softly while gently touching Rachel's shoulder. Rachel pulled her shoulder away so his hand was left stranded in mid-air.

Rachel opened the oven door and leaned down to inspect the lasagna. She grabbed a pair of oven mitts from the counter and lifted the lasagna out of the oven. She went to put it on the counter but realized she didn't have a hot pad. She stood for a few seconds and then turned toward Malcolm.

"Can you get a hot pad out for me?" she asked.

"Only if you promise to hear me out."

"Malcolm!"

"Is everything OK out there?" asked Beth from the living room.

"We're fine," said Malcolm reassuringly.

"We're *not* fine," yelled Rachel.

There was silence as they stood facing each other.

"It's just a job," said Malcolm.

"Working for Steven Davis."

"That's a good thing."

"Is it?"

"Yes it is. For one thing, it means a lot more money."

"Malcolm, why is it always about money with you."

"I don't think that's fair. I'm going to be doing communications, just like I do now. Only I will be getting paid more to do it. What's wrong with that? I don't get you."

"You don't get *me*?"

She put the lasagna pan on the stovetop and moved past Malcolm for a hot pad.

"Maybe we should talk about this later," Malcolm suggested.

"Fine with me. I'm not the one who raised it and I'm not the one who followed me into the kitchen to talk about it."

Malcolm didn't say anything. He stood a moment before turning and going back into the living room. The apartment was small enough that Malcolm knew Rob and Beth had heard every word.

"Sorry about that," he said.

"No problem," said Rob a little too quickly.

"Rob and I always fight in front of our friends," said Beth, though Malcolm wasn't quite sure if she was being reassuring or critical.

Dinner went as well as could be expected, meaning there were no more fights or arguments. Malcolm tried to carry on as if nothing had happened, but Rachel wouldn't cooperate. She was silent for the most part and terse when she wasn't. Beth seemed pleased with herself while Rob was just awkward. Mercifully, the evening ended early.

While Beth was putting on her coat and telling Rachel that they would have to return the favour, Rob held Malcolm back and said in a half-whisper: "I won't ask you any more about you-know-what, but we need to go for coffee so you can fill me in. I'll call you." He gave Malcolm a supportive slap on the shoulder.

Rachel cleaned up the kitchen in silence. Malcolm sat at the kitchen table and watched her.

"Sorry I didn't tell you about the job," said Malcolm.

"I don't want to talk about it," said Rachel, wiping the stovetop with a dishrag. She didn't sound angry, just tired.

"But you said we'd talk about it later."

"Yes. Just not tonight."

"When then?"

She turned to Malcolm.

"Malcolm, I'm tired. I want to go to bed. I don't want to talk about this now. I don't know when we will talk about it. Tomorrow maybe. It depends on how I feel."

Malcolm couldn't remember the last time they had fought.

"I just don't understand what you've got against me making more money."

"It's not about the money. Don't you get that? It's the fact that money is so important to you. It didn't used to be."

She was right: Malcolm hadn't gone into journalism for the money. But that was before journalism went in the tank and he was unemployed. He was lucky to have a job. But she would never understand that because she never worried about that.

"I just don't know why you'd take a job working for some-one like Davis."

So that was it. Throughout the election Rachel had posted pieces critical of Davis on her Facebook page—mostly from CBC and The Tyee. About how one or another of the companies he owned was unfair to its employees or mistreated workers at its factories in China or hired scab labour at its plants in the U.S.

"I'm just doing communications for him. That's all. He's the premier of British Columbia, elected by a majority of voters—"

"Well, I wasn't one of them."

Malcolm wanted to say, "I never would have guessed," but knew better.

"Did you vote for him?" she asked.

"Rachel, what has that to do with anything? The point I was trying to make is that he's the premier and he was elected by a majority of British Columbians. I don't think it's too much of a stretch to say that I'm working for them."

"Oh fuck off, Malcolm. That's such bullshit. Why can't you just admit you voted for him?"

"Okay, I did vote for him. Happy now?"

Rachel didn't say anything.

"Is that what this is about? You're mad because I voted for Davis?"

"Yes . . . no . . . I don't know." Rachel was suddenly subdued. She leaned against the stove as if she was exhausted. "I worry about you."

He was pleased at that.

"Well don't worry."

"I don't like the idea of you working for him. He's so . . . sleazy."

Silence.

"What do you want me to do? Do you want me to quit? I will."

He didn't believe she would ask him to quit.

"You still don't get it." She was frustrated. "It's not what I want; it's what you want." Her voice fell. "And what you want is different than what I want."

Rachel went to bed while Malcolm consoled himself with a beer, then another beer. By the time he climbed into bed he was drunk and he couldn't tell if Rachel was asleep or awake.

CHAPTER 3

JAMES BAY COFFEE and Books had a lived-in feel, partly because of the used books that lined the wood-panelled walls and partly because of its well-worn couches, tables and chairs tucked into scuffed corners and nicked crannies on two levels of the 1920s storefront. It attracted mostly people from the neighbourhood: older men with frayed, greying goatees and hair the texture of straw, wearing T-shirts, flannel jackets and jeans; middle-aged women in bulky wool sweaters, anoraks and hikers; twentysome-things, some in dreads, who never travelled alone and carried guitars and longboards; young moms in vegan Toms and colour-ful tattoos pushing oversized strollers. Paintings by local artists dotted the walls and Scrabble boards lay piled on a table by the window. If it were a car, James Bay Coffee and Books would be a 1996 Chevy Cavalier in need of new springs. Located mere blocks from the legislature, it might as well have been a continent away because no political types ever visited it, choosing instead to stop at the trendy Discovery Café, the uber-corporate Starbucks or the aptly named Serious Coffee. It was precisely for that reason that Rob thought it was a good place to meet Malcolm the morning after the dinner party.

"So tell me about your job," Rob said. "I couldn't very well ask you about it last night."

"Yeah, Rachel was pretty upset. She was still mad this morn-ing. Never said a word to me."

Rob shrugged. "She'll come around."

"I don't know. The only other time we had a big fight was when we were first dating. She wouldn't take my calls for a week."

"Give it some time. So when do you start?"

"Today. They gave me the morning to clean out my desk."

"Wow. That's fast."

"I've got a feeling it's just a sign of things to come."

"Where's your office?"

"In the legislature."

"Don't tell me you're in the West Annex."

"The West Annex?"

"The premier's office is in the West Annex. And the cabinet office. The chief of staff has an office there along with some other staff. I'm not sure if all the premier's staff are there. I've only been as far as the reception area; reporters aren't allowed any further than that."

"They just gave me a room number and told me to show up after lunch. I guess I'll be able to let you know this afternoon."

"We'll still be good—no matter what happens—right?"

"What do you mean? Why wouldn't we be?"

"Well, it can get pretty—" he paused while he searched for the right word "—intense at times around here; feelings can run high. I don't want that to happen with you and me."

"It won't be from my end," Malcolm said.

"You say that now," Rob said. "But I know best friends who stopped speaking to each other. I just want to make sure that doesn't happen with us. That doesn't mean I'll be going easy on you or your new boss . . ."

"I wouldn't expect anything else," said Malcolm.

"And if you've got any brown envelopes lying around . . ."

"You'll be the first number on my speed dial."

"That's what I like to hear."

"Hey, I've got a question for you: you didn't have anything to do with me getting this job, did you?"

"Me?"

"Yeah, they said I came highly recommended and I thought maybe it was you."

"No, not me," Rob said. "I know Davis well enough from his days as a Liberal cabinet minister, before he jumped to the UP. But we were never close. He was always stand-offish with the gallery, as if mixing with reporters was beneath him. Mind you, if he'd asked, I would have told him you were too good for him."

"Thanks. I wonder who it was?"

"Does it matter?"

"Not really. I was just curious."

Rob sipped his coffee.

"A word of advice—as a friend and someone who has covered more than his share of politics: watch your back. No matter what they say, no matter how nice they seem, these people are not your friends."

"Come on," Malcolm grinned.

"In politics, everyone is your friend, which is the same as no one is your friend. If it comes to throwing you under the bus they won't think twice. In fact, they'll climb behind the wheel."

Malcolm sat back and gave Rob a questioning look.

"I've seen it happen," Rob said.

"All I'm going to be doing is talking about all the good things government does for its citizens."

"Wonderful. Keep that outlook."

"Why wouldn't I?"

Rob shrugged.

"Politics changes people. Power changes people."

"Not me."

Malcolm had been in the legislature only once before, during summer holidays with his family. He was eight and his mother had insisted on taking an excruciatingly boring guided tour, so they had joined a group of Japanese tourists who kept asking to get their photos taken with him. It was awful. The best part was the enormous urinals that were taller than him. It was like they had been built for giants, water gushing down the white porcelain from over his head. Of course, his brother Adam had to ruin it by shoving him as he was taking a leak so that he spent the rest of the afternoon sulking around the Royal B.C. Museum trying to hide his soaked pants while Adam hissed in his ear that he looked like he'd pissed himself. Even the museum's giant hairy mammoth couldn't cheer him up.

Malcolm climbed the wide steps to the legislature's main entrance. Inside, the security office was on his right immediately opposite the information desk. Malcolm stood in the cramped office a moment or two before a guard came out of the back room.

"I was told to come here and get a pass," Malcolm said.

"A visitor's pass?" asked the guard.

"They didn't say. I'll be working here." Malcolm felt good saying that, then just for good measure added: "In the premier's office."

"What's your name?"

"Malcolm. Malcolm Bidwell."

The guard retreated to the back room and returned with a clipboard. She ran her finger slowly down the clipboard until she came to a stop.

"Malcolm Bidwell? Here you are." She looked up. "I'll need to take your photo."

Malcolm followed her into the back room where she pulled down a projector screen attached to the wall.

"If you will take off your coat and stand on the 'X', I'll get your picture."

A few minutes later the guard handed Malcolm his electronic security pass with his photo on the front. The image was blurry and the colour was off. He looked 40 years old.

"I'm supposed to meet someone in room 108," Malcolm said. "Can you tell me how to get there?

"Out the door, turn right, then right again and go until you come to the rotunda. Go through the rotunda and on the far side on the left in the corner are some stairs leading down to the first floor. Room 108 is just down the hall from there. Can't miss it."

"Is it in the West Annex?"

"No."

Malcolm couldn't help but feel disappointed.

The legislature was silent except for the soft echo of Malcolm's footfall on the gleaming Italian marble. In the hollow distance a door slammed. From above, airy voices cascaded down the sweeping staircases. A square of sunlight reflected off an ornate column at the edge of the expansive, empty rotunda; overhead, the copper-domed roof soared eight stories. Malcolm felt overcome by a sense of grace. It wouldn't last. Any moment now the sedate century-old granite building and its extensive grounds would be under siege from hordes of scuttling visitors.

Tourist season had been in full force since the first cruise ship docked at Ogden Point a month ago and disgorged thousands upon thousands of smartphone-clutching visitors into downtown Victoria. Now, every day the city faced a fresh onslaught. Under a canopy of flowering Japanese cherry trees lining Menzies Street immediately beside the legislature, the horse-drawn carriage tour drivers drove their huge Percherons, stamping and snorting in the dappled afternoon sun. Along the harbourfront causeway at the foot of the legislature, a shaggy one-man band stroked his foot-long beard and lifted his soft felt hat in grateful response to the warm applause from an appreciative audience; nearby a bagpiper in full Scottish regalia breathed noisy life into his instrument; while on the street above people rushed by on their way back to work without giving a second glance to the man playing Bach's Sonata No. 1 in G minor on his violin and dressed as Darth Vader. All around, artisans and artists of every description had spread their blankets and erected kiosks on which to display their work. There were carvers and jewellers, charcoal portrait artists and watercolour landscape painters, one fellow with a respirator and spray cans and another with safety goggles, metal tubing and a blow torch. In the centre a juggler drew gasps from overflowing crowds as he tossed his flaming kerosene-soaked batons high into the air while perched precariously atop a unicycle. On the water, jolly miniature ferries were loading up with passengers before casting off on their tours of the Inner Harbour and Gorge water-way. Up Government Street, merchants had wheeled out hangars of thin T-shirts and set up tables of imported souvenirs as music blasted from bookshelf speakers perched above their open door-ways. The carnival-like atmosphere that surrounded the legisla-ture made it seem less like a House of Parliament and more like a midway at a summer fair.

Malcolm got as far as the stairs and a door marked *No Public Access*. He twisted the handle and pushed. The door was locked. He tried it again. Nothing. He located the electronic pad on the wall just above the door handle, retrieved the security pass from his pocket and placed it against the pad. The pad's red light turned green and he heard a distinct "click". Malcolm turned the handle and pushed the door; it opened. At the bottom of the stairs he came to a narrow, windowless corridor bathed in a dim ochre light; exposed insulated duct pipes made the low ceiling seem even lower. Did the guard say right or left? He chose right. Walking past several closed office doors, he didn't see 108. The toneless pale brick walls absorbed the rhythm of his shoes and the thick, stale air stuck in the back of his throat like milk gone bad. He continued until he came to a second locked door. Using his pass to open it, he found himself in another long, windowless corridor with offices on his left and what looked like utility rooms on his right. He went until he came to another corridor on his right and took that. He ducked his head as he went through a low doorway and walked until he came to yet another corridor that seemed to run parallel to the first corridor. By now he was feeling a bit lost and slightly claustrophobic. Just then a woman emerged from a door down the corridor and came toward him.

"Excuse me," Malcolm said as she approached. "I'm trying to find room 108 . . ."

"108? I think that's where I'm going." She started to walk back the way Malcolm had come. She hadn't offered to show Malcolm the way, but Malcolm took her comment as a positive sign and hurried to catch up.

"I don't know any of the room numbers," the woman confided when Malcolm was alongside her. She was in her twenties and wore a tight, short black skirt and even tighter white blouse where a tug-of-war was being played out between a small white button and her breasts, threatening to lay bare an already half-exposed lace bra. "But I think we are in room 108 or pretty close. Who are you looking for?"

Malcolm looked at his notebook. "Jarrod Tapscott," he said as if he was reading the name for the first time. Of course, it wasn't the first time. Malcolm had repeated the name over and over, both in his mind and out loud. He had even gone so far as to Google Jarrod Tapscott, with mixed results. He had turned up a few United Party web pages where Jarrod Tapscott was mentioned, but no photos and little personal information. Piecing together bits and pieces from Facebook, LinkedIn and other websites, Malcolm learned that Jarrod Tapscott was originally from Kelowna and had graduated from Queen's University with a major in political science and a minor in history. From what Malcolm gathered, Tapscott was also in his twenties—young to be the premier's director of communications—and Malcolm had wondered whether he had the right Jarrod Tapscott. It was unlike Malcolm to feign a lapse of memory, but he couldn't help feeling that his easy recollection of Jarrod Tapscott's name would be a rebuke to this woman who couldn't even remember the number of the room where she worked.

"Oh, Jarrod. Yes, yes. I'll take you there, though I'm not sure he's back from Vancouver yet."

"Oh," said Malcolm. "Well, I was told to meet with him this afternoon."

The woman stopped and looked Malcolm up and down. "Who are you?"

"Malcolm Bidwell."

"Are you coming to work with us?"

"I'm going to work on the premier's communications team."

"Good," she said with genuine enthusiasm. "That means we'll be seeing a lot of each other." She started walking again and Malcolm wasn't quite sure what to make of her last statement.

"So you work with Jarrod?" he asked.

"Well, I worked with him before he became communications director. He was my boss: head of caucus research. You don't look familiar. Are you from Saskatchewan? I hear they've hired all sorts of Tories from Saskatchewan."

"No, not me. I grew up in Vancouver but I've been living in Victoria for the last year."

"Funny. I haven't seen you around. Did you work on the campaign?'

"No."

"What university did you go to?"

"UBC."

"Me too. You weren't in the Young Liberals, were you?" she asked as if confirming what she already knew.

Malcolm laughed. "Nope."

"I didn't think so. What's your name again?"

"Malcolm. Malcolm Bidwell."

"Malcolm," she said, lingering on his name. "That's not a very common name. I know only one other Malcolm: Malcolm Turnbull. His father is a former MLA. We were at UBC together. Not the father—Malcolm. After graduation, I came here and he went off to England to do a master's in economics. I've always wanted to go to England, especially London. I hear he's finished now and looking around for something to do. Here we are."

They came to a stop in front of a sturdy oak door with a lead glass pane that looked like it hadn't changed since the legislature was opened in 1898. The number 108 was on the archway directly above the door. Malcolm couldn't understand how he had missed it. The door opened into a large, cluttered room with a half-dozen desks lining the walls, separated by fabric dividers. Somewhere a steam radiator protested violently. Overhead, the ubiquitous air ducts hung low, casting cool shadows from a bank of fluorescent fixtures. A row of windows looked out onto an interior courtyard. Across the courtyard two men stood smoking.

"Jarrod!" the woman called.

"Here!" a voice shouted.

"He *is* here," the woman said with cheery surprise.

They followed the voice to the far corner and into a small office without windows.

"I thought you weren't back until Monday," she said.

"Maurice asked me to get materials ready for the swearing-in," said Tapscott, tapping away at his keyboard without looking up.

"Look who I found. Malcolm . . ."

"Bidwell," Malcolm said helpfully.

"Yes, Bidwell. He was wandering the catacombs of this place hopelessly and utterly lost."

Malcolm could feel the blood rush to his cheeks.

"Tapscott," said the young man, getting up. Malcolm extended his hand, but Tapscott ignored it, forcing Malcolm to awkwardly drop his arm to his side. Malcolm had been right: Jarrod Tapscott looked like he'd graduated from university in the last year or two. He was tall and thin with short-cropped brown hair combed forward in the current style, though Malcolm thought it glistened with too much product. He'd probably been in a rush this morning. He wore a close-fitting white dress shirt and tailored grey suit pants; the suit jacket hung crisply on a hanger on a clothes tree in the corner. His silk tie was tightly knotted and perfectly centred. Malcolm noticed Tapscott's fingers were pink as if freshly scrubbed and his fingernails were neatly clipped and bright white. Manicured?

In contrast to the workspace they had just come through, Tapscott's office was dingy with painted yellow brick walls and a low-slung ceiling crisscrossed by ducting. The only light came from a winking fluorescent fixture above a spotlessly clean desk. The desk was empty save for a computer terminal, telephone, and a box of Wet Ones. Malcolm wondered if neatness was a prerequisite for working for the premier. Facing the desk was a bookcase without any books. The top shelf held a bank of TVs silently tuned to news networks: CBC Newsworld, BC1, CTV News Channel and CNN.

"He'll be a wonderful addition," the woman said to Tapscott while staring at Malcolm. Malcolm was sure his face was glowing red.

"Thanks, Catherine. I can take it from here."

"You don't have to thank me," Catherine said softly to Malcolm, touching his arm. "But you can take me for coffee sometime."

After she had gone, Tapscott observed: "She likes you."

"I'm not quite sure why," confessed Malcolm.

"That's Catherine. She is very . . . welcoming. Can come across as a bit scattered. Don't let that fool you. Fabulous researcher. Smarter than you and me put together. I have to apologize. Had hoped to be better prepared for you. Just got back late yesterday. Off the campaign. Haven't had a chance to get organized yet."

Tapscott had a clipped, almost military, way of speaking, as if he was reading his own form of shorthand aloud. At first,

Malcolm had difficulty following him and was forced to listen closely; for a brief moment he wondered if Tapscott had developed this affected speech for that very reason, but in the end he put it down to too much time spent doing research.

"We're going to be here a while. Until we can sort out offices. Probably won't be in the West Annex. No room. Can't stay here with research. Need our own space. A matter of working with the folks who look after office allocation. As you can imagine, we're going to have a lot of new MLAs. Offices will be at a premium. Good problem to have though. Better than the alternative. So no desk for you. Or phone. I'm on it though."

"No problem," said Malcolm. "Anything I can do? To help?"

Malcolm heard himself unintentionally falling into Tapscott's clipped speech pattern and silently berated himself, worried that Tapscott might think he was mocking him.

"Not with that. I'm preparing materials for the cabinet swearing-in. Lot to do in two weeks. Could use a hand with the event side. Can you work with Angela on it?"

"Sure. Who's Angela?"

He'd done it again, but Tapscott either hadn't noticed or chose to ignore it, because he showed little response.

"Angela Chang. Boss's "body man". Official title is deputy chief of staff. But she does everything the Boss needs doing. Handles his calendar. Oversees events. Very handy with a Tide to Go."

It was only when Tapscott smiled that Malcolm realized he was making a joke.

"Also talk to Maurice. Maurice Lloyd. Chief of staff. Maybe start with him. Then talk to Angela."

"The Boss", Malcolm assumed, was Davis, but he didn't ask; it would only draw attention to the fact he wasn't one of them—and he was already feeling very much an outsider.

"Sounds good," he said.

"Let's get you somewhere to work. At least temporarily."

They walked to the office doorway where Tapscott stopped so suddenly Malcolm nearly bumped into him.

"Take any desk," Tapscott said, waving expansively. "Except Catherine's in the corner there. You'll have the place pretty much to yourself for a few days. Everyone returns from the campaign on Monday. Hopefully by then we'll have things sorted out. Any questions about the computer, where to find things on our hard drive, ask Catherine. Got to get back to my swearing-in materials."

Tapscott slid past Malcolm, taking care to avoid touching him, and reclaimed his desk.

"Thanks," Malcolm said.

Malcolm surveyed the office and selected a desk beneath a window where he had direct line of sight to Tapscott's office. Malcolm's desk was almost completely taken up with a computer and TV. He flipped on the TV. It was tuned to TSN. He surfed the channels until he came to BC1, Global's 24-hour news channel. Their legislative reporter, Joey Kapur, was speculating on who might be in cabinet.

Catherine came back in the room and sat at her desk.

"He didn't shake your hand," she said in a conspiratorial whisper.

Malcolm shook his head.

Catherine nodded knowingly. "He never does."

"No?"

"It's a phobia."

Malcolm raised his eyebrows.

"Afraid of germs," she said.

"You wouldn't know it by his office."

Catherine laughed.

"You were in the Young Liberals?" Malcolm asked.

"Before I joined the UP."

"What made you switch?"

"I could read the writing on the wall and I wanted a job in government."

"So it wasn't ideological?"

Catherine laughed. "Oh my God, no!"

Malcolm thought that she wasn't all that different than him.

"Why don't you use one of these?" she asked, motioning to desks near her. "That way we don't have to shout at each other across the room."

"I'm good here," said Malcolm. While they may share similarities, Catherine's interest in him was unsettling; he felt the more distance between them the better.

"Suit yourself." And as if to punish him, she ignored him the rest of the day.

That was fine with Malcolm because he had work to do. He arranged to see Maurice Lloyd the next morning. Angela Chang was in Vancouver. He left a message for her to call him. Then he spent much of the day scouring the United Party website, news releases, and clippings to brief himself on the freshly minted MLAs and the new government's agenda.

Late in the day, the phone at his desk rang and Malcolm answered it. It was Tapscott. Malcolm looked up. Through the doorway he saw Tapscott at his desk with the receiver pressed to his ear. He was turned away from Malcolm and looked like he was studying the yellow brick wall. He asked Malcolm to prepare a welcome note from the premier for a program for a China trade conference next month. ASAP. Then he hung up abruptly and went back to his computer without ever looking at Malcolm.

Malcolm called the com shop at Trade and Investment for some key stats, and experienced for the first time the power of the phrase "the premier's office". He'd seen it from the other side when he was in Education: moribund ministry staff suddenly coming to life, pulling out every stop, doing whatever was required, engaging whoever was needed, right up to and including the deputy minister and minister. No request was too small. It hadn't been like that at the News Daily. In fact, the opposite: staff ignored the publisher's requests as if they'd never been made and took cruel delight in pushing the editor to a purple-faced, spittle-flecked rage before acquiescing to some meaningless part of his plea.

Malcolm then combed through the United Party's 100-day platform for anything on international trade. He emailed a draft to Tapscott before the end of the day. In all, it had taken him less than an hour. Tapscott loved it and sent it straight on to Maurice for sign-off. By the time Malcolm logged off his computer and left, Catherine was nowhere to be seen.

On his way home Malcolm walked down to Fisherman's Wharf and bought two orders of halibut and chips. Then he stopped by Birdcage Confectionery and picked up a bouquet of freesias—Rachel's favourites. Malcolm tingled with anticipation: he was determined to make up with Rachel, even if it wasn't his fault. It was no one's fault; they just had different views. That's all. Life would be pretty damn boring if you agreed with your partner on everything. He didn't expect her to change and he didn't think it was right for her to expect him to change. He was pretty sure she felt the same.

Malcolm climbed the steps to their apartment two at a time and gave a quick twist and push on the door handle. Locked. Rachel was normally home by now. As he fumbled for the key in his jacket he thought perhaps Rachel was upstairs. Sometimes if she was upstairs she locked the door to be safe.

"I'm home!"

Silence. In the kitchen the fridge self-defrost clunked to a stop making the apartment feel emptier.

"Rachel!"

Nothing. Placing the flowers and fish and chips on the kitchen table, Malcolm removed his coat and threw it over a chair. Something must have come up to keep Rachel late at the office. A crisis of some kind: a client who had been evicted or was short of cash or lost her job. Was tonight her yoga night? Malcolm could never keep Rachel's schedule straight because it was constantly changing. She was always taking on new projects, meeting new people, making new friends. She could be exhausting, but the very thing about her that exhausted him also exhilarated him. She was an adventure, the kind where you never quite knew where you were going to end up but you knew getting there would be a lot of fun.

Malcolm put on the kettle for tea. No beer tonight—he wanted a clear head for the reconciliation. As he waited for the kettle to boil, he felt a vague unease. Had he misread Rachel? Had she been angrier than he thought? In a nanosecond their conversation from the previous night flashed forward and with it a tiny speck of concern. He decided to call her cell. It went straight to voicemail.

"Hi Rachel, it's me. Just wondering where you are. I've picked up something for dinner so you don't have to bother. Give me a shout when you get this."

It was 6PM. He turned on the TV to the news. The economy was still in the tank. Some things never changed. Davis was in Victoria for a briefing on the state of the province's finances. Funny that Tapscott never mentioned it. Davis said the province's books were in worse shape than the Liberals let on during the election. Of course they were. And if they weren't, he'd say it anyway. Said the Liberals' balanced budget may be "fairy dust". Reporters asked if it meant program cuts and public sector layoffs. Davis said it was too early to speculate but it was imperative that B.C. be put on a sound financial footing and his government would consider every means possible to achieve that. "Everything is on the table."

"That will send a shiver through the public service," Malcolm said out loud, as if Rachel were in the room. But he didn't feel the same worry: he was above all that now.

More cabinet speculation followed in a live hit with Kapur from his Victoria office. The window behind Kapur overlooked the legislature's rose garden. Was it a real window or just a prop? Malcolm guessed real. Kapur tossed out several "sure bets" for cabinet posts along with a couple of "possibilities" and by the time they had hit the quarter hour it had been all provincial politics. That wasn't normal. Crime and punishment were the standard fare for the first fifteen minutes—if it bleeds it leads—with politics usually held back until after the twenty- or twenty-five-minute mark. Still, it was better than the U.S. where many TV stations had shuttered their leg bureaus years ago. Global's sports billboard showed the Canucks clearing out their lockers following their second-round playoff loss.

After the news, Malcolm tried Rachel's cell again. Still no answer. He left another voicemail telling her that he's worried he hasn't heard from her and asks her to call as soon as she gets this message. Almost as soon as he hung up, his cell beeped with a text message. Rachel.

"Got ur messages. Im at Dads. Will call u tomorrow."

Malcolm immediately called her cell again, and again it went straight to voicemail. He hung up and called her Dad. As the phone rang Malcolm tried to remember the last time he had spoken with Andy. Malcolm and Andy didn't talk much; they both liked it that way. Rachel had tried to bring them closer by suggesting they do something together, just the two of them. So Andy invited Malcolm to tag along with him to the anarchist book fair at the Russian Hall. It ended badly after a belligerent woman Malcolm had mistaken for a man took a swing at him, missed and sent the Bakunin display flying.

When they did talk, Malcolm stayed away from politics because Andy would start on a Castro-length speech about the Prime Minister and big oil and tankers on B.C.'s coast and invariably wind up accusing Malcolm of not doing enough as a journalist to halt the impending ecological and economic disaster.

Instead, Malcolm steered the conversation toward the one thing, besides Rachel, that he and Andy had in common: Vancouver. Malcolm and Andy had both grown up in Vancouver. In fact, they'd attended the same high school, though thirty-five years apart. Andy's favourite Vancouver topic was life in the '60s. He talked and talked about places he'd been and people he'd known: how they turned Lifestream Natural Foods on 4th Avenue into a co-op; his first time at the Retinal Circus; freaking out on bad acid at the 1968 Easter Be-in at Lumberman's Arch; partying with The Grateful Dead at a motel on Kingsway. For a time Malcolm enjoyed the stories. Unfortunately, Andy liked to tell the same tales over and over to the point where Malcolm could repeat them almost verbatim. Still, it was better than 'oil-ageddon'.

Andy didn't believe in voicemail so you just had to let the phone ring and ring until he picked it up.

"Hello," Andy said when he finally answered.

He sounded like he'd just woken up. Mind you, that's how Andy always sounded. He'd been smoking a pack-a-day since he was fourteen.

"Andy. It's Malcolm. Can I speak to Rachel?"

"I'm not sure that's a good thing."

"What do you mean? Is that what Rachel told you?"

"No, Malcolm. It's what I'm saying."

Malcolm had never openly confronted Andy before, even when Andy routinely criticized Malcolm for working for the MSM: Main Stream Media. Malcolm felt it was easier to avoid an argument than deal with the messy emotional aftermath that might last for days and weeks, maybe even years. But not this time.

"Andy, with all due respect, this has nothing to do with you. Can you please ask Rachel to come to the phone?"

Malcolm half-expected Andy to lecture him, maybe even threaten him. But while he was an anarchist who believed Bakunin was right when he said the passion for destruction is a creative passion, Andy was also a pacifist who had a poster of Ghandi in his dining room and preached his philosophy of *ahimsa,* or non-violence. Malcolm always thought there must be quite a struggle going on within Andy.

Nothing.

"Andy?"

Silence.

"Andy, would you just get Rachel?"

"I'll ask her if she wants to talk to you. But I'm doing it for her. Not you, Malcolm."

Malcolm could hear Andy's feet scuffle across the hardwood floor and then muffled voices. Andy must have covered the phone with his hand. Suddenly, the sound was clear. It was Andy again.

"Rachel says she will call you tomorrow."

"All I want to do is talk to her. I don't understand what's so difficult about that."

"She'll call you tomorrow, Malcolm."

"Don't hang up. Andy?"

The line went dead.

"Fuck!"

Malcolm hit redial. The phone rang and rang. He let it ring for what seemed like minutes. No answer. He was tempted to lay the phone down and just let it ring. Then they'd have to answer. He hung up and called Rachel's cell again. Again, it went straight to voicemail.

"Rachel, I'm sorry for the fight we had and I want to make it up to you. Give me a call. I love you."

Then he sent her a text message: "Left u a v-mail. Call me. Love u."

She wrote back: "Need time to think. On my own. Call u tomorrow."

It was a good sign. Better than no response at all. He was feeling hopeful so he called her again. No answer. He didn't leave a voicemail. So he texted her again.

"Maybe I can help."

He waited. Nothing. Several minutes went by. He finally grabbed the plastic bag with the fish and chips and opened it. The fish was cold and the chips were soggy. He turned on the TV, sat on the couch and picked at the fish and chips with the phone nestled in his lap, hopeful that it would either ring or noti- fy him of a new text. He stayed up to watch the late news and sports. The Canucks were once again cleaning out their lockers and looked like he felt: dejected.

Next thing Malcolm knew a phone was ringing somewhere off in the distance. It kept ringing. Why didn't someone answer it? The ringing sounded closer now, clearer, and he woke up. He was still on the couch with the phone in his lap. It was ringing. He glanced at the number on the call display but had trouble focusing. It had to be Rachel.

"Hullo," he said sleepily.

"Malcolm! I need your help."

"Rachel? What's wrong?" His throat was dry. There was a pause.

"It's Catherine."

"Catherine?"

Malcolm was confused.

"From work."

It took him a second or two to place Catherine.

"Look, I'm sorry to bother you . . ."

Malcolm was wide awake now.

"What time is it?"

He looked at his watch.

"For fuck's sake, Catherine, it's three o'clock in the morning."
Silence.

"I know what time it is, Malcolm." Her tone was frosty, but there was something else that Malcolm couldn't put his finger on. "I wouldn't have called you if I didn't really need your help."

Desperation. That was it. It flashed through his mind that she could be a stalker. Calling him in the middle of the night. Tapscott said she was different. Was that code for dangerous?

"How did you get my number?"

"From work." Pause. "Everyone's number is on the system."

That would mean his address was on the system, too.

"Where are you?"

"I'm at home. I need your help. Can you come over right away?"

Malcolm was even more suspicious.

"What's wrong?"

"I think it's better if you just come over."

"It's three in the morning. I'm not going to come over to your—"

"Steven won't wake up."

"Steven?"

"Davis. The premier."

CHAPTER 4

CATHERINE LIVED IN the Orchard House high-rise, the tallest building in Victoria when it was completed in 1969—and the most unwelcome. A twenty-two-storey slab of concrete and glass that occupied the better part of a city block, the Orchard House squatted in James Bay like a sumo wrestler at a garden party. Opposition to it was so fierce that the city never allowed another high-rise like it. It was just around the corner from the legislature and only a few blocks from Malcolm's apartment. In fact, he passed it every day on his way to work. Now he took the elevator to the 16th floor. Catherine had buzzed him in, so when the elevator doors opened and he stepped into the hall she was watching for him from her apartment doorway. She was dressed in jeans and a T-shirt. He noticed she wasn't wearing a bra.

"He still hasn't woken up," she said.

Malcolm looked in the living room expecting to see the premier sprawled on the couch, maybe even lying in a heap on the floor. Nothing.

"Where is he?"

"In here."

Catherine led him down a narrow hall. Her hair was pushed flat at the back, like she had been sleeping on it. The door opened into her bedroom.

"Holy shit!" Malcolm said.

On the way over he had prepared himself for anything and everything. Still, it was a shock to see the new premier of the province—someone he had only ever seen on TV—like this. Steven Davis lay on the bed on his back with his head slumped to one side facing the door. His eyes were closed. He was naked except for a pair of boxer shorts that were twisted awkwardly, as if someone had struggled to put them on him while he had been lying there. Malcolm couldn't help but notice the enormous erection pushing at his shorts.

"How long has he been like this?" Malcolm asked.

"I don't know. Half an hour. Maybe more. I woke up and he was like this."

"You woke up?"

Catherine pursed her lips and stared at him.

"Have you called 911?"

"No."

He reached for his cellphone.

"No, don't!" She put her hand on his arm.

"What?" He looked at her.

"You can't call 911!"

"Why not?"

"That's why I called you."

"Catherine, he's unconscious. We need to call an ambulance. This is serious."

"No!"

"Then what do you want me to do?"

"I don't know. I thought we might be able to move him."

"Move him? But he needs medical help."

"Then we can call an ambulance. But after we've moved him."

"I don't know. Is that safe?"

"It's not like he's going to die. He's breathing fine. He just won't wake up."

Malcolm walked around the bed and leaned down and put his ear by Davis's nose. He lifted Davis's arm and let it drop. He felt his wrist for a pulse. After half a minute, he said, "His heartbeat is steady. We could just leave him and see if he wakes up."

"We can't."

"Why not?"

"He's not supposed to be here."

"No kidding."

She gave him a pained look.

"Sorry."

And he meant it. For the first time he felt sorry for her. He looked at Davis.

"So?" he asked, turning back to her. His voice had lost its edge.

"So what?"

Catherine hadn't seemed to notice the change.

"So how did this happen?"

"It's complicated."

Malcolm just looked at her and waited.

"Oh fuck," Catherine said, "what does it matter how it happened?"

"I think I have a right to know what I'm getting myself in for."

Catherine looked down then up, but there was no sense of embarrassment in her voice when she spoke.

"We were in a relationship—it started during the campaign. Somehow his wife found out and she demanded Steven end it and fire me. He agreed to end it, but wouldn't fire me, so she went to Maurice. I think Maurice was more worried about what might happen if our relationship became public during the election. After he'd finished swearing at me for fifteen minutes, he told me to go home. We were in Kamloops at a rally. He had Matt McDonaugh, Steven's press secretary, drive me to the airport and put me on a plane. I wasn't happy about it because I didn't think they should be able to tell me what to do with my personal life. But I went along because I didn't want it to be blamed for costing Steven the election."

"And now that the election is over, you're back together?"

"It wasn't like that. The other day he called and said he was going to be in Victoria and wanted to see me. But being apart had given me some time to think, and I told him that maybe it would be better if we didn't see each other anymore. We argued and I hung up. Then he texted me today and asked to come over. Just to talk."

Malcolm looked at Davis on the bed.

"You've got a funny way of talking."

Catherine frowned.

"I still think we should just leave him here and hope he wakes up."

Catherine shook her head.

"He's got a 7AM breakfast meeting with the transition team and then he's meeting with MLAs to discuss cabinet positions. What if he doesn't wake up in time? What if he's still lying here in my bed? What do we do then? I think it's better if we move him to his hotel room."

"Fuck! What a mess!"

Silence.

"Why me?" Malcolm asked.

"What?"

"Why call me? Why didn't you call Jarrod?"

"Jarrod? He wouldn't even shake your hand. Do you really think he'd be a help in a situation like this?"

"What about Maurice?"

"You're kidding."

"Well, there must be someone."

"They're all away. They won't be back until Monday. I was desperate."

"Thanks a lot."

"I wouldn't have called you, but I can't move him by myself."

Malcolm looked at Davis.

"So what happened?"

"I told you."

"Not about your relationship. About tonight. Tell me exactly what took place this evening."

"I got a text from Steven around four telling me that he'd like to see me. He said he was in meetings all day and would finish around 10."

The words seemed to flow easily out of Catherine now.

"He said he could come over after his last meeting. Like I said, I didn't think it was a good idea, but he insisted. He got here around 10:15. We started talking and one thing led to another. Afterwards, we were lying in bed half asleep. I went to snuggle next to him but he didn't respond. He just lay there. Usually he holds me. I tried again, but he still didn't respond. I realized something was wrong. I tried to wake him but he wouldn't wake up. That's when I called you."

"Has he had that the whole time?"

"What?"

"That." Malcolm pointed to his erection.

"Yes. He always takes something. He worries about not performing. I think it's the difference in our ages. Usually it's Viagra, though he tried Cialis once and didn't like it; he said it made his muscles ache. This time he said he was using something one of his old business partners brought back from Germany."

"What's it called?"

"I don't know."

Malcolm rooted through Davis's pants looking for a prescription bottle.

"Did he take it in front of you?"

"Yes, he took one just after he arrived and another about two."

"You were busy."

Catherine just looked at him blankly.

Malcolm threw the pants on the bed. "I can't find anything. He probably just took a larger dose than he should have. My advice is we wait a while and see what happens. It might just wear off. If he doesn't come around in an hour, then I'll help you get him back to his hotel."

"Why not just take him there now?"

"Because it's not going to be easy. What do you think's going to happen when we show up in the hotel lobby carrying the next premier of B.C.?"

"I thought about that. I have a car. We can take him down in the elevator to my car and then drive to the hotel parking lot. He's staying at the Grand Pacific. It's an underground lot. We can load him directly from the car into the elevator and into his room without having to go by the desk."

Malcolm thought about this. "It might work," he said.

"If we go now there is less chance we might bump into someone, like a jogger or the newspaper delivery boy," Catherine said.

Malcolm looked at his watch. It was nearly 4AM. She had a point: in the next hour or so the streets would start to come alive.

"Okay. But he can't go like that. Let's get him dressed."

Catherine gave a relieved smile. "Thanks, Malcolm. I really appreciate this."

"You're putting his pants on him, though," Malcolm said firmly.

Dressing Davis wasn't easy. Malcolm sat him up and held him while Catherine pulled one arm through a sleeve and then the other. Malcolm noticed how fit Davis was for his age. He must work out. Malcolm then lay Davis back down while Catherine started putting his pants on. She couldn't lift his leg and put his foot into the pant leg at the same time.

"Here, let me help get you started," Malcolm said, "but you're on your own after that."

Malcolm turned Davis so his legs fell over the side of the bed, then sat him up. Catherine bent down and threaded the pant legs on, one at a time. Malcolm then lifted Davis up and Catherine shook him into the pants like she was putting a pillowcase on a pillow. When she got to the erection she placed one hand on his penis and carefully bent it to one side while gently pulling at the pants with the other hand. It wasn't working.

"I could use some help here," she said without looking at Malcolm.

"That wasn't our deal. Besides, someone needs to hold him up."

"You could hold him with one hand and use the other to help with his pants."

"I could. But I won't."

"Bastard," Catherine said. She was puffing. She pushed roughly on Davis's erection and gave the pants a hard yank so they moved up to close to his waist.

"That should hold," she said as she hooked the waist clasp closed, sat on the bed and tucked her hair behind her ear.

"What about that?" Malcolm asked. He was looking at Davis's fly. The erection was protruding forcefully out the opening.

Catherine pushed at the erection while pulling at the zipper. She tried stuffing the offending appendage inside the zipper. The erection would not be subdued; she managed to get the fly only partway closed before she quit.

"Good enough," she said. "It's not like we will see anyone anyway."

Let's hope, thought Malcolm. He lay Davis down while Catherine put on his socks and shoes and stuffed his tie into the pocket of his suit jacket.

"Don't forget his watch," Malcolm said.

Catherine grabbed the watch off the bedside table and slipped it into Davis's pants pocket.

"I think that's it," she said, taking one last look around the bedroom.

Malcolm moved to the foot of the bed and stood beside Catherine. They both looked at the next premier of British Columbia draped across the bed, his shirt wrinkled and untucked, his pants bunched around his waist, his fly half-open, the grey boxer shorts visible, and beneath them a noticeable mound. Davis had a smile on his face.

"At least he's happy," said Malcolm. "Must have been all your work with his zipper."

"Are you always like this?" Catherine asked.

"Sorry. I get like this when I'm amped. Let's go."

Malcolm put Davis's arm around his neck and lifted him to his feet.

"He's heavier than he looks," Malcolm wheezed.

They carried Davis to the elevator and down to Catherine's car without incident. However, as they leaned Davis's body into the back seat they accidently banged his forehead on the doorframe.

"Ouch," said Malcolm. "If that doesn't wake him up, nothing will."

As if on cue, Davis mumbled softly as they lay him down in the back seat. Catherine went around, opened the other door, straightened his arm, and gently stroked his head.

The Grand Pacific was only a few blocks away on Belleville Street. Catherine used Davis's room key to get into the underground garage and parked right beside the elevator. She got out and pressed the up button while Malcolm gently unfolded Davis from the back seat. Catherine returned to the car; behind her the elevator pinged and the doors opened. They each grabbed one of Davis's arms and pulled him to a standing position outside the car, but before they could support him, his legs buckled and he collapsed in a tumble beside the rear tire.

"Come on, Stevie," Catherine said, reaching under his arm. "Up we go."

On TV Davis projected an air of power and strength and unwavering belief. And for all his charisma, he seemed cold and distant. So while it was shocking to see him in this state, it was even more shocking for Malcolm to see Catherine use terms of endearment like "Stevie" and to hear the warmth and affection in her voice.

The fall seemed to have an effect on Davis and he was able to gather his feet under him so that they made it into the elevator without further mishap. Catherine pressed the button for the 12th floor. The doors shut but the elevator didn't move.

"You need his room key," Malcolm said.

Catherine retrieved the card from her pocket and tapped the electronic pad several times, then pressed 12. With the whirring of the elevator, Davis started mumbling again, only louder. Catherine consoled him, laying his head on her shoulder and leaning against the brushed metallic rear of the elevator for support. Suddenly the elevator started to slow. Malcolm looked up expecting to see the number 12 illuminated. Instead, the number 8 lit up.

Without saying a word, Malcolm squared himself to the front so he was standing only an inch from the doors. The elevator shimmied to a stop. Malcolm wasn't sure what he would do if someone was waiting to get onto the elevator. Step out and ask them to take the next elevator? They would still see Davis. Tackle them? He could imagine the headlines: "Man attacked in luxury hotel". Better than: "New premier snared in sex scandal".

"Turn his head away from the door and kiss him," Malcolm said in a raspy whisper.

Catherine took Davis's head between her hands and twisted it toward her. Holding it tight, she tilted her head slightly and kissed him, her eyes wide open and watching the doors the whole time. Davis made a low moan.

The doors slid open. No one. Malcolm quickly punched the close doors button with his fist. He looked down and saw he had formed two fists. Then he hit the button again and again in rapid succession until finally, slowly, the obstinate doors began to reluctantly comply. When they had finally shut, Malcolm punched the button again.

He turned to look at Catherine and Davis. She was watching him with a smirk. He shrugged.

At the 12th floor, he held the door with one hand and told Catherine to wait while he checked the landing. Empty. He went back to help her with Davis. Swinging Davis's left arm around his neck and holding his hand firmly against his shoulder, he half-lifted, half-dragged Davis into the hallway. Davis mumbled incoherently in his ear, his breath like stiff feathers against his neck.

"What room?" he grunted.

"What?" Catherine asked.

"Room number!" Davis felt heavier than before.

"1205."

The trio moved haltingly down the hallway, Catherine trailing closely as if to recover anything that might fall. Malcolm had worked it out that if anyone asked what they were doing, he would say Davis was his father in town for a visit and he'd had a bit too much "fun". It wasn't great but it was all he could think of at four in the morning. Besides, it was partially true.

Catherine darted ahead so that when Malcolm and Davis reached 1205 the door was already open. They banged the door as they entered and the door swung back and hit Malcolm in the forehead.

"Fuck!" Malcolm said and he dragged Davis roughly to the bed and let him fall.

"Careful!" Catherine said.

Malcolm rubbed his head. "That hurt."

The next morning Malcolm felt like calling in sick, but it was impossible: he was meeting Maurice at nine. So he hauled himself out of bed, showered, shaved, and quickly drained two cups of coffee before setting off. As he passed the Orchard House he thought about Catherine and how he'd left her with Davis. It was only when he saw the flowers outside the Birdcage Confectionery that he remembered he hadn't heard from Rachel, and the pleasure he had from replaying the extraordinary events from the night before was stained with the guilt of only now having thought about Rachel.

Still, his mind turned back to Catherine. He had helped her undress Davis and get him into bed. She had thanked him and told him to go, that she would look after things. He had left her lying beside Davis, fully clothed, and had walked home by a different route. The weather had changed, the air was cold and damp, and mist had started to pool in Irving Park. By the time he got to his street, the fog had thickened and spread so that he could barely make out the street name on the signpost. Counting down the houses from the corner, he turned at his, the third house in. The walkway around to the side of the house was completely obscured by the dark and the fog so he went by memory, feeling his way forward with his feet, hand outstretched in case his memory wasn't as good as he thought it was, until he came to the steps to his apartment. As he unlocked the door and stepped inside, he noticed his face was dripping as if he had broken out in a cold sweat.

Chapter 5

"WHAT AM I going to do with you?"

Maurice Lloyd had pushed back his chair, placed his loafer-clad feet on the desk and folded his hands resolutely behind his head. The grimness of his mouth told Malcolm that the question was rhetorical so he sat quietly in his chair facing Maurice. An awkward silence filled the room.

"Morons!" Maurice finally growled as if talking to himself. "I'm surrounded by fucking morons!"

Removing his feet from the desk, he got up, marched across the room in three quick strides and yanked opened the office door.

"Jess—tell Jordan to get in here right away!"

"He's not in yet, Maurice."

"Then call him. I don't give a shit where he is. Just get him in here! Now!"

"Yes, Maurice."

Maurice slammed the door.

Maurice's office was part of the same suite of offices in the Sussex Building as Jordan Leopold's, though it was an upgrade of sorts. Maurice at least had framed artwork on the walls, large colour photographs of landscapes from around British Columbia: open grasslands of the Chilcotin, snow-capped mountains of the Rockies, thousand-year-old cedars on Haida Gwaii. But the colour wasn't quite right; they were faded as if from exposure to the sun. Or from age. On closer scrutiny, Malcolm recognized them as old promotional photos from Tourism BC, the provincial tourism marketing organization, and he recalled that Maurice had cut his teeth there in the heady days of the 1980s and the elation of Expo 86. Of course, Malcolm hadn't even been born, but years later he saw a family photo with his parents and Adam as a baby crowded around Expo Ernie, the robot mascot with the stylized blue Expo 86 logo on his chest. He remembered thinking how Expo Ernie seemed so dated, like watching the original Star Wars, so that it looked not just like a different time, but a different place. Not unlike the photos on Maurice's office walls.

Maurice also had his own executive assistant: Jessica Laird. Around Maurice, she was meek to the point of being a victim, but with anyone seeking access to the new premier's political adviser she was like a Rottweiler on steroids. When Malcolm had phoned the day before, she was not only frosty, she was openly hostile. She grilled him about the nature of the meeting and Malcolm's position. Even the use of Jarrod's name didn't have any effect; if anything, it only stiffened her resistance. Then, after what seemed like hours on the phone, she finally, grudgingly made an appointment for him.

He showed up ten minutes early only to be acknowledged with a perfunctory glance followed by a stiff wave for him to take a seat. Stubbornly, Malcolm lingered by her desk, observing that her appearance was as buttoned down as her manner. Her dark hair was pulled tight in a ponytail so that her thin face seemed even thinner. She wore a pantsuit with a blouse done up tight around her neck, no makeup or jewellery—a man's Rolex watch being her only concession to fashion. She looked older than her thirtysomething years and Malcolm wondered if that was deliberate. She raised her eyes without moving her head, annoyed that he was hovering near her desk, so he smiled and made an ingratiating remark that bounced off her teflon-plated exterior. He sighed to himself and dutifully sat down. After a few moments the door to the hallway opened and a small man with curly brown hair and glasses poked his head in. He looked vaguely familiar.

"Does Maurice have a moment?"

"Not until this afternoon, Mr. Watling."

Jeffrey Watling. Malcolm had read his bio on the party website. Newly elected in West Vancouver-Capilano. Part of the lawn-and-tennis-club set. He had founded his own investment firm and made millions before the 2008 economic collapse. Or was it from the collapse? Touted for a cabinet post, though a junior post.

"I need to get his view on something. It's urgent."

"Mmm." Jessica was unwavering.

"It's to do with the premier."

"Mmm."

"I called and left a message but he never returns my calls."

"The premier?"

"Maurice."

"Mmm."

"As I say, it's urgent."

"Mmm."

Watling paused. "What time is he free this afternoon?"

"I have an opening at 2:45."

"Okay. If that's the best you can do."

"Mmm."

"Thank you." And he fled.

Inside Maurice's office, Malcolm heard the door open, and when he turned he saw Jessica leaning into the room, the door handle still in her hand.

"Jordan's just come in."

She quickly closed the door without waiting for a reply.

Maurice sat at his desk looking at his computer. Malcolm wanted to ask about the photographs as a way of reaching out to Maurice, but he felt it was probably better not to say anything. Something had set Maurice off just after Malcolm had introduced himself and had told him he was there to get direction on the cabinet swearing-in ceremony.

There was a quiet knock at the door and Jordan Leopold entered the room as if he were walking barefoot on broken glass. He was wearing a pink shirt and matching tie. The tie had a fresh yellow stain like egg yolk or orange juice.

"You wanted to see me, Maurice?"

Maurice continued to stare at his computer without saying anything. Jordan looked at Malcolm and then back to Maurice. He stood in the doorway as if ready to make a quick exit.

After some time Maurice said: "Close the door, Jordan."

Jordan grimaced and shut the door carefully, noiselessly.

"Malcolm here was telling me that you interviewed him for the position with the Boss's communications team."

Silence.

"Yes," Jordan said.

Malcolm had never heard a single syllable stretched for so long.

"And how long did that interview last?"

Maurice continued to stare unblinkingly into the computer screen, every so often moving the mouse on his desk. Jordan looked at Malcolm. His face was now the colour of his shirt. Malcolm adjusted himself in his chair.

"Half an hour."

"Half an hour," Maurice repeated slowly.

"Maybe less."

"Maybe less," Maurice repeated. "So, twenty minutes?"

"Yes."

"You're sure."

Jordan looked at Malcolm.

"Maybe less."

"Maybe less than twenty minutes?"

"Yes."

"Ten minutes?"

Jordan swallowed hard. "Yes."

"You're sure?"

Jordan looked down at the floor.

"Yes." It was a short, dejected single syllable.

"Let me get this straight," Maurice said slowly to his computer screen. "You spent ten minutes interviewing Malcolm for a job in the office of the premier of British Columbia—"

"But Maurice—"

"A job providing crucial and highly sensitive communications advice to the highest—"

"He was—"

"—political office in the province?"

Maurice looked up from his computer.

"Yes?" he asked.

"But his father—"

Jordan leaned forward, hands outstretched, as if coaxing a response from Maurice.

"His father," Maurice echoed.

"Is—"

Jordan cocked his head slightly and raised his eyebrows as if he had said enough for Maurice to understand.

"Is," Maurice repeated.

Jordan nodded knowingly. Maurice stared blankly at him for what seemed like hours.

"Do you know Malcolm's last name?" Maurice finally asked.

Jordan looked at Malcolm. By now moist patches had appeared under his arms, making his pink shirt red.

"What?" Jordan looked confused.

"Malcolm," Maurice turned to Malcolm, "what's your last name?"

Jordan turned to Malcolm.

"Bidwell," said Malcolm slowly.

Jordan's eyes widened and his neck flamed.

"Not Turnbull?" he asked.

Malcolm shook his head.

"You're not Malcolm Turnbull?"

"No," Malcolm said softly.

Jordan's head spun towards Maurice as if it had come detached from his body.

"Maurice, I—"

Standing up, Maurice ignored Jordan and came around the desk, perching himself on the edge in an overly casual way so that his knee almost touched Malcolm's knee. He took off his glasses and held them up to the window and then put them back on again.

"Malcolm, as you can see there's been an unfortunate error," he said calmly but firmly. "The person we had intended to interview for this position was Malcolm *Turnbull*. This puts us both in an awkward position, but if you can give us a few hours, I'm sure we can arrange to have you returned to your previous position with the . . ."

"Ministry of Education," Jordan said quickly.

"Ministry of Education," Maurice repeated.

Malcolm sat back heavily in his chair. "I'm confused," he said. "So you're saying I don't have a job?"

"Yes. I mean, no. What I'm saying is, you don't have *this* job." Maurice was sounding less firm now. "We—Jordan—made a mistake. We had our eye on a fellow named Malcolm *Turnbull*, an exemplary candidate—not that you aren't—and somehow," Maurice looked at Jordan, "we interviewed you instead. We will make it up to you. Of course, all we ask is that you keep this confidential."

After a moment, his head still spinning, Malcolm said: "I don't know what to say . . ."

"I'm as surprised as you are," said Maurice, deftly aligning himself with Malcolm as one who had also been wronged.

"I guess I'm wondering what I'm supposed to tell my family," said Malcolm. "My friends? The people in Education?"

"I know this is very difficult," said Maurice, "but it wouldn't be good for anyone if it became public."

Was Maurice being clumsy or was he threatening him? Maurice didn't strike him as someone who was clumsy unless he meant to be.

"I'm not sure what you mean," Malcolm said, getting up.

He imagined it would be embarrassing for Maurice to have to explain how the party elected for its superior management skills got something as simple as a person's name wrong. It might even raise other questions—about the whole hiring process. Maybe even prompt media scrutiny of the people working in taxpayer-funded positions in the premier's office. It's certainly what he would do if he were in the press gallery. Is that what Maurice was worried about?

"Of course, if you don't like the Ministry of Education, I'm sure we can find you a position in another ministry," Maurice said soothingly. "I'd like to make this work for both of us."

"But you still haven't told me what I will say to people when they ask why I left."

Maurice shot Jordan a dark look.

Just then the door behind Maurice's desk opened and Steven Davis leaned into the room.

"Maurice, I need a word with you."

Even from across the room, Malcolm could make out bruising above Davis's eye and instinctively touched the welt on his temple.

"Premier, can you give me a couple of minutes? I'm almost done here."

"Now, Maurice."

With that Davis withdrew, leaving the door ajar. Maurice looked at Malcolm, then back at the open door. He scowled and reluctantly followed, closing the door behind him. A minute later Maurice returned, his face cloudy. He remained silent.

At last he said: "You can go, Jordan."

Jordan raced to the door, hastily slamming it on his way out.

Maurice moved to where Malcolm was standing, placed himself squarely in front of him, and leaned in so his face was only inches away from Malcolm's.

"What's your game?" he asked, his eyes flitting, studying Malcolm's face.

Malcolm was puzzled by the question.

"What?"

"You know perfectly well what I mean. What are you up to?"

"I don't understand."

Maurice slowly turned away and went back and sat looking at his computer.

"How do you know the Boss?" he asked abruptly.

Malcolm flinched and hoped Maurice hadn't noticed.

"Premier Davis?"

Maurice continued to stare at the computer screen.

"I don't. Know him. Personally. If that's what you mean."

"That's strange, because he knows you. He thinks you're perfect for the position. And if he says you're perfect, then you're perfect."

There was an uncomfortable pause.

"Does this mean I'm not going back to Education?" Malcolm asked warily.

"Apparently you're a smart boy, so you tell me."

Another awkward silence.

"Thank you," was about all Malcolm could think to say.

"Don't thank me," Maurice snapped. "I had nothing to do with this."

Malcolm decided his welcome, such as it was, had long since worn out, and he made straight for the door, careful not to seem in too great a hurry. Behind him, Maurice said something that Malcolm didn't catch.

"What?" Malcolm asked, stopping and turning.

"I said you'll be working out of the West Annex." Maurice looked up from the computer. "I want you close so I can keep an eye on you, Bidwell."

Malcolm closed the door as quietly as he could. As he waited for the elevator, he heard a door open down the hallway behind him and padded footsteps coming toward him. He couldn't bring himself to look. A sense of dread came over him as the footsteps stopped beside him. Maurice had had second thoughts. He turned, expecting to see Maurice. It was Davis. He ignored Malcolm and stood facing the elevator. Malcolm began to speak, but Davis lifted his hand slightly from his side without moving his head. The elevator chimed its arrival and the doors slid open. Malcolm waited for Davis to enter first and then followed. Davis stood at the front of the elevator almost directly in the middle of the doors. Malcolm took up a position in the corner. Davis waited until the doors closed before turning around.

"Thank you for your help last night."

"You're welcome," replied Malcolm. Clearly Catherine had told him. "You look better," he said, and immediately wished he hadn't, worried that Davis may take it as a judgment of his condition last night. Better than what? Better than comatose on a young woman's bed with a massive erection? Malcolm was never comfortable in these situations because he didn't have the easy way of those who always know the right things to say, though he liked that the next premier of British Columbia felt indebted enough to him to intervene on his behalf. It was his first experience with raw power and it felt exhilarating, even pleasurable.

"Catherine says you can be trusted. Is that true? Can you be trusted?"

"Absolutely," Malcolm answered.

"Good. Because in politics trust is all we have. The trust between government and voters. The trust between caucus and its leader. The trust between you and me. Trust is the glue that holds it all together. Break the trust and everything falls apart. The centre cannot hold."

Davis said it in a well-practised rhythm that suggested to Malcolm it wasn't the first time he'd made that speech. Nevertheless, he felt a special bond between them. The elevator reached the ground floor and the doors opened. Their bond had been sealed in the time it had taken the elevator to travel eight floors. Malcolm slipped past Davis and out of the elevator and turned around. Davis stuck out his hand and smiled a megawatt smile. Malcolm shook his hand.

"Welcome aboard, Malcolm Bidwell."

Before Malcolm could reply, the elevator doors started to close and he quickly retrieved his hand. He watched silently as the doors enveloped Davis and his body disappeared, leaving only the image of his megawatt smile.

By the time Malcolm had returned to the legislature, the others had already heard the news. Jarrod even came out of his office to greet Malcolm.

"Jessica just called over. Said we are going to have offices in the West Annex," Jarrod said excitedly. "Wonderful news! But what's this? About a mistaken identity?"

"Just some mix-up," said Malcolm. "How did you find out?"

"Word travels fast," Catherine said with a wink.

"Jordan and I were having breakfast at Floyd's," explained Jarrod. "He got the call from Jessica. He was in a state. Didn't even finish his eggs. I told him to give me a call. Let me know everything's okay. He phoned me when he got out of the meeting from hell."

"Well, it was all resolved," said Malcolm reassuringly, "though I didn't get a chance to talk to him about the swearing-in. What do you want me to do about that?"

"We can talk about that later," said Jarrod, quickly retreating once again to his office, as if he had had all the face-to-face conversation he could handle.

"The Boss was there," Malcolm said in a surreptitious whisper to Catherine. "He looked fine, almost as if last night had never happened."

"Yah, he came to about fifteen minutes after you left. He had a splitting headache, though I'm not sure it was his little pick-me-up or that awful bump he took getting into the car."

"He wasn't the only one who got a sore head last night," Malcolm said defensively.

"Ah, poor thing," she said with a mocking laugh. "Think of it as your shared experience. Something for your memoirs."

"I'm pretty sure he wouldn't want that included in mine or anyone else's memoirs."

Catherine pouted: "You don't sound very appreciative."

She didn't like to be criticized.

"So you talked to him?"

Catherine nodded. "I explained how you'd helped. He was worried because he doesn't know you, but I assured him there's nothing to worry about, you're totally cool. Then this morning when I heard from Jarrod that Maurice was going crazy and it somehow involved you, I called Steven. He said he'd look into it. And he did. Nice, huh?"

She smirked, satisfied with herself.

"We'll see," Malcolm said.

"What do you mean by that?"

"Maurice is pissed."

"So?"

"So he said he's going to be watching me."

"He watches everyone. Look at me; you don't see me fretting."

"Easy for you to say. Steven has your back."

"And yours."

"It's that simple?"

"It's that simple."

Malcolm considered this.

"Politics is all about who you know," said Catherine. "Look, why do you think I joined the United Party: to network."

"That sounds awfully calculating?"

Malcolm didn't mean it to sound as harsh as it came out.

"It's not calculating at all," Catherine said with a petulant downturn of her mouth. "It's just good business."

"Good business?"

Catherine nodded. "It got me this job and now I'm making even more contacts, which I will use when I'm ready to move into the private sector. I don't intend to stay in government my whole life, you know."

Malcolm considered the irony of Catherine's "contact" with Davis, but decided against pointing it out. He didn't want to be uncharitable. After all, Catherine had saved his job.

"So it looks like we're moving to the West Annex," said Malcolm.

"*You're* moving," said Catherine. "*I'm* not."

"You aren't?" Malcolm's disappointment was obvious.

Catherine shook her head. "I asked," she said with a tone of resignation. "There's no room in the West Annex. They said with all the new MLAs, we're going to get a bigger budget and more staff . . . so they're putting research in with caucus in the East Annex."

There was a pause before Catherine added: "I can't believe you've only been here one day. We've been through so much already. Promise to call me and fill me in on any juicy gossip?"

"You'll know what's going on long before me," Malcolm said with a wink.

"I'll give you a call whenever I hear anything," Catherine pledged.

"Just as long as it's not three o'clock in the morning," Malcolm said with smile.

"Sorry, I'm not the kind of girl who makes promises she knows she can't keep."

'Time to talk?' Malcolm texted Rachel. He was on his lunch break, sitting under an umbrella outside Murchie's on Government Street. Rachel hadn't called, and Malcolm had debated whether to take the initiative. He wanted to talk to her, but he didn't want to appear too eager. In the harsh light of the noon-day sun he thought about calling her but was afraid he might get Andy—he definitely didn't want to have that conversation again. A text was more impersonal but, he argued, she was the one who was supposed to be calling him. In that case, a text was just right, more of an inquiry than an appeal. What to write? He'd carefully weighed several alternatives, including: 'Time to talk?', 'Want to talk?', 'Give me a call', and 'When r u calling?' 'When r u calling?' seemed demanding and desperate, and though Malcolm felt a sense of desperation, it was less so than the previous evening when Rachel's absence had surprised him. Now he wondered if there wasn't more to it than his job. Maybe it was something else. Was this around the time her Mom ran off? He was surprised how it still affected Rachel. The only time he'd known her to be truly drunk was on the anniversary of her Mom leaving.

They had been living in the bush outside 100 Mile House—Andy, Rachel and her Mom—when one day her Mom up and left. Rachel was five. No goodbye. No nothing. Her Dad raised her on his own in a drafty shack and supported them by horse logging. They moved to Vancouver when she was in Grade 10 to take care of her ailing grandmother and after she died, they stayed on in the family home. Her father was still there. He'd used a small inheritance to open a fair trade coffee shop on Commercial Drive. Malcolm couldn't imagine anything worse. He told Rachel that if he were ever forced to work in a coffee shop she should just shoot him and put him out of his misery.

Malcolm finally decided on 'Time to talk?' It seemed to have the right balance. Now he just had to wait for her to respond.

Down the street, a clutch of Japanese girls were giggling self-consciously in front of the souvenir shop as they took turns having their photo taken with the giant stuffed black bear dressed in an RCMP uniform. Malcolm liked Murchie's because it was a few blocks up from the Inner Harbour, so it wasn't within easy walking distance for some tourists, yet it still had the energy of the Government Street tourist zone. The downside was that sometimes busloads of sightseers trooped past on their way to Chinatown.

Ding. A text. Rachel.

Malcolm picked up his phone from where it lay beside his coffee cup.

"C u this afternoon. On 1:30 bus."

Malcolm felt a rush of relief and joy. Relief that Rachel had decided to return home. Joy that he would see her. He missed her.

"Meet u at the station," he texted back.

The bus station was just down the street from the legislature and only about a ten minute walk from their apartment. Time had slowed to a shuffle and Malcolm found himself at the station a half hour early; the bus wasn't due until 5:30. He decided to wait outside but had second thoughts when a panhandler in a wheelchair and soiled baseball cap set up near the station entrance. The man, about 45 or 50 years old, asked for money in a screechy, sing-song voice: "Spare a little channnggge . . . spare a little channnggge." Feeling like everything in his life was working for him, Malcolm decided to share some of his good fortune and dropped a five-dollar bill into the man's upturned cap. The man looked at the cap and then looked away. No thank you. No nod of appreciation. Nothing. Malcolm wanted to retrieve his money and offer the panhandler some rude advice on being grateful, but instead he headed back inside the bus terminal to wait for Rachel, feeling less at peace with himself.

Malcolm met the bus as it wheeled into the terminal parking lot and squealed to a halt in front of the double glass doors. Scanning the tinted windows, he thought he could make out Rachel and followed her to the front of the bus, only to find it was a teenage girl who stepped down into the half-circle of an exuberant family. The bus emptied its passengers and Malcolm worried that Rachel had missed the bus until she finally emerged. There was a brief moment of awkwardness when Malcolm was suddenly confronted with how to greet her. He gave her a quick hug and then attempted to gloss over his discomfort by reaching for her carry-on.

"I thought we might drop your stuff at home and go out for a drink and a bite to eat," he said.

All afternoon he had vacillated about what they should do. His first thought had been to go for a walk and talk about what had happened, like one of their first dates when they had

strolled and chatted for so long, joyfully unaware of their surroundings, that they unexpectedly found themselves on
Commerical on the other side of Hastings amongst the hookers
in short skirts and knee-high boots and Johns in idling cars. The
conversation then had been exploratory—finding out who she
was, what she liked, her hopes and dreams. Her fears. It had all
been so new. It seemed so long ago.

Then he wondered if she would be hungry. Rachel needed
to eat or she got grumpy, and talking to her when she was
grumpy was like pushing a large boulder uphill. He contemplated
cooking her dinner, but he only did that on special occasions and
he didn't want to put that much emphasis on her return. He considered going for something to eat, but then it was pretty early
for dinner. So he landed on going for a drink and then dinner. A
drink might loosen them both up for any discussion about what
had happened. He knew he would certainly need a drink to settle
his uneasiness. Then they could have their talk.

"Can we do it tomorrow?" Rachel asked in a way that left
room for only one response. "I'm really tired. I thought we
might just go home and order in pizza. Do we have any beer?"

"Sure, we can just go home," Malcolm said, hiding his disappointment with breezy agreement. Her carry-on suddenly
seemed heavier, so he shifted it to his other hand.

"Dad says to say hi."

Not likely, Malcolm thought, recalling his last conversation
with Andy. But it was nice of Rachel to offer an olive branch.

So he reciprocated: "How's the coffee shop?"

"Good. He says the worse the economy gets, the more people drink coffee."

"That's good for him."

"Yes and no. He feels torn by it. He's doing well while others
struggle. You know Dad, always looking out for the other person."

"Does he still volunteer at the bookstore?"

"Yeah. Though he didn't go in yesterday because I was
home."

Malcolm had wanted to tell her about the previous night but
he worried about what she might think and, more importantly,

that she might say something to someone, even inadvertently, and betray "the trust". He also worried about the questions it would present, questions about this new friend—a female friend—who called him for help in the middle of the night. Questions about how this woman felt about Malcolm. Questions about how Malcolm felt about her. Questions for which Malcolm didn't yet have answers. He decided he couldn't tell Rachel. Then he was worried about not telling her. If it emerged sometime later, Rachel might wonder why he hadn't told her, maybe even conclude that he hadn't because he had something to hide. And she'd be right. Was it just Catherine that he wanted to hide, or was there something else? Something fundamental to their relationship. Betrayal. That was it. Betrayal. Malcolm felt he had betrayed Rachel. Not for helping Catherine, but because he'd enjoyed it so much. And it hadn't involved Rachel—not that she would have wanted to be involved. Malcolm felt guilty. There was no way he could tell Rachel. In the end, it didn't matter because Rachel ate the pizza, finished her beer and fell asleep on the couch before they had a chance to do much more than talk about the bus ride over.

CHAPTER 6

RACHEL EASED THE car up to the stop sign. At the church across the street the bald head of the minister glistened in the late-morning sun as he stood on the steps with his back to them and greeted a thin line of departing, grey-haired parishioners.

"That's where I went to Sunday school," Malcolm said.

"I know," Rachel said.

"I told you that before?"

"At least once."

Rachel pulled away from the intersection.

"Rev. Callaghan was the minister," Malcolm said.

Silence.

"He was a Newfoundlander. From Twillingate. He used to be a Catholic priest. But he quit."

"Being a priest?"

"Yup."

Silence.

"Was he married?"

"As a priest you mean?"

"Of course not as a priest. As a minister."

"Yeah. His wife taught Sunday school."

"Is that why he left the priesthood? To marry her?"

"I don't know. Maybe."

Silence.

"He loved Yeats. He used to quote him all the time. Said we were all slouching towards innocence."

"You mean Bethlehem."

"Huh?"

"Bethlehem. Slouching towards Bethlehem. That's the quote."

"No. He always said slouching towards innocence."

"Well he was wrong."

"I don't think so."

"Look it up."

Malcolm pulled his smartphone from his hip pocket.

After a moment Rachel asked: "Well?"

He resented the sharpness of her tone. She'd been like that all morning.

"I don't get it," Malcolm said. "He always talked about slouching towards innocence. He said we are all trying to get back to the Garden of Eden."

"Not Bethlehem?"

"No—don't miss the turn." Then letting loose his resentment: "I don't know why you didn't let me drive."

Tight-lipped, Rachel accelerated around the corner and sped down the narrow street, made narrower by the enormous sprawling chestnut trees crowding the curb and cars parked on either side.

"Careful!" he said as an older-model black BMW backed slowly out of a driveway in front of them. The driver, a wispy, white-haired woman, was looking the other way. Rachel slowed to a stop and waited. The old woman continued carefully backing up, oblivious to them. When she finally turned her head toward them her face froze in constricted bewilderment and she abruptly stopped, leaving the car stranded half out of the driveway and blocking the street.

Malcolm leaned forward and waved politely to her through the small windshield of their Toyota and the woman looked even more confused.

"Mrs. Thompson," Malcolm said. "I'm surprised she's still driving. She must be in her eighties."

The old woman jerked the car back into the driveway in a single hurried movement and Rachel crept past.

"I used to look after their dog when they went on holidays," said Malcolm. "An Airedale named Fred—or was that Mr. Thompson's name? I wonder if he's still alive."

"Mr. Thompson?"

"The dog."

Rachel turned into the driveway and parked behind a special edition Range Rover.

"Looks like Adam's already here," Malcolm said.

"How many are coming again?" asked Rachel.

"Mom said about thirty or so."

Rachel sighed.

"Just be yourself," said Malcolm.

"It's not me I'm worried about," Rachel said.

Malcolm reached into the back seat to grab the wine and flowers they'd brought.

"Careful," Rachel snapped as Malcolm swung the bouquet of flowers forward.

"Relax," Malcolm said, but immediately wished he hadn't because he could see it only set her more on edge.

As he got out of the car and looked across the street at a house half-demolished, Malcolm was struck once again by how much the neighbourhood had changed. Wealthy offshore investors had snapped up many of the 1940s stucco homes, like the one across the street, knocked them down and erected enormous residences with gated iron fences and security systems to shield them from their neighbours. Then they returned to Asia to manage their businesses, leaving their new "monster" houses vacant for long stretches. In the few homes that hadn't been knocked down, aging parents lived alone waiting for calls from their adult children who had moved out to the suburbs where it was more affordable. The once-vibrant street that had reverberated with the gleeful peal of children's voices was now eerily quiet.

Malcolm's parents' house was a reflection of the street: it bore little resemblance to the home he grew up in. In the first reno, the interior had been stripped down to the studs and reconfigured so that Malcolm never did get used to the new location of his bedroom on the far side of the house; the roofline was reshaped during the second major reconstruction, giving the house a post-modern look that copied many of the new houses on the street; and an oversized deck was most recently added off the kitchen, swallowing up what remained of the back yard. Malcolm's father argued that the additions were necessary for the house to maintain its value

in a market where 3,500-square-foot homes were now considered
the norm. To placate the Thompsons and the shrinking minority
of long-time neighbours, his parents had selected an updated version of the grey stucco cladding.

"Like putting lipstick on a pig," Rachel whispered to
Malcolm when they had been given the grand tour the year
before.

No sooner had the construction ended, than Malcolm's parents
saw their last child—Kyle—leave home. So they closed up all but
one of the bedrooms, covered the furniture in the living room and
dining room and, except for when they entertained, lived in the
'great room' and the kitchen. In a bit of twisted logic, Malcolm's
Dad reasoned that the yard, which had shrank to the size of a sim
card, needed a gardener. He had always looked after the yard himself, but now argued: "You can cover up things in a large yard, but
a small yard shows every imperfection." So every Wednesday a
Quebecois landscaper named Vernay, driving a dented green pick-
up, joined a convoy of other Quebecois landscapers in dented pick-
ups to cut the grass, weed the flower beds, and trim the laurel hedges
of the enormous homes that now lay claim to the neighbourhood.

"Happy anniversary!" Malcolm shouted as his Mom opened
the door. He held the wine and flowers wide and let his Mom
give him a warm embrace. Rachel smiled cautiously in the background.

"You're early," said Malcolm's Dad, appearing in the hallway. "I thought you said you were taking the eleven ferry."

"We wondered if you might need a hand getting ready, so
we came over on the nine," said Malcolm, handing the flowers
to his mother.

"Everything's under control," said Malcolm's Dad. "You
worried for nothing."

"These are lovely," said Malcolm's Mom. "I'll put them in
water right away. Thank you, Malcolm."

"And Rachel," Malcolm called after her.

"What have you got there?" asked Malcolm's Dad, eyeing
the wine.

"For you," Malcolm said and handed the bottle to him.

"We have plenty of wine here, you know."

"That's fine, Dad. If we don't drink it today we can have it another time."

"Adam brought a bottle, too. What do you two think—we never buy wine?" he muttered, taking the wine into the kitchen.

Malcolm half-turned to Rachel, raised his eyebrows and made a little moue, then followed his Dad into the kitchen. Through the patio door he saw that chairs had been set up around the perimeter of the deck. Malcolm's brother Adam was sitting in one, typing on his smartphone.

"Your brother brought wine, too," Malcolm's Dad said loudly from the kitchen, holding the bottle for Adam to see.

"Roy, just let it go," said Malcolm's Mom, snipping a stem and placing the flower carefully in the vase beside her.

Rachel hung back by the kitchen doorway while Malcolm went out onto the deck.

"How's the premier's number one spin doctor?" Adam asked before turning back to his smartphone.

"Chasing another ambulance?" Malcolm asked with a slight uplifting of his chin.

"I should be at the office," he said without looking up. "A deal I thought was done is going sideways."

Adam's phone started vibrating as he was typing.

"I've got to take this," he said and got up and went inside.

Malcolm's Dad came out onto the deck.

"Where's Adam?" he asked.

"He had to take a call. Some deal he's having trouble with."

"He better watch himself."

"What do you mean?"

"Some of those guys he's involved with . . . you need to count your fingers after shaking their hands."

"I thought he was doing boring white collar stuff . . . part-nerships . . . corporate governance . . . like that."

"He was, but he took on a new client a while back—an investment relations firm. They hooked him up with a mining stock promoter. Now he's got them all calling him. Adam Bidwell: legal adviser to Vancouver's penny stock promoters.

Not exactly what your mother and I had in mind when we sent him off to law school."

Roy Bidwell was senior accountant with a large wholesale food supplier. He'd taken the job right out of university. He liked to tell everyone that 1983 was the best year of his life: that was the year he began work, got married, and started a family—in that order. If nothing else, Roy was all about the proper order. Last month, he celebrated his thirtieth year with the company and received a gold mantle clock with his name inscribed on it. It occupied a position of prominence on the faux wood mantle over the gas fireplace in the great room.

"He'll be fine," Malcolm said because he could tell that his Dad was worried. "Adam's smart."

"There's school smart and there's people smart, and he's not people smart," grumbled Malcolm's Dad. "You're people smart. That's why I don't worry about you."

Someone had put Tony Bennett on the stereo and the party guests, many on their second or third drink, were swaying easily when Mr. McIntyre pushed his way toward Malcolm.

"Malcolm!"

"Hi, Mr. McIntyre."

"Call me Bob."

"Bob."

"Come here," he said and took Malcolm by the elbow and steered him into the dining room. There were four people standing over by the china cabinet talking, drinks in hand.

"Your father tells me you're working for the premier," McIntyre said.

He was holding his drink low, by his waist.

"That's right, Mr. McIntyre."

"Call me Bob."

"Bob."

"Well, you can't do that your whole life."

"No?"

"Of course you can't. And who'd want to? Jesus—all those former class presidents. Like being stuck in high school your whole life." He shook his head. "No, you want to get into business. Get a real job."

"Business?" asked Malcolm.

McIntyre nodded silently and leaned forward.

"Have you thought about gas?"

Malcolm could smell the alcohol on his breath.

"Excuse me?" Malcolm asked.

"G–A–S," McIntyre repeated slowly and smiled.

"I'm not sure what you mean," Malcolm said after a moment.

"Natural gas. Shale. Fracking. Compressed. Liquified. It's the future. You young kids today, you all want to work with computers. Forget computers. High tech companies come and go. Look at the trouble RIM is in. Hell, try finding a Compaq computer today. Go on. I dare you. You can't 'cause there aren't any. Gas. That's where the jobs are. Remember that. Will you?"

"I will, Mr. McIntyre."

"Call me Bob. No need to thank me." He lifted his glass to show Malcolm it was empty. "I need a refill."

Malcolm watched Mr. McIntyre lurch toward the kitchen, then checked his smartphone. It was a quiet Sunday politically. The premier was at home—or at least that's where his schedule said he would be. Lately, he'd started "going walkabout"— Maurice's words—showing up unannounced in public with "a fucking media conga line stretched out behind him"—Maurice's words again. Maurice liked to manage everything—even impromptu public appearances.

"How's Malcolm," said Uncle Jim, entering the dining room.

"Hi, Uncle Jim," said Malcolm, and he slipped his phone back into his pocket.

"Mary!" Uncle Jim yelled back into the living room. "Malcolm's here."

Malcolm's Aunt Mary came up to them and Malcolm gave her a hug. She was tiny and plump and her body had the feel of a warm, lumpy pillow.

"Malcolm, dear," Aunt Mary said. "Susan tells me you're in politics."

"Not really, Aunt Mary. I work in the provincial government . . . for the premier's office."

"Is that an elected position?"

"No, no. Though I work with cabinet ministers—and MLAs sometimes."

"So you're in cabinet?"

"No, no. I'm in communications."

The look on Aunt Mary's face indicated that this last explanation worked to only further perplex her.

"What's he like—the premier?" asked Uncle Jim.

"Incredibly hard-working."

"You've met the premier?" asked Aunt Mary.

"He works for him, Mary," said Uncle Jim with a note of exasperation.

"Oh," said Aunt Mary, as if that was the first time she had heard this. "He's such a nice man. A real family man."

"Yes," said Malcolm and thought wryly back to the first time he met the premier.

"Well, I voted for him," said Uncle Jim, "but I didn't vote for all those cuts he's making. Making seniors pay for bus passes was the last straw."

"We have to pay for bus passes?" asked Aunt Mary.

"Starting next April," Uncle Jim said.

"But we never take the bus," Aunt Mary said. "Why do we have to pay for a pass if we don't use the bus?"

"That's not the point," said Uncle Jim.

"Well, if it isn't it ought to be," said Aunt Mary with a self-congratulatory nod.

Adam joined them. He had an air of agreeability, as if they had been waiting for him to inject new life into the conversation.

"Things going better?" Malcolm asked.

"We'll see," said Adam with a crooked grin.

"Is Cathy here?" asked Aunt Mary, swivelling her head to survey the room.

"Nancy," Adam corrected her. "No, we're not together anymore."

"Oh dear," said Aunt Mary, as if receiving news of a death in the family. "And I so liked her."

"It was for the best—for both of us," said Adam trying to maintain his cheerful demeanor.

"She was such a nice girl," said Aunt Mary. "For the life of me I could never understand why she kept her hair so short, lovely blonde hair like that."

"She had dark hair," said Adam, and then for good measure added, "Long. Past her shoulders."

"So you're here alone," said Aunt Mary, at once making it clear that there could be nothing worse in the world. Both her daughters were married and had children who were already in their teens.

Adam was saved by his phone, which gave off a ringing sound like a stock market bell announcing the opening of trading. He glanced at the incoming number and grimaced.

"I've got to take this," he said and glided off toward the hallway.

"How are house prices in Victoria?" asked Uncle Jim.

"I don't know," said Malcolm. "We rent."

"Rent?" asked Uncle Jim as if he had never heard of such a thing. "What on earth for? You might as well flush your money down the toilet."

"Oh, Jim," said Aunt Mary, "for goodness sakes, leave the boy alone."

"He's not a boy. How old are you, Malcolm?"

"Twenty-five."

"Twenty-five, Mary. Do you know when I was twenty-five I already owned two homes? And do you know how I managed that?" Uncle Jim didn't wait for a response. "Never rented."

Malcolm's Dad passed by with a tray of fresh drinks.

"Roy, how come you're letting Malcolm rent?" Uncle Jim asked loudly, following him into the living room.

The anniversary cake came into the dining room held high by Mrs. Moore, a friend of Malcolm's parents who had lived down the street until 1990, just after Tiananmen Square kicked off another Vancouver land rush. She had sold her house to an anxious family from Hong Kong and moved out to White Rock. Mrs. Moore called everyone to gather around the cake and they sang Happy Anniversary to the tune of Happy Birthday. Then Malcolm's Mom and Dad lifted the silver knife with a bright red ribbon tied around its handle and ceremoniously cut the cake. Mrs. Moore quickly shooed them aside and took over the duty of serving the cake.

"Do you know how much your old house is worth today?" Uncle Jim asked Mrs. Moore as she sliced him a piece of the cake. "$2.4 million."

"Margaret doesn't want to hear about her old house," said Aunt Mary, elbowing Uncle Jim in the ribs.

"She sold it for $450,000 in 1990," Uncle Jim said, coming up to where Malcolm was leaning against the kitchen doorway. "If she'd kept it, she'd be a millionaire today," he added through a mouthful of chocolate cake. "That's why you want to own your own home, Malcolm."

Malcolm motioned that Uncle Jim had some icing on his cheek, and his uncle wiped it with the back of his hand and then licked his hand.

After everyone had been served, Malcolm's Mom went round with seconds herself. She stopped in front of Uncle Jim and Malcolm.

"We're so proud of Malcolm," she said, beaming.

Uncle Jim took the opportunity to help himself to another piece of cake while Aunt Mary scolded in the background.

"To be honest, we always wondered about journalism . . . such a nasty business."

"Oh, Mom . . ." Malcolm gently protested.

"No, it's true. Your father and I were so relieved when you got the job in the premier's office. That work with news-papers was so upsetting . . . like when you had to ask those people how they felt after their son has just died in that horrible house fire. I couldn't imagine someone asking me that. It would be unbearable."

"Mom, it wasn't that bad."

"Yes it was. I was shocked when you told me that . . . how you intruded into people's sorrow. That's no way to make a living. You're much better off where you are."

Adam hovered over his mother's shoulder looking for a second piece of cake.

"What are you talking about?" he asked, reaching out to take a slice of cake. He quickly popped the whole thing in his mouth.

"Adam, where are your manners?" Malcolm's Mom asked with mock indignation, but in fact enjoying the intimacy of a family moment. "We're talking about Malcolm's job."

"Oh," said Adam with feigned disinterest.

"I think public service is a calling," said Malcolm's Dad, who stopped briefly on his way to the kitchen to stock up on more drinks. "Unfortunately, we have too many people who don't treat it that way."

"We are so pleased that Malcolm felt the call," Malcolm's Mom said, trying to keep the conversation on a positive track.

"You weren't involved in that business with the fellow who hit the cop were you?" asked Adam.

"No," said Malcolm.

"It was unfortunate he had to resign," said Adam. "I thought he wasn't so bad. The pundits said he was a sure bet for cabinet. He might have survived if it had only been the speeding ticket—but not after sucker punching that cop. Did you see the video?"

How could he miss it? It was everywhere on social media. Gary Johnson, MLA for Surrey-Cloverdale and the government's first political casualty. The media reported that it had taken less than twenty-four hours. Actually, it was less than six hours. He was on his way home from his election-night celebration when his truck was pulled over for speeding. His wife was driving because Johnson had had a few. Johnson got into an argument with the RCMP officer and decked him. Broke his nose. His daughter videotaped the whole thing on her smartphone and posted it to her Facebook page from the back seat of the truck, apparently not fully appreciating the consequences.

"What about the size of his truck?" asked his Dad suddenly excited. "Who drives a truck that big these days? Can you imagine what it costs him to fill that?"

"Do they force him to resign in those circumstances, or does he do that voluntarily?" Adam persisted.

Malcolm knew the answer. Johnson had been given a choice: leave caucus or be turfed. He had balked and threatened to take it to a meeting of caucus, hoping he could ride it out. And he might have because he was popular with his colleagues. But he was no match for the premier, who had already contacted the caucus chair and lined up all the support he needed before he'd even met with Johnson.

"I'm not really part of those discussions," Malcolm said truthfully, while purposely not responding to Adam's question. It still surprised him how quickly he had adapted to the art of political communications—the non-answer answer.

"Lucky they have such a large majority, because if they continue to lose MLAs at that rate they're going to need it," Adam said with a crooked smile.

"Well, I say we're still better off with the United Party than the Liberals," Malcolm's Mom said forcefully as if she had to defend Malcolm.

"Has Roy given any thought to selling this place?" asked Uncle Jim. "I bet it would bring a bundle."

"Let's stop by my Dad's before we go to the ferry," Rachel said once they were in the car.

"We won't make the seven then," Malcolm said.

"I know, but I want to see Dad."

"As long as we're on the nine o'clock," Malcolm said firmly. "It's the last ferry." He wanted to say, "and I have to work tomorrow", but stopped short.

"Malcolm, look—your Dad and Mom have each other. Dad has only me."

Rachel started to tear up. Malcolm hadn't thought about how the party might affect her. His parents had been married thirty years. Never any doubts—at least none they'd ever voiced.

Her parents' relationship had broken down in a glaringly public way. Malcolm couldn't imagine living in a small community day after day with people who looked at him and saw a man whose wife had left him. Their pity would have been too much to take.

"Okay. Let's go see him."

When they arrived Andy was chatting with the neighbour next door, an older woman in a worn cardigan who was tending her garden.

"This is a nice surprise," Andy said, giving Rachel a long embrace.

Malcolm hadn't talked to Andy since their conversation on the phone two weeks ago, when Rachel had gone home, and he wondered now how Andy would react.

"Andy," Malcolm said, leaning forward and reaching out his hand but not moving closer.

Andy took a step toward Malcolm, clasped his hand and said coolly: "Malcolm."

"Hi, Mrs. Claridge," Rachel said and gave the older woman a warm hug. "You remember Malcolm, don't you?"

Mrs. Claridge removed the garden glove from her right hand and shook Malcolm's hand.

"We were just talking about how long I've lived beside you," said Mrs. Claridge. "I remember your Dad as a teenager. He was quite a handful. Of course, that was when my Ralph was still alive."

"Betty had a realtor around today," explained Andy. "Sold the Wimmers' house down the street and wanted to know if Betty was interested in selling. We figured he must have been talking to the Wimmers about who lived on the street. Anyway, it got us to reminiscing about the old days."

"You're not thinking of selling, are you?" asked Rachel.

"Where would I go?" asked Mrs. Claridge. "Into an old folks' home?" She frowned as though unsettled by the very idea.

Andy said, "I told her if she needs a hand around the place she can just call on me."

"Oh, I don't like to be a bother," Mrs. Claridge said mildly. "Your father already shovels my walk whenever it snows, and puts out my garbage and recycling. I have a young man from the university who cuts my lawn and prunes my fruit trees. I think I'll be alright for a while yet."

"Why don't we all go in and I'll put some tea on?" Andy suggested. "You, too, Betty."

"We can't stay long, Dad," Rachel said.

"We're not in that big a rush," said Malcolm. "We have time for a cup of tea."

Rachel smiled at him, and as they walked back to the house she easily slipped her arm through Andy's and leaned into him. Malcolm followed with Mrs. Claridge, taking comfort from the old woman's methodical, side-to-side gait, and from knowing Rachel was happy.

CHAPTER 7

"Unbelievable! Un-fucking-believable!"

Jarrod was shouting in his office. Malcolm poked his head through the doorway.

"Trouble?"

"Ten fucking days! Just to get connected to the government server. Can you believe it? Takes longer to connect my computer to the server than it takes Toshiba to make the fucking thing."

Jarrod's old computer had gone up in a puff of smoke. Literally. It caught fire one day and set off the smoke alarm so everyone had to evacuate the building.

Jessica squeezed past Malcolm and into the office.

"I told you to leave it to me," she tutted. "I'll call them again this morning."

Jessica was more obliging since they had moved into the West Annex, taking the communications team under her wing and helping guide them through the tangle of government services. She'd had the offices cleaned a second time, tracked down new desks and chairs, and secured a pallet of flat-screen TVs that were connected to cable so that now the news channel talking heads chattered constantly in the background of every office. Malcolm could hear the start of a Kevin O'Leary rant in his office, walk down the hall to the office of press secretary Matt McDonaugh, and not miss a word. Still, even Jessica couldn't get Jarrod's computer connected any quicker: it would be up and running in ten days, the client services supervisor told Jessica later that morning outside Malcolm's office. But only if everything went "smoothly".

"And that almost never happens," he sighed. He had the look of a man who was always disappointing people.

Marek Balicki, the premier's assistant director of issues management, who had been listening in, offered: "Nothing a good dose of free enterprise won't fix. God, I can't wait till we start to clear out this deadwood."

"If you have no other questions . . ." the client services supervisor said with a small, forced smile, as if he'd been through this before with countless premiers' staff—and would be through it again with countless more.

"No . . . no," said Jessica, unaccustomed to failure.

"Then I'll be in touch when I know more."

"We could be retired by then," Balicki said.

The comment sent the client services supervisor looking around for an exit.

"This way," Jessica said, comforted by being able to reassert her authority. She guided him to an oak door that led to the outer reception area and past the security desk.

Malcolm shared an office on the first floor of the West Annex with two other communications officers: Amanda Pedersen and Amy Li. He called them the two A's because they seemed interchangeable. They were both fresh out of university and daughters of prominent party supporters. Jarrod's office was next door. The rest of the floor housed offices for Maurice, Matt McDonaugh, Angela Chang, director of policy Suzy Charron, and the cerebral issues management team of director Glenn Franson and assistant director Marek Balicki. The premier's executive assistant, Rai Bains, was located in the large reception area, while Jessica had an office in an open area near Maurice. And, of course, the premier had the corner office overlooking the front lawn. "So he can see when it needs mowing," joked Balicki, though not so loudly that Maurice might hear.

By the end of the third week, Malcolm's work day had settled into a satisfying routine. He arrived at the office about 8AM, having used his electronic security pass to slip through the side door to the West Annex and greet the portly commissionaire at the desk with a cheery, "Good morning, Burt." Burt's response was always the same: seemingly startled into action by this welcome intrusion, he half-tumbled out of his padded leather chair to buzz Malcolm through the inner door before Malcolm could use his pass. It was a good-humoured ritual that both Malcolm and Burt acknowledged and appreciated, Malcolm for the sheer delight of being treated as a person of consequence, and Burt for the regard shown by Malcolm, the only person in the West Annex who knew his name. Once through the inner door, Malcolm was met by the reception area, the office's second—and stiffer—line of defence, though now it was easily scaled because Rai wouldn't be at her desk for another half hour.

Malcolm then poked his head into Franson and Balicki's office. Franson was all of 25 years old and already a seasoned political hand. Having worked on two campaigns, he knew more about politics and elections than others twice his age. He was hard-nosed and ruthless, and if given the slightest opening went straight for the jugular. One-half of the whiz kid team of Franson and Balicki. Balicki, also twenty-five and a veteran of two elections, was a kinder, gentler version of Franson. His forte was assembling bites of information and turning them into fact-bombs to use against the Opposition. Legend had it they started in research within days of each other and have been inseparable since. Balicki was outgoing, garrulous, and funny. Franson was reserved, serious and unsmiling. They made a perfect team.

Malcolm gave them a noiseless nod because they were in the middle of their daily issues call with "The Centre"—the newly established Public Affairs Program, or PAP as it quickly became known. Over the speakerphone, the dulcet voice of Gina Biocchetti—the former television reporter who days after the election exchanged her microphone for a senior post in government communications—ran down the issues of the day. Balicki returned Malcolm's nod with a smile and a broad wink; Franson just looked at Malcolm before turning away.

Franson and Balicki had already been working for two hours, mostly at home and in the car, constantly scanning media reports that were sent automatically to their smartphones. They were looking for any stories that might need an immediate government response. At this time of the morning, the reports were coming through every few seconds, sent by two dozen faceless communications staff hunkered across the street in a windowless room on the top floor of a squat, four-storey, pale pink concrete building that wouldn't have been out of place in the 1950s Soviet Union.

Once in the office, Franson and Balicki quickly scoured the media monitoring package that was produced and delivered every morning to their computer by the same faceless communications drones. The package included stories related to the provincial government from that morning's TV, radio, print and the web, as well as anything from the previous day that was published after the package had been put to bed, along with transcripts of the top-rated talk radio shows. Often running to more than 100 pages, the package covered everything from the Coquitlam mother whose daughter died after an ambulance ran out of gas on the way to the hospital, to the cougar shot by a conservation officer on a rural Port Hardy street.

Franson and Balicki then prepped a package for the Boss highlighting the key issues, including holding messaging for questions he might get from media that morning while he was out and about. Maurice also got a copy of the package and would weigh in with his thoughts on the messaging if he didn't like what Franson and Balicki had produced.

Malcolm avoided Maurice, who was always the first in, and went straight to his desk. He liked that time of the morning, when he had the office to himself. The two A's didn't arrive until 8:30, typically closer to 8:45, and then between stifled yawns and applying their makeup, spent the next twenty minutes deconstructing the previous night's romp through Victoria's club scene. Malcolm used the time to quietly flip through the stack of morning papers that had been dropped just inside the office doorway. He had the electronic editions on his computer, but he preferred hard copies. Rai had made a push to eliminate newspaper delivery as a way to save money, but Malcolm convinced Franson that it was helpful to see how stories actually played out in print. What seemed like an innocuous story online was a banner headline at the top of the page in print, and what might appear to be a major story in the e-edition ended up as a two-paragraph, single-column story tucked into the bottom corner in the hard copy. Still, as more readers switched to the online edition, it was only a matter of time before print editions went the way of hot lead and linotype.

The first floor, or "downstairs", was the political arm of the premier's office. "Upstairs" on the second floor was the domain of the public service led by deputy minister to the premier, Alwyn Upshall. Where Maurice operated by nuance, allusion and acts of concealment, Upshall managed by bluntness. In part, it was because of his size: at six-feet, four-inches and 260 pounds he lacked the physical presence for subtlety; and in part it was because of his face: like a well-worn catcher's mitt, it was deeply lined and perpetually tanned—the face of a man who met everything head-on. Gravity tugged heavily at his fleshy features, and his slick black hair was flecked with grey as if stuck with blowing ash from an ever-present, half-smoked cigarette that he planned to re-light as soon as he had a break. He constantly professed to be quitting smoking. Behind puffy cheeks and sagging eyelids, two watery black smears looked out on the world.

Upshall had a small staff of six or so, but the size didn't reflect his responsibilities: a $44-billion annual budget, nearly four times that of the province's largest publicly traded company; and with more than 30,000 government workers, he was the head of the province's largest employer.

The cabinet chambers were also located upstairs, occupying almost half the floor. You might say the ministers of the Crown were literally aged in oak, meeting as they did behind soundproofed, carved double oak doors, within oak-panelled walls, and around an enormous oval oak table with individual leather desk pads and pen sets. There, they debated, argued and devised the best way to govern British Columbia's 4.5 million residents—and to get re-elected. A narrow, spiral wrought-iron staircase provided private access between the two floors, a vestige of a previous century, its helical design and wobbly construction a metaphor for the complex, changing and sometimes unsteady relationship between upstairs and downstairs.

The first time Malcolm met Upshall—he demanded to be known by his last name—was in the tiny men's bathroom on the first floor at the bottom of the sweeping marble staircase that greeted the public entrance to the West Annex. He was stooped over the basin washing his hands, head bent and shoulders hunched in the way of a man who often finds himself in spaces that are too small.

"Upshall," he said gruffly as he dried his hands on a wad of paper towels, then stuck out a giant paw with fingers like Cohibas. He gripped Malcolm's hand quickly and tightly, as if afraid it might slip away.

"Malcolm . . . Malcolm Bidwell . . . part of the communications team," replied Malcolm. He tried to return the firm grip but found his fingers had been rolled together so he could only hang on as Upshall vigorously pumped his arm up and down like he was trying to draw water from a dry well. Upshall finally released him and Malcolm stepped back to collect himself. Meanwhile, Upshall removed his glasses, cleaned them on his tie, and put them back on, looking hard again at Malcolm. It was as if he needed to get a clearer view.

"Well, I won't hold that against you," Upshall finally said without smiling.

He was wearing a dark suit with shiny patches on the elbows. The suit was too big, even for him: the jacket hung on his shoulders like a hockey jersey and was unbuttoned, revealing pants that were cinched tight so they bunched at the waist, and legs that drooped into a pool on the floor. Malcolm gave a broad grin in defence, hoping that the remark was intended as a joke, but Upshall remained stone-faced.

"I look forward to working with you," Malcolm said, trying to make this a brief encounter.

There was an awkward moment. Malcolm wanted to get to the stall, but he had to wait until Upshall moved out of the way. Upshall, for his part, understood that he held the strategic high ground and was in no hurry to surrender it. Finally, Upshall shifted his bulk sufficiently to allow Malcolm past. As Malcolm opened the stall door Upshall turned and asked: "You're the new one, aren't you?"

Malcolm, his hand still on the door, was defensive. "Well, I've been here nearly a month now."

As he closed the door to the stall he couldn't shake the feeling that he would always be the new one. Always the outsider.

"Maurice just put this on my desk," Jarrod said, holding up a note. Malcolm went to reach for it, but Jarrod pulled it away. "Minister Visser needs a hand writing a speech. Apparently we fired everyone in his com shop. Not a single person left standing. Now he's demanding help. Fast. I can't because I'm swamped."

He swept his hand across his empty desk as if to supply proof.

"I need you to be his com shop. Until we can get more bodies over there."

Malcolm knew all about the firings: a third of communications staff across government had been let go late yesterday in what was being dubbed "Black Monday". Staff were called one-by-one into a meeting and handed a sealed envelope. Inside the envelope was one of two letters—either offering you a job or firing you. Don Henderson got a letter firing him. Malcolm tried to call him as soon as he heard, but there was no answer on his direct line and his cell phone was no longer in service. He finally called Janice, the office administrator. She was still choking back tears when she answered.

"They had security escort him out of the office with all his belongings in a cardboard box. Ten years of public service and they march you out the door like a criminal."

Janice had survived, along with several others in the office. She said Mackin had received an offer letter and would be accepting it.

"What else can you do?" she asked. "You know that better than anyone."

What did she mean by that?

"A few were talking about rejecting the offer," she said. "I told them they were crazy. Why stay after the election if you were only going to quit? Unless all they wanted was the severance package."

Malcolm tried to send Don an email, but his account had already been shut down.

Malcolm said to Jarrod: "It seems we're really good at firing people and but not so good at hiring them. Don't you think it should be the other way around?"

Jarrod squirmed uncomfortably in his chair, as if an unwilling conspirator caught in an act of disloyalty.

"I'll let Minister Visser know that you'll contact him," he said and returned his attention to his empty desk.

CHAPTER 8

ON HIS WAY to see Visser, Malcolm ran through what he knew about the new Minister of Advanced Education: longtime United Party member with a family history in the UP that stretched back several generations; the only elected UP member of the legislature back when the party was a true United Party, before it became a shell for fleeing Liberals; one of a tiny core of left-of-centre UP ministers in a cabinet dominated by the party's right; confounded both history and the experts by getting re-elected in what had been a swing riding; and, perhaps most interesting of all, considered by the punditry to be the "political conscience" of the party. And only as an afterthought: he used a wheelchair.

Malcolm opened the door to Visser's office.

". . . and I told her I couldn't possibly take her money."

Visser, who had his back to the door, was in the middle of telling his staff a story. Upon seeing Malcolm, a young woman started to get up, but Visser waved her to remain seated.

"Just a moment," he said over his shoulder without actually looking at Malcolm. "We're almost done."

Malcolm could have been the premier himself, but Visser didn't care. Returning his attention to his staff, he continued, "But I said I could let her buy me a coffee. And she did. That's how she became my constituency assistant. And later my wife."

The young woman beamed a broad smile and such an obvious look of admiration that Malcolm had the feeling it took all of her willpower not to reach out and hug Visser.

"Okay, back at it," Visser said easily, and the four staff members lifted themselves out of their reverie and returned to work.

At that point, Visser neatly spun his wheelchair to face Malcolm.

"You must be Malcolm. Thanks for coming. I can really use your help."

Malcolm tried not to look at the wheelchair, but the more he didn't look at it the more obvious he was.

"Ah yes, my wheelchair," Visser said matter-of-factly.

"I'm . . . I'm sorry," Malcolm said, his throat tightening.

The young woman coughed in embarrassment and Malcolm felt the convivial air of the staff coffee break leak out of the room.

"Lemme give you the sales pitch," Visser said, his voice changing to mimic a car salesman. "It's the latest model: titanium frame so it's strong but light." He gripped the bar and gave it a tug. "Adjustable camber for increased comfort . . . and Spinergy Spox wheels. It can go from one end of the legislature hallway to the other in about fifteen seconds—if the commissionaires aren't around."

"Nice," Malcolm said, nodding and smiling as Visser's warmth and charm put him at ease.

"I, on the other hand, am not as state-of-the-art. I've got an inflammation of the spinal cord that makes it impossible for me to get around without this chair. The doctors told me it could be permanent or it could go away tomorrow. That was six years ago."

Visser slapped the side of the chair in a way that was both appreciative and resentful. Malcolm had a sense of glimpsing something personal that he shouldn't have, like walking past a house and observing a private exchange in the window before the curtain was drawn.

There was a moment of strained silence before Malcolm said: "So you need someone to write a speech for you . . ."

"Right. It seems Maurice fired everyone in my com shop. Now I'm stuck without any communications support and I'm opening a new First Peoples House at SFU on Tuesday."

"Well, you're in luck, minister," Malcolm said. "I was a com officer in Education before going to work in the premier's office, so I know a little about the subject—more than forestry and mining, anyway. I haven't worked in government long, but I have written some speeches and lots of news releases. And I was a reporter with the News Daily in my previous life."

"Unless you're older than you look, that must have been a very brief life."

"It was," said Malcolm. "But long enough to get a number of stories under my belt. I know how to craft a narrative."

"Great! Exactly what I need."

Visser invited Malcolm into his office where he closed the door. Malcolm noted that neither his executive assistant nor his ministerial assistant were included in the meeting. Visser laid out in broad strokes what he wanted to say at the event, much of it pretty standard: recognition of First Nations and the value of their heritage and culture; the vital role of post-secondary education to the B.C. economy; the new government's plans for both First Nations and post-secondary education.

"The tone of the speech is my biggest concern. I want to fore-shadow the results of the core service review. Of course, the premier has his view and I have mine, so how we handle that will require some delicacy. And the worst thing is we don't have a lot of time."

"So you've already completed the review in advanced education?" Malcolm asked.

The review had only been announced in the days following the election, which was barely a month ago. Some ministries hadn't even started consulting with stakeholders.

"That's where I need your help framing my position," said Visser, at once answering, but not answering Malcolm.

"I'm sorry to be a bit slow, minister, but I thought the review wasn't going to cabinet's priorities planning committee until the end of August. Has that changed?"

"No. But you knew the review was ninety per cent complete before it even started? And the remaining ten per cent is, for the most part, cosmetic."

"I didn't know that," said Malcolm, almost inaudibly.

"Well, before the election, the premier and a hand-picked team did their own review. First they identified programs closely linked to the former government. The plan is to eliminate any of those programs that don't directly affect the public—"easy wins", they called them. It sends a message to voters that the UP is not the Liberal Party 2.0 and reinforces the message that the Liberals

mismanaged government. Then they targeted unionized government services that they want to decertify and privatize, like prison
guards—a bit of payback for union support of the NDP during
the election. In the final tranche they earmarked programs they
want to scrap but will likely generate a lot of public backlash.
They plan to do those early in the mandate to give the public
time to forget about them before the next election. The review
being carried out now is really just a matter of looking at the
books and confirming what they've planned. And, of course,
demonstrating that it was all done with the utmost fairness and
equity and in the public good."

"I see," Malcolm said.

"That last part was sarcasm," Visser said.

"I got that," Malcolm responded.

"Good. My problem is that I completely disagree with their
plan. While it's certainly worthwhile to scrutinize what services
we're offering and to examine what programs aren't being delivered efficiently and effectively, we shouldn't use politics as the
lens through which we view whether a program stays or goes.
We don't have a monopoly on good ideas. Just look at what he
wants to do with the student loan program. The NDP proposed
expanding it during the election, so he plans to cut funding pretty
much in half and link what's left to labour demand. A middle
class kid from Vanderhoof who wants to go to UBC to study
theatre won't get any funding, but a kid going to BCIT for sheet
metal working will—though not as much as he would have previously. More kids won't be able to afford a post-secondary education. Is that really the outcome we want? Not me. That's why
I plan to use this first speech to lay down a marker . . . make it
more difficult for the premier to cut funding and gut the student
loan program—among other programs."

He paused and looked at Malcolm.

"Are you comfortable with this, Malcolm? If you aren't,
then let me know now and you can walk out that door and we
never had this conversation."

Malcolm was feeling uneasy. He was fine with helping write
a speech, but he certainly didn't expect this. He should give

Maurice a heads up. If he didn't and Maurice found out, well he didn't want to think about that.

"Needless to say, I will take complete responsibility for the speech, if that's what's worrying you."

"It is a concern," Malcolm admitted. How did Visser know what he was thinking?

"Of course it is," Visser said. "You work in the premier's office. You're worried it would put you in an awkward position, to say the least. I wouldn't do that and I wouldn't ask it of you. I thought I would simply say that I added those comments after you delivered the speech to me. There was no way you could know. You could even give the speech to Maurice ahead of time—the one without my comments."

Malcolm thought for a moment.

"Couldn't you to just add the comments after I give you the speech?" Malcolm asked.

"Look, I'm not a writer," Visser said. "If I could do it myself I would. But I can't. I need your help."

Malcolm felt caught. Even if he didn't help Visser, he still knew what Visser was planning to do. So either way he would have to tell Maurice. Then what?

"Aren't you worried about what will happen to you?" Malcolm asked.

"Malcolm, I know much of politics is about compromise, but sometimes there are things you feel so strongly about that you have to stand up for them no matter what."

Malcolm tried to think of something he felt so strongly about that he would take a stand—no matter what. Nothing came to mind. Surely there was something he would take a stand on.

Visser continued: "My granddad used to say, 'If you don't stand for something, you'll fall for anything.' I would add that it's easy to stand up for what you believe in when it doesn't cost you anything. The real test of the strength of our convictions is when you have to pay dearly for them. My opposition to the core review may cost me, but that's the price that has to be paid."

Malcolm had all but made up his mind to tell Maurice, but now he wasn't so sure. There was a lot to like about Visser.

Gerald Morris was right. He was a nice guy. But Malcolm also knew that helping Visser could lose him his job. Was he willing to pay that price for someone he had just met? But it didn't feel like he had just met Visser. It had only been a half hour, but he felt like he'd known him all his life. They had a special connection. Still, one thing Malcolm had learned from Rob was there were no secrets at the legislature. It was just a matter of time. Some took hours, some days, some weeks, some years, but eventually every secret came out. Every one. He could only hope that his secret came out long after he had left government.

"Alright, minister," he said, before taking a deep breath and adding, "I'll give it a go."

"Wonderful. From now on, it's Mike. So tell me, Malcolm, how you're going to have me deliver the best speech since the Gettysburg Address?"

"Okay, minister—Mike—but let's aim for something a little more manageable. How about the best maiden speech by a minister in this government?"

"Deal," Visser said and reached out to shake Malcolm's hand.

"Do we want to call in your MA?" asked Malcolm.

"Not yet. Let's nail down a framework for the speech first. Then we'll get Eric in to work on some of the platform commitments that they want us to include in every speech. Just be careful what you say in front of Eric. He reports everything he hears to Maurice."

Malcolm cocked his head to one side.

"That's how Maurice keeps an eye on me. I'm sure Eric has already sent Maurice a note telling him that you're here."

"How can you be so sure I won't report what we're doing?" Malcolm asked. "I work for Maurice, too."

"You do, but you're not one of them."

"Oh no?"

Malcolm tried not to sound deflated. Was it that obvious?

"No. I haven't seen you at any of the party conferences or helping out on campaigns. I'm the longest serving United Party MLA in this government and I know everyone active in the UP, but I don't know you. Why is that? Obviously, the answer is that you haven't been active. I checked the membership list and you're not on it. So you aren't even a party member. That means you haven't drunk the Kool-Aid. Am I one hundred per cent certain? No. But in the end, we all have to trust someone. I've decided it might as well be you."

"It sounds to me like you're fighting against your own government—your own party."

"Not fighting, Malcolm, reforming. I'm out to reform the United Party."

"Have you thought that maybe you're in the wrong party?"

"I can't say that it hasn't crossed my mind. But the United Party is the party of my father and his father before him. I feel an obligation to help restore it to what it was before it was hijacked by Davis. I can't do that from the outside. And I can't do it alone. I have built a core base of support within the party—that's why Davis was compelled to appoint me to cabinet. You don't think he did that on his own, do you? But he also doesn't trust me as far as he can throw me. That's okay, though, because the feeling is mutual."

CHAPTER 9

ANY DOUBTS MALCOLM had about Visser's relationship with Maurice and Davis were abandoned when he returned to the office and found Jessica waiting.

"Maurice wants to see you right away."

Maurice was in a familiar pose, seated behind his computer staring at the screen.

"Malcolm, do you know who wrote the jingle for Mr. Clean?"

Malcolm was apprehensive around Maurice. Everyone was. How could you not be? Maurice was crazy. It was made worse by the fact that sometimes he could be so normal. If he were simply crazy all the time, consistently crazy, then you would know what to expect. But he wasn't. If anything, he was consistently unpredictable. And like all truly crazy people, anything could set him off. More often than not, there was no connection between what was said and Maurice's unhinging. Like a bolt of lightning from a clear blue sky. And his reaction was never the same: sometimes he would scream until his face went purple, the vein in his neck bulged, and his voice grew hoarse; other times he would launch into a subdued, rambling, speech that touched on everything from politics to pop culture; Maurice liked to think of himself as a pop culture observer and analyst, though Malcolm thought his tendencies were more compulsive.

"Uh, no."

"Come on, make a guess."

"Hmm, no idea."

"Really?"

Maurice frowned with disappointment, like a child who couldn't entice someone to play with him.

"My mother used to use it," Malcolm said, helpfully.

"Tom Cadden. He was thirty-four when he wrote it. I bet he didn't know at the time that it would become the longest running TV jingle ever."

Maurice began to sing the commercial: "Mr. Clean gets rid of dirt and grime and grease in just a minute. Mr. Clean will clean your whole house and everything that's in it."

Malcolm wondered—only half-jokingly—if Maurice was on some sort of medication but didn't say anything, waiting to see the direction this was headed. If there was a direction.

"You have to wonder what makes it so successful. The tune? It's pretty catchy in a way. Easy to remember, I guess. The words? They're nothing special. They rhyme, but what jingle doesn't? It came out in the late fifties . . . 1958. It was probably pretty trendy for the time. I wouldn't know because I wasn't even born then. But it still works today . . . fifty-five years later. Now that's longevity for you. That's branding!"

Maurice was always on about branding—brand management, brand reputation, brand engagement. He was like that guy in Forrest Gump talking about shrimp. What was his name? Bubba. Maurice was the Bubba of the B.C. legislature the way he was always talking about branding. He liked to tell everyone that the Boss was a brand, like he wasn't a real person but some product.

"But he's more than just a brand," Maurice would explain. "He's also the brand ambassador for the party and the government. He does a great job considering all his baggage."

Maurice held the view that politics is a profession where the less you've done the better.

"That way you don't have a record with which you can be attacked by the media, your opponents and those who envy the success of others."

University professor? Too smart. Businessperson? Too ambitious. Labour leader? Too partisan. Charity CEO? Too idealistic.

"The best politician is . . . a politician," he said. "One who has been a lifelong politician. Preferably one who has done nothing, so there is nothing with which they can be attacked. Everyone can identify with them. They can be whoever you want them to be. They are democracy's chameleons, changing with their surroundings."

He wasn't joking.

And if not a politician?

"Then a radio talk show host because they have a ready-made constituency. And radio is so ephemeral. *Never* a newspaper columnist, and especially never a political columnist. Opinions harden around them. Too sharply dividing. It's the nature of print—and the fundamental difference between oral and written communication."

Maurice waved at Malcolm.

"Come here, I want to show you something."

Malcolm walked to the side of his desk.

"No, come right around. You have to see the screen."

Malcolm stood directly behind Maurice.

"Do you know who that is?"

It was a black and white image of a man in his mid-thirties. He wore a black suit, white shirt and black tie. Malcolm wondered if the suit and tie were really black or if they were some dark colour that only showed up black in black-and-white photos. His hair was slicked back in the style of the 1950s. He wore thick black-rimmed glasses and stood at a dark wooden podium.

Malcolm shrugged. "Nope."

"That's Mike Visser."

"What! No way!"

"Not Mike Visser, the Minister of Advanced Education! His grandfather."

Malcolm could see the resemblance in his mouth, and also noticed a United Party banner behind his head on the wall in the background. It looked like he was standing in a dingy, dimly lit hall.

"That was 1958 . . . the same year Tom Cadden came out with the Mr. Clean jingle. Visser was speaking at a rally in Oak Bay. Fresh off the boat from Holland. He could barely speak English. 'Visser-the-fisher', they called him because Visser means fisher in Dutch. Ran for MLA four times and lost every time."

"You mean he was never elected?"

"Not once. In 1960 he couldn't even win the nomination. Pathetic. Let me show you something else."

He clicked the mouse and another image appeared. This time it was a colour image of a man in a grey suit amid a crowd of people. A woman reaching out to him had the unmistakeable big bleached hair and bangs of the 1980s.

"Mike Visser. The *son*," Maurice said with emphasis. "Mike's father. UP candidate in the 1983 election . . . when Shelley Jesperson was leader . . . the year the party didn't elect a single candidate. Got less than three per cent of the vote. I think he got even less. He certainly didn't get his deposit back. Never ran again."

Maurice closed the screen.

"They think they're a fucking political dynasty—like the Kennedys or the Bushes. The Visser kings. They couldn't even get elected until the grandson finally won a seat. Some dynasty."

He got up and walked over to the window. A horse and carriage clip-clopped lazily down the tree-shaded street, going in and out of the patches of sunlight that peeked through the leafy canopy, a string of cars backed up in frustration behind it.

"Jarrod says you're working on Mike's speech for Tuesday."

"That's right."

"I don't know how much you know about Mike . . ." Maurice stopped and turned and looked at Malcolm.

"I just met him. To be honest, Maurice, I barely knew his name."

"Jesus, you young people today don't have any sense of history. Well, as you saw, his Dad and his grandfather weren't very successful politicians. But they were running at a time when the party itself wasn't very successful. Let's be honest, it was a fucking disgrace. Convicted murderers got more votes. But that's changed. The party's changed. We attract more voters now because we're a bigger-tent party than we used to be. We're a party of all political stripes. I'm a former Social Crediter. Frank Richmond was a Conservative. The Boss was a Liberal. But we're all United Party members now. We believe in free enterprise, low taxes and small government. But some want to take us back to a time when the party represented very narrow interests."

Maurice stopped again and waited.

"Like Visser?" Malcolm ventured.

"Like Visser. And he's not alone. There are others—their numbers are small, but they have a disproportionately strong voice within the party. They have forced things . . . created issues for the Boss. My job is to look out for the Boss. Protect the brand. Your job, too."

Maurice looked at Malcolm.

"Right?" Maurice said forcefully. He wasn't asking a question, but seeking confirmation.

Malcolm nodded cautiously without saying anything. He had to be careful what he was agreeing to.

"So part of looking out for the Boss means keeping an eye on who is doing what. In your case, it's Mike Visser. Mike's giving his first speech next week, and I want to see it before he delivers it."

"No problem," Malcolm said, relieved. "I'll email it to you when I have a draft."

"Don't email it! I have one rule about email: I never use it. Don't email me anything. Ever."

"Nothing?" Malcolm was incredulous.

"Did you not just hear what I said? Nothing. Ever."

Malcolm wanted to ask how Maurice functioned without email. Malcolm couldn't imagine. It would be like working in the 1980s. But if he didn't like email there were other ways to share documents electronically.

"If you want, I could set up a Dropbox account and post the speech there," Malcolm offered helpfully. "Then you could see it online from anywhere right away."

"Dropbox?" asked Maurice.

"Yeah, it's . . . like . . . a cloud-based, file-sharing program." Malcolm could see that Maurice had no idea what he was talking about so he quickly added: "Really easy to use." As in any eight-year-old can use it—and millions do.

"Look, Malcolm, I don't need all that. I just want to see the speech. Give it to Jarrod when you have it. He'll print me off a copy." And then he added for emphasis: "A *paper* copy."

"No problem," Malcolm said.

He waited to see if there was anything else. Maurice had turned to look out the window, as if he had something on his mind. He turned back and seemed surprised that Malcolm was still there.

"Close the door on the way out," he said and returned to his desk.

On the way back to his office Malcolm dropped in on Jarrod.

"Did you know that Maurice doesn't use email?"

Malcolm moved a pen and perched himself on the edge of Jarrod's desk. Jarrod frowned, reached out and pulled the pen toward him protectively.

"He uses email," Jarrod said without taking his eyes off where Malcolm was sitting on his desk.

"He just told me not to send him Visser's speech by email because he never uses email. As in *never, ever*."

Jarrod pushed his chair away from his desk and then back again so that it was in the same position.

"He uses email," Jarrod repeated. "He's just very selective about it. Would you mind not sitting there? He doesn't want anything captured by FOI. You didn't email him, did you?"

"No," Malcolm said, lifting himself off Jarrod's desk. "He asked me to send Visser's speech to you. Then you're to make a paper copy for him. He stressed that he wants a *paper* copy."

Jarrod leaned forward with the pen. He studied the desk for a moment, then placed it in the same spot from where Malcolm had picked it up.

"He's paranoid about Freedom of Information requests," Jarrod said. "He thinks that's what helped bring down the Liberals. He should know—he was the one who used FOI like it was his personal service. He doesn't want the same thing to happen to us. The NDP have already filed requests. For the transition binders. Upshall's the same. Won't write anything down. Physically write anything on paper. He's afraid it will be FOI'd. But he likes email. Says it makes his life easier. Just deletes everything at the end of the day. Says it's all transitory."

"Transitory?"

"Yeah. FOI regulations allow you to delete any documents that are considered transitory."

"But everything can't be transitory."

Jarrod sneered. "I'll let you tell Upshall that."

He took out a Handi-Wipe from a drawer and picked up the pen and cleaned it, then cleaned the spot on the desk where Malcolm had sat. Then he carefully set it on the spot he had just cleaned. Then moved it slightly. Then slightly again.

"You must be Malcolm. Please come in."

A slim, fit woman held the door. She wore a pair of shorts over black leggings and a baggy v-neck sweater and scarf. In the shadow of the doorstep she might have been a university student, but as Malcolm stepped out of the dark and into the large, well-lighted foyer he saw that she was in her mid-thirties.

"No jacket?" she inquired.

"Nah. It's not bad out there. Even with the wind."

"I don't think I'll ever get used to Victoria. It's always so cool. I'm Claire, by the way. Mike's partner. Mike's in here."

Claire had the welcoming, unforced manner of a career politician's wife and Malcolm wondered how many people she had greeted over the years. Claire led Malcolm down a hallway past a wall of family photos and Malcolm thought he caught a glimpse of Mike's grandfather but couldn't be sure. There were large sepia-toned photographs in elaborate gilt frames with rounded glass that showed unsmiling people staring straight at the camera. Malcolm considered how they were so unlike today's digital photos that were posted to websites where they were seen by thousands of "friends", but would never grace the walls of a family home. As if they had no connection to the past.

"You're not from around here then?" asked Malcolm.

"No," Claire said. "Salmon Arm. They don't wear leggings and scarves in June up there, I can tell you."

She stopped at the doorway that opened into a spacious room. Visser was sitting on the couch with his laptop open, his wheelchair nearby, empty.

"Malcolm, thanks for coming. And thanks for giving up your Friday night. I really appreciate it. Especially so late."

"No problem," Malcolm said.

Rachel had a special staff meeting today after work anyway. Her non-profit was looking to expand into Vancouver, Kelowna and Calgary. Then they had gone for dinner and drinks afterwards. Malcolm had been invited to join them after his session with Visser.

"I read your first draft. It is very good. The structure is terrific. I've made a couple of tweaks here and there to get the tone right. And I added one of my favourite quotes. See what you think."

Malcolm sat next to Visser on the couch and took the laptop. He was glad Visser liked the draft and was curious what sections he had reworked.

"It's better," said Malcolm, handing the laptop back to Visser. "Though I wonder at the end if you aren't pulling your punches a bit too much."

"Where?" asked Visser, squinting at the laptop.

"Here," said Malcolm leaning over and pointing. "And here."

"So what would you put? I want to be careful, remember."

Malcolm took the laptop back and typed intermittently while Visser watched over his shoulder. Even before he had finished Visser said: "I like that a lot. That's much stronger."

After they had finished, Malcolm got up to go, but Visser encouraged him to stay for a drink.

"We don't have a lot of people over," he said. "A politician's social life can be pretty isolated. We go to a lot of events, but that's work really. It's hard to keep friends—real friends—because we spend half our life in our constituency and the other half here on the island. People back home get on with their own lives while we're over here, so when we see them it's a bit like we're just visitors. And here—well—everyone we know is a politician or in politics."

"Including me," said Malcolm.

"I guess that's right. But somehow, I don't think of you as being in politics."

"I'm not sure if that's a good thing or not."

"It's a good thing," said Visser laughing. "Don't get me wrong: politics can be awfully rewarding. You can do a lot of good for people, especially on a one-to-one level, and that's extremely satisfying. But this whole place—" he waved expansively "—can also get pretty claustrophobic. And sometimes it doesn't seem real, if you know what I mean."

Malcolm nodded. Even though he had only worked in government a few months, he did know what he meant.

"Scotch?" asked Visser.

"Beer if you have one," said Malcolm.

"Beer it is."

Visser shifted his body easily from the couch to the wheelchair and expertly glided out of the room and returned a few moments later with two beers in his lap.

"I have to tell you, Malcolm," Visser said as he handed him a beer, "that since I met you I've got a bit more of a spring in my step. You're good for me."

Malcolm could feel his face heat up; his ears particularly glowed red when he was embarrassed.

"Undeserved, but thank you," he said.

Visser leaned forward slightly.

"And in more ways than one," he said. He looked toward the open door before continuing in a quieter voice. "Claire and I want to have children, but we've been unable to—I've been unable to. I've been to any number of specialists who haven't been able to help me. But I'm actually starting to feel something. It's too early to say where it will all end up, but for the first time in years I'm hopeful."

Malcolm felt uncomfortable and wondered why Visser was sharing such intimate details. All he could think of saying was: "That's great."

"Don't say anything to Claire. I don't want to get her hopes up."

"I won't," Malcolm said. He couldn't imagine raising it with her. Then to try to show he wasn't as ill at ease as he felt, he added with a wink: "I thought she'd be the first to know."

"I'm not at that point yet," Visser said, as if he'd already said too much and his talking about it might ruin everything.

"Okay," said Malcolm somewhat apologetically. And then to change the subject: "How'd you two meet?"

"She answered my ad for a constituency assistant. My old CA split up with her husband and moved back to the Kootenays. Claire had been working at the local rec centre and was looking for a change. About a month into the job, I asked her out. The rest is, as they say . . ."

"And she's no longer your constit assistant, obviously."

"Right. I wanted her here with me when I'm in Victoria. It was hard for her at first, but she's fine with it now. Most of the MLAs leave their wives and families at home and rent an apartment here, but I didn't want to be away from her."

"So how long has it been?"

"Five years."

So she married him after he was in the wheelchair, thought Malcolm. That's true love. He wondered how he would have reacted if Rachel had been in a wheelchair when they first met. Five years. That would be five years without sex—and maybe a lifetime. He couldn't imagine it.

The first news reports came from Emma Ashby, the Vancouver Sun's education reporter, on her live Twitter feed.

"BC Ad Ed Min @MikeVisser says student loan funding will remain unchanged."

It wasn't until a minute or two later, between her sixth and seventh tweets, that Malcolm heard a loud "Fuck!" from Maurice's office. Malcolm, who had been following the Twitter coverage while working on a speech for the premier, figured Maurice must have only then glanced at Twitter. Either that, or he didn't follow Ashby and someone who did sent him the tweet. In any case, it prompted more shouting.

"Malcolm! Get in here!"

The two A's lifted their heads and exchanged knowing looks while trying unsuccessfully to suppress smiles. They resented Malcolm for his relationship with the Boss—even though he'd rarely seen him in his month in the PO. As he lifted himself out of his chair, Malcolm girded himself for what was to come.

"Jarrod! You too!"

Good. He wouldn't take the brunt of Maurice's wrath alone.

Maurice was waiting at his office with his hand on the door. Malcolm and Jarrod passed in front of him, like students called into the principal's office.

"No calls," he growled to Jessica, before closing the door behind him.

Jarrod fingered his tie nervously, and made a silent, hurried inquiry of Malcolm. Malcolm raised his eyebrows noncommittally, and noticed that Jarrod's tie was starting to fray in that one spot.

"Did you see what's just come through?" Maurice asked, moving to his computer as if for reassurance.

Malcolm and Jarrod looked at each other. Better to let Jarrod answer this one.

"No," Jarrod said.

"Fucking Visser just announced that we're not reducing student loans."

"I don't remember seeing that in his speech," Jarrod said, turning to Malcolm accusingly.

Maurice didn't seem to hear him.

"We're supposed to be in the fucking middle of a core fucking review of—"

Maurice's cellphone rang. In his month in the premier's office Malcolm could recall only a handful of times hearing Maurice's cellphone. Every time it was the Boss. Maurice pulled his smartphone from its plastic holster on his belt and looked at the number of the incoming call. He grimaced and squeezed his forehead so the lines bunched in the middle. Was Maurice getting permanent furrows? The ringtone went off again. Maurice turned his back to Malcolm and Jarrod before answering.

"Hello, sir."

Maurice's voice was calm, as if he hadn't been screaming just a few seconds before. Malcolm could hear an animated voice on the other end of the phone.

"Yes. No, Premier. I did. Yes, Premier. I understand. I'll call him. Yes, right away."

Maurice replaced the phone in its holster. He turned to Jarrod.

"Print me off a copy of Visser's speech. I shredded mine."

Malcolm looked at the shredder in the corner by the window. It was overflowing and bits of paper lay scattered on the floor like telltale chads in a Florida returning office. Beside him, Jarrod had already turned to go, so Malcolm turned to follow.

"Malcolm, stay behind. I want to talk to you."

Malcolm's chest tightened. He watched as Jarrod's back went through the doorway.

"Did Visser give you any indication he was going to talk about the student loan program?"

"No," Malcolm lied.

"Nothing? Not even a mention of it in passing?

Malcolm shook his head slowly and lied again. "Nope."

"What an asshole! At least he could have been man enough to tell us to our face what he was going to do."

Maurice made it sound like Visser had not only done this despicable thing to Maurice, but to Malcolm as well. Malcolm held his breath waiting for Maurice to go on.

"Okay," Maurice said, dismissing him.

Malcolm exhaled with relief and left.

He didn't hear from Visser until that evening. He was lying on the couch waiting for Rachel to finish labelling scarves before they watched an old episode of *Breaking Bad*. They'd seen it several times already, but found some comfort in watching it again.

"How are you doing?" Visser asked.

"How are *you* doing is more the question?" Malcolm answered.

"I'm fine. Davis called me this afternoon. Boy was he pissed. Can't say I was surprised. Still, it's a bit of a shock when the premier goes off on you. He was barely coherent."

"Wow," Malcolm said.

"He calmed down by the end of the call. Said we're a team and I can't be a lone wolf doing my own thing. Apparently other

ministers are upset because they weren't informed. I don't know
if that's true or just bullshit. I'm leaning toward bullshit."

"He called Maurice."

"Yeah. Maurice was all over Eric. I feel sorry for Eric. It
wasn't his fault. I'm meeting Maurice tomorrow at the cabinet
offices here in Vancouver."

"Good luck with that."

"Thanks. I'll need it. There'll be fireworks."

"He asked me if I knew anything about the student loan
announcement."

"And?"

"I said no, of course. He thought you might have mentioned
it to me. I told him no. Just so you know for tomorrow. He also
asked to see the last version of the speech that we had."

"I expect he's going to tell me that I can't say anything in
future without the green light from him or the premier."

"So what will you do?"

"What do you think? I have no intention of pulling punches."

"You've got guts, I'll say that much."

"Thanks. Talk soon. Oh, by the way, that problem I've had.
It's fixed itself."

"What?"

"Not completely. Let me just say that the plumbing is working better now."

"Congratulations, Mike."

"All credit to you, Malcolm."

"I don't believe it."

"Believe it. I didn't feel like this before you came along. I
better get going, Claire is calling for me."

Malcolm spent the next two weeks working every day with
Visser. Visser offered to set up a workspace for Malcolm in his
office but Malcolm politely declined. It wasn't that he didn't
want to—he enjoyed working with Visser. Visser was enthusiastic and generous and supportive: everything Maurice wasn't. It
made him feel like he finally had a purpose. But he also knew it
was short-lived. When they finally hired a new communications

team, he would be back at his desk in the West Annex where being too tight with Visser was career limiting. Nevertheless, they talked by phone a half-dozen times a day—Malcolm had Visser's direct line and cellphone on speed dial—and Malcolm visited Visser's home almost every night. But they were never seen together in public. And they never emailed. Malcolm thought about treating the emails as transitory and deleting them after he read them, like Upshall, but couldn't be sure they somehow wouldn't be backed up by the government server. The irony wasn't lost on him that he now suffered from the same paranoia as Maurice. When the new communications team was finally in place, Malcolm called Visser one last time.

"Hey," Malcolm said.

"Hey."

"How about those Blue Jays?" Malcolm asked.

It was a standing joke between them: Visser hated sports so Malcolm always asked him about them.

"They won last night."

"Don't tell me you watched it?"

"I can't lie. I asked it to be included with my morning briefing package."

There was a long silence.

"So you've got a new com director . . ." Malcolm said.

"He won't be as good as you."

"You haven't met him yet."

"I don't need to."

"He comes highly recommended."

"They'd have to be pretty foolish to hire someone who didn't come highly recommended."

Malcolm laughed because it was true, but then remembered his own hiring and wondered if Visser was referring to it. Malcolm had told Visser about it. He hadn't told anyone—not even Rachel. He could trust Visser. Though he didn't tell him why the premier intervened on his behalf, just that he did. And Visser never asked.

"You could come work for me," Visser said.

"You've got a com director."

"I'll fire him."

"You don't get to fire him."

"Then I'll make his life so miserable that he'll want to quit."

"I don't believe you."

"I will."

"You haven't got it in you."

"You'd be surprised what I have in me. Besides, how did you become such an expert on me in just two weeks?"

Silence.

"I had a great time working with you, Mike."

"It doesn't have to end, Malcolm."

"Everything comes to an end."

"Why work for Davis?"

"There's no sense going over this again."

"I still don't get it."

Malcolm wasn't quite sure he "got it" either. He was still torn. He had thought about it for the last two weeks. He hadn't talked about it with Rachel, because he was sure what her answer would be: work with Visser. But then she'd be disappointed when he didn't, and he couldn't stand any more of her disappointment.

He told himself he had to be realistic. Visser couldn't even guarantee he'd be in cabinet in a year. What then? Malcolm would be out of a job is what. Besides, how long can you remain idealistic and relevant in politics before you're just tilting at windmills?

With Davis he was sure of the next four years and maybe four more after that. Besides, with Davis he could just do his job, collect his paycheque, and at the end of the day close the door behind him and go home. He didn't have to worry about being idealistic or relevant. Or at least that's what he kept telling himself. And he knew that, like the key messages he drafted every day, if he just kept saying it long enough he'd eventually believe it.

PART TWO

(MARCH 2014)

CHAPTER 10

"HERE HE IS! Here he is!"

"Minister, we have a few questions for you!"

"Minister!—"

"Minister Watling can't speak to you."

"Minister, is it true that if the Army Navy Air Force Club can't—"

"Minister Watling isn't taking any questions."

"If the ANAF can't pay its rent you're going to—"

"I'm sorry, I have a previous engagement."

"You're going to throw the veterans into the street?"

Watling stops.

"Minister?"

Watling turns and a mass of cameras, microphones and notepads swarm him. Pink-faced and glistening in the insistent glare of the TV lights, he blinks nervously as reporters close around him, some of them pressing up against him. He tries to give himself some space but he can't because he is backed against a wall in the legislature hallway. He adjusts his glasses and pulls at his shirt collar as if it is too tight. He is alone. Where did his ministerial assistant go? There he is, pushed back into the shadow behind the lights, peering on tiptoe from the edge of the scrum; he might as well be on Mars. A media relations staffer from PAP dips and weaves and squeezes through, taking up a position by Watling's right shoulder, wielding her mini digital tape recorder in front of her like a Taser. The media take it as a signal to move closer. A few latecomers hurriedly fumble with their equipment and extend their arms, jabbing their tape recorders and microphones into the crowded tangle in front of Watling's face.

There is a brief pause as reporters ready themselves. Watling takes that moment to lean into the microphones and say: "It is patently untrue that we are throwing veterans into the street."

"What the fuck!" screamed Maurice. "I don't believe it! Tell me he didn't say that!"

Maurice was sitting at his desk watching the scrum on his computer. Behind him stood Glenn Franson, Jarrod Tapscott, Marek Balicki and Malcolm.

"It gets worse," Franson said. He was even more morose than usual.

"But minister," says one of the reporters closest to Watling, "isn't it true that your ministry told the ANAF they have to pay $24,000 in rent?"

The reporter waves a piece of paper in front of Watling.

"This letter says that if they don't pay the rent they will have to leave by April first next year. It's signed by your deputy minister."

Watling shifts uncomfortably from one foot to the other.

"Look," he says, trying to be reasonable, "there is a cost to taxpayers for all of the services we provide. I know people think government is free, but it isn't."

"Is he a fucking idiot?" yelled Maurice, holding his head with both hands.

He stood up, looking at the computer screen as if it were something foreign.

"So you *are* kicking these war heroes out?" shouts a reporter off-camera.

"Let me be perfectly clear: we are not kicking out any war heroes," says Watling.

"Why does he fucking well keep repeating the fucking negative?" screamed Maurice, his face blotchy red and the vein in his neck turning blue.

Reporters yell out, but it's impossible to hear the questions.

"So they can stay?" shouts one reporter over the others. It's Kapur and the other reporters defer to him. "So you're saying they can stay," he repeats.

"They can stay as long as they pay the rent," says Watling.

He looks more comfortable—almost smug—as if he is finally getting the reporters to understand.

"But the ANAF says it doesn't have the money to pay the rent," says a reporter.

"Last question!" barks the media relations staffer.

"They've been in the building rent-free since the end of World War One," says a voice that is louder and clearer than the others. It is obviously Gary Maitland, the person behind the camera—the same person who captured the scrum and posted it to his website, See it Now. He fancies himself as the Edward R. Murrow of the legislative press gallery. Malcolm heard he lives in his mother's basement.

"Through the Depression," says another reporter.

"Through World War Two," says the reporter beside Watling.

"Why are you forcing them to pay rent now?" asks Maitland.

Watling looks irritated, as if they have missed his point.

"I'm sorry," he says, though he doesn't sound sorry. He sounds like he's really annoyed. "But government isn't free."

"The minister has to go," says the media relations staffer, and she places a hand on Watling's shoulder and gently but forcefully guides him through the scrum and down the legislature hallway. The camera follows his back as the ministerial assistant scurries to catch up. Watling turns and says something to the media relations staffer and she quickly removes her hand from his back, and he continues walking.

"Fuck!" said Maurice. "I thought the scrum transcript was bad, but this . . . this is actual . . . fucking . . . shit."

The transcript was sent twenty minutes ago. Maurice was in a Treasury Board meeting when he saw the email and immediately stepped out and came downstairs where he huddled behind closed doors with his senior staff. Malcolm had knocked on the door and alerted them that Maitland had posted the video to his website and then stayed while they watched it.

"Where were you when all this was going on?" Maurice asked Jarrod.

Time to blame someone, Malcolm thought. Maurice was big on blame. It came with the territory: politics was all about blame. The parties were the worst offenders—they spent their days either blaming one another or thinking of ways to blame one another. Caucus, cabinet and the premier weren't any better, always trying to pin a mistake on a colleague—usually to gain political advantage but sometimes out of pure malice. The media fed into the whole process, encouraging the worst kind of "gotcha" politics. The result was cynical voters and young people who were turned off traditional democratic institutions. At the same time, Malcolm understood why Maurice did it: if he didn't find someone to blame, then he could end up getting blamed. Blame or be blamed.

"I was in my office," said Jarrod defensively, "monitoring media . . . how was I to know?"

"All I can say is that it was a good thing that media relations staffer from PAP was there or that scrum would still be going on," said Maurice.

The room went quiet.

"When did this break?" asked Maurice.

"The ANAF held a newser this morning," said Franson.

"I didn't see it on the calendar," Maurice said.

"It was last minute. The NDP helped set it up . . . they did a call-around to the gallery and local media. Don Forsyth was there."

Forsyth was the new NDP leader.

"So why didn't we know about it?" asked Maurice. "Matt?"

He looked around the room.

"Where's Matt?"

"Haven't seen him," said Franson, shrugging.

The others shook their heads.

"What the fuck!" said Maurice.

He walked to the door and yelled: "Jessica, find Matt and get him to call Glenn ASAP . . . Jesus Christ!"

He slammed the door, which seemed to make him feel better.

"Did Trevor give us a heads up on this rent issue?" he asked, continuing his interrogation.

Trevor Patterson, Watling's ministerial assistant. All the ministerial assistants—MAs—and the executive assistants—EAs—were political staff. Some of the stronger ministers—Frank Richmond, Ginny Jones—had enough political clout to hire their own staff. But most ministers relied on Maurice to appoint their staff. It meant that while staff worked for the ministers, they owed their allegiance to Maurice.

"No," said Franson. "He said he knew about it, but he didn't think it was a big deal . . . it was only $24,000."

"It's not the fucking amount," said Maurice. "It's the optics. These are people who fought for our country and it looks like we're balancing the budget on their backs."

"I was just . . ." said Franson, ducking his head.

"The NDP have posted a release showing one of the veterans on the sidewalk outside the ANAF in a wheelchair," said Malcolm, looking up from his smartphone. "He looks pretty old."

He handed his phone to Maurice.

"Holy fuck!" Maurice said. "This guy looks like he could die at any moment. Look at all those medals."

He gave the phone back to Malcolm. Franson came over and Malcolm showed him the photo.

"We're dead," Maurice said dejectedly. "Dead, dead, dead, dead, dead. Glenn, you better go meet with Jeffrey and make this go away. I've got to get back to Treasury Board."

"Make it go away?" asked Franson.

"Yes!"

"How? From everything I've seen we're making those veterans pay $24,000 a year rent or evicting them."

"For fuck's sake, we're not evicting them. Am I the only one who gets this? And we're not charging them any rent. Ever! They can continue to stay in the building for free for fucking eternity. Just make sure they know that and the media know that before QP."

Malcolm returned to his desk and a few minutes later Franson poked his head through the doorway.

"I can't reach Matt, so why don't you come with me?"

Malcolm's face must have looked as puzzled as he felt because Franson added: "Watling can be a bit of a pompous prick; it's good to have numbers."

The receptionist in Watling's office was up out of her chair before Malcolm had closed the door behind them. A visit from Glenn Franson wasn't common . . . and usually meant there was trouble.

"Hi Nicole, we're here to see Minister Watling," Franson said.

"I'm afraid he's in a meeting," said Nicole, wincing.

"He'll want to see us," Franson said.

Nicole knocked gently on the minister's door, opened it a crack and spoke to someone. The door immediately swung open and Trevor Patterson emerged.

"Glenn . . . I . . . we . . ." Patterson said, his face flushed.

"We're here about the ANAF," Franson said, talking right over him.

"We're just meeting about that now," said Patterson. "You're welcome to join us," he added, as if Franson needed an invitation.

"Who's in the meeting?" asked Franson.

"The minister, our com director, David Andrews, and our deputy minister, Alison Hunter. And me . . . of course."

Glenn considered this for a moment.

"Okay."

There was a remarkable calm in the room. Andrews and Hunter were seated around a large table and Watling was behind his desk leaning back in his chair in a triumphant pose, beaming. Malcolm had the feeling he viewed their visit as some sort of honour. Watling was the party's foremost bagman, reported to have raised more money for the last campaign than the next two largest fundraisers combined. All of those wealthy investors of his, Malcolm thought. The party brass were so grateful they rewarded him with a gift-wrapped nomination in one of the safest UP ridings in the province. To keep those dollars flowing, they followed up with a cabinet position, albeit a junior post: Minister of Community Affairs and Corporate Services.

"Welcome," Watling said. "We were just saying how this morning was a success. For everyone."

The deputy minister took her cue from Watling, crossing her legs and straightening her back while nodding encouragingly.

"Minister," said Franson, "Maurice asked me to meet with you . . . to sort out this ANAF issue."

The use of Maurice's name seemed to have the desired effect, for Watling sat forward to pay closer attention.

"I'm not sure what Maurice means by sorting out . . . I think the whole thing has gone pretty well."

"I agree," said Hunter, nodding more vigorously.

Franson remained unsmiling.

"And you?" he asked, turning to Andrews.

"I think the NDP will raise it during QP. I know I would."

"You communications people always see the negative in everything," Watling said.

"Trevor?" asked Franson without turning around.

Patterson didn't move from where he was standing behind Franson.

"It could go either way," he said. "It all depends on the opposition. If they have something better, they'll drop this . . . if not, then it could be a long QP."

"I'm not afraid of the NDP," said Watling with excessive bravado. "Bring 'em on."

"Quite right, Jeffrey," said the deputy minister, caught up in the moment. "Er . . . I mean . . . Minister."

"I don't see what the problem is," continued Watling. "We're on solid ground here. It's a sound business decision."

"Exactly," said the deputy minister, gathering herself. "It's strictly business. How do we justify giving the ANAF free rent when we have other properties where we charge rent? You could argue that those other properties are subsidizing the ANAF."

"Look," said Watling, leaning back again in his chair and putting the tips of his fingers together to form a tent, "we were asked to find savings within our budget. We did. We were asked to reduce waste and increase efficiencies. We did. And at the end of the day we will all be better off for it."

Malcolm had the feeling he was trying out a response for QP. Franson sat quietly, not moving.

"It's the top story on CBC and 'NW," Andrews said, looking up from his smartphone. "All of the major media have posted
it to their websites."

"Minister, you need to understand that this story will not go
away," said Franson. "It would be best if you dealt with it before
QP prep and definitely before QP."

Watling looked at his smartphone.

"QP prep is in fifteen minutes," he said.

QP prep was scheduled for 9AM Tuesdays and Thursdays and
11AM Mondays and Wednesdays when the House sat. It usually
lasted about a half hour or so, depending on what issues had surfaced that morning. Franson led the questioning and was reported
to be much tougher on cabinet ministers than the Opposition
ever was in the House. He made it a point of pride to keep score
of the questions he had successfully predicted would be raised in
QP—and he ruthlessly graded the ministers' responses.

"Can't we just prep for it?" asked Trevor.

"We can do all the prep in the world but it won't take away
from the fact that there is no way we can win on this," said Franson.

"I disagree," said Watling, bristling.

Franson wouldn't budge. "Minister, if you don't put an end
to this quickly, you'll be dealing with it for days . . . *we'll* be dealing with this for days. Maybe longer. We can't afford to let this
knock us off our agenda at a time when we really need to keep
our eye on the ball."

Malcolm saw how Franson obliquely referred to themes
that the premier had touched on in a recent speech to caucus—
sticking to their plan and not getting sidetracked by issues.
Malcolm remembered that speech clearly—Davis had upbraid-
ed the Minister for Social Development for her mishandling of
the seniors' bus pass debacle during the first session and said he
didn't want something similar to happen in this session.
Watling also apparently remembered the speech because he
quickly acquiesced.

"I'm a team player and will do what I'm asked."

The deputy minister's nodding slowed to a stop and she slid
down in her chair.

"Good," said Franson. "Let's get media up here right away."

"What about QP prep?" asked Watling.

"Marek is handling it today. I told him to tell the House Leader that you would be late."

Watling frowned, his face coloured, and he shot a glance at the deputy minister, who was suddenly fascinated by a spot on the table in front of her. While Franson had made it seem like Watling's choice, it was now clear to everyone that the decision had been made before they had even entered the room.

"David, will you give the gallery a call and ask them to come to the minister's office in about ten minutes? You can let them know the minister wants to clear up the ANAF story. That should be enough to get them here in a hurry."

Malcolm spoke up: "Minister, can I offer a couple of suggestions?"

"Who are you?" asked Watling rudely, still smarting from being handled by Franson.

"Malcolm Bidwell," said Franson. "He works with me in the PO."

"Great—another kid in short pants," said Watling.

"Minister, Malcolm's a former reporter with the News Daily . . . he knows media."

Ignoring the insult, Malcolm cleared his throat and said: "Minister, you have a habit of responding to a question by repeating it. For example, when you were asked about turning veterans into the street, you said you weren't turning veterans into the street. A better way to respond is to say that you are allowing the ANAF members to remain in the building under the existing agreement. Just don't repeat the turning-them-into-the-street part."

"David and Trevor are always telling me that," said Watling, "but I don't like to be seen as ducking a question. The people who voted for me expect me to be forthright . . . stand up for what I believe."

Franson jumped in: "It's not about being forthright, it's about presenting your position in the best light. You can still say what you believe—just don't repeat the negative part of the question because that may be the part the media use. Instead, go right to what you *are* doing. You can even use a bridging phrase like 'as a matter of fact' or 'in fact' or 'let me tell you what we are doing'. Come on, let's try it."

Watling got up and came around his desk and Franson moved in front of him. He held a pen as a microphone.

"Minister," he said, holding the pen in front of his mouth, "do you think it's right to turf war heroes—some of them in their eighties—out into the street just so you can cut costs in order to meet your budget target?"

Franson turned the pen back toward Watling.

"In fact," said Watling, leaning toward the pen, "let me tell you what we are doing. We are continuing the arrangement with the ANAF that we have had and that was first put in place by Premier John Oliver eighty-nine years ago."

"Good," said Franson. "I like the Oliver part. It reinforces that nothing has changed."

There was a knock on the door and the receptionist poked her head in.

"The media are here," she said.

Watling turned to Franson: "I'm going to say that I plan to meet with the ANAF president. I feel it would help if I can meet with him."

"Good idea. It will demonstrate that you're reaching out to them. Ready?"

Watling nodded.

"Malcolm and I will stay here."

Malcolm knew that their presence would only fuel the story. He could see the headline: 'Premier's office called in to douse minister's firestorm'.

Andrews led the way out of the room with Hunter, Watling and Patterson following closely behind. Malcolm could hear someone—he thought it might have been Rob—joke with the minister about putting an end to a good story. Malcolm and Franson waited in silence for the scrum to finish. After a few minutes, Watling and the others returned to the room in a shiver of excitement.

"I think that went really well," Watling said with a wide smile and his shoulders back.

"Set things right," agreed Hunter with a singular, businesslike nod.

Andrews's silence was less supportive, while Patterson tried to dampen expectations.

"There was just that bit of confusion about the options . . ."

"Options?" Franson asked, looking around. "What options?"

"The options the minister mentioned after he explained about the communications breakdown," offered Andrews.

"Communications breakdown?" repeated Franson, now sounding worried. He turned to Patterson: "Play the tape."

Patterson placed his tape recorder in the middle of the long table and hit play.

"Can you turn it up?" Franson asked even before the voices started.

All eyes were focused on the recorder.

"Minister, can we get you over here?" asked a voice. "It's a better backdrop."

One of the cameramen, Malcolm guessed. There were rustling sounds as the minister repositioned himself.

"Stand right here," said the same voice. "We've marked the spot on the floor for you . . . good . . . thanks . . . all set."

"Minister," said another voice, "we understand you want to clear things up about the ANAF."

"Way to ruin a good story!" yelled a voice in mock reproach. It was Rob.

"Yes, well, I'm sorry to disappoint you all," Watling said stiffly.

"So . . ." a voice said expectantly.

"Well, I think this whole thing is really just a . . . communications breakdown . . . yes, that's what it is," said Watling sounding as if the idea had just come to him.

"How so exactly?" asked a voice.

"Well, I haven't had a chance to speak to the president of the ANAF and I feel that if I would have spoken to him before all of this started, then we wouldn't have the problem we have, so in that sense it's a communications breakdown."

"What would you have told the president?" asked a reporter.

"Well, I want to say first that I plan to speak to the president—"

"Do you have a time for that?"

The reporters will want to be there, thought Malcolm.

"No, I haven't. I've asked my staff to call him and set something up. When I do speak to him I will explain why we made the decision we did."

"Will you tell him that he can stay in the building?"

"Of course I will tell him that."

"So you're saying now they can stay in the building?"

"We've said all along they can stay in the building—that's nothing new."

Malcolm detected a hardness creeping into Watling's voice as he grew more defensive. He glanced at Franson who hadn't taken his eyes off the tiny tape recorder that now looked awfully small in the middle of the large table.

"But they won't have to pay rent . . ." a reporter suggested helpfully.

"Well . . ." Watling hesitated. "We need to balance the budget so we will have to get the money from somewhere."

"So you *will* still make them pay," another reporter said with renewed enthusiasm.

It was like watching a six-year-old drive: Watling was careening all over the place.

"Ummm . . . if we don't have the money then we have to get it from somewhere . . . maybe we will have to look at other options."

"What other options?"

"Well, perhaps they want to move somewhere else."

Franson looked at Watling who was drawing circles on a blank sheet of paper.

"So you would provide them with another building?" The reporter's voice was less enthusiastic.

"Ummm . . . well that could form part of the discussion with the president. Perhaps there is somewhere else they would like to go."

"But, minister, why move them to another government building? Why not just let them stay where they are?"

"Ummm . . . well perhaps it wouldn't be another government property."

"So you're saying you would pay for a privately-owned building," asked a reporter.

Malcolm could hear the frustration in the reporters' questions. Voices in the background were getting louder—likely some of the reporters trying to figure out among themselves what Watling was saying.

"Ummm . . . there's really no money to pay for another building," Watling said.

There was a pause.

"So what are you saying, Minister?"

"Look, there's only so much money," said Watling.

Malcolm could hear his tone get sharper; it was the same tone he had taken in the earlier scrum.

"And it's my responsibility to meet my budget target," Watling continued. "I think when I meet with the president of the ANAF and explain that to him—he will understand."

"Thanks, everyone!" Trevor's voice said abruptly.

The recorder continued to run in the middle of the table and no one reached to shut it off.

Franson finally spoke in a quiet, steady voice: "Minister, we will have to do clean up on this. We can do it going into caucus."

Watling kept drawing his circles as if he hadn't been paying the slightest attention. But he had heard everything. Malcolm was sure of it.

The government caucus met for a half hour at 1PM on Mondays and Wednesdays during session—just before the House reconvened for the afternoon at 1:30. The press gallery used the occasion to stake out the caucus room at the end of the hall, down from the legislative chambers, and ask questions of ministers as they went in. Except it wasn't anything as organized—or as polite—as that. Reporters, unruly and raucous, roamed the hallway, some with cameramen in tow hoisting TV shoulder-cameras, others weighed down by bulky tape decks, the rest gripping digital tape recorders and notebooks, each on the lookout for a story, crowding the corridor, waiting for something to happen, always waiting for something to happen.

Commissionaires in white shirts, clipped black ties and military epaulettes patrolled the hallway trying unsuccessfully to exert some control over the chaos by issuing verbal cautions for reporters to stay off the red carpet, so as not to block access. Backbenchers sauntered through the maze of reporters untouched and largely unrecognized. Parliamentary secretaries, ministers of state, and ministers with minor portfolios lingered hopefully, unable to resist the allure of perhaps making the six o'clock news, yet knowing that they were only of interest if they had badly misstepped. Such was the case of the hapless Minister of Agriculture who, in only his second week on the job, had been arrested outside Kelowna for impaired driving while on the way back to his hotel from a dinner meeting with the B.C. Wine Institute. Rather than admit his mistake, apologize, and throw himself on the mercy of the court of public opinion, he tried to defend himself by arguing that his drinking had a purpose: he had been looking into how to increase sales of B.C. wines. The imprudent man was grilled by reporters both going into caucus and coming out again—a rare double-ender.

When scrums did happen, the languorous congestion of the hallways was replaced with laser-like urgency. Reporters hurried to block the path of a cabinet minister amid shouts and questions. Commissionaires struggled to keep the corridor open by calling out to clear the hallway and pushing the tightly bunched pack to one side, as if they were working, not in the hallows of government, but as *oshiya* on a Japanese subway station platform during rush hour.

Reporters passed the time between scrums swapping tales and chatting up government communications staff and stray political advisors, trying to inveigle any bits of information that might help fill their quota of stories. Government communications staff spent their time leaning against hallway walls trying to be inconspicuous yet helpful, clarifying for reporters, linking back to ministry communications shops for information to help support what ministers said in scrums, all the while trying to figure out what reporters were working on in order to alert ministers' offices so that ministers were prepared to respond when they arrived to make their run through the gauntlet. Opposition communications staff weaved their way through the reporters and government communicators like spies working behind enemy lines, monitoring scrums and sending back intelligence via smartphone for critics to use during Question Period.

Because of the caucus room's location in the corner of the legislature, where two hallways came together and two flights of stairs led to ministerial offices up and down, ministers often arrived at the same time from as many as four directions, sending reporters into fits as they were forced to decide who to interview. The hallway would become clogged with small scrums of reporters, ministers, communications staff, ministerial staff, and legislative security. With each new minister, reporters—their arms outstretched in one direction holding their microphone or tape recorder—would crane their necks in the other direction to see if the new arrival offered a better story.

It was into this creative anarchy that Watling waded that afternoon at exactly 12:54PM. He had been instructed to arrive just a few minutes before the meeting so he could use the start of caucus as a convenient excuse to keep his media scrum as brief as possible.

"A quick surgical strike," advised Franson. "Stop, let them surround you, give your statement and then move on. Whatever you do, don't take any questions. Trevor—"

Patterson quickly said, "Yup."

"You make sure you're right beside him—not in camera shot but close enough to move him through the crowd. Got it?"

"Right," Trevor said sharply as if responding to a military command.

"I've also given PAP a heads up and they will be taping the whole thing, so Trevor you don't have to worry about that. You're there to support the minister. We're all good, then? Minister?"

Watling nodded his agreement though Malcolm thought he looked less sure of himself than before. He could see it in his eyes. They drifted uncontrollably.

Franson usually attended caucus meetings, but this time said he would linger in the hallway to monitor the scrum, though from a distance.

"Will you be following up with the gallery?" asked Malcolm as they left the briefing.

"No. I don't know any of them and I'd be surprised if they know me."

"Will Matt be there?"

"I assume so."

Franson stopped and dialled Matt's cell. No answer.

"Where r u?" he texted him.

Nothing.

"You better come," he said to Malcolm. "If Matt's there, you can leave. We don't want too many people in the hallway—the gallery gets prickly when they think they're being managed. But if Matt isn't there, we'll need you to help shape the story and correct any misinformation from the NDP afterwards."

Watling wasn't any better in the scrum going into caucus. He was nervous, stammering and squinting into the challenging white light of the TV cameras. Almost immediately beads of perspiration bubbled on his forehead and formed a stream that trickled and pooled in the corner of his left eye giving him the appearance of being on the verge of crying. He tried again to claim it was all a breakdown in communications. Malcolm noticed the NDP communications staffer, a child-waif whose face was consumed by oversized glasses, on the edge of the scrum; she was smiling as she listened and tapped gleefully on her smartphone. The scrum descended into muddling incoherence with Watling lashing out about "wilful misunderstanding", before fleeing for the relative safety of the caucus room with Trevor running interference.

"I've got to get into caucus," Franson said glumly to Malcolm. "Let me know how it goes with the media."

"You mean how bad it is?"

Franson gave Malcolm a look of exasperation and turned away.

The media were harsh and unrelenting in their criticism. That would have been bad enough, but there was something else: they were taking turns mocking Watling—seeing who could one-up the other.

"No . . ." said Gary Maitland. "What we have here is . . . a failure to co–mun–i–cate," drawing out the last word.

"Jeffrey Watling would make a perfect Minister of Silly Walks," added Bev Hayden in her droll way.

Kapur said: "It's not that I *like* kicking war heroes out onto the street—"

"But you don't *dislike* it," rejoined Joanne Freeman of the Globe and Mail, smiling at her cleverness.

"—but everyone has to pay their way. What kind of world would we have where 87-year-old veterans in wheelchairs think budget targets don't apply to *them*."

"But minister," said Freeman, "are you kicking them out or are they staying?"

"He's doing both," said Hayden. "He's kicking them out and they're staying."

The last line got the loudest laugh of all.

Malcolm emailed Franson the bad news: "Not good. Media having a field day. Clean up?"

He waited outside the caucus room door for a reply. The hallway had gone eerily quiet; the reporters had retreated to their offices upstairs to await the start of QP, leaving only the commissionaires and government communications staff to wander the corridor, like parade marshals after the parade.

Malcolm moved down the hallway toward the main corridor keeping an eye on his smartphone for Franson's response. On the other side of the corridor, by the bulletin board opposite the main doors to the chambers, Province newspaper columnist Raymond White was in a hushed conversation with Opposition House Leader Megan Greenfield. Malcolm checked his phone again; Franson had responded: "Coming to see you."

By the time Malcolm had looked up, Franson was already halfway down the hallway. Maurice was with him. It was that bad.

Franson said: "We're going to have to have another—"

"What a pile of shit," interrupted Maurice.

"Quiet please!" hissed a commissionaire.

"Alright," Maurice said to the commissionaire who had started to approach them. "Keep your shirt on . . . I'm leaving."

He took a look around him as if he'd lost something.

"Where's Matt?"

Malcolm shook his head.

"That's why I've got Malcolm working the halls," Franson said.

"Jesus Christ! I shouldn't need a fucking GPS to find my goddamn press secretary!"

"Sir!" growled the commissionaire. He had come up behind Maurice and gripped his elbow.

"Get your fucking hands off me or you'll be cleaning toilets in the museum basement," Maurice said.

The commissionaire didn't budge.

"Sir, this is the Speaker's Corridor. If you want to have a conversation you need to take it around the corner."

"Do you know who I am?"

"Sir, the rules apply equally to everyone. If you have a concern, I suggest you take it up with the Speaker."

"Don't worry," huffed Maurice, "you can bet I'll be raising this with Len."

Franson intervened: "We'll set up another avail with Watling after QP. But not here . . . and definitely not at the blue curtain."

The blue curtain was a tatty, faded velvet curtain that looked like it had been salvaged from a 1960s movie theatre. A backdrop for media interviews, it hung against a wall in an alcove at the entrance to the legislative library opposite the chambers and facing, with no hint of irony, the men's toilets. Media liked it because it was convenient: they could interview a minister and then quickly interview the Opposition critic, who was usually hovering nearby. They also liked it because it carried with it a legacy of celebrated interviews that media loved to relive and, at the back of their minds, hoped might be replayed, creating a new legacy that would be the stuff of stories told by reporters for years to come. Blue-curtain interviews often drew an audience of MLAs and staffers, adding to the drama—and the stakes. Some ministers handled the pressure, seeming to rise to the occasion so that they gave the appearance of actually enjoying it, while others saw their political careers end in a burst of flames. It was clear Franson was worried that Watling would be in the latter category, though Malcolm wondered if, given his recent performances, he would be more fizzle than fireworks.

"In his office then?" asked Malcolm.

"Yes. I've told him to stay in the House until he receives word from us. We'll send a note in when the hallways are clear."

Question Period was a disaster. It was Watling's first time on his feet in QP and he made the mistake of trying to verbally joust with the Opposition. He was clearly modelling Frank Richmond, the beefy former RCMP officer turned developer whom Watling openly admired. Richmond's approach in QP was to feign indignation that the NDP would have the temerity to even question him, make a blistering attack on the failure of the NDP to form government ("always the bridesmaid, never the bride"), then abruptly sit down without making any reference to the actual question. It infuriated and frustrated the Opposition. It worked best with questions about programs and policies. It was less successful when the questions involved real people; then it made Richmond look arrogant and hard-hearted, as if he had not only deliberately ignored these poor individuals, but had indirectly attacked them for being failures, like the NDP. Watling had obviously overlooked this.

As soon as the bell rang ending Question Period, the press gallery raced down the stairs from their seats high above the chambers to wait for Watling to emerge. They circled around the main doors while keeping an eye on the side door in case Watling tried to slip past them.

Tina Bancroft, the Opposition critic, was quickly corralled as she emerged from the House, and shepherded to the blue curtain. Malcolm monitored the scrum from the wall beside the men's toilets. Bancroft was scathing in her criticism of Watling and the government, accusing the premier of personally directing the eviction: "How else do you explain the minister's response?"

Malcolm sent a summary to Maurice and Franson, and told reporters that Watling would take questions in about ten or fifteen minutes in his office.

"We'll just wait for him to come out and get him at the blue curtain," countered CTV's Terri Calhoun.

"Why isn't he coming out?" asked Kapur, peering through the bevelled glass panels of the chamber door.

"He has House duty," said Malcolm, not knowing if that was true or not. If he didn't have House duty, he did now. "But we've arranged with the House leader to take a few minutes . . . in his office."

"Probably scared to come out," Scott Whittaker of Canadian Press said.

Behind Scott, Malcolm noticed the Globe's Joanne Freeman leaning over the small shelf at the bulletin board writing a note. She quickly folded it and handed it to a page standing at the entrance to the chamber. A minute later Watling emerged through the revolving main door to the House and was immediately surrounded by media.

Malcolm was stunned. This wasn't the plan. He tried to call Franson, but a commissionaire reminded him that use of phones in the Speaker's Corridor was not permitted—he would have to go around the corner. Malcolm decided he couldn't leave Watling on his own with the media so he sent Franson a quick text: "Watling just came out of House. Media have him."

Then he went to see what he could do for Watling. The media were trying to coax Watling to the blue curtain, but Watling was looking around, dazed and uncomprehending.

"Excuse me . . . excuse me . . . thank you," Malcolm said as he pushed through the pack of reporters and cameras. "Minister . . . there's a call for you . . . in your office."

Watling looked at Malcolm like a drowning man at a life preserver. But the gallery wasn't giving up without a fight.

"What call?" demanded Calhoun.

Malcolm could feel all the eyes of the reporters on him.

"It's personal. Minister, we need to go."

Reporters grumbled and Malcolm heard someone cough the word "bullshit". Nevertheless, Malcolm reached out his hand to Watling. For a moment he thought Watling was going to take it, which wouldn't have looked good on TV. But Watling caught himself and pushed his way toward Malcolm.

"Minister, the NDP have called for you to resign over this," asked Rob. "Are you going to resign?"

Malcolm glanced back over his shoulder to see Rob looking not at Watling, but directly at Malcolm. Malcolm stopped, allowed Watling to exit the scrum and then said: "Minister Watling will address all of your questions in exactly ten minutes in his office. Thank you."

Malcolm walked beside Watling to the end of the corridor without saying anything. He texted Franson to let him know they were heading to Watling's office. As they turned to go upstairs, Watling said: "Do I really have a personal matter I have to deal with?"

"You do now."

A long pause.

"Thank you . . . for getting me out of that."

"No problem, Minister."

Franson and Trevor Patterson were waiting for them when they got to Watling's office.

"What happened?" asked Franson.

"I got a note asking me to come out, so I came out," said Watling. "When I came out the media swarmed me."

"I think Joanne sent him the note," said Malcolm. "I saw her write something and hand it to a page. It was just a mixup."

"Did the note say it was from Joanne?" asked Franson.

Watling reached into his pocket and pulled out the note and handed it to Franson.

"It says it's from Joanne right here," Franson said, showing it to Watling.

"I didn't see that," said Watling. "I just saw a note asking me to come out and thought it was from Trevor."

"Look, we only have a few minutes before the media will be here," said Malcolm sternly. "I think we better prep the minister."

Malcolm took the lead, laying out three things Watling had to tell the reporters.

"One—you apologize unreservedly for the distress this has caused veterans. No hedging, no qualifications. You need to be authentic, so sound like you mean it. Two—the ANAF can continue to stay in the building as long as they want. Period. Three—you will provide the building rent-free just like government has for the last eighty-nine years. That's it. Nothing else. If reporters ask you anything—anything at all—you just keep repeating that the ANAF will be able to stay in the building as long as they want—for free. OK?"

Watling nodded.

"Oh, and if they ask about your personal call—"

"Yes . . . ?"

"Tell them it's personal."

"What personal call?" asked Franson.

"I can't tell you—it's personal," responded Watling, smiling for the first time that afternoon. Then he looked at Malcolm. "Right, Malcolm?"

"Absolutely right, Minister."

CHAPTER 11

WATLING FOUND A place in the pantheon of legislature mythology alongside Bill Smith, B.C.'s eccentric second premier and newspaper publisher, who ran and was famously elected under the name Amor de Cosmos or "Lover of the Universe"; and Bill Vander Zalm, the scandal-plagued, charismatic 1980s premier who lived in a castle in the middle of a biblical theme park called Fantasy Gardens. "Watling" also became a neologism, though its definition depended on its context: cabinet ministers clamoured for media training courses, fearful that they might be next to "pull a Watling"; the press gallery prowled the hallways looking for "the next Watling"; and the Opposition NDP scoured ministry budget estimates hoping to uncover "a Watling".

Word rapidly spread that Malcolm had played a pivotal role in helping to defuse the situation, and his star began to rise. Visser was the first to call, right after the weekly caucus meeting later that evening. Malcolm and Rachel were at a movie, so he left a voice message.

"Malcolm! Your ears must be burning—and in more ways than one. Everyone in caucus is talking about how you single-handedly pulled Jeffrey Watling's political career from the ANAF fiery wreckage. They say you were truly heroic, although Jeffrey being Jeffrey, I'm not sure you've done the government a favour—or the voters for that matter. I guess heroes can't choose who they save."

No sooner had Visser hung up than Watling himself left a message pleading with him to take a job in his office as either his com director or MA. He could have his pick.

"I talked to the premier, but he wouldn't commit," Watling said. "He says he needs to talk to you first. Tell him you'll do it."

The next morning, Rob texted him that the press gallery was using his photo for a dart board.

"We were having fun with MJW until u showed up," he wrote. "Thanks a lot!"

Nowhere did Malcolm's star rise higher than with the premier himself. In his ten months in the West Annex, Malcolm had met with the Boss on a number of occasions, but their conversations had been restricted to whatever Malcolm was working on at the time: a speech for the truck loggers' convention; a Q and A on an upcoming trade mission to China; a news release for the opening of the new Burnaby Hospital emergency department. Their times together were scheduled into Davis's tightly controlled calendar, never impromptu, and never alone—Maurice hovering intrusively nearby giving his view on whatever was being discussed. Davis was efficient, businesslike, and distant. Malcolm took that as a signal that their brief shared history in those early hours in Catherine's Orchard House apartment was to remain firmly buried in the past.

That changed a couple of days after "the Watling incident". Malcolm was slumped forward in his chair, languorously leaning on an elbow, newspapers spread open in front of him across the desk, alone in the early-morning office: the two A's hadn't arrived and wouldn't for another ten minutes or so—later if they had been out last night. This was a time of quiet stillness, when the day was still new and brimming with hope.

"Do you think it's over?"

Malcolm instantly recognized the over-rehearsed voice that pierced the calm and looked up to see Davis eyeing him. Pulling up a chair, Davis put his feet on the edge of Malcolm's desktop, tilted back, his hands behind his head, elbows sticking out as if relaxing on the deck at his summer cottage. This was clearly going to be more than a quick "good morning" courtesy call.

Davis had the lean, angular, polished good looks of Lance Armstrong, along with the self-assurance that routinely trespassed on arrogance, and the same emotionless eyes that concealed any hint of ethical failings.

Malcolm hesitated. "Not quite. The good news is it's off the news pages and onto the op-ed pages," he said, sitting up straighter. "Should only be another day or two in print unless the

NDP get more creative with their letters to the editor. It's pretty well run its course in the talk shows, though Hayden and Kapur will have one last kick at it on Friday."

Friday was the day when Hayden and Kapur took to the radio airwaves as political commentators offering their take on the week in politics. "Half-entertainment, half-politics," the show's host pitched in the billboards. "Half-wits," Maurice rejoined whenever he heard the promo.

"That's assuming nothing happens that will kick it up again," Malcolm added.

Davis smiled his Cheshire cat grin.

"We shouldn't hear anything more from Jeffrey," Davis said. "He's busy with a number of events in his riding that will keep him away from the legislature for the rest of the week and maybe even into next week."

"Good," said Malcolm nodding approvingly. "It'll help keep things quiet."

"Touch wood," said Davis, and he pushed awkwardly forward to knock twice on Malcolm's fibreboard desk.

The superstitions of politicians and their staff were still something of a mystery to Malcolm. He was introduced to it during last summer's session when he'd talked about how well things were going and Franson jumped down his throat. The next day the NDP had their first strong Question Period, and Franson blamed Malcolm. He wasn't joking.

Davis was no less serious. He carried fourteen cents in his pocket at all times—two nickels and four pennies—the change he had on him the night he was elected premier. He would only carry the same coins from that night, no substitutes would do, and he always had them in his left pocket, the pocket they were in when he was declared premier. One day he lost one of the coins—a penny—and made staff stay for hours searching for it. Everyone was forced into service—Maurice included. After a fruitless hour of looking, Malcolm suggested simply replacing the penny.

"One penny is the same as any other," Malcolm insisted.

"Is it?" asked Davis.

"You believe these coins got you elected? These specific coins?"

"Everything is connected," Davis said. "No matter how insignificant. Change one thing and it changes everything."

"But if everything counts, then nothing counts."

"That's not true. Not true at all. Why would you say that?"

"Just something someone told me once."

"Well they're wrong. If nothing counts then the things we do, the choices we make, don't matter. But if everything counts, then every choice matters. It's all about the choices we make."

"What they said was that in politics everyone is your friend, which is the same as no one is your friend."

"They don't know what they're talking about. Try making your way in politics without friends. You won't get far. I didn't get to be premier without them."

Jessica recovered the lost talisman on the spiral staircase, wedged between the tread and the railing. Davis took one look at it, verified that it was the wayward coin, thanked everyone for their help, and slipped it into his pocket—his left pocket.

Because he always carried coins, Davis had developed a vulgar habit of jingling them. And when he wasn't jingling them, he was fingering them, turning them over and over, rubbing the raised lettering and the image of the maple leaf and beaver, which to an unknowing eye might have looked like he was touching himself.

Davis got up from Malcolm's desk and placed his left hand in the silk pocket of his bespoke suit. The jingling started, quietly at first, then louder. Abruptly the two A's entered the room, both talking at the same time, which Malcolm accepted as completely natural because they never listened to anyone anyway. They didn't notice Davis until one of the A's, Amy perhaps, saw him and stopped short and simultaneously quit talking in mid-sentence. The other—Amanda maybe—continued past her, rattling on:

"—the cutest brown buckle—"

"Ladies . . ." Davis interrupted, taking his hand from his pocket and reaching out to them.

Amanda pulled up short, sounding like she'd swallowed the brown buckle she had been describing.

"I need this room for a few more minutes," Davis said, and he guided them out the door, his hand almost caressing one of their waists. One of the A's—possibly Amanda or maybe it was Amy—half-turned to give Malcolm a sly, knowing smile, as if she'd caught him doing something he shouldn't have. The look unnerved Malcolm and in his mind he ran through his work for the last week, trying for the life of him to see if there was anything he'd done that might have prompted this visit from Davis. Davis closed the door.

"So, Malcolm, let me get to the point of why I stopped by."

There is a point to this visit, thought Malcolm, and he braced himself.

"I'm off tomorrow to Toronto and New York to meet with credit rating agencies and bond holders. Then I'm onto Washington to hold some American hands—they're fretting again over softwood lumber. I had planned to take Matt to handle media, but I've decided you should make the trip instead. I talked to Maurice about it and he agrees. We both think you did a great job on the Watling issue and are ready for a new challenge. I know you've been working on some of the materials so it shouldn't be a steep learning curve. Maurice says he will get together with you and Glenn this afternoon to go over the rest of the communications and bring you up to speed on the issues. Rai has given Jessica all the details around schedules, flights, hotels, etc."

Malcolm didn't know what to say. He'd never flown on a business trip before. He sat perfectly still and tried to think of something; nothing came, the sweetness of the early-morning silence now turned sour. Finally, he gave a single nod of his head.

Davis waited a few beats before concluding: "Okay, then."

Malcolm felt the pressure to say something—anything—and finally blurted: "I've never been to Washington."

Davis gave him a quizzical look and Malcolm cursed himself for making it sound like a family holiday and not a business trip. As Davis opened the door to go, the two A's nearly fell into the room from where they were pressed tight trying to hear.

"Oh, one more thing," Davis turned back to Malcolm. "You're not going to work for Jeffrey Watling. You work for me. Understood?"

Malcolm nodded.

"Ladies," Davis said, giving them his third- or fourth-rate smile, the one he usually reserved for his wife, "thank you for the use of your office. It's all yours."

They giggled and said in unison, "Thank you, Premier," then followed his back as it went down the hall and around the corner, as if they were afraid to turn away in case he might look back at them.

"Sooo, it sounds like Malcolm has been a bad boy," said one of the A's.

"Definitely *not* going to work for Jeffrey Watling," said the other, mimicking the premier.

"Bad, bad, bad," said the first, wagging her perfectly manicured finger.

For some reason they thought this was extraordinarily funny and their raucous, mocking laughter cascaded across the room, ebbing just as Jessica marched into the office holding a Starbucks coffee triumphantly in front of her like a baton majorette leading a parade.

"I was out and thought you might like this," she said to Malcolm. "Lots of sugar, right?"

Malcolm was bewildered. Looking past Jessica, he glimpsed that the two A's shared his confusion: Jessica never got anyone but Maurice a coffee. Ever. First the Boss and now Jessica: his morning had definitely taken a different turn.

"No?" Jessica asked, her arm dropping in unison with the corners of her mouth.

"No . . . I mean yes . . . that's right," Malcolm said, carefully accepting the paper cup with the ubiquitous green logo with both hands as if it were priceless china. "Thank you very much, Jessica," he said, landing uncertainly on her name.

"I've got you and Glenn in to see Maurice at 2:30," Jessica continued. "Maurice said you'd need about an hour. And I'm just finalizing the changes to the travel documents. Matt always takes the first flight over in the morning, but I'd recommend you overnight at the Fairmont—the one at the airport, not the one downtown. Then you're right at Vancouver airport in case the flights here are delayed. It's supposed to be fine, but you never know. Is that what you'd like to do?"

Malcolm shifted uneasily under the weight of Jessica's help-fulness. The Boss usually scheduled a media avail at the airport just before he left. Always in front of the Bill Reid canoe. Genius by association. Malcolm assumed there would be one tomorrow.

"Probably, but I need to see the communications materials and the schedule before I'll know for sure."

"Of course. I don't mean to rush you. Let me know. I've booked the hotel and flight over for you in case they get full, but I can always change them. Is the coffee okay?"

Malcolm took a sip. It was syrupy sweet. She must have poured half the jar of sugar in it.

"Perfect," he lied and smiled. "Thanks, Jessica," he said, landing more firmly on her name.

After Jessica had gone, Malcolm turned to the two A's: "Sorry, what was it you were asking me?"

The girls looked at each other with a gloominess usually reserved for chipped nails or broken heels, then turned away so as not to afford Malcolm even the slimmest satisfaction, though their slumped shoulders couldn't disguise their disappointment.

Malcolm's smartphone vibrated with a new text. Rob.

"Time 4 coffee?"

Malcolm looked at his watch. 8:45. Then at the syrupy cof-fee-filled paper cup on his desk.

"Absolutely" Malcolm typed. "Where?"

"Serious"

"K"

Malcolm knew that Rob would want to be back for 10 when the House started. Estimates—the Opposition's line-by-line review of the government's budget—were continuing, and while Rob and the other gallery members only loosely tracked the esti-mates of minor ministries—quickly scanning through the Hansard "blues" later that day or the next to make sure they didn't miss anything—they took more interest in the larger min-istries where the back-and-forth between distrustful Opposition critics and self-justifying ministers had greater potential for a story. Reporters rarely sat in the House, except for Question Period and perhaps final reading of major pieces of legislation. Otherwise, they kept a watchful eye on the proceedings on their computers at their desks in the press gallery office, continuing to make telephone calls, carry out research and gossip. Today, the ministries of health and agriculture were up. Community affairs and corporate services had been scheduled but was pulled at the last minute for obvious reasons.

As Malcolm pushed his way into the line-up just inside the door at Serious Coffee he half-regretted not suggesting they meet at the James Bay Coffee Co. a block further up; it would have been a lot quieter. But he took consolation in the fact he stood a good chance of bumping into political staffers or media, putting his newfound public profile on display. From a small table near the bathroom Rob waved above the confusion and Malcolm squeezed his way past the impatient crowd waiting for their morning Americanos and lattes to come up, their mood resembling that of an unruly bar at last call.

"I've already ordered," Rob said. "It's crazy in here."

"I'll just grab a coffee," Malcolm said, taking off his coat and dropping it over the back of the chair. "Back in a minute."

He fought his way to the counter and ordered a drip coffee so he wouldn't have to wait. On his return to the table, Rob waved again and motioned that his order was ready so Malcolm retrieved it from in front of several anxious people pressing forward against the edge of the counter.

"What's new?" Malcolm asked.

"Same old, same old," Rob responded. "I think I would have been better off as a plumber—at least I'd always have work."

In twenty-five years in the newspaper business Rob had never been out of work but he always talked as if he could be at any moment.

"So what's the problem now?"

"Everything," said Rob with a sigh. "The newspaper business is so fucked up. Last week they had us in for training on how to use these new video cameras. They want us to take videos and post them to YouTube. All part of this move to 'Digital Now'."

"Is there any money in that?"

Rob ignored the question.

"They've got a whole procedure for us to follow. Social media is king. When I have a story they want me to tweet it first. Then post the video to YouTube. Then tweet that. If not a video, then a photo that I post to Instagram. Then tweet that. Then I write something short and snappy for the website. Then I write the actual story for the print edition, and finally I blog. It's crazy. I'm a reporter, not a fucking webmaster. I used to write stories that helped bring down governments. Now I tweet."

Malcolm didn't understand Rob's complaint. But then he'd never worked in the "Golden Age" of newspapers. He thought Digital Now made sense, especially because everyone had a smartphone. If you thought about it, smartphones were the new newspapers—only better. They gave you access to videos as well as the usual text and photos. And they were interactive. You could explore other areas of the web thanks to embedded links and call up old and related stories with a click. And if you wanted to make a comment you could still do it "old school" by firing off a letter to the editor, or you could use the new technology and respond in the comments section of a story on the website. You could even have a personal dialogue with individual reporters on Facebook and Twitter. And you could bet more people would see your tweet or YouTube video or web story or blog than would ever read the paper. For the first time, Malcolm thought Rob sounded old.

"Malcolm—"

Malcolm looked up. A man in his early twenties who was going prematurely bald stood pinched-kneed by their table nervously holding a coffee to go.

"Jason. Jason Isfeld. Just wanted to say hi."

"Hi," Malcolm said tentatively.

"I work with Catherine in research."

"Oh yeah."

"We were talking about you this morning."

Malcolm leaned back. It was all he could do not to look over at Rob.

"I wondered," he said, turning to look briefly at Rob but quickly focussing again on Malcolm, "if you have any advice on how I might land something in the PO? I'm looking for a change."

"That's really not my area," Malcolm said, cooler now and sitting up.

He hadn't anticipated the personal demands that might come with his raised profile.

"I just thought you could help me out."

"Let me think about it," Malcolm said, already determined to forget about it.

"Great. Why don't I leave you my card?"

"Ahhh . . . sure," Malcolm said, not sounding at all sure, and feeling put upon.

"Maybe you can put a good word in for me."

"I don't even know you."

"You know what I mean," the young man said with an overly generous wink. "Thanks a lot. I'll be sure to say hi to Catherine for you."

"You do that," Malcolm said.

It had been weeks since Malcolm had spoken to Catherine, but the distance between them seemed greater because of their physical separation. The friendship that had been so vivid in those first days had faded and now they only spoke infrequently. He bumped into her every so often when he went for drinks with the rest of the premier's office, and she always said they should get together for a coffee to catch up, but they never did.

"You don't have any intention of calling him do you?" Rob said.

"I won't have to: he'll call me. He's like all the others—in a big hurry to get ahead. What is he? Twenty-two? Stepped right out of university and thanks to someone he knows—probably his father or an uncle who's on the party executive or a family friend who's a big donor—got a job that pays him forty or fifty thousand a year. He's been there two months and can't understand why he hasn't been promoted already. Talk about entitlement."

"You sound like me."

"Whaddya mean?" Malcolm asked.

Rob laughed.

"Old."

"I am old—compared to everyone else I work with. Do you know what they call us? Caucus and cabinet ministers? The kids in short pants—and those are the ones who like us. The ones who don't like us talk about us shitting in our Huggies."

"And the kids with training wheels."

"Haven't heard that one."

"I happened to pass Walt Field this morning in the hallway when he was telling Blair Simpson that Davis was taking away your training wheels."

Malcolm smiled and relaxed.

"I'm going with him on his trip back east. Doing media."

"That's great!" Rob said. "So is Matt going with you?"

"Nope. Riding solo."

"Congrats."

"Thanks."

"Is it permanent?"

"Are you asking as a reporter or my friend?"

"Both," Rob laughed. "You know that reporters are like cops: always on duty. It's not an occupation; it's a state of mind."

"Well then, for the record, it isn't permanent. They thought I did a good job with Watling so they're giving me a chance to show what else I can do. Hey, are you going over for the presser at the airport tomorrow?"

Malcolm had checked and the news conference was set for 10AM in front of The Spirit of Haida Gwaii jade canoe in the international terminal.

"No. The Mad Hatter has frozen all travel. We'll pick it up off the wire. Looks like we're going to be doing a lot more of that. He's even removed the water coolers to save money."

"The water coolers?" Malcolm asked incredulously. "Come on."

"Would I make that up?" Rob asked.

"Anyway," Malcolm continued, "we've got a videographer filming it. So if you want it, it'll be posted on the government YouTube page."

"Thanks, but no thanks. You'll only include the boring clips. I won't get to see when Davis slips and falls into the canoe or if he does a Watling."

Malcolm shrugged. "Better than nothing."

"I'm not so sure," said Rob.

On their walk back to the leg, Rob asked about Rachel.

"I can't remember the last time I saw her," he said. "I think it was the night you told us you got your job in the PO. We never get together."

Malcolm felt awkward. Rob and Beth had called a couple of times and asked them over, but nothing was ever finalized.

"Yeah, it just hasn't worked out," Malcolm said.

There was a reason it hadn't worked out: Rachel didn't like Beth. She said she was smug, pushy, and a know-it-all, and that she couldn't imagine her as a friend. But Malcolm couldn't say that. So instead he messaged or *massaged* what he said, just as he did when he wrote key messages for issues notes for the Boss. With issues, it was more about what *wasn't* said, than what *was* said. And as he walked past the fountain at the rear of the leg and up the stairs to the legislature entrance, he was aware for the first time that he had started incorporating communications techniques into his everyday life. It was natural, he told himself, like a philosophy prof who thinks philosophically, or a novelist who views life as a narrative, or even, as Rob said, a reporter who is never off duty. It's a state of mind.

"Yeah, that's probably for the best," said Rob as they reached the Speaker's Corridor. "Beth mentioned that she doesn't have a lot in common with Rachel. But that doesn't mean you and I can't still be friends."

"Absolutely," said Malcolm.

Just then the sergeant-at-arms emerged from the Speaker's Office holding the ceremonial mace in front of him, turned sharply right and marched stiffly down the corridor with the

Speaker, the Clerk of the House, and assistant clerks in tow, on their way to the chamber for the start of the day's proceedings.

"Make way for Mr. Speaker!" the sergeant-at-arms shouted with a fanfare that would not have been out of place if the year was 1377 and it was the first speaker of England's House of Commons, Sir Thomas Hungerford. But it was 2014 and the speaker was the improbable Len Trout, a rough, bowling ball of a man who, before he was elected to the legislature, managed a tire shop alongside the two-lane highway that ran through the village of Canal Flats in the shadow of the Rocky Mountains, literally in another time zone from Victoria. With his starched wing collar and white tabs, flapping arms, and black robe fluttering as he puffed to keep up with the sergeant-at-arms, he resembled a penguin trying to take flight. The Clerk of the House, tall and gaunt, whose unflinching stride proclaimed his superiority, was hard on his heels. After waiting for them to pass, Rob climbed the stairs to the press gallery offices and Malcolm turned and headed toward the causeway that would return him to the West Annex.

Rachel was sunk into the corner of the couch, feet stretched out on the coffee table, laptop open in front of her.

"Good day?" she asked.

This was pro forma. When he came home from work she would ask how his day went and he might talk about some of the people in his office—Jarrod was a favourite. Rachel, who had never met Jarrod, suggested that he might be slightly Asperger's. The two A's were also a recurring theme—Rachel and Malcolm never tired of marveling at their latest clubbing exploits, which were so different from their own social lives. They had a tacit understanding that any talk of what Malcolm actually did, while not off limits, was to be avoided.

But not tonight. Tonight Malcolm was feeling a full wind in his sails, that and a couple of pints from celebratory drinks after work at the Swifty. So he told her about his success with Watling and she listened carefully, unfolding her legs from the coffee table and putting down the laptop beside her on the couch. At the end, as Malcolm waited for her congratulations, there was silence.

"So," Rachel asked methodically as if trying to understand, "your job was to get this minister—Watling—off?"

"Well, yes and no," Malcolm said. "It was to get him off as you say, but more importantly to make the issue go away."

"Because it was making the government look bad."

"Worse than bad."

"Seems to me the government deserved to look bad, throwing those veterans out of their club."

"It did," agreed Malcolm. "That's why we needed to fix it. Make it right."

"But you made it right only because you were forced to."

"Well . . ." he said. He hadn't expected this. Even Rob had acknowledged what a good job he had done.

"It sounds like this Watling still believes he was right to close the ANAF club."

She's missing the point, Malcolm thought. It wasn't about Watling or the government or even the ANAF. It was about him. What he did. Why couldn't she see that?

"If it hadn't become an issue, would they have closed the ANAF club?" she asked.

Malcolm knew the answer and, more to the point, knew she knew the answer.

"They didn't close it, though."

"But they would have if they could have."

It was Malcolm's turn to be silent.

"Do *you* think they should have closed the club?" Rachel asked.

"No."

"Because it was the right thing or because it was an issue?"

"Both."

She finally smiled, got up and came over and gave him a hug.

"Congratulations," she said, her head on his chest.

Malcolm sensed there was something else.

"Malcolm?"

Here it comes.

"What?"

"What happens when it isn't the right thing?"

"You worry too much."

But it was a question he had asked himself. And he still didn't have an answer.

CHAPTER 12

MALCOLM OPENED HIS eyes. The bright red numerals on the digital clock that stared at him from the bedside table were shuddering. With his face half-buried in the overstuffed pillow, he could only see the clock with one eye and it occurred to him that he might be able to see more clearly if he lifted his head but his head felt awfully heavy, too heavy, like it was full of sand, and so he lay there and wondered how he would lift his awfully heavy, sand-filled head, and instead closed one eye and opened it again hoping that the numerals would stop moving long enough for him to focus on them.

2:13. Or 2:18.

Before he'd gone to bed he had turned off the room thermostat after his experience in Toronto two days earlier when the constantly blowing air had dried out his throat and he woke up feeling like he'd spent the night in a wind tunnel. But now it was hot and stuffy and he couldn't sleep, the air in the Washington, D.C. hotel room thick. A base drum thumped in his head in time with his heart and he was feeling nauseous and regretful. He shouldn't have had so many beers. It was their last night and Angela, who could usually be counted on to keep the Boss company, had arranged to meet up with a university friend now working for a U.S. congresswoman, so Malcolm felt obliged to stay up with Davis.

Malcolm had kicked off the single blanket but he was still sweating under the roiled sheet. He should get up and turn the air on but instead he lay there and considered whether it was worth getting up. Maybe he should try to fall back to sleep. No. He hurled himself out of bed, the room lunging toward him, his foot tangled in something on the floor, something soft—the blanket—nearly falling but managing to catch himself. He kicked at the blanket and then kicked at it again.

"Fuck!"

He winced. His eyeballs felt gritty and sore. He decided to get a drink of water; somewhere he'd heard that drinking a glass of water before going to bed helped prevent a hangover. He'd already been to bed . . . maybe it was too late . . . couldn't hurt. He'd left the curtains open so the lights of the city cast a glow across the room, enough for him to find a glass on the hotel dresser. He made his way to the bathroom. He couldn't bring himself to turn on its fluorescent light, all shards and sharp edges, so he fumbled in the faint darkness until he found the tap. The sound of rushing water almost made him sick but he gulped some air, filled the glass, and followed the light of the city back into the hotel room.

He went to the window and looked out over the black ribbon of the C&O Canal. Behind it was the Potomac, its winding outline traced by the red tail lights of vehicles on the George Washington Memorial Parkway, and in the distance the orange streetlights of Virginia. He had asked for a view of Capitol Hill or the Washington Monument, but the clerk at the hotel check-in said the rooms faced the wrong way.

"There are no views of the Capitol or the Monument," he said, frowning so that his thick, black eyebrows formed a solid line.

Recalling the unibrow made Malcolm smile but he still felt queasy. He took a sip of water. Then another. He still had three-quarters of a glass. How could anyone drink a whole glass of water after a night of drinking? He placed the glass on the bedside table and eased back into bed, hoping he could fall asleep quickly and dreading his 6AM wake-up call.

The gleaming marble staircase led up and opened onto a landing without an end. A doorway turned into a room bathed in red light and there was a sense of danger, of someone or something lurking in the room, unseen. A party, and for the first time Malcolm was aware of himself as he made his way from group to group. Adam was there and Catherine and he asked about Rachel, but a voice that he recognized but couldn't place told

him that she had . . . then he couldn't make out what the voice
was saying. He felt he'd lost something and couldn't find it. The
doorway was no longer there but the room was the same, though
changed, turned blue and cold, with no obvious way out. In the
distance, the muffled sounds of the party mingled with a ringing
and Malcolm wondered why someone wasn't answering their
phone. The question hung there, drifting, while Malcolm stirred
from his sleep and the ringing grew clearer, louder, and he realized it was in his room. He opened his eyes and looked at the
clock: 3:34. Or 8:84. The numerals were still blurry but at least
they had stopped shuddering. Must be 3:34. Only an hour since
he was last awake. From his back, he swung his arm sideways,
grabbing for his cellphone where it lay on the bedside table,
knocking the glass of water onto the floor.

"Shit! Hullo."

His tongue was thick and fuzzy like he'd been chewing cotton balls.

"Malcolm!"

"Yeah," he said. He closed his eyes.

"Fraser. We've got a big problem."

"What?"

"The minister's been arrested."

"What?"

Malcolm quickly opened his eyes. Too quickly. The ceiling
swayed unevenly.

"Minister Chapman has been arrested. He's in jail."

"What happened?"

"He was picked up with a prostitute."

Malcolm sat upright.

"Fuck off!"

He had sat up too quickly and now the room slipped and
shimmied in the night-light of the city.

"Well, it wasn't actually a prostitute. Turned out to be a
cop. Two cops. A sting."

"Wow," Malcolm exhaled.

The phone went silent.

"Where is he now?"

"I told you—in jail."

Fraser sounded exasperated, but there was also a hint of panic in his voice. Malcolm didn't like many of the ministerial assistants. The combination of political partisanship and power brought out the ugly frat-boy qualities in them. It was worse with the women, who seemed to have something to prove. But he liked Fraser.

"Right," Malcolm said, trying to clear his head. Everything seemed both harsh and muffled, even Fraser's voice. "Does the premier know?"

"The minister didn't say. I don't think so. I didn't ask."

Malcolm would have to call the premier. Fuck!

"Yeah, no problem," Malcolm lied. "Tell me exactly what happened."

The Boss would have a million-and-one questions and Malcolm had to be able to answer every one.

"I'm not totally sure because I didn't talk long with the minister, but this is what the police are saying—"

"To who? . . . saying to who?"

"What do you mean?"

"Who are the police saying this to?"

Malcolm wondered if media were already on the story. The room had stopped quivering.

"To me . . . this is what they told me."

"Okay . . . sorry . . . go on . . . start right from the beginning," he said. "How you heard the minister had been arrested."

"He called me—"

"When was that?"

"I was just going to tell you."

"Okay . . . sorry . . . go ahead."

"He called me about fifteen minutes ago . . . around 3:25 . . . actually it was 3:23. I remember because I looked at my cell when it rang and I saw it was the minister. I've never had a call from him this late before. He said he'd been arrested and was in jail and could I come and get him—"

"So you got him? He's been released?"

"Uh, no. That was only fifteen minutes ago. Like I told you."

Exasperated again.

"Oh, right."

Fuck, Malcolm wished he hadn't had so much to drink last night.

"He's being held overnight and he'll be released later this morning . . . after eight."

"Oh."

Malcolm thought that turning on the bedside lamp might help make things clearer so he reached over and turned it on. The light hurt his eyes so he held his other arm up to shield them.

"He didn't tell me any more than that. I had to ask the police what he'd been arrested for. I think he was too embarrassed to tell me."

"No kidding."

"Anyway, I called the police to find out what happened and they—"

"Who'd you talk to?"

"A guy named Entwhistle. He was very good. A sergeant. He said the MPD—"

"Who?"

Malcolm could feel his mind getting sharper. Talking helped.

"Metropolitan Police Department . . . the Washington police."

"Right."

"Anyway, he said there have been complaints—community activists demanding police crack down on the sex trade—so the MPD have been carrying out undercover stings. He says they're always picking up political types. But then it's Washington, what would you expect? Software developers? Speaking of which, in this case, they advertised online, which kinda surprised me."

"What do you mean?"

"Well the minister's not exactly web savvy. He barely knows how to retrieve his own email. He's forever downloading documents and losing them on his hard drive. I spend half my time trying to find where he's filed them. Anyway, the minister arranged to meet two prostitutes at a nearby hotel—"

"So not here?"

"No, I guess he thought he might get caught."

"Now there's an irony," he said, bringing his arm down from where it shielded his eyes. He was used to the light now.

The phone went quiet again.

"So what happened next?" Malcolm asked.

"He went to the hotel room and met two men—"

"Men?"

"Yeah, that's what the police say. He met two men and was undressing when the two men announced that they were cops."

"I didn't know Chapman was gay."

"Neither did I. I don't think anyone did. Does. Certainly not his wife and kids. This will devastate them. When he called to say he'd been arrested I think he was crying."

"Boy, to be outed in a police sting."

Malcolm felt sorry for Chapman . . . living a lie . . . hiding his true self. We all keep some part of ourselves private, thought Malcolm. No one lives fully in the public sphere. It's just that something like sexual orientation is so fundamental to who you are, to your being. How do you live a full life keeping that hidden? He tried to think about what part of his self he kept hidden.

"Now you see why I said we've got a big problem," said Fraser.

"The problem isn't that he's gay," Malcolm said, trying to figure out how to manage the situation. "The problem is that he lied about it. He deceived his family, friends, colleagues, voters. People will accept that he's gay. They won't accept that he hasn't been truthful with them. That's going to be the toughest to explain."

"Well, that and the fact he cheated on his wife and was arrested for buying sex from two prostitutes," said Fraser.

"Well, when you put it like that . . ."

"Look, his being gay may not be an issue in Victoria or Vancouver, but he's an evangelical Christian from the Valley's Bible Belt. There are no gays out there—at least none who admit it. I wouldn't be surprised if his constituents try to recall him. They nearly strung up a school trustee last December for suggesting Christmas concerts be called Holiday concerts."

"Okay, I want to be clear when I call the premier. So there were two men?"

"Yeah."

"Anything else?"

"No."

"Are you sure? Nothing weird or sensational?"

"This not sensational enough for you?"

Malcolm laughed but stopped quickly when his head throbbed.

"You know what I mean," said Malcolm. "Nothing that will surface in a day or two and bite us in the ass? We're going to want to release everything—and I mean everything—in one big shitty dump. All at once. I don't want this to be one of those issues where new revelations trickle out and it never has a chance to die and it keeps going for days and weeks on end. So no interns he's propositioned? No staff he's screwed? No jilted ex-lovers waiting to tell their stories?"

"Malcolm, I barely spoke to him. I'll talk to him again when I pick him up later this morning. I'll let you know then if there's anything else."

"Okay. In the meantime, I'll give the premier a call and see if I can wake Maurice and then let you know what the plan is."

Malcolm got off the phone and wondered if he should walk down the hall to the Boss's room or call him. He decided to walk down. He pulled on some jeans and a t-shirt and grabbed his phone and hotel room key.

The Boss's room was a corner suite at the end of the corridor. Conscious of the early hour, Malcolm knocked softly on the door so as not to wake other guests. No answer. He tried again, louder this time. Behind the door, he could hear some movement but still the door didn't open. He moved so he was directly in front of the peephole in case the Boss was trying to see who was knocking at this hour. Finally he heard the security chain being disengaged and the deadbolt unlocked. The door opened a crack and Davis's face appeared, eyes half-closed, squinting at Malcolm, the room dark behind him.

"Sorry to wake you, Premier," Malcolm said in a half-whisper. "But I thought you'd want to know that we have a major issue that can't wait until morning."

Malcolm had practised that explanation while he was getting dressed.

"What is it?" asked Davis in a voice that sounded like a cement mixer starting up.

"I don't think I should tell you out here," said Malcolm, looking around.

Sound travelled in the hallways; if the TV wasn't on, he could hear everything people said as they passed by his room. Davis didn't move. A light went on behind him throwing his face into shadow.

Someone else was in the room. A door closed. Malcolm strained to hear.

"I'll come to your room in a few minutes," Davis said, his voice hardening. "I just need to get some clothes on."

"Okay."

Davis shut the door and turned the deadbolt.

Slowly retracing his steps, Malcolm hesitated at the door to his room. He swiped the keycard in the door. The green light winked at him knowingly. As if he had to convince himself of what had just happened, he stopped, turned, and held the door ajar, looking back down the hallway toward the corner suite. Nothing. He stepped forward and let his hotel room door pull itself shut. Someone was in the room. But who?

Malcolm heard a door open and close and he waited for Davis to knock but he didn't. So Malcolm quietly opened the door of his room and peered down the hallway toward the corner suite. Nothing. Then he heard the whirr of the elevator and turned the other way just in time to catch the back of a kitchen-sink blonde in thigh-high black leather boots step through the sliding elevator doors. What stayed with Malcolm, and would remain with him throughout the rest of the morning and keep recurring to him on the flight back to Vancouver, was the image of the woman's tight-fitting leopard-print skirt that barely covered her bum—the same leopard-print skirt he had seen in front of the hotel the evening before.

Fraser and Chapman had joined Malcolm and the Boss for a drink the night before in the hotel bar. Chapman had only stayed for one drink before saying he had "work to do." Davis, Fraser and Malcolm continued on, with Fraser dominating the conversation with the Boss, anxious to make an impression, and the Boss calling him "Frasier" as if he were the fictional TV character. They finally called it a night, the Boss heading off to his room and "Frasier" out for a final smoke and asking Malcolm to keep him company. The two huddled in the protection of the hotel entrance out of the icy March wind blowing off the Potomac when a cab pulled up and the leopard-print blonde got out and headed straight through the lobby to the hotel elevator.

"Dial-a-hooker," Fraser had said, trying to be clever.

A series of crisp knocks loud enough to waken everyone on the floor interrupted Malcolm's thoughts.

"So what's happened?" asked Davis briskly, pushing his way into Malcolm's hotel room.

He was clearly not happy to have been dragged from his bed at 3:45 in the morning. Malcolm explained about Chapman, expressing concern for the impact on his wife and children.

"Fuck the family," said Davis. "They've probably known about him all along. If they haven't, they should have. We have a news conference tomorrow at the Vancouver airport. It was supposed to bookend the trip. Show off our successes. We'll have to cancel it otherwise we won't be able to talk about anything but fucking Chapman. Have you spoken to Maurice?"

"No. I thought you'd want to know first."

"Get him on the phone."

Malcolm dialled Maurice's smartphone and it went to voice-mail.

Malcolm said: "Maurice—"

"Maurice," Davis said, grabbing the phone from Malcolm, "Call me ASA-fucking-P! We've got trouble."

He handed the phone back to Malcolm and Malcolm hit the red phone symbol that ended the call.

"What do we do about the minister?" asked Malcolm.

Davis sat down on the chair in front of the desk.

"Nothing. He's fucking toxic."

"He will be released at 8AM, so that should give him plenty of time to make the flight at 11."

"I forgot about that. I can't be on the same flight as him. He'll have to take a later flight."

"Do you want me to help manage his media or leave it to caucus and the party?"

"I don't want you anywhere near him. You work for me, remember? If you get involved in any way, it will look like I'm involved—like I'm defending him. In fact, I don't want caucus communications involved. I don't even want the party involved. This is strictly a personal issue. Nothing to do with politics. He's on his own."

Malcolm thought about how Chapman would cope with the media onslaught. It wouldn't be easy. A newser in the controlled environment of a downtown Vancouver hotel would be best, the media corralled and contained behind a roped off area well back from the minister. He should be standing with his wife beside him—but only if she's willing. The kids, too, if they're old enough. Maybe not the kids—too unpredictable. Definitely not the airport, where everything is moving: the planes, the people, even the luggage. Moving might be okay for radio and print, but not for TV. Bad visual. Bad. Bad. Bad.

He'd seen airport interviews where the subjects walk as they talk to the media. Maybe they're just heading to get their luggage or to their car. But it looks awful. Communications rule of thumb: if you're walking, you're not talking; if you're talking, you're not walking. It looks like you're trying to avoid the media, like you've got something to hide, like you're running away. Malcolm had seen some actually try to run, thinking if they can get away they won't have to answer any embarrassing questions. What they don't understand is that the media love runners. Runners make for better stories. There's no need for the media to prove anything. It's all there on camera: the subject running away. He wouldn't run if he wasn't guilty. When they finally do catch up with them—and the media always catch up with them—they not only have to answer the embarrassing questions the media didn't get to ask earlier, but now they have to answer why they ran. And you can bet the media will re-run all that footage of them running away—and not just on the six o'clock news, but on the Internet. Hell, it might even go viral. No, he wouldn't want the minister interviewed in the airport. Maybe he should try flying into Seattle and driving across the border. It was worth a shot.

"Do you want to speak with the minister?" Malcolm asked. "To find out his side of the story? It could be by phone."

"Only to fire his ass."

"I wonder if it wouldn't be wise to hear him out. The media will want to know when you found out and they'll judge every-thing you do after that, so we should be very careful about each step we take."

"So you think I should talk with him?"

"I don't know. I just mean that everything will be scruti-nized later: what did you know and when did you know it, that kind of thing. So we want to do all the right things."

"I don't agree: we don't have to do all the right things, we just need to do everything right. There's a difference."

Malcolm looked at Davis. His eyes seemed to absorb all the light, like black holes.

"Okay," Malcolm said. "So let's do everything right. I think it would be good to be able to say that you heard the minister's side of the story. That would show you've acted fairly, that you're a reasonable person and didn't make the decision to fire him without having heard the evidence."

"But I don't care what he says. I *am* firing him. He's a political fucking Fukushima, pissing radioactivity all over the rest of us."

"Yes, of course. Then after you've heard him out, you can tell him he's been removed from cabinet—"

"And caucus. He'll sit as a fucking independent. I don't want him anywhere near the party."

"You could then release a statement immediately after talk-ing to him."

"Me?"

"It would show that you're in control . . . that you're a deci-sive leader . . ."

Malcolm hesitated before he continued, the image of the woman in the leopard-print micro-skirt still fresh.

". . . that you won't put up with unethical behaviour. Of course, it will ignite a media firestorm for the minister who will be left without any communications support."

Davis stood up and went toward the window, looking out at the twinkling lights, his hand slowly turning the coins in his pocket.

"I like it," he said finally, without turning around. "The party will take a hit, but I could come out of this with a bump in my personal ratings."

Malcolm could see a faint smile reflected in the window before Davis turned to the sound of Malcolm's phone.

"Maurice," said Malcolm.

"Put him on speaker," said the premier.

"Maurice," Davis said, the faint smile reappearing. "We have an issue, but Malcolm here has put together a very solid approach that I think just may work for us."

Maurice agreed with the plan and said he would contact the caucus chair, who would inform Chapman he was being turfed, but not until after Davis had spoken to Chapman. Then the statement could go out. Maurice suggested Glenn Franson draft the statement.

"No, I think Malcolm should draft the statement," said the premier, looking approvingly at Malcolm. "He'll work on it here and send it to you."

Maurice said he would arrange with Fraser to have Chapman call the premier immediately upon his release at 8AM. He would also instruct Fraser to cancel Chapman's airline ticket and not provide any further support for Chapman once the premier had relieved him of his cabinet duties.

"Let the bastard find his own way home," said Maurice coldly.

In the end, Davis came out of it looking just as Malcolm had predicted: a decisive leader with a firm hand. Political columnists portrayed him as a leader willing to take a stand against ethical wrong-doing regardless of the personal consequences.

Editorialists were nearly unanimous in commending him for disclosing Chapman's arrest himself, agreeing that while it was a difficult decision it was the right thing to do. And talk show hosts and their callers uniformly condemned the decline in moral standards among politicians—the premier excepted.

Maurice, Davis and the rest of the premier's office congratulated themselves on a trip that couldn't have had a better result. Even the softwood talks, though pushed to the business sections of the print media and CBC's regional noon talk shows, were favourably received.

And Davis was right about his personal popularity. Polling showed his approval rating jumped by ten points to its highest level since the election.

Chapman wasn't as fortunate. He returned home to a media circus at YVR. His wife had already packed the kids and moved out. She later gave an exclusive interview to Global TV followed by a round of media interviews. And just when it seemed the dust had settled, she kicked it up again with an appearance on Dr. Phil, a segment entitled "Marriage Meltdown: When Your Husband Cheats with Another Man", followed by a round of daytime talk shows in major U.S. markets. It took on another life in Canada when the national media picked up the story, a story they had all but ignored previously; it was as if they needed the U.S. media to validate their coverage. The national media pushed it to another level, first reporting on the arrest and then reporting on the U.S. media coverage of the arrest.

Under the intense media glare, Chapman resigned his seat. He weathered the initial assault when the story played "straight-up" ("Well, not that straight," Maurice joked) on the nightly newscasts, but he couldn't withstand the melodrama and accompanying vilification of daytime TV.

Malcolm convinced himself that Chapman was better off out of politics, free to live his life true to himself—his real self, not his political self. And he pushed down any questions he had about Davis and the blonde in the leopard-print skirt, leaving them unasked, so that it wasn't long before he couldn't remember why he'd ever had any questions in the first place.

CHAPTER 13

JESSICA HUNG UP the telephone, made a sour face, and marched into Jarrod's office as solemnly as if she were part of a funeral procession.

"I finally got through to the help desk but there was no one there, so I left a message. I'm not sure when they'll get back to me. Their answering machine said they are experiencing an unusually high volume of calls."

"What the hell!" Jarrod exploded. "It's only 8:15. They can't be that busy already."

"That's what the help desk always says," said Malcolm. "It's their standard response."

"I don't understand," said Jessica. "We're a high priority client. We're supposed to be able to get immediate help 24/7."

"Great!" shouted Jarrod. "Just fucking great! Things were supposed to get better when we outsourced the government network."

"The GlobalTech deal saved taxpayers millions," Jessica said, as if she was personally responsible for the contract.

"What good is that if the network doesn't work?" yelled Jarrod. "Fuck! I'm trapped in GlobalTech hell."

"Let me have a look," offered Jessica.

"It won't do any good," said Jarrod, getting up quickly. "There's nothing there."

"You're even missing the 'J' drive!" Jessica exclaimed, unable to suppress her surprise.

"I've got nothing! Absolutely fuck all!"

"It's probably the server."

"But you're on the same server. And you've got access to all the drives."

"Maybe it's something to do with your connection," suggested Malcolm.

Jessica went around to the back of the computer and checked all the wires.

"I can't see anything," she said.

"You don't think it's the computer, do you?" asked Malcolm feigning innocence, knowing full well this was a sore point for both Jessica and Jarrod.

"It can't be," Jessica said. "GlobalTech assured me they'd checked it out before they delivered it."

"What are you on—your fourth computer now?" asked Malcolm.

"Fifth," Jarrod responded, "or sixth—I've lost count."

He was suddenly deflated. Jessica gave Malcolm an exaggerated frown, as if gently admonishing a favourite child. It had been almost a year since Malcolm had moved into the West Annex and yet it was only in the last few months that he had come to feel like one of them, a full-on member of the premier's team and a trusted advisor to ministers and their political staff.

At first, the political staff hadn't been sure what to make of him. On the surface, he was an outsider: he'd never worked alongside them in the trenches of an election campaign, where loyalties were forged and tested and proved over the twenty-nine days, so that when they emerged out the other end they were closer for the shared experience, not friends necessarily, maybe not even likeminded, but connected to each other by an emotional bond. Yet, he was also an insider—potentially the ultimate insider—by virtue of his relationship with the Boss. The undefined nature of the relationship only added to his stature and was a source of considerable speculation. Some guessed he knew the family—perhaps he was one of Michael's friends. Others said he was too old for that and suggested he had to be a former colleague from the Boss's early days as a condo developer. That was pooh-poohed by still others who said Malcolm was too young for that. A few who had lived through party purges and bore the scars to prove it whispered that he was placed among them for a purpose as yet unknown but which couldn't be good for anyone, and advised those who knew what was good for them to keep their distance.

Most had kept their distance: they were civil enough, but not warm, and never inviting. Malcolm's handling of Watling had helped to close the distance, but it was his work on the Chapman issue that not only brought him into the political inner circle, but placed him squarely at the side of Steven Davis. In government, where clout increases the closer you are to the premier, there wasn't a more powerful place to be. He was now a bona fide star at "The Rockpile", where even the Opposition knew his name.

Outside the legislature, in the world of car loans, house repairs and getting the kids off to school, it was a different story. There, where the who's-in-and-who's-out of the premier's office goes unobserved unless it involves a scandal, Malcolm was just another anonymous government worker doing whatever government workers do. Even his parents would have been hard-pressed to explain what he did, but then they had never bothered to ask because as far as they were concerned Malcolm's "government job" was only temporary. Not a real job like his older brother's, or his father's. Those were career jobs. Lawyer. Accountant. Jobs you could do for the rest of your life. Even his younger brother the archeologist would eventually have a real job. But working for a politician? It was something you did until something permanent came along.

After his failure to impress Rachel with the Watling incident, Malcolm had carefully constructed a firewall between his home life and his work life. Chapman was a case in point. Malcolm took care to avoid any reference to Chapman; he still felt twinges of guilt about the part he'd played in the former minister's down-fall. And if Rachel was aware of Chapman, she never let on. As a result, Malcolm led two distinct lives: one at work and one at home.

His closer relationship with the political staff had not come without a cost. Malcolm had noticed that as he had become tighter with his colleagues at work, he grew more distant from Rachel at home. Even though he never mentioned work, he wondered if Rachel had somehow sensed a change in him and had instinctively responded by pulling away. Or maybe it was him; maybe he was pulling away. Or maybe it was both of them.

Malcolm couldn't be sure, but he also realized that he wasn't unhappy about it—and that worried him as much as the growing gulf between them.

"Quit being naughty," Jessica said without meaning it.

Malcolm grinned and returned a shrug of forgiveness. Glenn Franson poked his head through the doorway.

"Malcolm, can I talk to you?" he asked.

"Sure thing," Malcolm replied.

On his way in to work Malcolm had detected an increased level of anxiety as he passed Franson and Balicki's office. No wonder, considering how all morning his smartphone had lit up like a prairie lightning storm as the news about Dalton spread from print to web to radio to TV.

The RCMP were investigating the province's top cop, Justice Minister Wade Dalton, for "dirty tricks" during the last election campaign. Malcolm had thought the News Daily must have searched its photo bank for hours to find the most incriminating image it could of Dalton. He was staring sideways into the camera and the look on his face was of someone caught redhanded. Had it been Photoshopped? They wouldn't dare.

Franson went into his office and closed the door. He looked dejected. He always looked dejected—it was the nature of someone who spent his waking hours dealing with messes: either preventing them, sweeping them under the rug, or mopping them up. But this morning he looked even more doleful than usual. On the TV beside Franson, the Global Morning Show was finishing up a cooking segment. The chubby male co-host was covered in chocolate icing and licking his fingers while the closed captioning showed him saying "Mmmmm". His trim and tidy female co-host kept her distance, her face pitiless.

"What's up?" Malcolm asked.

Franson seemed to reconsider and motioned with his head for Malcolm to follow him. They went back into the hall and out the side door that led to Menzies Street, where Franson stopped and lit a cigarette. A sign posted on the door said, "NO SMOKING WITHIN 10 METRES OF DOORWAY". Malcolm noticed a clutter of cigarette butts on the grass beside the sidewalk.

"You worked at the News Daily, right?"

Franson took a deep drag on his cigarette.

"Yup."

"Then you know Rob Ryland."

It was one of those comments that hovered between a statement and a question.

"Sure. I worked with him one summer on a series of First Nations stories."

"So you know him pretty well?"

Pure question.

"I see him around the buildings. We still go for coffee."

He didn't tell Franson that Rob called him almost every day to chat; Franson didn't need to know everything.

"That's what I heard," Franson said, his lips parting to form a smile without any warmth or humour; it was purposeful, intended to send a message.

Malcolm shouldn't have been surprised, but he was. Not about Franson knowing he was friends with Rob. No, what surprised Malcolm was that Franson wanted him to know that he knew. He was telling Malcolm that he knew more than Malcolm might think. It was also a test and a caution: a test to see if Malcolm was telling him the truth; a caution to always tell him the truth because Malcolm could never be sure just what Franson knew.

Malcolm had passed the test by adhering to his first commandment in communications: thou shalt not lie. It wasn't an ethical or moral principle of his, just good communications practice. Always tell the truth—that way you're never caught out, never have to explain a lie. Of course, that didn't mean you always told the *whole* truth. The skill in communications, the real talent, was knowing how much—and what parts—of the truth to tell.

"So you think you could ask him to go for coffee this morning?" Franson asked.

"Why?"

Franson inhaled on his cigarette and glanced furtively to his right and left, as if someone might be watching. Malcolm followed his glance and shifted uneasily.

"You see that story he did on Dalton?"

Malcolm nodded. How could he miss it? Front page, banner headline: "RCMP INVESTIGATE DALTON FOR DIRTY TRICKS". A worker in Dalton's campaign office had gone to the RCMP with evidence that Dalton had orchestrated a series of mishaps that had plagued his NDP opponent during the last election campaign. The RCMP were looking into whether the actions were criminal or violations of The Election Act. The RCMP wouldn't officially comment. Rob had quoted an anonymous police source—probably one of his contacts from his years on the crime beat. The campaign worker referred Rob to his lawyer, who also wouldn't comment. There had been no response from Dalton, the government, or the party, and no indication Rob had tried to contact them. Malcolm had wondered about that. Normally Rob would get a response from one of them, even if it was only to say that he was running the story and ask them if they had anything to say. He was probably worried they'd tip off other media.

He also noted that the News Daily normally would have posted the story to their website the night before, but had held back until the print edition was out. That was a common enough tactic a few years ago when print was still king, but not lately with the surge of digital. Clearly, they felt they had an exclusive and so it wasn't as urgent to rush it to the web to beat out their competitors.

They were right; it was an exclusive. As soon as the story was out, every other news outlet picked it up. Now it was leading the news every half hour on both CKNW and CBC, and was the top story on Global's morning news—before they went to their cooking segment.

The morning radio talk shows had been scrambling to find someone—anyone—to speak to it. He'd heard a political scientist from UBC vainly trying to sound knowledgeable on CBC's morning show out of Vancouver. It would blow up the schedules of the mid-morning and afternoon talk shows as well. They will try to get Dalton and the campaign worker, but if they aren't talking then they'll go after the NDP candidate who lost or someone from the NDP because they will be more than willing to talk, if they haven't called them already. They will also try to get someone from the United Party, the government and the RCMP. As a last resort they'll give Rob a call and ask him to come on to talk about the story. But that would only be a last resort. It's always better to talk directly to the people involved.

They'd have to be careful though because it wasn't some junior minister; it was the justice minister, who had a sharp legal mind and even sharper political elbows. Dalton had been one of the first Liberals to jump to the United Party, bringing with him a group of young, well-to-do MLAs who had gone to university together. Once in Opposition, they took delight in heckling the Liberal government in the House. Dubbed the "frat pack" by media, their name was a playful twist on the federal Liberal rat pack who had made Brian Mulroney's life miserable in the House of Commons during the 1980s. Now Dalton was also UP House Leader, in charge of shaping government's agenda inside the legislature.

"We have something . . ." Franson stopped to correct himself, ". . . a document for him."

He took another long drag on his cigarette and tossed it onto the sidewalk where he ground it into the concrete with the sharply pointed toe of his Franceschetti blucher. High-end foreign-made shoes were the latest must-have among young politicos. Then he kicked the butt onto the grass where it joined the clutter of filters.

"We thought that you'd be the best person to give it to him."

"On Dalton?"

"No. Something else."

"A brown envelope?" Malcolm asked.

Franson shrugged.

"Why don't you give it to him?"

"I don't know him."

"Well, Matt then?"

"Look . . . we just thought since you worked with him he might not see it as so . . . political . . . coming from you."

Malcolm considered this.

"What's in this brown-envelope-that-isn't-a-brown-envelope?"

Franson frowned, fished into his outer jacket pocket and took out a pack of cigarettes. He lit another cigarette. Now it was his turn to look uneasy.

"Information on an NDP MLA," he said, blowing smoke as he spoke.

Behind Franson, across the street at The Embassy Inn, an older couple got out of a cab and waited on the sidewalk for the driver to unload their luggage. Instead the driver reached down and popped the trunk lid, glancing impatiently in the mirror as the man struggled to lift the bags out of the trunk.

"Anyone I know?"

Franson clenched the cigarette in his teeth as he reached into his inside jacket pocket and removed a folded photocopy.

"It'll provide balance," he explained, handing it to Malcolm.

More like a diversion, Malcolm thought as took the document and scanned it.

"Rob's not stupid," Malcolm finally said. "He'll see this is political even if it comes from me."

Franson's lips tightened.

"So you won't do it?"

"Oh no, I'll do it," Malcolm said. "Just because it's political doesn't mean it still isn't a good story."

"Good. One more thing." Franson leaned in confidingly. "It's not a hundred per cent."

"What do you mean?"

"Just what I said."

"You mean it's not true?"

"It's true enough . . . it's just not the whole story. But you can't tell Rob that."

On the other side of the street the older couple had come back out of The Embassy Inn, pulling their luggage, the woman in front, moving quickly, the man following, slumped with weariness and resignation. They passed a carriage driver standing on the sidewalk eating an apple.

"I'm confused," Malcolm said.

"What's to be confused about? We want you to give this to Rob. That's it. Nothing else."

Something wasn't right.

"Look, Glenn, just be straight with me. What's going on?"

Franson's lower lip pushed up to make a frown and his forehead contracted to form a solid crease above his eyes.

"Okay. You know we're getting hammered with the Dalton story and we want to change the channel."

Malcolm nodded.

"But we don't have anything . . . nothing that would pull the dogs off Dalton. Except perhaps . . ." he motioned to the document " . . . this. Problem is the RCMP looked into it at the time and said there was nothing to it. We think there's a story there—even if it's only the fact they investigated."

Malcolm had never seen Franson like this—the confusing flush of metaphors, blurting out things he shouldn't. For the first time, Franson seemed to be acting his age.

"It's pretty weak," Malcolm said after letting enough time pass to show that he hadn't rushed to judgment. "If the RCMP say there's nothing to it I can't see Rob doing a story just because *we* think it's news."

"He might if you asked him."

There it was. What this was all about.

"I'm . . ."

Malcolm didn't know what to say—he was caught: he desperately wanted to be a team player, but he couldn't feed Rob a bullshit story. Maybe someone else. But not Rob.

"The Boss said you'd do it," Franson said. "I told him I didn't think you would. That you and Rob are pretty tight."

Malcolm wondered just how much Franson knew about his friendship with Rob.

"So the Boss thinks this is okay?"

"Absolutely. It was his idea."

Across Menzies, under an arch of trees not quite fully leafed out, a great grey draft horse in harness nuzzled the arm of the apple-eating carriage driver, attempting to convince her to give him the rest of her apple. After initially resisting, the driver relented.

"Okay," Malcolm said.

"One more thing."

"What?"

"Well, two more things: we want the story out tomorrow and he needs to run it clean."

"Clean?"

"Yah . . . without comment from the NDP."

"I'm pretty sure he'll get reaction from the NDP; it's standard practice."

"He didn't get one from us on the Dalton story."

"That was unusual."

"No it wasn't. We often ask the gallery to run it clean or we threaten to give the story to someone who will."

Malcolm couldn't imagine telling a reporter when a story should appear, let alone how to write it.

"It's important," Franson added. "We can own the story."

"We'll own it anyway."

"It's not the same. If it runs clean the accusation will sit out there unanswered, maybe even through a couple of news cycles. It'll catch the NDP flatfooted. They will be forced to scramble. It could be the afternoon before they're able to cobble together a decent response."

"Kinda like us this morning," Malcolm observed dryly.

"Exactly," Franson said, not in the least defensive.

It wasn't personal for Franson; it was politics.

The single sheet of photocopied paper lay in the middle of the table, like an uninvited guest who had become the centre of attention.

Without taking his eyes off it, Rob asked, "Where did you say you got this?"

"This" was a copy of an RCMP file on Don Forsyth, Leader of the Opposition. The report was dated a year ago, shortly before the election, and showed the Mounties received a complaint that a charity chaired by Forsyth was diverting funds earmarked for housing for people with developmental disabilities into the coffers of the local NDP constituency. The complainant wasn't identified.

"Someone I work with," said Malcolm, hoping that Rob would just leave it at that.

They were seated in the far corner of James Bay Coffee and Books, tucked up against a wall, away from the prying eyes of anyone walking by the plate glass windows that faced the street. The only other person in the place was a young woman who sat at a small table with her back to them, a bright green tattoo of a parrot twisting across her bare shoulders, its blazing red eyes never leaving Malcolm and Rob.

"And how did they get it?"

"I don't know. They didn't say."

All true.

Malcolm was a jangle of nerves.

"It must have come from someone in the RCMP," Rob said. "Or maybe the Justice Ministry—there are a lot of ex-Mounties there who are still tight with the Force."

He looked up at Malcolm.

"Fuck, this a great story," he said.

His eyes went back to studying the photocopy in front of him.

"If it's real," Rob added.

In politics, information is currency. And misinformation is counterfeit currency. In the digital age, it had become harder than ever to tell the difference.

"What makes you think it isn't real?" asked Malcolm, his lower jaw tightening as he once again debated whether to tell Rob the whole truth.

Malcolm had vacillated all morning between never even mentioning the story and telling him everything. If he buried the file he would be letting everyone down: Franson, his colleagues, the Boss. And then there were the repercussions—it would certainly trigger a fall from grace, from the inner circle. Oh, he'd still work in the premier's office, and people on the outside—people like his parents and Rachel, even Rob—might think because he worked there he was a political insider, but he wouldn't be. How could he be if he wasn't someone they could turn to in a tight spot, someone they could rely on when it counted most, someone they could trust?

He thought about the best way to get Rob to do the story. At first, he considered telling him everything. *Everything*. If he didn't, there was the danger Rob would make one call to the RCMP and find out the investigation had gone nowhere. End of story. But telling Rob everything would mean exposing himself, laying himself bare: that he was prepared to do something under-handed, certainly unethical, maybe even illegal. And for what? For political gain. It was bad enough that he was willing to trade on his personal friendship—but he would be asking Rob to join him. He couldn't do that. And he was sure Rob wouldn't agree anyway, friendship or no friendship. In the end, he decided just to play it straight and hope for the best.

"There's not much to go on—just a complaint," said Rob. "And the timing is curious, to say the least."

"I told them you'd see it was political," Malcolm said, then quickly added: "but I also said you'd never let that get in the way of a good story."

Rob twisted his head sideways to look at Malcolm.

"You scare me, buddy."

Malcolm gave a lopsided grin.

"Just doing my job."

Rob grinned back. He turned the paper over.

"It looks like this is only part of the file. Is there more?"

"Unfortunately, that's all I've got. Sorry."

"If you come across anything else . . ."

"You'll be the first one I call."

"The first one you call? Are you shopping this around?"

"No, you've got an exclusive . . . but only if you run it tomorrow."

"Fuck off!"

Malcolm was prepared for Rob's reaction; he would have responded the same way.

"What's the problem?"

"I'm already working on a follow-up for my Dalton story. I don't have time to do that and this."

"I never thought I'd hear you complaining about having too many stories."

"What if I hold off on this for a few days? It'll give me more time to—"

"Uh uh. The deal is ASAP . . . tomorrow at the latest. Otherwise we give it to Kapur. We want it out there."

"To bigfoot the Dalton story. Right?"

Malcolm had told Franson that it was not only unlikely they could quash the Dalton story, but naïve. And it was typical of the premier to think they could. He believed that everything was simple, and that people overthought things, making them more complex than they needed to be.

The best-case scenario with the Forsyth file would be that they would succeed in muddying the political waters, which would prompt a pox on both their houses. Of course it wouldn't do much for public confidence in politicians. No wonder voter turnout was so low.

In response to Rob's question, Malcolm did what all good communications people do when they don't want to answer a question—he ignored it. Then he shifted gears by asking his own question.

"You don't want the story?" Malcolm asked.

Rob paused.

"Why Kapur?"

"Mmm?"

"You guys give everything to Kapur."

"Global's the big dog."

"So why not just give this to him?"

Malcolm shrugged and looked away.

"It was you, wasn't it?" asked Rob. "I'm glad I've got you in my corner. Thanks, buddy."

Malcolm looked down at his coffee mug. He couldn't look at Rob. He could still say something. Tell Rob it was all a put-up. If not that, then tell him to forget the whole thing. It was all a mistake. But he didn't. He didn't say anything. He just sat there. He heard Rob saying something:

" . . . won't allow me much time to run it down."

Was that doubt creeping into Rob's voice? But as quickly as it appeared, it was gone.

"Fucking Kapur," Rob muttered.

"One more thing . . ." Malcolm said.

Rob looked at him as if steeling himself for a blow.

"What?"

"You need to run it clean."

"You're kidding me."

Malcolm shook his head.

Rob was silent, then finally said: "Do you know what the NDP will do when they see it? They'll put my balls in a vice and then dance a fucking jig on them with cork boots. You of all people should know that."

Malcolm gave a weak smile.

"Remember what you told me in this coffee shop a year ago? You said that we couldn't let work get in the way of our friendship; that if you were tough on Davis you were just doing your job. Well, it works both ways. I'm just doing my job."

"Yeah," said Rob, "but do you have to be so fucking good at it?"

Malcolm left Rob and went straight back to work where he looked for Franson. He wasn't in his office, so Malcolm sat down at his computer and started working on a speech the Boss had to give to the Vancouver Board of Trade.

"How'd it go?"

Franson was standing in his doorway.

"Fine," Malcolm said, trying to sound positive. "He said he'll have something in tomorrow's paper."

Franson greeted the news the way he greeted everything: with a straight face.

"I've got a question for you," Malcolm said. "Why Rob?"

"What?"

"Why give the story to Rob? I know you said it was because I know him. But why not Kapur? Matt's got a great relationship with him—maybe better. And the News Daily has what—60,000 readers? Global has ten times that many viewers."

"We couldn't risk it with Global," Franson said in a voice without emotion.

"What do you mean?"

"We don't want to jeopardize our relationship with them. They're too important to us."

"What about the News Daily?" Malcolm asked.

Franson shrugged. "Who gives a shit about the News Daily? It's only print."

Malcolm walked home quickly in the downpour. He'd forgotten his umbrella in the hallway when he left that morning, and now the rain was bouncing off the streets and sidewalks and running down the gutters. When he reached the Birdcage he ducked under the red canvas awning that was sagging under the wet and stamped his feet. His shoes were soaked and he could feel his socks sticking to the insoles. He waited a minute, hoping for a break but the rain kept pelting down. Bracing himself, he stepped out and nearly knocked over a woman walking her dog. Malcolm apologized as the woman reached down to reassure her small dog and straighten his bright blue Gortex doggie raincoat. When she stood up, he saw it was Catherine.

"Hi," he said, brightening. "How are you?"

He was surprised at how good it felt to see her.

"Better if I didn't have to walk Henry."

"I didn't know you got a dog."

"It's not mine," Catherine said. "It's my neighbour's. She's visiting her granddaughter in Halifax and asked me to look after him while she's away."

A delivery truck turned the corner in front of them, spraying Malcolm with a wash of water.

Catherine laughed. "Look at you," she said. "You're drenched."

Malcolm looked down. His pants were dark and the soggy cuffs collapsed around his ankles from the weight of the water. Rain streamed down his face, dripping from the end of his nose.

"Come on," Catherine grabbed his arm. "You can dry off at my place."

"It's okay. I'm only a few blocks away."

"Don't be silly. I'm right across the street. Come on. At least until the rain lets up."

Catherine made a dash for the crosswalk, tugging a reluctant Henry. Malcolm knew he should go home, that Rachel was expecting him, that if he went with Catherine he was just using the rain as an excuse to see her. He felt an unmistakeable tug from Catherine, as if he was on the end of that leash and not Henry. She had the same energy and vitality that had first attracted him to Rachel. Both women knew where they were going and what they wanted out of life, and they weren't afraid to reach out for it.

But Rachel seemed pale now in comparison, eclipsed by . . . what? Something had changed. What wasn't the same anymore? It wasn't one single thing, but a cumulation of things. Her desire to change the world now seemed less altruistic and more judgmental. Her work with refugees, that he once viewed as romantic— even humanitarian—now struck him as mundane. And it wasn't just what she did. He once thought her style was unique; now he wished she'd shop anywhere other than the hemp store. He realized that he simply wasn't as attracted to her anymore. Then it dawned on him that maybe she hadn't changed—maybe he had changed. And it wasn't a bad thing. Maybe it was a good thing. For everyone. He dashed across the street and caught up with Catherine.

"You better take those clothes off, or you'll catch your death," Catherine yelled from her bedroom.

Malcolm felt strange to be in Catherine's apartment again, as if it was both familiar and new to him.

"Here," she said coming down the hallway. "You can wear these. I think they should fit you."

She handed him a pair of pants and a shirt, and Malcolm stared at them.

"You always have men's clothes in your apartment?"

He had tried to say it lightly but his voice had an edge to it that he wasn't able to hide. She looked at him unblinkingly and frowned, and he immediately wished he could retract what he'd said.

"Sorry," he said, accepting the clothes. "I didn't mean that."

"Yes you did. You just can't help yourself, can you?"

"Only with you, it seems. I don't have that problem with anyone else."

"I don't know whether to be hurt or flattered."

"You should be flattered. Definitely flattered."

Catherine smiled widely.

"Now you're doing a much better job."

"That's because I mean it."

"I'm glad."

There was that tug again, and Malcolm allowed himself to be pulled along, delighting in its effects on him, heightened by the frisson of being illicit. He saw that she had changed into a T-shirt and yoga pants.

Was this a seduction or was she just being helpful? He could-n't be sure. There was a rise of doubt followed by apprehension. Perhaps it was all in his head and her offer to dry off at her place had been just that: a genuine reaching out that she would do for any colleague. When he thought about it like that he was posi-tive there was nothing to her invitation. The sexual hum of the room quieted and Malcolm stood shivering in the cold damp of his clothes.

"I should go," he said, holding the dry pants and shirt out for her to take.

"Don't be silly."

"Are you sure?"

"Of course."

He stood there uncertainly, still unclear what it meant. Catherine looked at him for several seconds in her unwavering way.

"Good God, you're so stupid!" she finally said, reaching out and firmly grasping his hand. "But that's what makes you so adorable."

She pulled him toward the bedroom and Malcolm allowed himself to be pulled.

Malcolm left while Catherine was in the shower. He'd told her he would let himself out and she didn't object. He picked up his pants off the floor and felt for his cell phone. Dead. The perfect excuse if Rachel had tried to call him. His pants were still wet; he should have hung them up, but that was the last thing on his mind when he—or rather she—took them off. He found his shoes where he'd removed them by the front door. They had left a puddle, as if offering a gentle reproach.

Tucking in his shirt, he felt a sharper sense of guilt as he considered what he'd tell Rachel. Normally, she always asked where he had been and wanted to know what he'd been doing, but she wasn't as interested anymore. It was as if it all required too much energy, and these days that was one thing she didn't have. Still, he better have something to tell her just in case. He couldn't say he was working late, because she may have called his office phone. He couldn't have gone for a walk, not in this weather. A bar? On his own? If not, then with who? Then it hit him: the library! That was it! He'd gone to the library.

Grabbing his coat, Malcolm pulled the door securely shut behind him. He didn't actually have to go to the library, he could just tell Rachel he went there. She'd never know, but that wasn't good enough: he needed to be physically in the library, to pass through the glass doors and wander down the rows of books so that when he told Rachel he wouldn't be lying. He would be secure in the truth. Part of the truth, anyway.

He ran all the way. The rain had stopped and the streets had filled with people so that he had to dodge through the crowded sidewalk along Douglas Street, and was sometimes forced out onto the road to get around knots of pedestrians moving at a more relaxed pace now that the rain had quit. As he turned the corner up Broughton Street he grew anxious: maybe the library was closed. Didn't he read somewhere that they'd reduced their hours because of budget cuts? It seemed more important than ever that it be open. He ran even faster, narrowly avoiding a man coming out of a coffee shop carrying a cardboard tray of drinks. Where was he going with those at this time of day? In front of the library, Malcolm stopped at the bottom of the steps and leaned down and put his hands on his knees to catch his breath. A man emerged from the library with books. Still open. With a feeling of elation, he bounded up the steps and rushed through the sliding glass doors, safe at last.

"I was at the library," Malcolm shouted moments after closing the front door to their apartment. Nothing. Was Rachel even home? It was like they were roommates simply sharing the same living space. Funny how fast things can change. He went through the kitchen into the living room where Rachel lay sprawled on the couch going over some papers from work.

"I was at the library," Malcolm repeated.

"Rob called."

No hi. No why were you at the library? No nothing.

"He said he tried your cell but it went straight to voicemail. So he called mine."

"Yeah, it was dead. I didn't realize it until I was already at the library. Boy, it was crowded. Crazy really. I got Yeat's *Second Coming*. The one with 'slouching towards innocence'."

Rachel didn't smile.

"I had a hard time finding it. I finally asked a librarian. She found it in a book of poems called *Michael Robartes and the Dancer*—"

He held the book for her to see. Rachel didn't even look up.

"Rob said you need to call him as soon as you get in. He sounded pissed."

Malcolm's head pulled back.

"What makes you say that?" he asked, challenging her, as if she had accused him. Rachel twisted her head to look at him. Her eyes were listless, as if they said, "Don't believe me. What do I care?"

"The way he was on the phone. He barely said two words. I didn't even finish saying goodbye before he hung up. He was definitely pissed."

Malcolm swallowed hard. He needed to call Rob, but he couldn't do it from the living room—not with Rachel right there.

"I'll give him a call," he said.

Rachel had already turned back to her papers.

"Can I use your phone?"

She grabbed it from the coffee table and held it out for him.

Malcolm climbed the stairs two at a time, sat on the bed and stared at the phone. He had known all along it would come to this, but he was still unprepared. It took all of half a ring for Rob to answer.

"What the fuck, Malcolm?"

Rachel was right: he was pissed. Malcolm stood up.

"What do you mean?"

"You know fucking well what I mean. That piece of shit story you sold me."

Malcolm's chest pounded uncontrollably.

"What?"

"Would you stop it, Malcolm!"

Now Malcolm's throat tightened.

"Something was wrong with the story?" he asked.

The words came out in gulps.

"Oh no, there was nothing wrong with the story," Rob said, the edges of his voice seeping sarcasm. "It was a fucking peach of a story. A giant fucking peach. That's what it was. Malcolm and his giant fucking peach! Only problem, Malcolm, was there no peach!"

Malcolm wondered if Rob had been drinking. He listened for any background noise. Quiet. He wasn't at the bar. At home? Not at his office? He'd never known Rob to drink at work.

"What do you mean?"

Malcolm didn't know what else to say. He couldn't let Rob know that he knew. He had to ride this out.

"It's all bullshit!" Rob shouted, stumbling over the word bullshit.

He's been drinking alright.

"Where have you been?" Rob asked accusingly. "I've been trying to get hold of you for hours."

"My phone died."

Malcolm thought back to the library where he had felt safe. It seemed a long time ago.

"Really, Malcolm? Is that the best you can do?"

"What do you want me to do?"

Silence. Malcolm waited.

"Why did you give me that bullshit story?" Rob asked finally.

Malcolm could still hear traces of anger in Rob's voice, but there was also an unexpected calmness that was even more disquieting.

"I didn't know," Malcolm lied.

Malcolm heard himself and he wasn't convinced. Neither was Rob.

"Not good enough. Not good enough by a long shot. You fucked me over."

"Why would I do that?"

"Good question. That's what I've been asking myself for the last few hours. Why would my buddy, my friend, Malcolm do this to me? And you know what I came up with? You're one of them. You'll do anything to anyone. Well, it worked. I bought it, all of it. I wrote it without getting a response from Forsyth or the NDP. Told my editor the source was solid, so we could post the story as is and add to it as I got reaction."

Malcolm's fears were multiplying, piling one on top of the other, like stones filling his chest, forcing air out. He tried to settle himself, take a deep breath, but couldn't. Panicked. Pulse racing. Lightheaded. Unsteady.

"Well, I got reaction all right. As soon as it went online Forysth himself called me. Not even his fucking press secretary. Said there was no investigation. Said the single page you gave me wasn't the whole story. There was a second page of the report that vindicated him. Said it was a put-up job to discredit him right before the election. He emailed me the other page and told me to call the RCMP if I didn't believe him. I did. They said there was nothing to it. End of story. Well, not quite the end of the story. Forsyth's threatening legal action against me and the paper. Defamation. We've already pulled the story and posted a retraction and apology on our website. I'm just glad Forsyth got to me early enough to pull it from the print edition."

Gripped by dismay, Malcolm couldn't think or speak.

"So you can't even be bothered to deny it?"

Silence.

"You know what really bugs me—and there's a lot about this that bugs me—is that we were friends and you used our friendship . . ."

The words "were friends" jumped out at Malcolm—not "are friends".

" . . . telling me that you're giving me this exclusive . . . that you went to bat for me . . . convinced your boss to give it to me and not Kapur. That was a nice touch. And I believed you! Boy, did I believe you. But you know what I think? I think you never had any intention of giving it to Kapur because you didn't want to burn your "big dog". Better to fuck over Rob and the News Daily . . . it's only the island . . . all NDP anyway . . . nothing to lose . . . except a friendship. Thanks, Malcolm."

Click. The line went dead.

Malcolm felt for the edge of the bed and sat down, the cell phone still in his hand. He remained there for three or four minutes, his mind and body numb. What to do? His fingers jabbed at the touchscreen on his phone.

"Glenn—"

"Hello, Malcolm." Franson's voice was its usual flat self.

"The News Daily has pulled the story."

"I saw that."

"They've put out a retraction and apology."

"I saw that, too."

"Rob's really pissed."

"I'm not surprised."

"You aren't?"

"No."

"You knew he'd be pissed?"

"Well, I know I'd be pissed if I had to print a retraction and apology."

"That story was bullshit," Malcolm lamented.

He bent forward, his head in his hands, the smartphone to his ear.

"That's not accurate, Malcolm."

Malcolm's mind was slow. He couldn't think.

"But we both know the RCMP didn't find anything."

"Yes. But they investigated."

"But they dismissed it because there was nothing to it. It was made up. Manufactured. A lie. Not even rumour. You knew that. I knew that."

"What I know is that the RCMP carried out an investigation. That's what I know."

"What bullshit!"

"Look, I'm not going to sit here and argue with you about it. You did what you had to do. End of story. It's just too bad the story never made the print edition. That would have helped us."

Malcolm stood up, steady on his feet. His breathing was back to normal.

"But it wasn't true," he moaned.

"You're wrong: it was true. What we—what you—gave Rob was true. Someone had laid a complaint with the RCMP. That's what you gave Rob. It's not our job to verify that. If anyone didn't do his job it was Rob."

Malcolm was growing weary of this endless spiralling rationalization. He felt like a dog chasing his tail.

"How could he? We asked him to run it clean."

"Did you ask him not to go to the RCMP?"

"No."

"No. We only asked him to run it clean. How he understands that is on him."

"Well he doesn't see it that way. He blames me. He says it's my fault for giving him a bullshit story."

Malcolm's accusing tone had changed. He was feeling regretful.

"Of course he'd say it's your fault. Have you ever known a reporter who likes to admit they made a mistake? He'll be more careful next time."

"There won't be a next time."

"In politics there's always a next time."

Silence.

"It's no big deal. It's only the News Daily."

Silence.

"Malcolm?"

"What?"

Malcolm's voice was as flat as Franson's.

"A word of advice for you: in this job you have no friends."

Silence.

"Tell Rob we'll see if we can make it up to him. Sometime down the road."

"That would be great," Malcolm said, relieved.

"Just don't promise anything."

Malcolm rolled off of Rachel, retrieved his underwear from the bottom of the bed, quickly put them on, and lay on his back staring at the ceiling. Rachel turned over on her side so that she was closer to him.

"Are you okay?"

She sounded genuinely concerned. She reached out her hand and laid it on his stomach.

"Sure. Why?"

Her fingers began slowly walking towards his boxers. "Because you've never had this problem before. I thought maybe something's bothering you."

"Like what?"

Her fingers stopped and she removed her hand.

"You don't have to be so defensive."

"Sorry," he said, more a reflex than actually meaning it.

"Is it to do with Rob? I heard you arguing on the phone."

"I don't want to talk about it."

That wasn't completely true. Malcolm wanted to talk about it, just not with Rachel. He was afraid of what she'd say. Or wouldn't say. Either way, she would be judging him.

"You used to be able to talk to me," Rachel said, reaching out to rub his neck.

"It's something I have to deal with myself," he said, pulling away.

That also wasn't completely true. He needed someone who would tell him that everyone fucks up, that he's only human, that it would all work out. But Rachel wasn't that person. There were certain things she would never accept—and how he had used his friendship with Rob was one of them.

"Is that why you were late coming home?"

"Would you just leave it!" he said, too vehemently.

She turned away, pulling the covers over her shoulder.

Chapter 14

YOU READ IT HERE FIRST
REPORTER LEFT HOLDING POLITICAL BARF BAG
POSTED BY RAYMOND WHITE ★ MAY 2, 2014

YOU CAN BET News Daily legislative reporter Rob Ryland had a nasty case of indigestion yesterday after getting a taste of B.C.-style politics.

It all started when Ryland received a brown envelope courtesy of one of his many sources. Now that's not news. Everyone knows the Davis government is leaking secrets faster than Edward Snowden on speed dial thanks to disgruntled public service workers who are still steamed over last year's contract stripping.

But this brown envelope was different: it targeted the opposition NDP. Inside was an RCMP file containing damning allegations about NDP leader Don Forsyth. Talk about a police takedown! The only thing missing was a TV camera outside his house.

Ryland, who knows a juicy tip when he sees one, immediately posted a story with a link to the file. Just one problem: there was no story. Seems the RCMP looked into the allegations and ruled them out. Only Ryland forgot to ask. Now everybody is pointing fingers.

"I was led to believe this was solid," Ryland said to me on the phone. "So I wrote a brief for the web and intended to follow up with the RCMP. But before I could, Forsyth called me to say he'd been cleared of any wrongdoing. We have since removed the story from our site."

Oops.

Forsyth is blaming Davis and the United Party, saying they were behind the original allegations.

"It was a smear job in the run-up to the election," he told me. "Now they're trying the same thing a year later."

But the UP is suggesting it may just be New Democrat infighting.

"I wouldn't be surprised if it was bad blood left over from the party leadership race," Davis's press secretary Matt McDonaugh told me. "It's pretty clear there is a split in the NDP, and everyone knows they are notorious for eating their own."

A United Party poison pill or a NDP feeding frenzy? Whatever it was, Ryland was the one left holding the political barf bag.

MAY 2, 2014
10:04AM
OFF THE LEDGE
ED DANIELS SHOW

Ed: I'm Ed Daniels and I welcome you on this beautiful May morning on the Simpson Radio Network. It's time for our regular Friday political panel Off the Ledge, with Bev Hayden, political columnist for The Vancouver Sun, and Joey Kapur, Victoria Bureau Chief for Global TV News.

Bev and Joey, things are certainly heating up over in Victoria. Earlier this week, we learned that Justice Minister Wade Dalton, a senior cabinet minister, United Party House Leader, and close personal friend of Premier Steven Davis, is the subject of an RCMP investigation over alleged election misdeeds. And then we had the odd story about NDP leader Don Forsyth's own alleged run-in with the law. I emphasize alleged because it seems there's not as much to the story. Bev, what do you make of these developments?

Bev: Well you know Ed, there's never any shortage of scandal over here in Victoria. Unfortunately for the Davis government it's had more than its fair share as it comes up on its first anniversary in power. There was the MLA from Cloverdale—

Joey: Gary Johnson.

Bev: —who I guess you could say punched his ticket to the backbench by slugging an RCMP officer on election night. The

RCMP laying charges there—they don't take kindly to people assaulting their members. Johnson is fighting the charge—

Ed: Oh no.

Bev: Sorry, Ed, it was too good to pass up. In any event, there have been a number of postponements as he keeps changing lawyers—

Joey: Apparently he can't get along with any of them.

Bev: It now looks like his case will go ahead in July. Then there was Forests Minister Jeremy Chapman—

Joey: He's sitting as an independent—

Bev: —who was charged, if you recall, with soliciting on a trade mission to Washington. That case is still to come before the courts. As I understand it, Chapman may argue entrapment.

Joey: But he is out of cabinet and out of government.

Bev: Out of the party as well.

Joey: And let's not forget about Henry Rawlings—

Bev: The former Minister for Social Development—

Joey: —under RCMP investigation for activities that took place during his term as mayor of Clearwater.

Bev: Clearbrook.

Joey: That's what I said.

Bev: No, you said Clearwater.

Joey: I meant Clearbrook.

Ed: So we've had an MLA and two cabinet ministers resign in the first year.

Joey: Though only Chapman is sitting as an independent.

Bev: Yes, Rawlings and Johnson are still in the UP caucus.

Ed: And now Wade Dalton. The justice minister.

Joey: Yes, it's a nasty business, this one. Dalton's campaign manager, Sarbjit Sharma, apparently had a falling out with the justice minister. If you recall, a few months after the election Ray White had a piece about Sharma in the Province newspaper where Sharma complained that he was promised work in the new government.

Bev: But that never materialized.

Joey: No. Sharma said Dalton reneged on his promise. Now we have Sharma claiming Dalton engaged in dirty tricks during the election.

Ed: Bev, is there something to this or is this just a disgruntled former staffer?

Bev: Well, Ed, it may be a bit of both. Certainly Sharma is unhappy with Dalton. That much is clear. What's not clear is what Dalton is supposed to have done.

Joey: Sharma says he sabotaged his NDP opponent.

Bev: I was just getting to that.

Ed: Alright, Joey, I assume as Dalton's campaign manager Sharma would know a lot about what went on during the election.

Joey: You're right, Ed. He knows where all the bodies are buried, and he's offering to show the RCMP where they are.

Bev: Not only where they are—he's ready to help dig them up.

Ed: But we don't know the details yet?

Joey: We don't, but we know there were a couple of nasty incidents during the election. One involved a rally outside a Sikh temple where the police were called.

Bev: And remember, Dalton only won that election by 540 votes.

Joey: It was closer to 600.

Ed. It was close, in any event. Bev, maybe you can tell us where you think this will go. Will it have any legs?

Bev: It all depends on what the RCMP uncovers. They are being extremely tight-lipped.

Joey: That's normal in investigations involving a cabinet minister.

Bev: But they seem even more close-mouthed than usual.

Ed: I see the government has appointed a special prosecutor to handle the case, Ted Irving, a Toronto criminal lawyer.

Bev: That's what they do in cases involving politicians—to ensure transparency. It is especially important in this case that he come from outside B.C. because it involves the justice minister, who is responsible for Crown prosecutors.

Ed: So Irving will ensure there is an independent review of any potential charges that the RCMP may recommend.

Bev: He will also prosecute the case if it goes to court.

Joey: Irving is known as a real straight shooter. Highly respected in the Ontario legal community and among the police there.

Bev: What's unusual is that Dalton hasn't stepped aside while the RCMP and special prosecutor carry out their work.

Joey: That is normally what happens in these cases. Certainly the NDP are calling for it—have been calling for it from the moment it became public.

Ed: But isn't that what the Opposition always does—calls for somebody to resign every time there's a hint of trouble?

Joey: Yes, but in this case I think they're justified.

Bev: What's even more surprising is that the premier hasn't asked Dalton to step aside. Now I know they are personal friends—they shared an apartment for the first year together in Opposition—but certainly Davis must know that Dalton can't stay on as justice minister. It's simply untenable.

Joey: He's even hearing that from within his own party.

Bev: And not just anyone in the party: Mike Visser, the Minister for Advanced Education and a member of cabinet.

Ed: Joey, what about Mike Visser?

Joey: Ed, it's almost unheard of for a cabinet minister to speak out in this way. When they're sworn in as a minister of the Crown they're expected to maintain cabinet solidarity.

Bev: But cabinet solidarity on government policies. This isn't about a government policy.

Joey: Still, it was a surprise when Visser told reporters this morning that Dalton needs to step aside, not only because it's the right thing to do, but for the sake of the party and the govern-ment. He says he fears the UP will be consumed by the issue as long as Dalton remains justice minister.

Ed: Does he have a point?

Bev: He does. The NDP have been hammering away at Dalton in Question Period all week—and we have a long way to go before the House rises. Now we're hearing United Party backbenchers are getting restless; they say this is pushing the gov-ernment off its agenda. Davis needs to tread carefully here or he could lose his caucus—or at the very least split it.

Joey: Yes, there is no doubt there is growing support for Visser. Now the premier's people are suggesting that Visser's comments are really just bad blood lingering from the last leadership race when Dalton threw his support behind Davis, assuring him of the win over Visser.

Ed: Speaking of bad blood, the premier's press secretary suggested this week that bad blood within the NDP was to blame for the disclosure of the Don Forsyth investigation, or non-investigation as it turned out.

Bev: It seems the premier's office is going green: they keep recycling the same response.

Joey: If you listened carefully to Matt McDonaugh, Davis's press secretary, he didn't actually say it was bad blood, he said he wouldn't be surprised if it was bad blood. It's a subtle difference.

Bev: It was deliberately intended to turn the attention away from the United Party and onto the NDP. Ed, I'm less inclined to think it was NDP infighting, but I also don't think the United Party would be so ham-fisted in managing this.

Joey: I'm hearing rumblings about a rogue RCMP officer with political aspirations. It would certainly explain how that RCMP file found its way to News Daily reporter Rob Ryland, who ran with the story without checking with the cops.

Bev: Rob's a real pro . . . longtime legislative reporter. It just shows you the pressure reporters are under these days to rush their stories to the web.

Joey: In the old days, we'd run down a story before it went to print or air. Today, you literally watch a reporter write the story in real time, adding to it as he or she goes. It's a different world.

Ed: That's a topic for another day. Right now we have to cut away for a break. When we come back we'll go straight to our phone lines so have your questions ready for Bev and Joey.

Malcolm's cellphone buzzed to life, jittering atop the desktop. A new message. Malcolm ignored it and returned to reading the clippings package that had been emailed a few minutes before. He was surprised his name hadn't been mentioned in any of the stories. They'd put it down to a "rogue RCMP officer".

Had Rob deliberately kept him out of it? Malcolm felt hopeful that they could still be friends. But then he remembered that Rob hadn't called since, when was it, Tuesday? Three days. It seemed longer.

Rob had called every morning for the last six months. They would run through the latest political goings-on in Victoria, each sharing what they knew: facts, gossip, rumour, good-news stories the UP were pitching, bad-news stories the New Democrats were shopping around, speculation. Malcolm would then pass along some of what he'd heard, especially anything about the NDP, during the daily morning staff meeting. It had helped to establish his reputation for having a finger on the political pulse of the legislature.

Feeling guilt and regret for that time, now lost, perhaps irrevocably, Malcolm reached for his phone to check the last message. Catherine. He put the phone back on the desk without looking at the message. He didn't have to; it would be the same as all the messages he'd been receiving from her for days: "Call me".

He'd intended to call Catherine before now, but it was taking him longer to work out how he felt about her. There was an obvious attraction, but what did it mean? Was it just sex? Or something more? And what was he going to do about it? Catherine certainly seemed willing, but what about Davis? Where did he fit in all this? He hadn't had the nerve to ask Catherine. And what about Rachel? He still had feelings for her, made stronger by their shared history. They had enjoyed a lot of good times together. And they'd made plans for many more. Maybe plans was too strong a word—it was more an understanding that they would be together; that what they had wasn't temporary, but for the longer term. They'd even talked of kids: how many and whether they preferred boys or girls. He wanted girls; she wanted boys. Now that seemed so long ago. Did anything really last anymore? It was all a mess—he was a mess—even more reason for him not to call Catherine.

His eyes rested on the clippings open on his computer screen and his mind returned to Rob. Their friendship, too, was a mess. And it wasn't just Forsyth; it had started to change before then.

Small things, like the way he had more to offer Rob on their morning calls than Rob had to offer him. And the way he knew more about how government worked. Rob had only a partial view of government: from the outside. He thought he knew government, but he didn't, not really. Government was more than MLAs and org charts. Malcolm saw government from the inside; its networks, relationships, nuances. It gave him a more complete picture—more than that, an understanding—than Rob would ever have. That's the way life is, Malcolm thought: always changing, shifting, moving. Never staying in one place.

Malcolm looked at the phone and felt a mix of hope and despair: hope that he and Rob could still be friends of a sort; despair in knowing that even if they were friends, it would never again be the friendship they once had.

Chapter 15

OUTSIDE THE BOSS'S office, Malcolm sat patiently checking email on his smartphone. Next to him were McDonaugh and Franson, also on their phones. Jarrod wasn't invited, which would make him pissy for the rest of the day.

They'd been waiting five minutes. Without explanation, they had been led into the Boss's office by Jessica, using Maurice's connecting door. But then Rai, the premier's executive assistant, hearing them, took exception to Jessica's familiarity, which resulted in an awkward and tense standoff until Rai, in a chilly display of authority, made them come out and sit on the leather couches in the reception area.

Malcolm wondered why they were here, because it was Friday morning and that meant the Boss was in Vancouver; he always left immediately following the Thursday afternoon sitting—if he was there at all. He'd taken to avoiding the House as much as possible, as if it were beneath him to submit to daily questions from the Opposition. Since the budget was introduced in the third week of February, he'd adopted a new persona: corporate CEO of the Province of British Columbia. It was a role he was familiar with from his life before politics, a role he seemed born to. He was always a bit uneasy as a politician, wearing it like a baggy second skin that he desperately wanted to shed. Now he was constantly on the move: Vancouver to meet with business leaders, New York to shore up bond holder confidence, Beijing on a trade mission—anywhere but Victoria. In his absence, Dalton had been doing his bidding in the House, in caucus and in cabinet; like a puppeteer pulling strings from above. But the RCMP investigation had loosened Dalton's grip on the strings and the puppets were starting to take on a life of their own.

"Maitland has posted a piece on how many days the premier has been absent from the House," Malcolm said, checking his Twitter feed. "He's attached a running calendar that he's going to update daily."

"Fuck Maitland!" Franson said. "What's his readership? Two? We never respond to anything he prints and we ignore his requests for interviews. I don't know why you even monitor his shit."

"Because the gallery reads him."

"They all follow him," agreed McDonaugh.

Malcolm could see McDonaugh had opened Maitland's website on his smartphone.

"We should prep some bullets," McDonaugh said. "The gallery love stories like this—they're easy for the public to understand. They'll frame it that the premier is giving the finger to democracy, to the people's house."

"Fine," Franson said reluctantly. "But the gallery are only worried about their collective asses: they need the premier there to justify their existence to their editors. Really, do voters want him in the House flapping his gums with a bunch of politicians or out doing the peoples' business?"

"I'm not sure I'd message it quite that way," Malcolm said.

McDonaugh laughed and Franson's chin sank deeper into his chest. It was another ten minutes before they heard the familiar slam of the heavy double oak exterior doors that led from the covered exterior walkway connecting the main building to the West Annex. The commissionaire in the outer reception area must have been more alert than usual because almost simultaneously a buzzer sounded opening the lock on the inside door to the premier's office reception area and the premier burst through with Maurice close behind and Const. Charles Hadley, his RCMP security detail, trying to keep up. They were walking quickly. The premier looked flushed; Maurice was glum.

"Give us a minute," Maurice said as he hurried by and into the premier's office where he closed the door.

Hadley, in plainclothes, stood square-shouldered by the door, and when he turned his head Malcolm could see the cord from his earpiece disappearing into his jacket collar. He wondered what he was listening to because he was the only member of the detail.

The RCMP detail was added in the fall after the premier received the first threats. The following spring the premier moved out of the family home on southwest Marine Drive when he woke to an intruder in the kitchen. The RCMP said they couldn't assure the security of the house—too many entries—so he moved to a condo in Yaletown with a single private entrance. His wife now spent most of her time there, rarely making the trip over to their apartment in Victoria during session, the glamour of being the premier's wife apparently having lost its lustre.

A minute turned into five minutes. The door to the premier's office finally opened with a sigh and Maurice signaled for them to come in. The premier stood by his now infamous desk that filled the corner of the office by the window. Custom made in Germany, the glass and steel desk reflected a glinting vulgarity and pretension. After the media posted photos showing the desk being moved into the premier's office, a small group of B.C. cabinet makers demanded the premier get rid of the desk and instead use one made in B.C.

"Who knew we had cabinet makers in B.C.?" the premier asked with a bemused smile while watching them protesting on the lawn outside his window.

Before long they were joined by protesters angry about the decline of the forest industry and who insisted on a desk made from B.C. wood; others who wanted a desk created by First Nations carvers as part of the province's reconciliation and reparation for past wrongs; and still others who argued for a desk made from recycled plastic, the latter carrying placards with the word *desk* pasted clumsily over another word. Later, the word peeled off and fluttered high in the air before coming to rest under the redwood tree by the statue of Queen Victoria, where it joined empty yogurt containers, chocolate bar wrappers, and discarded newspapers.

Over Maurice's objections, the premier invited the protesters in to meet with him—and to see the desk. They crowded into the office where the premier shifted easily between the role of empathetic listener—carefully hearing each of the arguments—and master manipulator—skillfully and deftly playing one faction against the other. In the end, the cabinet makers emerged to tell the waiting media that while they couldn't agree with the premier's choice of desk, they wanted to thank him for taking the time to hear their concerns. The premier joked that he felt a kinship since he himself was "a cabinet maker, though of a different sort". The protesters even smiled and posed with the premier for the TV cameras, which Malcolm knew was more important than anything they might have said, because in a few days—maybe even in a few hours—the words might be forgotten, but the smiling faces would not.

Those were the early days of the mandate, the honeymoon period, when voters were still willing to give the premier the benefit of the doubt. The honeymoon had since long ended, and there were no smiling faces in the premier's office this Friday afternoon.

"I've just met with Wade and we've decided to try to ride this out," the premier said.

Malcolm guessed that Dalton would not step aside.

"I've also talked to Mike and asked him to give us some time. He said he'll think about it over the weekend. I'm not hopeful."

He was right not to be hopeful. The premier was in a weakened position and Visser was clearly using this as an opportunity to make inroads into his base. Malcolm had already been hearing from ministerial staffers that some members of cabinet were openly questioning the premier's decision to stand by Dalton. If ministers were wavering, then caucus was probably falling apart.

"That asshole," said Maurice. "He's never supported you."

"You can't blame him," said the premier with surprising equanimity. "It's nothing more than what I'd do in his shoes. So we have to assume that by Monday we could be facing a full-fledged caucus revolt."

"I wouldn't go that far," Maurice protested.

"I'm talking worst-case," the premier said.

Franson spoke up: "I don't mean to point out the obvious, but wouldn't the easiest way to resolve this be for Minister

Dalton to step aside—only until the RCMP investigation is over. Then he could be brought back into cabinet."

"Maurice and I have already had this discussion," said the premier firmly. "He won't step aside and I won't ask him to."

"Mallory won't let him," Maurice said.

"Mallory only has Wade's best interests at heart—as any wife would," the premier quickly replied.

"More like Mallory's best interests," McDonaugh said quietly to himself, but loud enough for Malcolm to hear.

"So we're in a box," the premier said. "Maurice and I have talked and we think the best plan is to call a special caucus meeting on Monday evening—after the House rises. It will give us the weekend to reach out to MLAs and build support. It won't be easy because Mike has been canvassing members all week, so he's got a head start on us."

"Will that give us enough time?" asked Franson.

"We can't leave it any later," said Maurice, "or we risk caucus splintering. As it is, we'll have a tough time holding them together until Monday."

"We'll have to work fast," said the premier. "I want to get it out there that I am willing to play hardball on this. I want caucus to know that they need to think long and hard about the choice they make on Monday. Maurice is going to be calling constituency executives and party members to get them to put pressure on their MLAs. Glenn, you handle the MAs and EAs and caucus communications. Matt, I want you to take the lead on media. I want them running stories about how I'm not just going to bat for Wade, but that I'm willing to go to the wall for him."

"Are you?" asked Matt.

"For now," said the premier. "But I want the media and caucus to think I'm willing to stake the premiership on this question. Malcolm, I want you to meet with Mike."

Malcolm's heart leaped.

"Why Malcolm?" asked Franson.

"Mike likes him," the premier explained. He turned to Malcolm: "Apparently, he was impressed with you when you went over to help out with communications last year, isn't that right, Maurice."

"That's right, Premier," said Maurice as if he were confirming Malcolm just killed his mother. "Eric says Mike couldn't stop talking about Malcolm. Still talks about him."

"I'm not sure what I can do," said Malcolm. The hesitation in his voice was clear. "Especially if you've already talked to him."

"I just need to keep the pressure on him—and I don't think Maurice is the best choice."

Maurice gravely nodded, but the effect was such that you couldn't be sure if he was in agreement or disagreement, which was perfect for politics, and which Malcolm filed away for his own use when the time was right.

"Don't worry, you won't be alone. I've got Ginny and Tom talking to him as well, making an appeal for cabinet solidarity. It won't be so much what you say to him, but the fact I've sent you. I want him to know we're putting on a full-court press."

Hardball, going to bat, full-court press: the premier reverted to the safety of sports metaphors whenever he was anxious. Despite an MBA from Cornell, Davis was really a jock who saw everything as a game to be won; he used to play basketball in high school and was good enough to get a scholarship, though only to a Canadian university and which he quickly rejected.

There was a damp chill in the air; the cool spring had lingered into May so that on this overcast Friday afternoon the three Beacon Hill tennis courts were deserted except for a lone pair of players on the far court. Pock, pock, pock: the rhythmic back-and-forth sound of tennis followed Malcolm and Visser as they made their way down narrow Nursery Road beneath the soft green hue of the plane trees. Anyone watching them would think that they made an odd pair: one tall and gangly, the other squat in his wheelchair.

Ahead lay the cricket pavilion and field, a vestige of Victoria's colonial past when 27-year-old Royal Navy Captain Walter Grant arrived in the summer of 1849 by canoe from the mainland carrying with him his cricket bat and ball, and proceeded to carve a field out of the Beacon Hill wilderness. Cricket had

been played on the site ever since. On this day, half a dozen players were practising: one lobbed a ball toward the stumps and bails
while a batsman gingerly swung and sent long looping balls out
into the waiting hands of players scattered in the field.

"You ever play cricket?" asked Visser.

"No, but I like to watch it," Malcolm said. "When I first
came to Victoria, I'd ride my bike down here on a sunny day and
sit on that grassy slope and try to figure it out."

"And did you? Figure it out?"

"It took me awhile, but I managed it."

Malcolm liked cricket: the formality of the white uniforms,
the sense of order, the symmetry.

"I'm not surprised," Visser said. "You've got a knack for fig-
uring things out. I've never understood the game. Give me hockey any day."

"Those days seem so long ago," Malcolm said wistfully.

"A lot has changed," agreed Visser. "You've changed.
You're now the premier's go-to guy. Maurice can't like that.
Better keep your head up."

"Maybe it's Maurice who should keep his head up,"
Malcolm said, trying to be funny, but it didn't sound funny; it
sounded like a boast.

Visser wheeled to a stop and took a long look at Malcolm
who kept on walking. Then Malcolm stopped and turned and
waited for Visser to catch up.

"So," Visser said, his voice hardening as he wheeled alongside Malcolm, "I don't hear from you for six months and then
out of the blue you want to meet. Let me guess: Wade Dalton?"

Malcolm felt the heat on his cheeks. He nodded.

"Davis sent you to try to persuade me to back off, right?"

Malcolm shrugged.

"Pretty much."

There was no use in pretending otherwise. A shout went up
and Visser instinctively turned to see. Malcolm followed his gaze.
The batsman had hit a ball a long way, past the ring of fielders,
so that when it landed it rolled up the grassy slope on the other
side of the field.

"He's already had Ginny Jones and Tom Puttock call me," Visser said as he watched a fielder race to retrieve the ball and throw it in. "I have to say they weren't very convincing, their appeal for cabinet solidarity. This has nothing to do with cabinet solidarity. It's not even a cabinet matter. It's about conflict of interest and the perception of a conflict."

He waited a few seconds as if weighing whether to continue, then turned back toward Malcolm with a renewed vigor.

"But I'm anxious to hear what you have to say. So Mr. Hotshot, convince me."

He settled back in his wheelchair expectantly.

Malcolm said: "I'm here to tell you that the premier is willing to go to any lengths to keep Dalton in cabinet."

Visser nodded. "Do you believe that?"

"It doesn't matter what I believe; I'm here to tell you what the premier said."

"But I'm curious what you think. Do you think he will risk losing caucus rather than fire Dalton?"

"He said he is willing to go to any lengths."

"Yes, but I've come to learn, after many years in politics, that what people say and what they actually do are quite different things. How about this then: if he loses caucus, do you think Davis will really quit before he will fire Dalton?"

Malcolm thought about this for a moment. He really didn't want to answer. He reverted to his communications default.

"It's not for me to speculate."

"Oh, come on, Malcolm. You've worked beside him for a year now; surely you have some sense, some inkling, of the man and how far he's willing to go. I'm not asking you to bet your life on it. I just want to know what your gut says."

Malcolm looked back to the cricket pitch where a new batsman was gearing up to take his place in front of the wicket. He felt himself at a crossroads, as if what he answered would put him on a particular path: yes, and he was on Davis's path; no, and he was on Visser's path.

"Life is about choices," said Visser, as if he could read Malcolm's mind. "You may think you don't have to make a choice, that you can just keep floating along wherever the wind or the current takes you, but not making a choice is also a choice."

Malcolm smiled: "Still the philosopher, I see."

"No matter," Visser said, wheeling away and starting toward the pavilion. "You've told me what I want to know."

Malcolm rushed to catch up.

"What do you mean?"

"If you were so sure about Davis resigning over this you would have said so right away. The fact you're hesitating tells me he isn't as firm on this as he—and you—would like me to believe."

Malcolm stopped. It was his turn to stare after Visser. Visser half turned in his wheelchair to see why Malcolm had stopped.

"Don't worry," he said. "You didn't tell me anything I didn't already know. Do you think I believed for a second he would resign over this? If he was truly going to resign he wouldn't have to send you, Ginny and Tom to convince me. The man doth protest too much. Besides, why would I stop? Either way I win."

"How so?"

"Davis has only so much political capital. If he resigns, I win. If he doesn't resign, he will have expended a lot of political capital trying to keep caucus onside—and I still win."

They started walking again. In the background, the bowler had just knocked a bail off a stump and the wicket-keeper stooped to retrieve it.

"What do you think, Malcolm?" Visser asked. "Do you think Dalton should step aside . . . not just for the good of the party, but because it's the right thing to do?"

"I'm not so sure it's that easy," Malcolm said.

"To do the right thing?"

"No. To know what is the right thing. Have you thought that maybe for the premier standing by a friend is the right thing to do?"

"So you're saying right and wrong are relative?"

"No. I'm saying there is more than one factor to consider when making a decision about what is right and what is wrong. It isn't so black and white."

"You're giving Davis too much credit—this isn't about friendship. It's about politics. That's all the man knows."

"And maybe you're not giving him enough credit."

They had come to a crossroads: ahead was the end of Nursery Road, a dead end; to the right, a narrow path of faded wood chips led up the hill past the pavilion into the centre of the park; to the left, the path stretched down across the grass ending at a row of parked cars along the street in the distance.

"It looks like we've reached the end of our walk," Visser said.

"We can continue down here back toward Cook Street," Malcolm suggested.

He didn't want it to end like this, with them arguing.

"No, I think we've said everything we need to say."

"How's Claire?" Malcolm asked, as if to contradict him.

"Fine," Visser said too sharply.

Pause.

"We're still trying to have a baby. But it's up and down. More down than up, thanks to me."

He gave a listless laugh.

"I'm sorry to hear that," said Malcolm. "Wish her well for me."

Visser nodded, turned and slowly pushed himself back down Nursery Road. Malcolm watched and thought how the gray, forlorn figure in the wheelchair contrasted against the effortless athleticism of the cricket players dressed in white. Then he turned and took the path towards the street.

8:35 Monday morning and the rain was coming down sideways in gusting sheets. The winds had cancelled the float planes from downtown Vancouver, and ferry sailings out of Tsawwassen were delayed. McDonaugh, Franson and Malcolm were sitting in the dark cloud that had settled over Maurice's office. They were waiting for the premier to come on the line. With the float planes grounded, he was on his way to Vancouver airport to get the earliest flight he could. It was becoming clearer that he wouldn't be there in time for the morning sitting at 10. Not a good start to the day.

The premier had put Maurice on hold while he talked to Roger Fenwick, an MLA from Prince George and Davis caucus stalwart. Fenwick had been working the phones over the weekend and was now updating the premier. Maurice had placed the speakerphone on mute. He was sitting behind his desk, poised to release the mute button as soon as the premier returned.

"Roger," Maurice grumbled impatiently, the fingers of his left hand lightly tapping his desk as if he was playing the piano. "Why does he have to always go on ad-fucking-nauseam? He just needs to tell him where we are with caucus. Nothing else. Jesus, I bet he can't even take a dump without going into every excruciating detail."

Another minute or two went by.

"Okay, Maurice, let's go," the premier's voice said abruptly from the speakerphone.

Maurice stopped playing his imaginary sonata and punched the mute button.

"Thank goodness," Maurice said. "I wasn't sure Roger was ever going to let you off. What a fucking windbag."

"I asked Roger to stay on the line to fill you in personally, so I've linked him into this call."

Maurice sat back and stared at the phone as if it had suddenly grown tentacles.

"Hello, Maurice," said a gravelly voice.

Maurice recovered well.

"Hello, Roger," he said icily. "So what have you got to tell us?"

"I'll try to keep it short," Roger said.

"Always a first time for everything," Maurice snapped.

Roger ignored him. Caucus was not happy with Dalton remaining as minister. They were still smarting from the public backlash to the government's first sitting when they slashed public services to balance the budget. The MLAs, many of them elected for the first time, had expected a gentler entry into government. Instead, they faced protests in front of their constituency offices and angry letters to the editor in their hometown newspapers. They couldn't even go to the grocery store without someone accosting them. The second budget, just released, introduced new rate hikes on everything from auto insurance to medical premiums and another round of cutbacks thinly disguised as a reorganization of services. MLAs were finding it a hard sell at home, so the last thing they wanted was to take on a battle they felt was unnecessary.

"If that was the short version, I'd hate to see the long one," muttered Maurice.

"I think you might have cut out on us there, Maurice," said the premier. "What was that you said?"

"It's not good news," Maurice said, as if Roger was to blame. "Is there anything they like?"

"They like the tax cuts," Roger said.

The premier: "Thanks, Roger. I appreciate all your work on this. Talk to you soon."

"Always a pleasure, premier."

Maurice gave the phone the finger. A beep indicated Roger's participation had ended.

"That's pretty much what I heard all weekend," said the premier.

"Premier," Maurice said, "I don't think you want to get to the point where you have caucus rise up against you and you have to back down. You lose them once and you might never get them back."

"So what do you suggest?"

"Deal with it before this afternoon's caucus meeting . . . before we get them all in one room."

"You mean cancel the meeting tonight?"

"Yes. You need to act before it looks like they pushed you. You need to own this decision. Not them."

"So when are you thinking?"

"Release it this morning—before caucus and QP."

"That's tight. Will I have enough time to meet with Wade?"

"You'll need to call him now."

"I'd prefer to do it in person."

"I'm afraid you don't have that luxury, Premier."

Pause.

"Are Malcolm and Matt there?"

"Yes."

"Malcolm, prepare a statement and make it brief; Matt, we'll do media this morning in my office right after the statement is out."

"Premier, are we also going to announce who's replacing Minister Dalton?" Malcolm asked.

"Yes, Ginny is going to be doing double duty."

"Have you spoken with her?" Franson asked.

"Yes, I talked to her about it on Friday when I asked her to talk to Mike."

The premier had been preparing for this all along. Malcolm looked at Maurice for a reaction, but Maurice's face didn't show anything. He must have known.

"She's already in cabinet," Maurice explained to Malcolm and the others in the room, "so no need for a trip to Government House."

Malcolm prepared a two–paragraph statement, but before he had a chance to give it to Maurice the news was already out. Joanne Freeman of the Globe and Mail tweeted it and in seconds everyone else in the gallery was tweeting it. Of course, everyone followed Wade Dalton, but Joanne was the only one following Mallory Dalton and Mallory was the first out with the news on Twitter: "Premier just fired father of my kids over the phone. I could spit nails. Friendship counts for nothing."

Malcolm rushed into Maurice's office with the statement.

"The Dalton announcement is on Twitter," he said, handing the statement to Maurice.

Maurice looked confused, as if he was trying to understand what Malcolm had said, when Franson leaned his head into the office.

"Mallory has just told everyone Dalton was fired."

Maurice's face went purple.

"What?" he asked.

"On Twitter," said Franson.

Malcolm showed Maurice his smartphone.

"She must have been with Dalton when the premier called," said Franson.

Maurice's own smartphone rang. He looked at the caller ID. He let the phone ring again as he visibly calmed himself before answering.

"Premier," he said. "Yes, I just saw it. Yes, I'll call him right away. Okay."

Maurice took the phone slowly away from his ear.

"Mallory is still tweeting," Malcolm said.

"What's she saying?" asked Maurice.

"'Wade was widely acknowledged as a great justice minister. It's so unfair to him. But he has been utterly gracious and took it like a man.'"

"Here's another one," Franson said: "'Maybe Wade should have backed Mike Visser. Then again, it's not too late.'"

"Fucking hell!" yelled Maurice and furiously worked his smartphone. He pressed the touchscreen, then pressed it again and again until finally he dropped it on his desk and yelled: "Jessica!"

Jessica was already at the door, apparently having anticipated the request.

"Minister Dalton is waiting for you on line one, Maurice."

Without saying anything, Maurice reached for his desk phone.

"Wade, what the fuck is Mallory doing?"

Pause.

"Well, tell her, and for God's sake get her off Twitter. No. As far as I know we are still saying you resigned."

He slammed down the receiver.

Malcolm: "She's tripled her number of followers in the last few minutes."

Maurice: "What does that mean?"

Franson: "Half the NDP caucus is retweeting her. It's got its own hashtag."

Maurice: "What does that mean?"

Malcolm: "*Hashtag Dalton fired* is trending."

"For fuck's sake, what does that mean?" Maurice yelled.

Malcolm: "It's going viral. It's out of our control."

"This is a disaster," moaned Maurice.

Malcolm: "She's posted another tweet: 'Wade is thoroughly decent and not bitter. I can't say the same. I'm heartbroken.'"

"Is she drunk?" asked Maurice so seriously that it drew a rare half-smile from Franson.

"Well, there is an upside to it," said Franson. "It's now perfectly clear that the premier forced Dalton to resign. That should help keep caucus onside."

Maurice's face brightened and he stood up in front of his chair.

"If he wants, the premier can have it both ways," Malcolm added. "He can still show support for Minister Dalton in public by saying that he resigned, while everyone knows, thanks to Mallory, that the premier forced him to. He'll come off as loyal but tough. It could be a win–win."

"You're right," Maurice said, smiling for the first time. "I'm not sure we could have planned this any better."

"Mallory has another tweet," said Franson. "'Have been told to zip it and stop tweeting, at least about my hubby. Funny they didn't mind when I tweeted my support for the premier.' And here's another one—"

"I thought she said she was going to stop tweeting," Maurice said, exasperated.

Franson continued: "'Shall only tweet about Beyonce and other safe subjects. Apparently my fifteen minutes is up.'"

"Thank fucking Christ!" said Maurice as he slumped into his chair exhausted.

Catherine's text read: "We're at the Swifty." It was the last day of session and everyone had gone for drinks to celebrate. Politicians and deputy ministers drank at the Pacific Lounge in the imposing Hotel Grand Pacific across the street from the Legislature; the Swiftsure, in the dowdy Days Inn a block further west, was the pub of choice for political staffers and government workers. Malcolm found Catherine at a large table—actually two tables pulled together—on the lower level. It annoyed him that two researchers—they couldn't have been any older that 22— were hanging over the arms of her chair vying for her attention. Even more annoying was that she seemed to be enjoying it. The rest of the table was made up of a mix of caucus types, communications folks and ministerial staffers, all of them under 25. The kids in short pants. He greeted them and sat at a vacant chair across from her and next to Ginny Jones's EA. Immediately he felt a bare foot push between his legs and snug itself into his crotch. He glanced across the table but she was occupied by the two boys. He waited a few minutes for the waitress to take his order but she was busy so he got up and went to the bar to get his own drink. While the bartender poured his beer he felt a woman's breasts pushing against him.

"Don't," he said. He was still annoyed. "Not here."

"Okay."

Catherine tucked her hand into the back of his belt and began walking toward the exit, her arm extended as if pulling a disobedient dog on a leash. He felt himself being dragged backwards. The bartender put the beer on the counter and looked at him questioningly.

"I'll be right back," Malcolm said to the bartender.

Catherine tugged Malcolm around the corner opposite the men's room, pushed him up against the wall, and kissed him. She tasted of beer and Malcolm wondered if she was drunk. Bas Dhillon, the former reporter turned lobbyist, came out of the washroom and said: "I'll have some of that."

"What's up?" Malcolm asked when she finally stopped kissing him.

"I'm just happy to see you," she said, and reached down and fondled him. "Let's get out of here."

"I just bought a beer."

"Leave it."

"I've got to pay for it."

"Okay. But hurry up."

Malcolm put a $10 bill on the counter and turned to go when he glimpsed, not a face, but a vague familiarity. There it was, over in the corner, a table of Rachel's co-workers just settling in. He quickly scanned the table. Rachel wasn't there. Not yet, anyway. She hadn't mentioned she was going for drinks, but it could have been a last-minute thing. She could be on her way—or worse, just stopped for a quick pee before sitting down.

Malcolm panicked and frantically looked back toward the exit. Catherine was still waiting by the bathrooms. No Rachel. Yet. Out of nowhere another fear lunged at him and he swung his head toward the table. Then back at the exit again. Then back to the table. He was sure that from where they sat they couldn't have seen Catherine and him by the bathroom. At least, he was pretty sure. Someone from the table waved to him. Amber, the volunteer coordinator. He waved back and was wondering if he should go over and say something to her when a waiter slid past him and made his way toward the table. She wasn't waving at him—she was just trying to get the waiter's attention. Malcolm slipped out of the exit feeling both guilt and betrayal but, more than anything else, a profound sense of relief.

In the months that followed, Malcolm replayed that scene at the Swifty over and over in his head, as if tracing the scar from an old wound. He was still surprised by how suddenly it all happened.

It was the following Monday. June 2nd. He'd gone to work that morning and everything was fine with Rachel. It wasn't like they'd had a fight. Just the opposite: they hadn't argued for months. Nothing. As far as Malcolm was concerned, it was like any other Monday—until on his way home from work he walked up their street to find Rachel packing everything she owned into Amber's tiny blue Yaris.

She hadn't said a word to him about leaving. Nothing. No warning. Nothing.

He confronted her on the sidewalk by the car.

"What're you doing?"

She just continued to calmly load her things. That was what got to him: she was so calm. No yelling, no screaming, no tears. Nothing. It was like she didn't feel anything. That was the most painful: their relationship ending not with a bang, but a whimper. It was too much for him.

He went around to the front of the car and put both hands on the hood as if to try to stop it from moving. By now Rachel was sitting in the front seat. He shouted at her.

"Rachel! Talk to me. Why are you doing this?"

She just looked straight ahead, expressionless. It was if he wasn't there; he didn't exist. He slammed the hood.

"Hey!" Amber yelled, getting out of the car. "There's no need for that!"

She took out her smartphone and held it in front of her, as if to ward him off. He thought she was taking a video of him, but then she said: "Here."

She wanted him to take the phone. He put his hand out to get it. Why? What was on it that she wanted him to see? He pulled his hand back.

"Here," she said again and took his hand and placed the phone in it.

It was open to her Facebook page. There was a photo of him and Catherine. At the Swifty. They were kissing and Catherine had her hand down the back of his pants. Who posted this? Amber? Before he could see, Amber pulled her phone back.

"Asshole!" she said, and slammed her driver's door shut.

Malcolm raced around to Rachel's window. He tapped on the glass.

"Rachel, please roll down the window."

He wasn't angry—he was desperate. Pleading. He placed both hands against the window, fingers spread wide as if he was imprisoned and desperate to get out.

"Rachel, please! Let's talk."

But she acted like she couldn't hear him. He thought about opening the door—it wasn't locked—but it didn't seem right. Finally, she said something to Amber and turned back to him and rolled down the window.

"Rachel, I can explain," Malcolm said.

She shook her head. "I don't want you to explain."

"You don't?"

"No."

"Why not?" He hadn't expected this. The ground felt like it was shifting beneath him.

"Because I don't believe you."

"What do you mean? You haven't even heard what I have to say."

"Whatever you're going to say, it won't be the truth."

"I've never lied to you." Back on solid footing now.

"Malcolm, there's a difference between never lying and being true."

Malcolm looked at her blankly.

"Tell me you've been true to me."

The grass beneath him seemed to turn to quicksand. He felt he was being pulled under.

It was Rachel who finally spoke: "Your problem, Malcolm, is you can't even be true to yourself. You need to start being true to yourself before you can be true to me."

The window hummed closed, Amber started the car, and they drove off. All he could do was stand and watch as the car reached the end of the street and stopped before turning right; the last thing he remembered thinking was that she didn't signal.

PART THREE

(DECEMBER 2014)

Chapter 16

As Malcolm padded down the red carpet of the Speaker's Corridor past the darkened frosted glass door of the clerk's office, a boisterous clamour tumbled down the wide staircase, filling the legislature hallway with possibilities. The press gallery Christmas party was a fixture of the parliamentary social season, and Malcolm had eagerly looked forward to it for weeks—even more so after yesterday's announcement.

Located on the top floor at the rear of the legislature, the gallery offices were more attic than penthouse. The grand marble staircase that led up from the Speaker's Corridor faded to a pale imitation on the second flight—flanked on one side by a worn oak bannister and on the other by a wall of yellowed, black-and-white, wood-framed photos of reporters in baggy suits, short ties, and cheap haircuts—an affectionate family album chronicling gallery members through the years. There was Vancouver Sun legend Marjorie Nichols, who Premier Dave Barrett once snarled was a "venomous bitch", her nicotine-stained fingers tap, tap, tapping with a sure touch on her weighty Underwood, an ever-present cigarette in an ashtray beside her trailing smoke into the air. In another, Jim Hume stared out from a group of similarly fresh-faced men, eager to make their mark, their arms draped casually over each other's shoulders in a display of friendship that masked their intense rivalry.

At the top of the stairs, Malcolm pushed through people spilling out the doorway and onto the landing. Inside had the hallmarks of a university party—a crush of predominantly 20-somethings packed into what looked like the cramped foyer of a down-at-the-mouth 1940s men's club that apparently hadn't seen a cleaner in decades. Only these 20-somethings were dressed in the legislature's business uniform of tailored dark suits, colour-coordinated ties, and crisp white shirts. Each held a drink in one hand and a smartphone in the other, and when they weren't drinking, they were checking for texts, or taking photos and videos of themselves and posting them to their Facebook pages and Twitter feeds for all their friends to see. Against the scuffed wood-panelled wall, a gaudy orange and lime green floral sofa from the 1970s sagged dangerously under the weight of five young people who were trying to shoehorn a sixth in beside them, as if it were a telephone booth or VW Beetle.

Malcolm was absorbed and propelled forward. He thought someone shouted something to him, but he couldn't make out who among the mass of bodies. The crowd was especially thick to his left where three reporters were furiously pouring drinks behind a makeshift bar. On the opposite wall, someone had opened a window and a small group were perched on the ledge six stories above ground, leaning out precariously, smoking.

Malcolm worked his way towards a doorway on the other side where the crowd was thinner and which led to a larger room where the reporters had their desks. He had been here several times, most recently yesterday to make his formal introductions, and he liked the shabbiness of the place with its stale air still smelling of steaks and cigars from another time in a not-so-foreign past when it was a cafeteria, and he welcomed its familiar, lived-in feel, from the beat-up desks to the piles of newspapers that had slid wilfully across the floor. But he also knew that he didn't belong here. He was a visitor, welcome of course, but lacking the sense of ownership that comes with possession. In different circumstances, he might have had an office here, carved out a career for himself amid the dimness and the dust. He knew he should be feeling jubilant, but the crowded noisy room only amplified his sense of regret.

"Ah, the premier's new mouthpiece."

Malcolm turned and found himself within inches of Bev Hayden. Bev was infamous for invading your personal space to try to make you feel uncomfortable in the hope that you would be thrown off and say something unguarded. Ministers were routinely warned about her during media training sessions and instructed not to get caught against a wall with her or there would be no escape.

"Bev, I missed you yesterday," Malcolm said, maintaining his ground. "I'd come by to say hello."

"I hope it wasn't here, because I don't have an office here," she said in a way that came across as both dismissive and superior.

"No," Malcolm reassured her. "I went to your office."

Bev occupied half of the top floor of the old armoury behind the legislature, a squat, three-storey, warehouse-like brick building built in 1894 and as structurally sound as a house of cards. The other half of the floor was taken up by Joey Kapur. Bev and Joey. Joey and Bev. They were like an old married couple who take comfort from living together in the same house but occupy separate rooms. Their disconnection from the rest of the gallery had the whiff of elitism and, when combined with their status as the reigning *doyens*, could sometimes turn the gallery's usual mood of sardonic camaraderie to an air of shared resentment.

The gallery president was the official head of the legislative reporters, responsible for fielding complaints from the clerk over gallery members blocking the hallways during scrums, and tussling with the sergeant-at-arms over how many additional cameras would be permitted in the legislature during the prime minister's visit. But Bev and Joey wielded the real power. A sure sign of their influence within government circles: they were known only by their first names. Even the newest ministerial assistant routinely referred to them as Bev and Joey, as if talking about Elvis or Oprah or Madonna.

"I hope you last longer than the last press secretary," Bev said without sneering. It was the season of peace and goodwill after all.

"Whatever else, Matt was good at his job," said Malcolm, taking a quick glance around to see if anyone was listening. He had to be careful in these early days because Matt still had a loyal following, especially among political staffers who had worked with him on last year's election.

Bev motioned with her head to a trio of reporters huddled in the corner away from the surging crowd and said: "We were trying to think of the last time a premier's press secretary was caught *flagrante delicto* only eighteen months into a mandate. It's got to be a new record!"

Bev chuckled at her own needling joke and Malcolm gave what he hoped was a non-committal smile.

"Still, I can't say I'm not grateful—he's provided me with enough material for a couple of columns—and there will be more to come when he goes to trial."

It was all Bev could do to refrain from rubbing her hands in glee.

"Any word on if more charges are being contemplated?"

Bev slipped the question in as a request, but Malcolm sensed that the enquiry was more probing than Bev wanted to let on.

"I haven't heard anything about that," said Malcolm, which was true. What he didn't say was that as part of their investigation police were interviewing other political staff, and now believed that Matt had not acted alone, though it was still too early to say whether others would be charged. Malcolm knew it was only a matter of time before this latest development became public. He had suggested the premier's office quietly let a reporter know so that the story broke over Christmas when voters were preoccupied with Santa Claus and turkey, but Maurice worried that if it became known they had leaked the story they could be accused of interfering with the police investigation. Malcolm had suggested someone at arms-length could handle the leak, but Maurice wanted everything kept tightly under his control. Now, Malcolm wondered if Bev had known the answer to her own question all along and was testing him. He glanced down at his smartphone. Bev's latest column hadn't been posted yet; he'd have to make sure to track that during the evening—he didn't want any surprises.

"Well, if anything comes up, be sure to let me know," said Bev, adding, "Welcome aboard," before seeking refuge with the three reporters in the corner.

Malcolm sent the media monitoring staff a note asking them to let him know as soon as Bev's column was posted.

"Am I allowed to speak to the new press secretary to the premier, or are you too busy talking shop with Bev?"

Catherine stood directly in front of Malcolm.

"Hey," Malcolm said smiling widely. "As a matter of fact, *she* was talking to *me*."

Malcolm glanced over at Bev to make sure she couldn't hear. Bev had her back to him and seemed to be regaling the other reporters with a story, likely about some long-forgotten politician.

"I don't believe it!"

"It's true. I was just standing here and she approached me."

"Aren't you special," Catherine said, stretching out the last word.

"It doesn't have anything to do with me—at least not me as a person. It's all about the position. Yesterday she barely knew my name; today she's my new best friend."

"Of course it's all about the position. People don't want to be the premier's best friend because he's Steven Davis. They want to be Steven Davis's best friend because he's the premier. Stupid."

Malcolm shrugged.

"Oh, there's Nicole," she said, standing on tiptoes and lifting her chin to see over the top of the sea of bobbing heads. "I'm going to say hello."

Malcolm turned his attention back to the party. He wanted to make sure he spoke with Rob; he hadn't seen him yet. As he surveyed the room, he caught the eye of Joey Kapur getting a fresh beer from a cooler beneath one of the reporter's desks. Joey made straight for him.

"Tim says you came by yesterday," Joey said when he finally reached him. Tim Winthrop. Joey's camera operator. A tall, laconic man with a slow gait who could move surprisingly quickly when the occasion required. More than one cabinet minister had made the mistake of thinking they could outrun Tim down a packed legislative hallway only to find out they had underestimated him.

"I just wanted to say hi."

"So you're taking over from Matt?"

Joey was in his mid-50s with a shock of black hair that refused to succumb to a comb, giving him an aging boyish appearance, like a south Asian Beach Boy in a sportscoat.

"Yup."

"I can't believe he was dealing drugs out of the premier's office."

"It was a grow-op on Cowichan Lake. The last time I looked that was about an hour north of here."

"Yeah, but he was Davis's spokesperson for the last year and a half—even longer if you count the time he worked for him in the previous Liberal government. Matt was as close publicly to the premier as you can get without sitting in his lap."

Joey's point hadn't been lost on the public. The good news was that internal polling taken immediately after Matt's arrest showed only a small percentage of people—the usual crank conspiracy theorists—thought the premier knew about the drugs. The bad news was that a majority thought he should have known.

"I called him the other day when this all broke, but his phone was already cut off. I tried his home but there was no answer. You don't have a number for him, do you? Matt and I were pretty close. We go way back . . . we started in the gallery together, back when he was still working for CP."

"Sorry. I can give you his lawyer's number, if that helps."

"Tried that. He's not letting him do media."

"I thought you wanted to talk to him . . . as a friend?"

"Oh sure. But my news director is chewing my ass to get an interview before CTV does. Terri hasn't talked to him, has she?"

Terri Calhoun. CTV legislative reporter. She worked twice as hard as Joey, but when your newscast attracts only a sixth of the audience of your competitor you have to work harder.

"I don't know, but I can check around and see what I can find out."

"I already called Maurice, but he didn't have anything. I don't believe him."

"Sorry, I can't help you with that."

In the two days since the story broke, Maurice hadn't mentioned Matt once; it was like he had never existed. Joey took a drink from his beer.

"So you've been with the PO only eighteen months. And now you're the press secretary."

Malcolm shrugged.

"How old are you?"

"Twenty-six."

"Jesus Christ, the Liberals were at the end of their second term before they brought in the kiddie corps. You guys started out with everyone in diapers." He motioned with his arm. "Look at this place."

Malcolm frowned and decided to change the subject.

"I saw your cast tonight. The rebirth of the NDP? Really?"

"I'm just reporting what the polls tell us."

"We've only been in power eighteen months," protested Malcolm. "The NDP and Liberals were each in power ten years. Give us some time."

"Fair enough, but you better start turning it around soon or you'll never be able to climb out of the hole you've dug."

"You're offering political advice now?"

"Free for the taking, won't charge you a penny," he said cheerily. Then his face took on a sombre appearance and he put his hand under Malcolm's elbow.

"Come here for a minute," he said, guiding Malcolm to a spot nearby where they couldn't be overheard. "You're in a position to hear about all sorts of breaking news before everyone else . . ."

Malcolm tilted his head slightly as if trying to understand what Joey was getting at.

"Not political news," Joey said, "things like that three-year-old who died in that mine last year in the East Kootenays."

Malcolm recalled the disaster: a toddler had wandered into an abandoned coal mine shaft.

"Matt would give me a heads up on anything like that. It helps me stay on the right side of my news director. I just want to make sure that we can continue that."

So that's how Global managed to break so many stories, Malcolm thought. He wondered what Matt got in return, but decided not to ask, assuming that if he was doing a favour for Joey, the favour would be returned in some way. He doubted whether the *quid pro quo* would be anything so obvious as favourable coverage, but it could be something as subtle as giving Malcolm the benefit of the doubt on a story or a heads up on a nasty NDP piece, or even a chance to rebut one of Global's "drive-bys".

Drive-bys were the worst kind of story. They came out of nowhere and usually targeted hospitals because life and death made the most compelling TV. They all had similar narratives: someone received terrible care because they were forced to wait for their surgery, or because they couldn't get the procedure that could save their life, or because the operation was botched, or because the nurses/doctors/lab techs were overworked and understaffed. Or all of the above. And if the patient was near death or a child, all the better. The United Party had perfected the drive-by during the final years of the Liberals and it had contributed to the erosion of public confidence in the health system: just what they needed to win an election. Now the NDP were tapping into their friends in the hospital unions to provide them with their own drive-bys.

Drive-bys were impossible to defend against. The most effective response was to have someone on camera in the story, but reporters, if they called at all, would often call late in the day when it was next to impossible to get someone on camera in time. Then all you got was a statement read by the news anchor at the end of the piece after the weeping mother and her flaxen-haired tot—they were always called tots—had already ripped the viewers' hearts out. You'd follow up by trying to get someone on camera for the late-night cast—if the cameraman hadn't already fucked off home. It wasn't much but it was something. Not only did the 11PM cast have fewer viewers, but by then the damage had been done. And in more ways than one, because you'd already had a call from Maurice, who screamed at you and suggested that a lobotomized chimpanzee on crystal meth could do a better job.

"Absolutely," Malcolm said, knowing that if he got a heads up from Joey he could at least try to push his way into the story. "I'll keep you informed and all I ask is that you keep me in the loop."

"Right," Joey replied. "Matt used to give me a call every morning to . . . let me know what's going on."

"Sounds good to me."

Joey smiled with quiet relief, relaxing his shoulders, dropping his hands and spreading his feet wide so his weight was on his back foot.

"You don't have a beer," he said. "Let me get you one." He wandered off to the cooler behind the desk.

While Malcolm waited, he felt a hand on his waist.

"You're still coming by later?" Catherine asked quietly, her lips brushing his ear and her hand drifting around to his stomach.

Malcolm nodded. "I'll be there. Have you seen Rob Ryland?"

"He was over in the corner earlier. There he is—pouring drinks behind the bar," she said.

Her hand slid down his front like a snake, lacking intimacy. Malcolm caught it before it reached his crotch and held it by his side.

"You're no fun. Where's your sense of adventure?" she said, pulling her hand free, turning and walking away.

"Here you go," Joey said, handing him a beer. "Who's that?"

"Her? Catherine. Works in research."

"We don't have anyone who looks like that in our research section."

Joey's eyes followed Catherine as she made her way through the crowd.

"Listen, I'm just going to see if I can catch up with Rob," Malcolm said, and moved through the crowd in the direction of the bar. He didn't get far before a hand pulled his shoulder and, when he turned, he saw it belonged to Elliott Jeffries.

Elliott and Chris O'Riordan were the radio guys. Elliott worked for CBC and Chris for CKNW, and like Joey and Bev, they weren't housed with the rest of the gallery but instead occupied the "radio room", which wasn't actually a room but a series

of windowless, airless cubbyholes in the basement of the legislature that were about as far from the gallery as possible while still
being in the same building. Turn off the bare fluorescent bulb
overhead and you couldn't see your hand in front of your face,
only the tiny twinkling lights from a bank of radio equipment
hooked to a computer that hummed along one wall. There was
barely enough room to turn around, partly because of the size
and partly because of the paper. There was paper everywhere—
taped to the walls, pinned on a bulletin board, stacked on shelving, covering half the desk, piled on top of a filing cabinet, and
lurking ominously in the corner like it was making plans to take
over the rest of the room.

"Say, do you know if Matt is doing any media?" Elliott asked
anxiously.

"No, I don't."

"I just heard Joey is trying to get hold of him. If Matt's doing
any media, you'll let Chris and me know, too. Right?"

Chris's face loomed over Elliott's shoulder.

"Yah, none of that shit that Matt used to pull."

Chris tripped over each word and for emphasis tilted forward
and belligerently shook his beer bottle in Malcolm's face.

"Crown Counsel is handling Matt's case—and they're independent of government," said Malcolm. "Matt has a lawyer. You
should speak with him. We have nothing to do with it."

"But if you hear, you'll let us know, right?" pressed Elliott.

"Yah," echoed Chris menacingly.

"Yes, I will let you know," Malcolm said and thought to
himself: *but I didn't say when I'd let you know.* Turning toward the
bar, he said, "I just need to talk to Rob."

"Mind if we tag along?" asked Elliott.

"Yeah. No. Sure. But it's not shop talk—unless you count
catching up on some of the people we worked with together at
the News Daily shop talk."

Chris took a long swallow from his beer, said he wanted to
get another, and spun off. Malcolm started moving towards the
bar, leaving Elliott by himself, but only for a moment before
he buttonholed a passing MA with a question about First

Nations. The crowd had thinned so Malcolm found it easier to reach Rob.

"Can I buy you a beer?" he asked.

Rob took a moment to consider the request, then opened a beer and told the other two reporters behind the bar he was taking a break. He led Malcolm through to the other room where small pockets of people huddled in the corners talking. They stopped beside Rob's desk.

"I never got to thank you for the heads up on the Browning story," Rob said.

"I told you I'd make it up to you. It just took a little while."

"It was a good story. Tim really liked it. He loves when we scoop the Sun and Province."

"Good. He was never easy to please."

"So now you're press secretary."

"I happened to be in the right place at the right time."

"You're too modest. They like you."

Malcolm laughed.

"Yeah, hard to understand, huh?"

The irony seemed to escape Rob, who said: "Not at all. You're smart. You've got good instincts. You're great under pressure. And you're ambitious. I'd say you're perfect for them."

Malcolm thought he could have added: *and you'll fuck over your best friend.*

"You could have more experience, but they like them young."

"Joey told me that we're all still in diapers."

"Yeah, well, he was young once," Rob laughed. "And it wasn't pretty. I know. I was there."

Malcolm smiled. "So are we okay?" He needed to know last spring was behind them.

"You talking about Forsyth? That was what? Eight, nine months ago? A lifetime in politics . . . and newspapers," Rob said.

Malcolm noted that he didn't say he was over it. It was only natural that Rob would still feel some bitterness.

"I just want you to know that you can count on me," Malcolm said. "I know you don't believe that, but it's true. I will share things with Maurice and Davis—but not everything. I couldn't do this job very well if I didn't keep some things to myself. And that means what you and the other reporters tell me. But it works the other way, too: you need to keep some things I tell you to yourself."

Rob considered this for a moment before responding.

"You can understand if I'm a little gun-shy—"

"Look—"

"Let me finish. It's going to take some time before we have a working relationship that we're both comfortable with. But I'm willing to give it a shot. What choice do I have?"

"What choice do we both have? You have a job to do. I have a job to do. We need each other."

Rob thought for a moment before lifting his beer bottle.

"Alright. Here's to needing each other."

It wasn't a ringing endorsement, but it was an endorsement. Malcolm brought his bottle up and it clinked hollowly. Someone turned up the music: *Please Come Home for Christmas.*

"Sorry to hear about you and Rachel," Rob said.

"Yeah."

"Beth and I both thought that you two would be together forever."

"Yeah."

"We talked about how perfect you were for each other."

"Yeah."

"I guess nothing is perfect."

CHAPTER 17

"MALCOLM!" YELLED JEFFREY Watling. "Did you call me?"

"No, Minister."

"When did you call?"

"I didn't call you, Minister."

"You didn't call me?"

"No, Minister."

"Are you sure?"

"Yes, Minister."

"Did you leave a message?"

"No, Minister."

"You didn't leave a message?"

"No, Minister."

"This fucking phone."

"What's that, Minister?"

"I've got a new phone and it isn't working."

"What's wrong with it?"

"It misses calls and it doesn't record messages."

"It misses calls?"

"And doesn't record messages."

"That doesn't sound good. Hang up and I'll try calling you."

Malcolm waited a moment before dialling Watling's number. There was no answer. It rang and rang but didn't go to voicemail. Malcolm hung up. Behind him the patio door slid open allowing the fizz and pop of the party to escape.

"What are you doing out here?" Adam asked.

"Helping someone figure out how to work their new phone."

"When you're done, come and see me."

"Okay."

Malcolm stood under the overhang on the deck of his parents' home, his back pressed against the siding, trying to keep out of the rain. April is supposed to be the cruellest month, but December was putting up a stiff challenge. They were in the midst of another Pineapple Express: it had rained every day for two weeks. It was funny to hear Vancouverites talk about the rain. Like the Inuit, who were supposed to have fifty words for snow, Vancouverites seemed to have fifty words for rain: drizzle, downpour, mist, sprinkle, showers. How about mizzle? And they parsed them all: light showers, intermittent showers, heavy showers. Right now, Malcolm would describe the rain as pissing. Inside, his parents were hosting their annual Christmas open house for family, friends and neighbours. His phone rang again.

"Malcolm, are you there?"

"Yes, Minister."

"This fucking phone. I'm going to throw it in the ocean. I never got your call."

"Could you see that I called?"

"Yes, it showed up as a missed call. That's the only way I knew you called."

"Have you checked the ringer volume?"

"I tried calling the help line, but it was no use. I couldn't understand them."

"They don't speak English?"

"They speak English but it might as well have been Mandarin. I couldn't follow their directions. Hold on while I check the ringer volume."

Malcolm waited a moment.

"Jesus Christ!"

"What's wrong, Minister?"

"I missed another call."

"Do you need to call them back?"

"I'm taking this fucking phone back all right."

"Okay, Minister."

"Thanks, Malcolm. And remember, if you ever want a job there's one here for you."

Malcolm found Adam in the kitchen pouring himself a Scotch from his Dad's liquor supply marshalled for the occasion on the island in the middle of the room.

"I can't take any more egg nog," Adam said as he downed half the glass of Scotch then topped it up again.

"Are you okay?" asked Malcolm.

"Actually, I need a favour from you."

Adam never asked for favours. He never asked for help of any kind. It wasn't in his nature.

"Can I borrow some money from you?"

"Sure," Malcolm said, reaching for his wallet, "how much do you need?"

"Ten thousand dollars."

The kitchen door swung open and Malcolm's mom swept in with an air of determination and went straight to the fridge and opened the freezer, took a quick look inside, then closed it again.

"Malcolm, we need more ice for the ice bucket. Would you be a dear and get some from the freezer downstairs and fill it?"

"I'll be right back," Malcolm told Adam.

When he returned, Adam was in the living room with his girlfriend Emma and Aunt Mary. Aunt Mary was showing Emma her knitted cardigan with the nativity scene.

"You see what happens when you do it up," said Aunt Mary, buttoning her sweater. "The lambs kiss."

"That's so sweet," Emma said.

"I could knit you one," Aunt Mary offered.

"Oh no, don't go to all that trouble for me."

"It's no trouble."

"Aren't you allergic to wool?" asked Adam, trying valiantly to rescue Emma.

"I could make it out of cotton or polyester," Aunt Mary said.

"Sorry to barge in," said Malcolm. "Adam, can I see you for a moment?"

Emma used the interruption to make her escape, so when Aunt Mary turned back she was gone. Disappointed, Aunt Mary joined Uncle Jim, who was staring out the front window at the house across the street with a sold sign on the front lawn.

"You want to borrow ten grand?"

"Just for a couple of weeks. Until the new year. That's when I get my Christmas bonus."

"I would, but I don't have ten grand."

"Couldn't you get a line of credit?"

"I guess I could. I could ask my bank anyway. Why don't you?"

"I've maxed out my line of credit, credit cards, everything. They're coming to take my Rover on Monday."

"What the hell happened?"

"It's a long story. The short version is my investments didn't pay off—yet. I'm still hopeful."

"Wow. Have you told Dad and Mom?"

"No. And whatever you do, don't tell them. I don't want to disappoint them."

"Alright. I'll go into my bank first thing Monday."

"Thanks, Malcolm. I really appreciate it."

As the afternoon wore on, the headiness of the first few hours subsided, like a can of pop gone flat; the rain seemed to beat down any residual enthusiasm; guests made their polite goodbyes, fewer newcomers arrived. So when the doorbell rang in a single, clear loud burst, it seemed more likely to toll an end to the party than signal a note of renewed hope and optimism.

"Malcolm!" shouted his Dad excitedly from the entranceway while exclaiming: "Please come in! Please come in!"

His Mom came bustling across the living room and grabbed his arm.

"You better come," she said with a mixture of urgency and apprehension.

The commotion created a welcome diversion for the handful of people still there. But before Malcolm and his Mom could reach the foyer they were met by his Dad and, following close behind, Premier Steven Davis.

"Malcolm, I thought I would stop by and wish you and your family a Merry Christmas," said Davis. "I'll only stay for a minute; I don't want to disrupt your little gathering."

"You must stay," Malcom's Dad said. "It's our annual Christmas open house. Everyone is welcome."

"Are you sure?" Davis asked with feigned reluctance.

"Of course, said Malcolm's Dad. "Everyone is welcome," he repeated reassuringly.

"Alright then," Davis agreed, as if it had been anything but a foregone conclusion.

Malcolm's Dad hurried off to get Davis a drink while Malcolm's Mom offered him a plate of Christmas baking.

"Malcolm is one of our rising stars," Davis said in the booming, hollow voice that he used for giving speeches, "and an indispensable member of my team."

Malcolm's Mom beamed.

"We are delighted he's working with you," she said, and then as she forced another shortbread on him: "Much better than that newspaper job he had."

Malcolm shuttled Davis around to meet family, friends and neighbours, and the party buzzed with anticipation and excitement. Davis worked the room as deftly as he worked a party conference. Aunt Mary showed him the lambs on her cardigan and offered to knit one for his wife. Uncle Jim told him the house across the street had sold for $3.7 million and asked what he planned to do about foreign owners snapping up Vancouver real estate.

Davis greeted each guest with a smile and enthusiastic handshake and looked them straight in the eye with undivided attention, giving the impression they were the most important person in the room. Adam and Emma were near the end, so Davis used it as an opportunity to linger. Eventually the talk turned to books they had recently read.

"I just read Yeats's *Michael Robartes and the Dancer*," Malcolm said. "Took me four months but I finally finished it."

It was his feeble homage to Rachel and their time together. It was the least he could do.

"I love Yeats," said Emma.

"I think the last book I read was Harry Potter," said Adam. "I can't seem to find the time."

"I don't read books," said Davis flatly.

"Really?" said Emma.

"I spend all my time on the Internet. It has everything."

"Well, maybe not everything," Malcolm said carefully. He didn't want to appear to be contradicting his boss.

"Everything I need," Davis qualified.

"So what do you read on the Internet?" asked Emma.

"Wikipedia."

"You only read Wikipedia?" asked Adam.

"And YouTube."

"YouTube?" asked Emma.

"Well, I don't read YouTube, but that's where I get a lot of my information."

"Is there anything you read that's not on the Internet?" asked Adam.

"PowerPoints," said Davis.

"PowerPoints?" asked Emma.

"Government reports, policies, proposals," Davis said. "I have to read those, but I have them sent to me as PowerPoint presentations. PowerPoint is the new briefing note. I tell them if they can't put it in a PowerPoint then it isn't worth considering."

Emma laughed, but then realized that Davis wasn't joking.

"So I take it you don't read fiction," she said.

"Novels aren't real," Davis said. "Real life is real. Why waste my time with something that is make-believe?"

"But fiction can give you insights into the human condition that you can't get elsewhere," Emma said, rather desperately Malcolm thought. He liked her for that and wondered what she saw in Adam.

"I get all the insights into the human condition that I need every day on YouTube," Davis said. "And in the legislature," he added, laughing.

The premier stayed for about an hour, lending the party an aura of celebrity. Malcolm knew he would be the talk of the neighbourhood for weeks and that those who missed this year's party would be sure to be there for next year's.

"What a delight!" Malcolm's Mom said as she closed the door on the last guest. "I can't remember a more successful open house."

"Incredible that Steven made time for it," said Malcolm's Dad. "Such a busy man, but then isn't that always the way: the busier they are the more they seem to do."

Emma and Adam put on their coats and got ready to leave. In their after-party euphoria his parents seemed to have forgotten them, so Malcolm saw them to the door.

"Your boss is an interesting guy," Adam said, in a way that indicated he meant more than he was saying.

"How so?" asked Malcolm.

"Well, he came to Dad and Mom's Christmas party."

"He's always making impromptu public appearances," Malcolm said, though he had been surprised to see him. "Kind of like this, where he just hangs out with people."

Emma and Adam shouted their goodbyes to Malcolm's Mom and Dad. Malcolm closed the door behind them and stood for a moment in the entranceway. Unlike the others, he wasn't leaving. He was sleeping in his old bed upstairs. He couldn't remember the last time he had slept in it—on his own. That's when he realized why Davis had come to the party. He was lonely. Malcolm wondered how many close friends—real friends—Davis had. Not many, he guessed.

Malcolm spent Christmas at home with his parents, the three of them and a turkey dinner for twelve. He was forced to eat leftovers for days. The holidays should have been a triumph, what with his new job and all, but Malcolm didn't feel triumphant; he felt forlorn, and if anything, his success only seemed to make it worse.

He had wanted to spend Christmas with Catherine, but she had gone to Puerta Vallarta. He'd tried to invite himself along and while she never said no, she never said yes either; she just kept putting it off until she was gone. Malcolm suspected it was Davis: he always went to Puerta Vallarta just after Christmas.

In mid-January, when Catherine had returned from Mexico, they met at the Swifty for a drink. The bar was quiet, even for the post-holiday lull.

"Why won't you move in with me?" Malcolm asked.

"Do we have to have this conversation again?"

"Yes."

"I don't want to move in with you," Catherine said.

"You just want to sleep with me."

"Something like that."

"But just when it suits you."

"Doesn't it suit you?"

"Yes. No. I want to wake up in the morning and have you beside me."

"But we have that now."

"Not all the time."

"I'm not so sure all the time is a good idea."

"Why not?"

"Because after a while we'd get bored of each other and then start fighting and then split up."

"That's what you think would happen?"

"Yes."

"It doesn't have to be like that."

"I like having a place of my own that I can go back to when I want."

"It's because you're still sleeping with Davis, isn't it?"

"Look, Malcolm, I like you. We have fun together. But I'm not interested in moving in with you."

"I bet you'd move in with Davis if you could."

"I'm not interested in moving in with anyone. Okay?"

"What if I said I want you to choose: Davis or me."

"Don't be silly."

"It's not silly. You go off to Mexico with him and I'm left here on my own."

"Is that what this is about?"

Malcolm shrugged.

"I'm sorry you're upset," Catherine said. "But I don't think it's fair that you want me to change. I don't ask you to change."

"But I would change for you."

"No you wouldn't."

"I would."

"How can you say that when you won't even change now and agree that I should stay in my own apartment?"

Malcolm thought for a moment.

"That was very clever of you."

Catherine smiled with satisfaction.

"Oh, don't feel so sorry for yourself. Finish your drink and we'll go back to my place and I promise tomorrow I will wake up in bed next to you."

Catherine's smartphone rang. From where he was standing, Malcolm could see it glowing on the bedside table where she always placed it when they had sex. He looked down at the top of Catherine's head as she knelt in front of him. After what must have been the fourth ring it quit. A few seconds later it rang again. Her head turned ever so slightly toward the phone.

"Don't answer it," he said.

Too late. She was already up and moving across to the phone. Malcolm remained on the other side of the room, the bed between them.

She looked at the number on the display and then said warmly, "Hello you."

There was a pause as she looked briefly at Malcolm then turned her back to him and said softly: "I'm in the middle of something right now." Pause. "Yes." Pause. "Yes." Soft giggles. "Of course." She hung up without saying goodbye.

Catherine came around the bed to Malcolm.

"Oh, look at you." With businesslike efficiency she stroked him. When that didn't work she knelt down in front of him and took him in her mouth. Nothing. She persisted. It was no use. After a minute or so she stood up.

"I don't know what's going on," Malcolm said defensively. He covered himself with his hands.

Catherine went into the bathroom. He could hear her brushing her teeth. Malcolm stood there lost, his mind vacant. Then he picked up his underwear and pants from the floor and slowly put them on, hoping Catherine would come out of the bathroom and ask him what he was doing, ask him to take off his pants and come to bed. But she didn't. She came out and began getting dressed. She was going out. He closed the door quietly behind him as he left.

CHAPTER 18

"THERE'S A FIRST Nations protest near Anahim Lake," Chris DeFrias said.

"When isn't there a First Nations protest?" asked Franson from his perch high on a platform at the front, like a supreme court judge. The roomful of political staffers laughed loudly, at once mocking DeFrias and thankful they weren't him. Franson was unwavering. "Next!"

A half-dozen hands went up. Malcolm, sitting next to Franson, sensed an uneasy anticipation on the forty or so faces below him. Several people leaned conspicuously against the walls: there were never enough seats for everyone so latecomers were forced to play a perverse game of musical chairs, desperately grabbing for a vacant seat, losing out, and rushing to try to secure another before it, too, was filled. Those who lost were forced to stand, a mild form of public shaming. Malcolm wouldn't have been surprised if Franson instructed caucus staff to remove some of the chairs each morning to ensure there weren't enough for everyone.

"Emily," Franson said.

"There's a rally today at noon at Robson Square demanding more funding for mental health," said Emily Fairchild. "The Opposition is speaking at it."

"Okay," Franson said, making a note.

"You've got your minister doing media today?" asked Maurice, who, like Malcolm, sat on the dais with Franson at the issues session that kicked off every morning when the House was sitting.

"Yes," said Fairchild, "both before and after the rally."

"Good," Franson said. "Next! Shannon."

"The report on the Mount Timson mine is coming out today."

"Is it bad?" asked Franson.

"We haven't seen it yet, but expect it to be," Shannon said. "The mine wasn't compliant when the spill happened and the Opposition has been linking it to cutbacks in mine inspectors."

Franson made a note.

"Send me your communications materials," he said. "Next!"

Pause.

"Richard."

Every head turned to look at Richard Cates, crimson-faced and standing by himself at the very back of the room. This was what they had been waiting for. They had all read the morning clippings package.

"Bev had a piece on our missing briefing binder," said Cates in a voice that sounded like someone was standing on his throat.

"Yes," said Franson with a terrible iciness. It seemed like hours before he finally said, "Next!"

It hadn't been a good start to the session and the loss of the briefing binder promised to make it worse. Cates, ministerial assistant to Education Minister Henry Solvang, had left the binder in a staff washroom at a school where they had been making an announcement. The confidential binder contained highly sensitive information, including a communications plan to neutralize the B.C. Teachers' Federation, the province's obstreperous teachers union and one of the government's sharpest critics. It also held a PowerPoint showing the best way to handle the press gallery, right down to a how to stall them by keeping your minister in the House ("tell them they have House duty") until you could sneak them out the side door. But most damaging of all was a memo directing political staffers on how to prepare ministers for the spring session.

The memo was part of Maurice's new "tough love" approach with cabinet and an effort to rein in the bureaucracy. There was a feeling within the PO that the government's precipitous drop in the polls was a result of sloppiness in the first year; they blamed the ministers for having too much autonomy, which in turn led to deputy ministers having too much say—providing direction to ministers instead of taking it. There was also the persistent worry that the public service—still riddled with Liberal supporters—was out of step with its political masters.

The memo was actually a "check list", like some David Letterman Top Ten. The list contained the usual: "TOP ISSUES" and "URGENT POLICY MATTERS". Everything in UPPER CASE to reflect the importance. But it also included Maurice's new control measures: "WHO TO APPOINT", "WHAT TO AVOID: PET BRUEAUCRATIC PROJECTS", and "WHO TO AVOID: BUREAUCRATS WHO CAN'T TAKE NO (OR YES) FOR AN ANSWER".

Normally, Upshall would have had a hand in putting together the memo but he had been deliberately left out of the loop. He only found out when deputy ministers started calling to ask why he hadn't given them a heads up. Malcolm guessed he wouldn't be around much longer. Another month or two. Tops.

The most controversial part of the memo was a political hit list: "WHO TO ENGAGE OR AVOID: FRIENDS AND ENEMIES". It included businesses, NGOs, unions, municipal governments—even media. Franson had advised against it.

"Ministerial binders always get FOI'd," he said.

"It's advice to cabinet," countered Maurice. "We can sever it under Section 13.1".

"Or you could just give it verbally," Franson suggested.

"It will have more impact if they see it in writing," said Maurice.

He couldn't have been more right, though not in the way he intended. The Opposition were ecstatic: the memo provided them with enough ammunition to fill a month of Question Periods. The gallery were apoplectic: they prided themselves on being unbiased and independent, so being included on a partisan list—even if the list was only for use within government circles— was insulting and humiliating, though less insulting and humiliating for those identified as "enemies" than those considered "friends". What offended the media most was government's brazen manipulation: no one liked to be played for a fool—especially reporters who thought themselves too smart by half; worse still was to be seen by everyone to have been played for a fool. Even the so-called media "friends" weren't so friendly anymore.

The disclosure put the government on its heels for the remainder of the session as the Opposition, abetted by a now-prickly gallery, launched attack after attack. Inside caucus, tempers frayed and anger flared. In cabinet, hope waned, resentment grew, and a weariness set in that was more typical of a government in the fourth year of its term—not the second. The session dragged on and on, until finally they crawled out the other end of the long, dark tunnel. Only it wasn't the end.

"Fucking Victoria," Davis said.

Malcolm and Davis walked side-by-side in the rose garden tucked behind the West Annex. The din of drums and pipes, of brass and boots, still echoed from the Victoria Day parade down Douglas Street the week before. The parade marked Queen Victoria's birthday, a uniquely Canadian holiday celebrating the semi-reclusive British monarch who had been dead for more than a century. It was odd, really, that she should be honoured with a holiday in Canada, because in all her 81 years she never actually set foot in the country. Even odder was that the holiday didn't take place on her birthday of May 24, but on the last Monday before May 25.

More importantly for most, the holiday kicked off the beginning of the Canadian summer, a time for cottages and camping, barbecues and beaches. So by all rights, Davis should have been in a bright mood on this, the last day of the legislative session heading into a welcome summer hiatus. But he wasn't.

"The fucking legislature," Davis muttered.

At the best of times the decorum in the B.C. legislature was more like a frontier logging camp than a seat of government, punctuated with heckling, jeers and catcalls, and dominated by the rough and tumble of Question Period. But this session was worse than usual as the NDP, seeing a government in trouble, sharpened its attack.

No one had a clearer view of it all than the clerk of the house in his position in the middle of the legislature, between the government on one side and the opposition on the other. This no-man's land separating the warring sides was a distance of two sword lengths, a tradition handed down from the days when swords were a required accessory for the well-dressed politician. More than a few times this session Malcolm thought the clerk must have been thankful for the change in fashion.

"The fucking NDP," Davis spat.

The premier's mood was doubly black because he was in the final day of estimates where he was forced to defend his office's budget for the coming year.

"The goal is get out of here unscathed," Upshall reminded him once again before they started. "The easiest way to do that is by giving them as little information as possible; the more information they have the more they will use it against us. So answer the question that is asked—but only that question. Nothing else. And whatever you do, don't rise to their bait. It's only an attempt to throw you off your game."

Upshall had literally written the book on how to survive estimates: he had provided pages of detailed instructions to his deputy ministers, right down to where to sit (on the right of the minister) and how to pass notes (inconspicuously under their arm without looking at them). The instructions even recommended deputies and ministers synchronize their bathroom breaks so as not to leave ministers unattended in the House.

"I'm surprised he didn't tell them to hold their dicks for them, too," Maurice sneered as he leafed through the instructions.

After some back-and-forth negotiations between the Government and Opposition House leaders, the two sides agreed that the premier's estimates would be limited to two days and, as usual, would close the debate on government estimates. Upshall called the deal "reassuring" and "a sign of conciliation and cooperation."

But it was apparent from the first question that the Opposition were feeling anything but conciliatory and cooperative. They began with a bombshell: the premier's office had on its payroll a staff member who was also a registered lobbyist. Brent Atkins was based out of the Vancouver office and promoted LNG to markets in Asia. He had worked on Davis's campaign and before that was a lobbyist for the oil and gas industry—only he hadn't removed himself from the lobbyist registry.

"It's a clear conflict of interest," Forsyth said, "at the very heart of the premier's office."

Maurice, who was tracking the debate from his office, picked up the phone and fired Atkins even before he knew if the claim were true. Then he stormed into Franson's office and ranted about "Brent-fucking-Atkins" while Franson frantically scoured the lobbyist registry website to verify the allegation.

"It's true," Franson said.

He quickly pounded out three bullets of messaging, saying them out loud as he typed for Maurice to amend and approve. He fired them off to Upshall, who was in the chamber and who discreetly slid a note under the premier's arm while looking the other way. The premier then stood and declared that it was an "administrative oversight" that had since been corrected.

But the Opposition had established the narrative and spent the morning probing Atkins' relationship with the premier before moving on to first the premier's and then the party's connections to the oil and gas industry, including political donations. In the afternoon they expanded on the basic narrative by rigorously detailing "friends and insiders" who had been appointed to positions paid for by the taxpayer, and comparing their salaries and benefits to cuts made to social services.

On the second day, against Upshall's advice, the premier decided the best way to blunt the attack was to try to frustrate the Opposition by reverting to the "rope-a-dope". He deliberately delayed providing an answer and when he did finally stand and respond he said only one word: "Yes." Another question. Another long delay. Another single word: "No." The debate slowed to a wobble and very nearly toppled into boredom. By the noon-hour break it was the leader of the Opposition's turn to seethe. But Davis took little satisfaction in his small victory. He couldn't understand why the Opposition didn't just get out of his way and let him govern.

"Who does Forsyth think he is?" Davis asked Malcolm as they looped a second time around the rose garden.

Davis stopped in the bright sun to admire his new Stefano Bemer Oxfords. At 2,000 euros, they were his not-so-guilty pleasure. Made in Florence from Russian reindeer—and not just any Russian reindeer, but one from 1786 whose hide was recovered from a sailing ship that sank off the coast of Plymouth and was preserved using tanning methods of the period.

"Does he forget that they lost the election?" Davis asked, taking out a tissue and bending and wiping an imaginary mark off the toe of his shoe.

Malcolm wanted to reply that the election was two years ago—an eternity in politics; that Forsyth was only doing his job as Opposition leader; that Davis was only doing his job as premier; that it was all just theatre and everyone had their part to play. But not today. Today he listened. Today, that's what the premier needed: someone to listen.

They walked to the end of the rose garden where a tour bus had pulled up and Chinese tourists streamed out to take photos of themselves with the flowers. Some of the men stepped off the bus and immediately stooped to light cigarettes, while some of the women, with umbrellas to protect them from the sun, wandered aimlessly arm-in-arm as if they were not quite sure what they were supposed to be looking at and not really caring.

Malcolm and the premier left the garden to the tourists and walked around to the back of the legislature, past the temporary signs warning of nesting crows. A man in a suit hurried by with his head down and holding the ubiquitous black hard-cover notebook that marked him as a civil servant. As they reached the steps of the legislative library a young couple stopped the premier and asked him to take a photo of them in front of the fountain. The premier thought they wanted a photo with him, so he handed the camera to Malcolm and tried to insert himself between the pair. The man tried unsuccessfully to get the premier to understand, until finally, in desperation, he positioned the premier out of the frame and quickly instructed Malcolm to take the photo. The premier seemed not to notice that he wasn't included.

Malcolm and the premier resumed their walk, turning the corner and continuing along the sidewalk in the shade of a red maple toward the news kiosk. Just then, from behind, over his shoulder, something dark fell.

"Ahh!" Davis cried and doubled over holding his head. On the ground behind him a large crow struggled on its back. It made a gurgling sound like a baby. Its feet kicked frantically. In its beak was something furry. For a moment, Malcolm thought the bird had caught a small rodent—a deer mouse or a shrew perhaps. Then he looked more closely and saw that it wasn't alive. It was a chunk of . . . hair.

"Fuck!" Davis screamed and pulled his hand away. He had a bright gash on his temple and the hair surrounding it was dark and wet. From the gash poured blood. It flowed into his right eye, then over and down his ear, hanging from his earlobe like a bright red earring; then, as if in slow motion, it fell to the ground.

Davis looked at his hand and the blood, and his face contorted with rage. He turned one way, then the other. The crow was still on its back, gurgling. Davis wiped furiously at the blood streaming down his face, streaking it across his cheeks. Then, like an injured bull, he snorted and put his head down and rushed at the crow, running over it. The crow rolled over several times and came to a rest on its stomach, its left wing lying limp and outstretched on the ground. Davis stopped and turned and came back to the crow and stood over it. He nudged it with the toe of his treasured Stefano Bemer Oxfords.

The crow didn't move.

"Premier, are you alright?" Malcolm asked and immediately thought it was a stupid question. Of course he wasn't alright.

In a daze, Davis stood over the dead crow.

"Premier, we should get your head looked at right away," Malcolm said.

He walked over to Davis and led him away and up the steps and through the side door into the legislature. Malcolm took him down the long hallway toward the information desk, thinking there must be someone there who knew first aid. Davis said nothing the whole time. Before they could reach the information desk, they met one of the ministerial executive coordinators. Malcolm couldn't remember her name, only that this was her first job out of high school.

"Oh my God!" she said, her mouth open. "What happened?"

"An attack," Malcolm said. "By the kiosk."

"No!"

"I've got to get him some help," he said as he continued to guide Davis down the hallway to the information desk where the man staffing the desk immediately called 911. They sat Davis down and someone ran to the bathroom to get some paper towel. Within seconds Malcolm heard an ambulance siren in the distance. They must have been nearby, he thought.

The ambulance crew arrived as the person came back with the paper towel. The attendants said he needed to go to the hospital. But Davis refused to go.

"I have to finish estimates," he said.

So they treated him right there. They cleaned the wound and bandaged it.

"I have to finish estimates," Davis repeated over and over as if trying to memorize the line.

By now Maurice and Upshall had arrived, along with the rest of the premier's staff.

"I have to finish estimates," Davis said.

Upshall assured him they could delay estimates, though Maurice seemed less certain. Malcolm tried to step back but the premier gripped his arm, silently insisting he stay by his side.

Word of the incident spread throughout the buildings so that a large crowd gathered around the information desk. Malcolm noted that several NDP staffers were monitoring the situation. NDP House leader, Tony Sanchez, pushed his way through to where the premier was seated. When he saw Davis with a white gauze pad taped to his head and his shirt soaked with blood, he stopped short.

"Good God," he said. "Are you alright?"

"Does he look alright?" Maurice asked, seeming to spoil for a fight.

Davis was still dazed, but coming around.

"I'll be fine," he said. "I may need a bit more time before we resume estimates."

"Of course," Sanchez said. "Take all the time you need. We can postpone it until next week."

"Just what you'd want," Maurice said. "To extend the session."

Davis lifted his hand to wave off Maurice.

"What about the attacker?" Sanchez asked.

"Dead," Davis said.

"No!" said Sanchez, clearly shocked.

A murmur raced through the crowd. Davis nodded grimly.

"Where is he?" asked Sanchez.

"Out there," Davis said, and pointed down the corridor without looking.

"What are the police doing?" Sanchez asked.

"Oh, I don't think we need the police," said Davis.

"What do you mean?" asked Sanchez. "You haven't called the police?"

He looked around.

"Of course we need the police," he said. "A man has just been killed."

"Not a man," Davis said.

"A woman?" Sanchez asked.

"No," said Davis.

"What?"

"It wasn't a person."

"It wasn't? But I thought someone attacked you."

Sanchez looked around for confirmation and received several nods from the crowd. Malcolm wondered where he would have heard that, and then remembered the executive coordinator in the hallway. What did he tell her? Did he mention the crow?

"A bird," Davis said.

Now that he said it out loud it seemed that an attack by a bird didn't warrant such a display. Davis dropped his head.

"It was a crow."

"A crow?" Sanchez asked as if he wasn't sure he believed him.

The premier nodded.

"It was big," he added.

"A crow," Sanchez said, deflated.

"Huge," Davis said weakly.

He turned to Malcolm for support but the air had already come out of the crowd. There was no getting it back.

"Well, I can see why we don't need the police," said Sanchez, drawing laughs from some; the crowd began to thin.

"Shall we say a two o'clock start," Maurice said to Sanchez.

"Is that enough time for the premier?" Sanchez asked.

Davis nodded.

"Two o'clock it is then," said Sanchez.

On the way back to the office Maurice persuaded the premier not to change his shirt or put on a fresh bandage, even though blood has started to seep through the gauze.

"That will be the narrative," he said. "How you were attacked and were patched up and went straight into estimates. You'll be a legend."

Davis smiled.

"I've always wanted to be a legend."

Malcolm couldn't tell if Davis was serious or not. Maurice turned out to be right: Davis's courage in the face of personal injury was the story—not Brent Atkins, not the long list of friends and insiders he had placed in plum positions, not the $45,000 he spent on his German-engineered credenza at a time when he was cutting services and laying off staff. In fact, the tactic was so successful the NDP halted estimates before the allotted time.

"They had to cut their losses," Maurice said gleefully. "How could they continue to attack the premier when he's sitting there with a bandage on his head and blood on his shirt? It would only win more public sympathy for him and make them look callous and hard-hearted."

However, there was little time to savour the victory. No sooner did they emerge from estimates than a YouTube video appeared of the premier killing the crow. Malcolm viewed the video with Franson, Balicki and Maurice standing over him.

"Jesus, pretty gruesome," said Balicki when they had finished.

They watched it a second time. In the dispassionate eye of the video the killing looked worse. The video was posted by "Billythekid".

"Who is this Billythekid?" asked Maurice. "Did you see him taking the video?"

Malcolm shook his head.

"There were lots of tourists. It could have been any of them."

By 6PM the video had more than 10,000 views. Four hours later, it had more than 70,000 views. The next night Jimmy Kimmel used the video in his monologue alongside a blurry video of the latest Rob Ford night on the town.

"Linked to Rob–fucking–Ford," Maurice said, shaking his head. "Could it get any worse?"

It could and it did. A local animal rights activist complained to the SPCA, which agreed to investigate, and that meant a special prosecutor had to be appointed in the event charges were recommended. Overnight the premier went from victim to accused. Maurice was sure Billythekid was a New Democrat.

"A hundred fucking dollars says this was a set up."

It didn't help when someone posted a photo to Instagram of the Stefano Bemer Oxfords with the hashtag "themurderweapon". A video went up on Vine showing the moment the premier ran over the crow. It was only six seconds but it looped over and over making it look like Davis ran over the bird again and again and, for all anyone knew, was still running over the bird. Malcolm found it impossible to tear himself away, and watched it again and again.

Local animal rights supporters staged a protest on the lawn of the legislature. "Crows have rights too", said one sign. Another said: "Premier Crow Killer". A third said, "Davis = murderer".

Malcolm and Davis were formally interviewed, and two weeks later the SPCA recommended Davis be charged. The recommendation went to the special prosecutor, Kieran Tiehon. Tiehon approved the charge in a one-paragraph information bulletin: "Steven Wallace Davis is charged with one count of animal cruelty under Section 445.1(1)a of the Criminal Code of

Canada: Every one commits an offence who wilfully causes or, being the owner, wilfully permits to be caused unnecessary pain, suffering or injury to an animal or a bird."

It led the news on every TV station in the province; it even topped the national newscasts later that evening. At first, the piece on Global seemed almost lighthearted. Partly it was the oddity of the charge and the fact it involved the highest political office in the province. Partly it was the impish special prosecutor: Tiehon turned out to be a garrulous Irishman who despite living in Canada for forty years had not lost his accent. He was dwarfed by cameras and media as he answered questions in his flickering lilt.

But the tone turned menacing when the Global news reader paused, looked straight into the camera and, in his deepest baritone, issued a warning that the video they were about to show was not suitable for all viewers. Malcolm thought if they didn't have viewers' attention before, they certainly did now. The video showed Davis killing the crow. The only good thing was that unlike the Vine video it didn't keep looping. Then Davis appeared on screen amid a swarm of cameras and was as brief as he had been during estimates. Will he resign? No. Will he step aside while the case is before the courts, as the Opposition demands? No. Will he plead guilty?

"I am the injured party here," he declared, turning to the cameras so they can see the bandage on his head.

It was a nice touch that Maurice had suggested.

Davis also appeared on camera without his lawyer. That was Maurice's idea, too: he thought the visual with his lawyer would make Davis look guilty by association.

"In the public's mind, why would you need a lawyer unless you've done something wrong?" Maurice asked.

Jeff Imrie, the high-profile—and high-priced—Vancouver criminal defence lawyer hired to defend the premier, objected to the characterization.

"Who are you always seen with on camera?" asked Maurice.

Imrie shrugged: "Clients."

"Exactly," said Maurice. "And who are they? Murderers. Gangsters. Drug dealers. All criminals."

Imrie pointed out that he would have to accompany Davis at some point during the trial.

"Not necessarily," Maurice said.

But he wanted Imrie to still do media, just on his own.

"We'll get double the camera time," Maurice said.

He was right: after Davis's clip there was a clip of Imrie, who told media that the premier would plead not guilty by reason of self-defence.

"He was viciously attacked," Imrie said. "And he had every right to defend himself."

But he wouldn't say anything more, telling reporters that he would make his case before the courts.

In the meantime, Maurice had the premier's communications and research staff working overtime to gather anything that may be useful, no matter how obscure. Franson interviewed an avian veterinarian, Malcolm sought out a crow expert from the University of Guelph. The research team tracked down every record of a crow attack. Imrie suggested also looking into previous crow incidents at the legislature.

"There may be enough of a pattern to be actionable," he advised.

"You mean sue ourselves?" Franson asked.

"The Speaker," Imrie said. "He's responsible for the legislative grounds."

Davis was hesitant.

"Will the public even make the distinction?" he asked.

"It's only as a last resort," said Imrie. "To support our case that you are not at fault."

"I don't know," the premier said. "Even accepting what you say, how would it look going after one of our own?"

But Maurice liked the idea; he'd been cool to the Speaker ever since he ruled against the government's attempt to restrict debate on the budget.

At his arraignment, Davis was accompanied by his wife. It was the first time they'd been seen together in public for months.

Grace's only stipulation was that they park a block or two from the courthouse: she didn't want to be photographed getting out of the car.

"It's so unflattering," she explained.

Maurice had suggested Grace be there.

"It's important to show the premier has the support of his family," he said. "It would be great if Michael and Jennifer could come."

"We can't very well fly Michael home," Grace said.

Michael was a student at one of the "Little Ivies". Davis had called in some favours and made a considerable donation to the school. But all the connections and money in the world couldn't turn Michael into a strong student. Worried about Michael's failing prospects, Davis had forced him to remain on the New England campus for the summer and enrol in remedial courses.

"But I suppose we could always take Jennifer out of class," Grace said, then turned to Davis, "though you know how the head of school hates that."

Maurice wanted Jennifer, but only if she wasn't in her school uniform.

"We want you to look like an average family, and the average family can't afford to send their children to exclusive private schools."

"It will take more than a change of clothes to make us look average," said Grace.

In the end, they decided that Grace would be enough support.

"Whatever you do, wear something understated—no Versace," Maurice said.

"I'm not sure I have anything that isn't couture," Grace said. "But I suppose I could always buy something for this one time."

CHAPTER 19

MALCOLM WAS CHATTING with the reporters outside the courthouse waiting for Davis. There was a nervous excitement in the air.

"What time is he supposed to be here?" one of the TV cameramen asked.

"The arraignment is at nine," Malcolm said, "the same as the last time you asked."

The talk among the reporters was quick and light. They needed an outlet for all their energy, like hockey players anxiously tapping their sticks waiting for the national anthem to end and the puck to drop. Then Davis and Grace appeared from around the corner. The TV cameramen and reporters saw them coming and ran up the street to meet them and Malcolm followed. Grace smiled broadly for the cameras, as if she were back on the campaign trail and not accompanying her husband into court. She was dressed in a red linen suit with a sheer blouse that did not strike Malcolm as understated.

Imrie waited for them at the top of the courthouse steps, briefcase in hand, holding the door open. He had to fight to follow them in ahead of the clatter of media. Cameramen shouldered each other through the adjoining door and raced down the hallway to get ahead of the couple. Malcolm peered over and around heads, lost at the rear of the pack.

Inside the courtroom, Imrie asked the judge to dismiss the case outright, even though he had advised Maurice and the premier against making such a request. He had argued that an arraignment was a pre-trial hearing where the Crown stated the charge and the defendant entered a plea.

"It's not the proper venue to seek a dismissal," Imrie explained. "It will make us look amateurish."

But Maurice insisted: "We want it to be abundantly clear right from the get-go that it's our view there are no grounds for this charge and that we are going to aggressively fight it."

"It will just put the judge off us," Imrie cautioned, knowing that would make the premier anxious.

The premier had been hoping this would all go away as soon as it got in front of a judge. He rationalized that the SPCA had to proceed with charges because of the expectations from their supporters, not to mention the impact such a high-profile case would have on donations. And the special prosecutor, well, everyone knew the Irish couldn't resist the spotlight—and there was no brighter spotlight than a courtroom with a sitting premier in the defendant's box. But a judge, a judge would see right away that this wasn't right. He would see it for what it really was: a terrible miscarriage of justice. Especially a judge like Bernie Lapin.

But Bernie Lapin didn't see it for what it was. Like everyone else, he was blinded by the glare of the TV lights. He stared menacingly at Imrie, smoothed his white collar, and welcomed the media to his courtroom. He cautioned them that video recordings were not permitted and that audio may only be recorded for the purpose of verifying their notes. Malcolm wondered what he would do next, spell his name for them?

Then Lapin looked past Imrie to the premier and explained that he couldn't dismiss the case because he couldn't determine whether the Crown had sufficient evidence to set the matter down for trial. For that he would need a preliminary inquiry— unless the defendant wished to proceed to trial by direct indictment. Imrie, who wasn't used to being ignored, said he did not wish to go directly to trial, but asked the judge to set the date for the preliminary hearing as early as possible because the premier was under a cloud and deserved the opportunity to clear himself as soon as he could. Lapin agreed and set the matter for the following Tuesday.

Outside, the Victoria Police had cordoned off one of the lanes on Blanshard Street in front of the courthouse with metal barricades to accommodate the satellite news trucks. Panel vans were lined end to end down the street, their shiny white satellite dishes tilted skyward. The lane had been turned into a parking lot snaking with thick black TV cable. A crowd had gathered to watch.

Moments after Lapin set the date for the preliminary inquiry, several TV reporters rushed out and down the steps and took up positions in front of waiting TV cameras. They were each lined up with their backs to the courthouse steps, one eye over their shoulder anxiously watching the glass outer doors of the courthouse, the other on a TV camera perched atop a tripod in front of them. The sidewalk swelled with anticipation, the traffic behind them on Blanshard Street an insistent murmur.

Abruptly the doors burst open and the air was filled with shouts as a mob of media backed out. In the middle, surrounded, were the premier, Grace, and Imrie. The mob stopped atop the courthouse steps blocking Davis's way; some reporters were pushed down the steps so they were forced to scramble around the perimeter of the mob, circling, trying frantically to get a vantage point of the premier. Below them, the TV reporters signalled to their cameramen to begin their live reports.

In the week between the arraignment and preliminary inquiry, the airwaves and social media filled with commentators offering their opinions on everything from the trial to Grace Davis's blouse. CBC took its coverage to another level: *Quirks and Quarks* broadcast a segment about the life cycle of crows, which extolled the cooperative way crows raise their young; on *The National* Rex Murphy recounted the story of Aeschylus and how a crow in the Dardia Mountains of Greece, thinking Aeschylus's bald head was a stone, dropped a tortoise from a great height and killed him: "a tragedy of monumental proportions for the *pater* of tragedy"; and *Q* explored the word crow in pop music, beginning with Counting Crows and Sheryl Crow, and closing with a live in-studio performance by Vancouver's Pugs and Crows Band.

The size of the government's clippings package doubled, then tripled. The media monitoring unit couldn't keep up and conscripted staff from ministry communications offices. They moved to a 24/7 schedule. Transcripts started appearing at all hours. No one seemed to be sleeping, including Maurice, who got crankier and crankier as they counted down the days to the inquiry.

But before they could get to Tuesday, Judge Lapin removed himself from the case. A year earlier, he had attended a dinner that was also a fundraiser for the United Party. A photo of Lapin and Davis laughing together at the dinner had surfaced on a blog. The judge told the media that he knew it was a fundraiser and only went when he was invited at the last minute by a friend whose wife had fallen ill and couldn't attend. Standing in front of the very TV cameras he courted only a few days before, he argued that since he never paid for the ticket—and thus did not make a donation—he could not be in a conflict. Whether the judge was in a real conflict was moot: in the court of public opinion, he was in a perceived conflict and that was enough for the Chief Judge to advise him to recuse himself.

Another week went by, it was now July, and they waited for a new judge to be named. The legislature was empty save for tourists: ministers were out making announcements and MLAs were on the barbecue circuit back in their ridings; pages and interns had turned in their pass keys; commissionaires were reduced to skeleton staffing; even the press gallery, having finished their round of post-mortems, had vacated the buildings. Taking their place were Queen Victoria, Francis Rattenbury and Sir James Douglas—or at least the students who portrayed them as part of the Parliamentary Players' summer guided tours. One set of actors for another, thought Malcolm.

The premier's head had healed to the point where he didn't need the bandage, but Maurice advised him to keep wearing it, at least until after the preliminary hearing. Government had also ground to a halt while the premier's office focused completely on the case. Finally, a new judge was appointed: Judge Cheryl Stanton. No one knew anything about her, except she was young for a judge.

"Have you seen her?" Davis asked, holding up the The Province newspaper where her photo occupied a third of the page. "She's very attractive. Hardly looks like a lawyer, let alone a judge. Model would be more like it."

"Whatever you do, don't mention her appearance," Imrie warned.

He was out of sorts these days: blunter and easily agitated. Malcolm wondered if it wasn't more trouble defending politicians than gangsters.

"She is as tough as she is smart—and she's very smart. I've seen her eviscerate a very good lawyer who made the mistake of complimenting her hair."

"Who am I going to mention it to?" Davis asked.

But that afternoon CKNW's Chris O'Riordan tweeted that Davis thought Judge Stanton could be Scarlett Johansson's doppelganger. Maurice was not happy, but then he was perpetually unhappy these days.

"Imrie has been on the phone to me," Maurice told them. "He's steaming. I explained to him that the premier bumped into Chris at Starbucks and they got to talking. It just came out. He couldn't help himself."

Maurice at first suggested they claim the premier was misquoted, that the comments were "taken out of context". Franson was skeptical.

"Misquoted and taken out of context aren't the same thing anyway. It's either one or the other."

"I'm not sure how you can claim that comparing her to Scarlett Johansson was taken out of context," Malcolm said. "And if you do, no one will believe it."

Davis agreed.

"Why should I deny it? Anyone can see that she looks like Scarlett Johansson. For God's sake, it's a compliment."

The look on Maurice's face told you he wasn't comforted. To be safe, he sequestered Davis in his Victoria apartment for the rest of the week with strict instructions not to talk to media. Meanwhile, Grace was reluctant to return to Victoria for the hearing. Maurice worried her absence would be read as a lack of support, so he arranged for a team of political supporters to show up outside the courthouse.

On the morning of the preliminary inquiry Malcolm went into work early. Franson and Balicki were already at their desks; Franson told Malcolm he had just sent out the issues scan.

"It looks like a light day, which is too bad," said Franson. "Nothing to distract media from the court case."

"Is it too much to ask for a plane crash?" asked Balicki. "Just one. That's all."

"Into the courthouse," suggested Franson. "Make it easy for the media to cover."

"What about the Boss?" asked Malcolm.

"He'd be under a desk with the judge," laughed Balicki.

"I mean how's he doing?" asked Malcolm.

Franson and Balicki looked at each other and shrugged.

"Who's accompanying him to the courthouse?"

"Grace, the last I heard, but double check with Maurice," said Franson.

Maurice was studying his computer screen when Malcolm poked his head around the half-open door.

"Who's going with the Boss this morning?" he asked.

"Right now? No one. Grace just called to say she missed the ferry. I don't believe her—she was never coming over."

"What are you going to do?"

"I don't know. I tried calling some cabinet members but they're all busy making announcements."

No one wants to be seen with him, thought Malcolm.

"He can't go on his own."

"No."

"Why don't you go?" suggested Malcolm.

Maurice was silent before he finally answered: "I'm too political. It would make more sense if you did because you were with him when it happened and you're the press secretary."

Malcolm had the feeling that, like everyone else, Maurice wanted to distance himself from the premier. Politics is a rough sport. But Malcolm was determined not to be like everyone else.

"Okay."

"You will?" asked Maurice.

"Sure."

Maurice didn't hide his relief, and told him to meet the premier at the end of the block opposite the news trucks and walk in with him.

As he came over the top of the hill, Malcolm could see demonstrators carrying placards—actually the backs of demonstrators and the backs of placards because they were turned away from him. They faced a large group of people, mainly young men in suits and ties and young women in smart outfits who looked a lot like the MAs and EAs at the legislature. The sea of placards and the well-dressed group were yelling at each other. Between them, separating them, was a thin black line of uniformed police. Around the perimeter, reporters and cameramen jockeyed for the best positions.

Above the roar of the demonstration Malcolm heard his name. There it was again.

"Malcolm!"

He turned and looked down a side street where a car was parked in the shade of an oak tree. The driver's side door was open and half out of the car was the Boss. He waved Malcolm toward him.

"Where have you been?" the premier asked.

He was clearly distressed.

"Maurice told me to meet you here at 9:30." He looked at his watch. "It's only 25 after."

"Oh," Davis said.

"What's all this about?" Malcolm asked, nodding toward the crowd.

"Animal rights activists. They showed up with placards and a banner. The police were called after they got into a scuffle with our supporters. How am I going to get into the courthouse?"

Malcolm saw the banner, fluttering in the breeze above the heads. In large, upper case letters it read: JUSTICE FOR ALL INCLUDES CROWS!

Like the banner, most of the protest signs looked professionally made. They all said the same thing: "Animal abuse is nothing to crow about".

"Let me go have a look," Malcolm said.

He started towards the crowd and felt a hand on his arm.

"Don't be long," the premier said. "I'm supposed to meet Imrie."

"I'll be right back," Malcolm assured him.

By now the demonstrators had spilled onto Blanshard Street, stopping traffic. Several taunted honking drivers by first showing them their placards, then sitting on their car hoods, their backs to the drivers. Police tried to push the demonstrators back onto the sidewalk. A driver of a Mercedes got out of his car and tried to help the police. Shoving a demonstrator to the ground, he was quickly surrounded by others waving placards and shouting at him. A TV crew rushed to capture the confrontation, but the cameraman stumbled and, as if in slow motion, he hit the ground, his TV camera skidding across the pavement and slowly coming to rest against the car tire.

Malcolm wondered if it was too late to call Hadley. Maurice didn't want Davis to look like he needed security, but if there were ever a time when he truly needed protection, it was now. Malcolm thought about asking one of the policemen for help, but reconsidered: if Maurice didn't want the premier on TV with a plainclothes RCMP officer, then he certainly wouldn't want him on the six o'clock news brought into court by uniformed police, surrounded by a crowd of shouting demonstrators.

He looked above the bobbing white placards to the front doors of the courthouse. The steps were clear, thanks to a cordon of police, but the problem was getting to the steps. As he considered how to move the premier swiftly through the crowd, he noticed Imrie had come out of the front doors and was motioning to him. A second later his smartphone rang.

"Malcolm," Imrie said. "Where's the premier?"

"In his car. Parked on Burdett."

"Don't try to come in the front doors. I'll meet you at the side doors, off Burdett. It's clear there."

Malcolm returned to find Davis hunkered down inside his vehicle, his hand shielding his face, as if afraid someone might recognize him.

"Imrie says the back way is clear. Let's go."

But the back door wasn't clear: a TV cameraman and solitary protester had staked it out. The protester had propped his sign against the stairs and was chatting with the cameraman, who had placed the TV camera on the ground between his legs. They looked bored, but as Malcolm and Davis approached, the cameraman recognized the premier and hurriedly heaved the heavy camera to his shoulder. The protester turned and reached for his placard, then stopped as if he couldn't make up his mind what to do, and reached into the back pocket of his jeans for his smartphone. But he couldn't get it out. His jeans were tight and the phone was wedged into the pocket. By the time he had it free Malcolm and Davis were at the top of the steps where Imrie was waiting with the door open. As the glass door swung shut Malcolm could hear the protester shouting into the phone:

"He's here! Davis is at the back door!"

Inside, the long hallway was empty.

"The police have kept the placards outside," Imrie explained. "However, some of the protesters are in court."

"Are any of the premier's supporters in court?" Malcolm asked.

"Yes," Imrie said. "When I saw the animal rights people lining up to get in I directed some of our supporters to get in line."

"Good going," said Davis with a grim smile, his first smile that morning.

Supporters weren't necessary to defend against the charge itself: that would be won or lost with the legal arguments. But they were important for shaping the narrative that would appear in the media and, in turn, embed itself in the public consciousness. If the courtroom was full of people opposing Davis, reporters would say so, and readers and viewers may be left with the impression that the public didn't support Davis. But if Davis could stack the courtroom with his supporters, then he could create a different public perception. It was no different than running an election campaign, which was why Davis was smiling. This was what he knew, he was on his turf now.

Judge Stanton swept into court, her red and black gown fluttering behind her as if it had trouble keeping up. The red of her gown matched her shoes and lipstick. She was more attractive in person than in her photos. Once she was seated the court clerk, a doughy-faced man with a belly that slid over his belt, called the case: Regina vs Davis.

With a sanguine brusqueness Stanton invited the special prosecutor to lay out his evidence. Kiehon spent the next hour putting forward the charge. He told the court he would not call on any witnesses at this point—a small concession to the premier's position—but submitted statements from the premier and Malcolm and a half dozen others. The climax of his presentation was the infamous YouTube video. The video was taken by a cruise ship passenger from Fort Sumner, New Mexico, who had also provided an affidavit. Some of the animal rights demonstrators cried out "Shame!" when the video showed Davis running over the crow. Compelled to respond, the premier's supporters cheered. Furious, Stanton immediately instructed Kiehon and Imrie to approach the bench. She wagged her finger at them and then waved them away. Kiehon continued to put forward his case. When he was done, Stanton asked Imrie if he wanted to respond.

"Judge—"

It was one of the animal rights activists. He was in the front row, standing up and leaning over the railing.

"I'm sorry, sir," Stanton said. "You can't speak during the proceedings."

"But Judge I have information that is vital to this case."

Stanton looked at Kiehon who was shaking his head and looked embarrassed.

"Mr. Kiehon?"

Kiehon slowly stood.

"Your Honour, the Crown has presented its case," Kiehon said and then sat back down.

"Judge—"

"Sir, I have to warn you not to say anything more. If you persist you will be removed from the court."

"Fuck you, bitch!"

It wasn't the man speaking—though he was smiling as if amused by the remark—but a sparkplug of a woman sitting next to him.

"Order!" shouted Stanton. "This is a court of law!"

"Judge, we just want our right to be heard," said the man.

"And who are you?" asked Stanton.

"We belong to CROW: the Committee to Restore Order in the World. We speak on behalf of the crow that was killed."

Stanton looked at Kiehon, then Imrie. They both smiled uncomfortably.

"I'm sorry, but you don't have standing in this court. This is a charge under the Criminal Code of Canada, and as such falls under the jurisdiction of the Crown, represented by Mr. Kiehon. He is responsible for making the people's case."

"He represents the people, but who speaks for the crow?" asked the man.

"The crow?" Stanton asked.

"Yes, who speaks for it?"

A murmur of support rose from the protesters seated behind the man.

"I'm sorry, you are out of order," said Stanton.

"You're out of order!" yelled the sparkplug standing up and pointing her finger at the judge. "This whole system is out of order if it can't protect against the abuse of animals."

Shouts of encouragement erupted from the other protesters. "YOU TELL HER . . . ANIMALS HAVE RIGHTS . . . DON'T WEAR FUR."

"Excuse me! Excuse me!"

Stanton's face had coloured, and she was half out of her chair banging her gavel.

"This is a court of law," she said loudly. "This is not Speaker's Corner where anyone can get up on their soapbox and say whatever they please. We have the rule of law and that must be adhered to. So I respectfully ask you to refrain from making any more comments or I will halt these proceedings and have the court officers remove you."

"You're part of the problem!" yelled another person.

Malcolm thought it was a young man with a scruffy goatee in the middle row, but he wasn't sure.

"Who said that?" Stanton asked.

No one responded. Stanton shook with fury. She took a moment to collect herself and it provided the demonstrators with an opening.

"She's wearing leather shoes." It was a woman in the third row. She pointed at Stanton. "Blood shoes."

"Animal killer," yelled another person.

This ignited the crowd.

"ANIMAL KILLER . . . ANIMAL KILLER . . . ANIMAL KILLER," the protesters chanted.

They stood now. Some were shouting. The premier's supporters on the other side of the courtroom were at a loss what to do. Some started jeering the protesters. One lifted his leg, and Malcolm thought he was mocking them by pretending to pee on them, but it was worse than that: he was showing them his shoes. His *leather* shoes.

The goateed animal rights protester leapt across the aisle and wrestled with the supporter, reaching to try to tear off his shoe. Two other supporters jumped to the aid of their friend prompting the animal rights activists to flood en masse across the aisle in retaliation. There was a lot of pushing and shoving and shouting. People fell backwards onto the benches with others on top of them. It was all happening so quickly. Malcolm sensed someone next to him. He turned. The sparkplug. Her face was contorted into a mask of hate. She shoved her nose to within inches of his. He smelled the strong odour of rotting garlic from her open mouth. Malcolm stood up. He was nearly a foot taller than her, but her ferocity mixed with the garlic made him feel like vomiting. And he did. All down the front of the sparkplug. The sparkplug lifted her hands as if in surrender and retreated while Malcolm slumped onto the bench.

Judge Stanton stared wide-eyed from her elevated perch at the front of the courtroom, banging her gavel but not saying anything. Imrie had pulled the premier closer to him and they watched with apprehension. Kiehon slouched beside the court reporter with his hand in his pocket and a grin on his face. The sheriffs tried to separate the combatants but there were too many of them. The media were elated. One of the TV reporters left and was quickly followed by the others. They returned with their cameramen and trailed by a dozen police officers who waded into the public gallery. Malcolm learned later that the police overheard the reporters tell their camera crews about the scene inside the courthouse.

Eventually the police cleared the courtroom, except for the lawyers, the premier, Malcolm, and reporters. The cameramen tried to stay, but Stanton was in no mood to be resisted.

"Arrest them for contempt of court," she said angrily to the police.

When the police tried to determine who she meant, she waved: "All of them! Arrest all of them."

Instead, the police herded the cameramen out of the courtroom and let the doors close behind them. The sheriffs took up positions in front of the doors. The courtroom was now so quiet Malcolm could hear the hum of the fluorescent lights.

Judge Stanton scanned the courtroom left to right and back again.

"Mr. Imrie, I believe we were about to hear from you."

But before Imrie could start, Kiehon was standing.

"Your Honour, may I say something before Mr. Imrie begins?"

"Do you have more evidence, Mr. Kiehon?"

"No, your Honour."

"Then I do believe it is Mr. Imrie's turn."

"But your Honour—"

"Mr. Kiehon, I am in no mood for any more courtroom antics."

"Your Honour, it has a bearing on the proceedings."

Imrie stood up.

"Your Honour, I'm fine with hearing what Mr. Kiehon has to say."

Stanton sighed: "All right, Mr. Kiehon, the floor is yours."

"Thank you, your Honour. I will be brief. I wish to enter a stay of proceedings in the case of Regina versus Davis."

"Mr. Kiehon, I cannot compel you to do so, but may I ask your reason for entering the stay?" said Stanton.

"Your Honour, after seeing the outburst today, I cannot see how it is in the public interest to continue with these proceedings. In fact, I think the public interest is poorly served by continuing."

"Mr. Imrie, do you have any comment?"

"Your Honour, I would like time to confer with my client before responding."

"All right, will fifteen minutes be enough time?"

Imrie nodded.

"Then we will take a short break, goodness knows we could all use one."

Imrie and Davis sat down and Davis motioned for Malcolm to join them.

"What do you think?" Davis asked Imrie.

"I think we should argue against a stay."

"Why? Won't it mean I'm free to go?"

"Yes and no. They won't proceed with the charge against you at this time, but they could always bring it back. They have a year."

"Do you think they will?"

"As it stands now? No. But that doesn't mean things can't change. They would have a year to present new evidence . . . perhaps someone steps forward . . . who knows. Anything can happen in a year. The worst thing is the uncertainty. And it would leave a political cloud over your head."

"Hmm. So what are my options?"

"Well, we could request that the judge dismiss your case outright, citing insufficient evidence, or we could oppose the stay, arguing that it denies you your day in court . . . your opportunity to tell your side of the story before a judge. That would assume we want to continue with the case."

"What's your advice?"

"I suggest we seek an outright dismissal."

"Fine by me."

When the court reconvened, Imrie told Stanton they opposed the stay of proceedings and asked the judge to dismiss the case outright. Stanton turned to Kiehon.

"Mr. Kiehon?"

"The Crown would prefer to stay the charge."

"I'm inclined to agree with you, Mr. Kiehon—"

"Your Honour!" said Imrie, leaping to his feet.

"Hear me out, Mr Imrie. I am inclined to agree with Mr. Kiehon that this case is not in the public interest. Having said that, my feeling is that if the charge is not in the public interest, then the case should be dismissed—"

"Your Honour!"

It was Kiehon's turn to protest.

"Please, Mr. Kiehon. I can't help but wonder if this case would ever have reached this court if the plaintiff were not the premier of British Columbia—"

"Your Honour—"

"Mr. Kiehon, you had your say and now it is my turn. I can't help but wonder, too, if the scene we saw in this courtroom today would have taken place if the plaintiff did not occupy the highest political office in the province. I refuse to have this court used as a platform for people wishing to further their own causes—no matter what those causes may be. It is a court of law and should be respected as such.

"As an aside, I can't think of a case in recent memory where a defendant has been under greater scrutiny or which has generated more publicity. And, with due respect to the views of many of those in the courtroom today, I believe any reasonable person would agree that Mr. Davis has endured quite enough. No, I think that on merit—or perhaps more accurately lack of merit—the law is clear. Case dismissed."

Davis stood and shook Imrie's hand then turned to shake Malcolm's hand. As he did he leaned in and whispered: "And Maurice was worried about my comments about the judge. I'd say they had the desired effect. I think I might see if she's free for lunch."

Chapter 20

Davis's success in the courtroom did not translate into success with the public or, more accurately, with voters. Within minutes of the decision, Twitter, Facebook and the blogosphere were besieged by angry protests. By day's end, an online petition demanding Davis's resignation had 10,000 signatures.

Stunned by the backlash, Maurice hastily called a meeting. Malcolm, Franson and Davis huddled in the premier's office where they listened to Maurice outline a strategy to regain control of the political agenda, both inside and outside the legislature.

"The first step is a cabinet shuffle," he said. "The goal is to reassert the premier's hold on caucus. We're going to do that three ways: cut fucking Visser off at the knees, reward our supporters with seats at the cabinet table, and increase the number of MLAs beholden to the premier by appointing them to parliamentary secretariats."

The latter were largely ceremonial. With few responsibilities, little power and no staff, the secretariats came with a hefty salary hike that less charitable observers might have construed as a payoff. By the time Maurice would be finished, about the only MLAs left on the backbench would be either adversaries, grossly incompetent, or under police investigation, which were surprisingly still quite a few.

"The second step is to schedule a fall sitting," Maurice said. "We'll introduce a populist legislative program that will set the Opposition back on their heels and bring the public onside again. It will be expensive, but necessary."

Davis loved it. "Great work, Maurice. But we'll need to move quickly."

"I agree," Maurice said. "I think we should announce the new cabinet on Monday."

"Monday doesn't leave us much time," Davis said. It was already Thursday.

"That's why I went ahead and drafted a list of possibilities for cabinet and the secretariats," Maurice said. He handed them to the premier.

"You've got Roger penciled in for a secretariat," Davis said. "I want him in cabinet."

Maurice frowned but didn't say anything, silently acquiescing.

"One more thing," Davis said. "I've contacted someone to work with me personally, to help me rehabilitate my image. Sherri Tomarillo."

"Sherri Tomarillo?" Maurice echoed. "What is she, a communications consultant?"

"Not quite," Davis said. "An image consultant."

Franson had already Googled her. "Her website says she combines image consulting with a holistic approach to client management."

"What does that mean?" asked Maurice.

"It says she uses unique listening and communication skills to work in depth with clients so their outer image reflects their distinctive beauty within. It looks like she also promotes some sort of herbal remedy."

Davis grinned sheepishly. "It was Grace's idea. She said I looked dumpy during the court case. I'm meeting with Sherri this afternoon. I'll tell her it's a rush job, that I need a fresh image in time for Monday's cabinet announcement."

But Monday was still four days away, an eternity in both politics and social media, the latter of which had become judge, jury, and executioner: "taking on the role," one anonymous blogger boasted, "that the justice system has abdicated." It didn't help that the video clip of Davis killing the crow was now so ingrained in the public consciousness that he was forever and a day identified as an animal abuser. "The kind of man who kicks puppies," as one political strategist unhelpfully observed.

Davis's political support crumbled day by day so that by Sunday he had lost much of his cabinet, the majority of caucus, and everyone on the party executive. On Monday, instead of unveiling a new cabinet, he held a news conference to announce he was resigning. He said he would stay on in a "caretaker capacity" until a new leader had been selected.

"What do you think of his new look?" Malcolm asked Franson as they watched the conference.

Sherri Tomarillo had insisted on personally dressing the premier for the event. A confusion of bangles and upswept dyed brick-red hair, she stood nearby, hands clasped in front of her face in admiration of her creation.

"Is that a hemp suit he's wearing?" Franson asked.

"Bamboo," Malcolm said. "Apparently it's part of the holistic approach, aligning his inner beauty with his outer beauty."

Davis's image consultant had not gone unnoticed. The next day the NDP made a request under the Freedom of Information Act for any and all material related to the contract for Sherri Tomarillo. Despite the fact that by law government had thirty days to respond, requests to the premier's office routinely took months, sometimes years, and even then the documents released were either incomplete or so thoroughly blacked out they were, for all intents useless. So it surprised everyone that the day after the NDP filed their request, they held a news conference to unveil a sheaf of leaked documents related to Sherri Tomarillo. The documents showed Tomarillo had been awarded three contracts each of $25,000. The NDP argued the contracts were excessive—"$75,000 for a weekend's work"—and were structured to circumvent the government's tendering rules that required any contract over $25,000 go to a competitive bid.

"Premier's new image cost taxpayers $75,000" said the Vancouver Sun's banner headline. The Province had stacked its headline so that it occupied half the front page: "Premier's shocking $75,000 makeover". The other half was a file photo of Davis sitting in a makeup chair, a cloth bib tied around his neck, being prepped for a TV interview.

That afternoon, the auditor general initiated a formal investigation into the awarding of the contracts, citing apparent irregularities.

Maurice launched an investigation of his own—into how the documents were leaked in the first place. He took the extraordinary step of hiring a private detective, who showed up on Thursday at the West Annex wearing a bulging suitcoat and pulling a square black suitcase on rollers.

"He's giving everyone a lie detector test," Jessica said, nervously eying the premier's office where the detective was setting up.

"Is he allowed to do that?" asked Jarrod.

"Maurice says it's voluntary," Jessica said.

"You don't have to take it," said Franson, "if you don't want to keep your job."

"But I didn't have access to the contracts," said Jarrod.

"Then you don't have anything to worry about, do you?" Franson said.

"I still don't see why I should be forced to take it."

The detective's name was John Eugene and he was a tall, grim, bald man without eyebrows or facial hair of any kind.

"Eugene. What is that? Scottish?" Malcolm asked.

Malcolm sat in a chair beside the premier's desk while Eugene sat in the premier's chair so that they were almost beside each other but facing in opposite directions.

"Turkish," Eugene said. "Eugenides originally. My grandfather changed it when he emigrated."

On the desk in front of Eugene was a laptop, positioned so Malcolm could see Eugene but not the screen. Eugene briskly explained that he was investigating the leak of the Tomarillo contracts. As he advised Malcolm of his constitutional rights and his right to an attorney, he studied Malcolm's face. Malcolm wondered what he was searching for. He told Malcolm his participation was voluntary. Malcolm smiled thinly and Eugene tapped something into the laptop that was beside the computer screen.

"What are you doing?" Malcolm asked.

"Taking notes."

He confirmed Malcolm's job title and how long he had worked in the premier's office, and asked for a brief description of what he did. Then he went through a long explanation of the polygraph, its components and how each worked. Malcolm wondered if this was all designed to get Malcolm to let down his guard.

"Is there a test after?" asked Malcolm with a smile, determined to show he had nothing to hide: nothing to hide and nothing to fear.

"Do you have any questions about the polygraph?" Eugene asked.

Malcolm shook his head.

Eugene then asked Malcolm to describe his role in the contracts. Malcolm said he didn't have a role because he had never seen the contracts.

"Did you have access to the contracts, say on a shared drive?" Eugene asked.

"No," Malcolm said. "Jessica manages those records."

Finally, Eugene went over the list of questions he was going to ask, taking time to discuss each of them with Malcolm.

"We're now going to move into the test phase," Eugene said. "I'm going to hook up the components we reviewed earlier."

He unrolled a blood pressure cuff and wrapped it around Malcolm's upper arm, over his shirt.

"This will record your heart rate, blood pressure and blood volume," Eugene said.

Next, he fastened two coiled rubber tubes across his chest, one just below his armpits and another above his naval, to record his breathing pattern. Finally, he hooked two electrodes, one to each of two fingers on his left hand, to measure sweat gland activity. As he was positioning the electrodes Malcolm noticed Eugene didn't have any hair on his hands. His skin was completely smooth. It struck him that Eugene's whole body might be hairless.

"I just need to calibrate it," Eugene said.

"I hope that doesn't involve an electric shock," Malcolm joked weakly.

Unsmiling, Eugene tapped more notes into his computer.

"First, I'm going to ask you a question that I want you to answer truthfully. Is this the month of July?"

Malcolm said, "Yes, it's July 17th."

"Please answer just yes or no. Nothing else," Eugene instructed. "Again, is this the month of July?"

"Yes," Malcolm said.

"Next, I'm going to ask you a question that I want you to deliberately lie to. It's called a stim test. Is this the month of January?"

Malcolm answered yes.

Eugene got up and moved the blood pressure cuff lower on Malcolm's arm. He said he needed to repeat the stim test. He asked him if this was the month of November. Malcolm answered yes again.

"Good, the device was able to detect that you were lying," Eugene said slowly and deliberately, pausing for effect, as if to impress on Malcolm that it was useless to try to fool the machine. "We're ready to begin. As I said earlier, there will be three tests of about five minutes each. The same questions each time. After each test you will rest for a couple of minutes. Understand?"

Malcolm nodded.

"Is this the month of July?" Eugene asked, no longer looking at Malcolm, but focused on the computer screen the whole time.

"Yes."

"Are you going to tell a lie on this test?"

"No."

The questions proceeded as expected, alternating between questions relevant to the investigation and "control questions" used to compare responses.

"Did you leak information related to the Sherri Tomarillo contracts?"

"No."

"Have you ever betrayed anyone?"

Malcolm had gone over this question earlier with Eugene. It was the kind of question that he always cautioned against giving a simple 'yes' or 'no' to when he ran his media training sessions.

"Complex questions require responses that provide context and nuance," Malcolm would always say. "How can you do that in a single word? You can't. So don't."

In this case, "betrayal" was such a loaded word. What did it really mean? Treachery? Duplicity? Or one of a dozen other things? There were also degrees of betrayal: some betrayals were worse than others. A straightforward 'yes' or 'no' answer didn't provide that distinction. Then there was context. Malcolm could argue there were times when betrayal was not only the most acceptable course of action, but the most moral. How could you convey that with 'yes' or 'no'?

"It depends what you mean," Malcolm finally said.

"A simple yes or no, please," Eugene insisted. He reached into his coat pocket and pulled out a package of dried currants, and tore it open.

"But the question isn't as simple as 'yes' or 'no'," Malcolm said.

Eugene popped a currant in his mouth and began typing on the laptop.

Malcolm weighed his options. He wanted to ask if Eugene would skip the question. But would even asking him be considered an admission of guilt? These fucking 'yes' or 'no' questions. He wanted to say 'yes'—it was the most truthful response—but he couldn't; Maurice would take it as a confession.

"No," Malcolm finally said. It was a soft no. An indecisive no.

Then he remembered what Rachel had said: "You can't even be true to yourself."

She had seen right through him. She'd always been like that. It was what he had loved most about her: that she saw him for exactly what he was and, for a time at least, had still loved him. If she were here, standing beside him, he knew what she would say. She'd say he had made the worst kind of betrayal, because it was a betrayal of himself.

"I'd like to change my answer," Malcolm said.

Eugene looked up from where he was retrieving a currant from its package. "Change your answer?" he asked.

"Yes," Malcolm said.

Eugene let the currant fall back into its package, placed the package on the desk and quickly began tapping at the laptop. When he'd finished, he looked at what he had written.

"This is highly unusual," he said. He got up and inspected the blood pressure cuff on Malcolm's arm, and made sure the electrodes were firmly attached to Malcolm's fingers, then sat down again.

"I will repeat the question," Eugene said. He paused. "Have you ever betrayed anyone?"

"Yes," Malcolm said. He watched as Eugene monitored the response on the computer screen. Eugene waited a moment before resuming.

"Did you leak information related to the Sherri Tomarillo contracts?"

"No."

Eugene was now more deliberate in his questioning.

"Do you know anyone who leaked information related to the Sherri Tomarillo contracts?"

Malcolm paused.

"No."

"Have you ever leaked information you shouldn't have?"

Malcolm paused again.

"Yes," he said crisply.

"Do you support Premier Steven Davis?"

"Yes."

Less crisp.

Following the three tests, Eugene pursed his lips and leaned forward to look closely at the computer screen before getting up stiffly and, without speaking, methodically unhooking the components from Malcolm.

"I'll go over the results with you," Eugene said. "Move your chair around."

Malcolm moved his chair so he could see the computer screen.

"There are a couple of areas of concern."

Malcolm had expected this.

"The first is your response to the question about whether you have betrayed anyone. You changed your answer. That is something I will report to Maurice. As well, both answers can't be true, so you either lied initially or you lied later. The results indicate that your first response was a lie."

He pointed to a line on the screen.

"The second area of concern is your response to the question about whether you leaked information you shouldn't have."

"But I admitted I have," Malcolm said.

"Precisely," Eugene responded. "And that's what I will report to Maurice."

"Are there any other concerns?"

"One other. I asked you if you knew anyone who leaked information about the Tomarillo contracts? You said no. Here is how the machine recorded your response." Eugene pointed to another line on the screen. Malcolm looked at the screen.

"So what does that mean?"

"Your response is consistent with other responses where you lied."

"What are you saying?" Malcolm demanded. "That I leaked the contracts?"

"Mm . . . it's not what I say. It's what the polygraph says."

"That's bullshit!" Malcolm said and stood up so he was looking down on Eugene and the computer screen. "I didn't leak those contracts. How could I? I didn't have access."

"I'm just telling you what the polygraph says," Eugene repeated.

Malcolm swung open the door and stormed out.

"What a bunch of bullshit!"

Jessica flitted anxiously as Malcolm approached and Jarrod peered from his office doorway, each afraid to ask what happened, but each knowing. It was Franson who said accusingly, "So you failed."

"Fuck off!" Malcolm said and went straight into Maurice's office.

Maurice was sitting behind his desk in front of his computer screen.

"Your fucking private detective says I leaked the contracts."

Maurice sat up straight.

"Did you?"

"Of course I didn't. I've never seen them. How could I? It doesn't make sense."

"Jessica!" Maurice yelled.

Jessica appeared at the door.

"Ask Mr. Eugene to come in here."

Eugene came into the room with a printout of the test results and laid them on the desk in front of Maurice.

"Firstly, he lied about question seven. That's this one here." Eugene pointed to some lines on the printout. "But then he changed his answer." Maurice looked at Malcolm.

"There are also discrepancies here," Eugene said, pointing to the printout, "and here. They should be the same as the others, but as you can see they're not."

Malcolm strained to see what Eugene was pointing to but the graphs were too small and he was too far away.

"You will also want to note his response to question twelve, about leaking information he shouldn't have."

Maurice nodded and smiled, tight-lipped.

"I will have a more fulsome report once I've finished testing everyone," Eugene said.

"We've done all the testing we need to do," Maurice said.

"If you're sure," Eugene said.

"I'm sure," Maurice said. "Now I need to speak to Malcolm alone."

Eugene collected the papers and left, closing the door as he went.

"Maurice . . ."

"You're fired," Maurice said. "I want you out of the building immediately."

"It wasn't me," Malcolm protested.

"Give me your pass," Maurice demanded, standing up and reaching out his hand. Malcolm took his pass from where it hung on a lanyard around his neck and handed it over. "Jessica will box up your things and send them to your home."

"Maurice . . ."

Maurice radiated a vile dislike.

"Visser resigned from cabinet," he said, "while you were taking your lie detector test, which I think is highly ironic. My guess is he's going to run for the leadership and wants to distance himself from the Boss. But then you probably already know that."

"What do you mean?" Malcolm asked.

"I couldn't put my finger on it but I knew something wasn't right with you the first time I met you. Remember? I told the Boss you couldn't be trusted, but he wouldn't believe me, didn't want to believe me. Well he does now. Visser told him today about how you helped him with his speech when he was first appointed Minister of Advanced Education—"

"I was asked to help him."

"—and how you lied about knowing what was in the speech. You knew exactly what was in it because you wrote it. All of it."

Unsteady, Malcolm reached out for Maurice's desk. It seemed to rise up, dreamlike, from the ground to meet his hand.

"Visser told us everything: how you collaborated with him while you were working here. How you helped him to deliberately undermine the Boss. How you passed along crucial information. How you even went to his house. So it really didn't matter if you passed the lie detector test or not. I was going to fire you regardless. Now get out."

Burt, the commissionaire, was waiting for Malcolm outside Maurice's office. Franson, Jarrod and Balicki were all watching from their doorways. Jessica had her head down.

"Can I just drop some things off at my desk and get my coat?" Maurice asked.

Burt nodded.

Malcolm took his cellphone from his pocket and laid it on his desk. It vibrated with a new text message. He picked it up again. It was from Davis. One word: "Trust."

Outside, Malcolm looked across the covered walkway at the side entrance to the legislature.

"Can you do me a favour, Burt?" he asked, nodding to the doors. "They took my card. I'd like to say goodbye to the gallery."

Burt glanced warily back at the West Annex and shrugged. "I guess there's no harm."

Malcolm followed Burt across to the towering twin oak doors where Burt quickly, almost surreptitiously, swiped his card against the plastic pad and turned and retreated to the safety of the West Annex. Malcolm pulled on the heavy door and walked down the broad expanse of hallway, surprisingly empty of tourists for the time of year. With a wistful gaze he took it all in: the pale filtered light from above, the rose-pink Tennessee marble, the neoclassical columns with their lavish scrolls in gold and silver leaf, the swooping arches of doorways that led to more doorways. The building was here before he'd come and would be here after he'd gone—after all of them had gone: politicians, political staff, bureaucrats, reporters, public; the only constant being the next generation of politicians, political staff, bureaucrats, reporters; and the next; and the next.

By the balustrade under the rotunda, he waited, as he had so often before, for the echo of his footsteps to catch up; but this time they were lost among the voices of tourists coming up the stairs. He left before they could trample on his memories.

It was mid-summer, so he wasn't sure any of the reporters would even be in the gallery, but he thought he would see anyway. He wasn't sure why he wanted to say goodbye. It wasn't like him to be so sentimental. Then he realized that without his card he couldn't get through the locked doors that led to the gallery. Even if he could somehow get through the doors, he'd be bound to run into commissionaires and they would be all over him for not having his pass visible. When they found out he didn't even have a pass anymore he'd be returned to the public area.

He was forced to retrace his steps and push his way through the tourists who suddenly seemed to be everywhere. He went quickly down the hall and out the other side of the building onto Government Street. He saw the Ministry of Education building rising up in the distance and he thought back to the day when he was hired into the premier's office. It seemed so long ago now. He wondered what Gerald Morris was up to these days and was tempted to call on him for old times' sake. To let him know that he had been right. But he worried that Gerald might not be there. He might not even be working in government. There was comfort in not knowing, so he walked up a block and crossed over in front of The Birdcage with its familiar red awning and flowers lining the sidewalk. He stopped at the corner and glanced up at Catherine's apartment. He hadn't heard from her in months. Mind you, he hadn't called her. It was as if they both knew that whatever they had—if they ever had anything—was over.

Malcolm spent the afternoon at a loss of what to do. He was suddenly free of any demands on him. He had a sense of drifting. There was really nothing keeping him in Victoria. Perhaps he should move back to Vancouver. Start fresh.

Around 5PM there was a knock at his door. He wondered if Rob had heard and come by to see how he was doing. But when he opened the door it wasn't Rob.

"Hello, Malcolm," Jessica said. "I brought your things. May I come in? I won't stay long."

Malcolm opened the door wider and Jessica moved past him and into the hallway. He took the cardboard box from her.

"Do you want to sit down?"

"No. Like I said, I won't be long."

Pause.

Jessica continued: "You knew, didn't you?"

"Yes."

"I just wanted to say I'm sorry for what happened to you."

"They were going to fire me anyway."

"But you could have told them it was me."

"Look—don't try to make me out as some sort of hero. I told them I didn't have access to the contracts, that you were responsible for them. They just didn't want to listen."

"Still, it was more than the others would have done."

Malcolm shrugged.

"I'm just sorry that you got caught up in all this."

"Why did you do it?"

"The contracts, you mean?"

Malcolm nodded.

"It had gotten completely out of control. Taxpayers paying for his hotel room at the Grand Pacific was one thing. But that image consultant was too much . . . and the hookers."

"Hookers?"

"You didn't know?"

"Know what?"

"He charged them to his travel expenses. That should be coming out soon too."

"Why would a man with his wealth charge hookers as a travel expense?"

"Power," Jessica said. "Carelessness. After a while they think they can do anything."

"They'll know it wasn't me."

"Yes."

Malcolm studied her face.

"You want to get caught," he said, as if it had suddenly occurred to him.

Jessica smiled.

"Why?" he asked. "Why are you doing this?"

"Because it's the right thing to do."

"But why now?"

"I should have released them sooner. I regret that. But I was afraid of losing my job."

"But Davis is already leaving."

"Yes, but he is staying on as caretaker. Who knows how long that will be? This will make sure it isn't long. The United Party is bigger than Steven Davis, though he never believed that."

"And you get to distance yourself from him and position yourself for a job with the new premier."

"It's not like that."

"What's it like then?"

"I'm trying to do the right thing and you make it seem self-serving."

"It's just your timing seems awfully convenient."

"I should go," she said sharply as if she was dismissing him. She moved toward the door.

"Yes," Malcolm agreed.

Without a phone Malcolm felt disconnected. No, it was worse than disconnected. Disconnected would be like being cut off in the middle of your phone conversation. You could always hit redial and get reconnected. But he didn't even have a phone. He felt cut off.

He went out and bought a phone, the first one he saw. But then he didn't know who to call. Visser? What would he say? Rob? Maybe. Just to give him his new number. But not now. Rob would be full of questions, searching questions, questions with sharp edges. He wanted softness and comfort. He wanted Rachel. He wanted to tell her what had happened. Hear her voice. She'd always known what to say to make him feel better. But he didn't have the nerve.

"Hello?"

"Minister Watling? It's Malcolm."

"Malcolm, I didn't recognize your number."

"It's a new phone."

"Of course."

"So far it seems to be working fine—but then no one's called me yet."

Watling chuckled lightly so his voice seemed to float.

"How are things?" Malcolm asked, forcing himself to sound cheerful.

"Things are getting very exciting, Malcolm. In about an hour I'm announcing I'm running for leader of the party."

"What?" Malcolm was dumbfounded. "That's sudden. I mean, the premier only resigned on—what was it?"

"Monday," said Watling.

"Was it Monday? I suppose it was. The days all seem to run together for me right now."

"It actually hasn't been all that sudden," Watling said.

"What do you mean?"

"You can't put together a leadership bid without doing the groundwork. Not if you want to be successful."

Malcolm was stunned. In government everyone seemed to know everyone else's business. Within the party it was even worse; it was impossible to keep anything secret. Yet Malcolm had heard nothing about Watling's plans. Not a whisper. Not even the whisper of a whisper.

"Well congratulations," Malcolm said.

"Thank you. And I was sorry to hear about what happened to you. I've always had the greatest respect for your abilities."

"I appreciate that, Minister."

"Enough with the 'Minister'. In another hour I will be plain old Jeffrey Watling, backbench MLA."

"So it sounds like you have everything under control."

"Oh there are always loose ends that need tying up."

"Who's doing your media relations?"

"David. You know him. My communications director—former communications director."

Pause.

"Malcolm . . ."

Malcolm waited.

"I'd love to have you on my team . . ."

Malcolm realized that Watling thought he had called looking for a job. But Malcolm was done with politics—he was firm on that. Nevertheless, he was interested in hearing what Watling had to offer, if only to help boost his sagging spirits.

"I'm putting myself forward as a new face, someone who will take the party in a new direction with new ideas. The question is how do I do that with Steven Davis's former press secretary at my side?"

Was he or wasn't he offering him a job?

"There is no getting around the fact that you will remind people of Davis."

And that's something no leadership candidate wants, thought Malcolm.

"As much as I'd love to have you on my team, Malcolm, I can't take the risk. I need to do everything I can to put myself in a position to win. That means not creating unnecessary issues. You, of all people, know that."

Malcolm wouldn't have taken the job, but that didn't lessen his disappointment in not being offered it. It had come to this: he was a liability. Even Jeffrey Watling didn't want him.

Chapter 21

THE LATCH CLUNKED, the green wood door, worn and soft on its hinges, scraped across the black and white chequered linoleum, its glass rattling loosely in the frame, and a young man in a newsboy cap and three-day beard stepped in.

"Hey, Malcolm."

Malcolm looked up from his newspaper.

"Hi, Troy. How's it going?"

"Slow."

"Ah."

"That kind of morning."

"Yeah.

Pause.

"The usual?"

"Yeah."

Pause.

"Better make it a double."

"That kind of morning, huh?"

"Yeah."

"Yeah."

Malcolm closed the newspaper and picked up the spotless stainless steel portafilter. He nuzzled the basket against the scarred belly of the grinder and flipped a switch, provoking a growl from the machine and soon after a flow of freshly ground beans. He filled the basket, gently tapped it on the side, filled it some more, and tapped it again. He grabbed a tamper, wedged the portafilter against the side of the counter, and packed the coffee, starting off with the force of a punch and finishing with a caresse, singing softly to himself as he did so. He inspected the level of the coffee, then wiped his finger around the rim of the basket. In a single motion, he jammed the portafilter into the La Cimbali, wrenched it sideways and hit the start button. The thick, creamy, reddish-black liquid piled into the two demitasse cups waiting open-mouthed under the spouts. Like a protective parent, Malcolm hovered, intently watching, gauging just the right moment to hit the button and stop the process.

"Here you go," he said.

Troy was studying the front page of the newspaper.

"So Watling's the new premier, huh?"

"Looks that way," said Malcolm.

"Do you follow politics?"

"Used to. Not so much anymore."

"I stay away from politics. It's not healthy."

"No?"

"All those toxins."

"Toxins?"

"Too much negativity."

"Ah."

"Focus on the positive. Positive feelings release endorphins."

"Endorphins?"

"It's all about endorphins."

"Ah."

"Life, I mean."

"Life."

"Yes."

"Yes."

"There are no endorphins in politics."

"I never thought of it that way."

"Most people don't."

"I guess not."

Troy paid Malcolm, then pulled a lighter and package of cigarettes out of his pocket. He picked up his coffee.

"Thanks, Malcolm."

It had been a busy morning; Malcolm had barely had time to glance at the paper. He looked at it again. Watling won on the second ballot, easily beating Ginny Jones. The photo that occupied the whole of the front page above the fold showed a grinning Watling holding his wife's hand, their arms thrust into the air. Directly behind, between Watling and his wife, her eyes focused on Watling, was Catherine.

Visser hadn't run. Maurice had got it wrong. Visser hadn't quit cabinet to run for the leadership: he quit because he was leaving politics altogether. He gave no reason, but the afternoon he announced his resignation, he said goodbye to his tearful staff, packed all his personal possessions into a single cardboard box, and left. The only remaining trace of him was his brass nameplate on the office door, and by the end of the day that, too, was gone.

Malcolm had heard he'd moved back to Vancouver. One day he bumped into him at the Granville Island market. He was with Claire, who had put on weight and, surprisingly, looked even happier than before. The bigger surprise was Visser: he was walking. He used a cane, though he said he wouldn't need it once he regained the muscle in his legs. It was an awkward meeting because Malcolm and Visser had not parted on good terms. Visser asked how he was doing.

"Fine," Malcolm told him.

Then Visser just blurted out: "I did it for you."

"Huh?" Malcolm asked.

"Davis. I told Davis . . . to try to help you."

"Help me? What do you mean?"

"I don't know. From yourself—you're your own worst enemy, Malcolm—from taking the wrong path."

"You thought I had taken the wrong path?"

"Yes. Hadn't you?"

"I hadn't thought about it."

"That was your problem: you always focused on the task at hand. Head down and hard at it. Never looking up to see where you were and where you were going, never taking time to think about the choices you were making."

"So you're telling me you got me fired for my own good?"

"Yes. And I'd do it again. We'd argued the last time we were together and I was still angry with you. It took me a while to get past that. But Claire made me realize that I owed you."

"Owed me? For what?"

Claire put her arm around Visser and pulled him close.

"For this," she said, rubbing her stomach and grinning.

"You're pregnant!" Malcolm shouted.

"You didn't notice?" Claire asked, laughing. "For someone so smart you can be so stupid."

Visser just grinned.

"He was a different man once he met you, Malcolm."

"But politics was your life."

"There are other things in life," Visser said. "It took Claire getting pregnant for me to see that. Once I realized that, I felt I owed it to you to help you see that, too. You're a good man, Malcolm. You just need to see that for yourself."

Malcolm looked at the front page photo again and folded the paper and put it with the others in the stand.

"Do you think things happen for a reason?" Malcolm asked.

The coffee shop was closed and he was wiping down the tables and chairs.

"Like fate?" asked Andy. He was at the counter preparing the bank deposit.

"Yeah. I guess."

Malcolm and Andy always closed the shop together. At first, Andy had insisted that Malcolm go home, he could close up by himself, he'd been doing it on his own since he'd started the business. But Malcolm had nothing to go home to, so he began to stay behind to help out. He liked this time of day, when everyone had left and the shop was quiet while only a few feet away Commercial Drive rumbled with traffic. It was spiritual, like being in a church in the middle of a city.

Initially, he and Andy worked in silence, but after a week or so they began talking. About anything and everything. Now, Malcolm looked forward to the end of the day and their talk.

"Yeah," Andy said, looking up from his tallying. "I think things happen for a reason. Though I don't believe in fate. There is no choice with fate. Your life is determined for you. It is what it is. I'm more about grace. With grace, you have a choice. You either accept it or not. It's up to you. The biggest problem with fate is there's no room for mercy. Grace is all about mercy. Mercy. Forgiveness. Redemption. And we could all use more of that."

Malcolm finished wiping the chairs, then started turning them upside down on the tables.

"Why?" asked Andy.

"I bumped into some old friends and it got me to thinking about how life can take different turns."

Andy put the cash in the bank bag, sealed it and stood up.

"I talked to Rachel," he said.

In their time together at in the coffee shop, Rachel's name had come up maybe half a dozen times—and then only in passing. And always by Andy. Malcolm feared that if he brought her up he might have to explain what had happened. And he didn't want that.

"What?"

"I said I talked to Rachel."

Malcolm went and got the broom and dustpan from the closet and started sweeping the floor.

"I told her I don't want her to end up like me," Andy said.

Malcolm stopped sweeping and looked at Andy.

"What do you mean by that?"

"For a long time I blamed Rachel's mom for what happened. But I was as much to blame—maybe more. I knew everything back then; you couldn't tell me anything. I was the one who wanted to live off the land. She didn't want to. It wasn't her thing. But she went because of me."

He paused for a moment, as if remembering what it was like then.

"She would have gone anywhere with me."

Andy opened the dishwasher and began unloading cups. Malcolm finished sweeping. Then he got out the mop and bucket and started washing the floor. The mood in the coffee shop had chilled. Malcolm's mop sloshed across the floor, its syncopated rhythm filling the strained silence.

After a while Andy said, "It was my fault."

Malcolm stopped mopping the floor.

"She left because of me."

Malcolm knew better than to say anything.

"She would have stayed," Andy said. "She wanted to stay. But I wouldn't let her. I was angry and I didn't want to let go of that anger. I felt I had a right to be angry. She'd betrayed me. I couldn't bring myself to forgive her. That's not the best frame of mind to make a decision that will affect you for the rest of your life. If I had to do it over again, I'd do it differently."

Malcolm returned to mopping the same spot on the floor. He had already gone over it three or four times.

"That's what I told Rachel. Don't do what I did. Don't end up like me."

Malcolm rinsed the mop and bucket and put them away. He slowly put on his coat.

"Is that why you offered me this job?"

Andy nodded.

"I thought you disliked me."

"It wasn't that I disliked you as much as I didn't like you. There's a difference."

"So why offer me a job?"

Andy closed the dishwasher.

"It was my chance to do things differently."

Silence.

Andy said, "If it makes you feel any better, I like you now. You're different than you were. Nicer. Maybe I just know you better."

Malcolm thought about that for a moment and started for the door to leave.

"How long are you going to wait before you call her?" Andy asked.

Malcolm turned to face Andy.

"What?"

"You heard me. When are you going to call her?"

Malcolm shrugged.

"That's why you took this job, isn't it? To try to get back together with her?"

Malcolm nodded.

"So what are you waiting for?"

Malcolm had asked himself that question every day since he had returned to Vancouver. And the answer was always the same.

"What if she says no?"

"You won't know that unless you talk to her."

"But if she says no then it's over."

Andy laughed a short, sharp laugh.

"Something can't be over that isn't even started."

"You know what I mean."

Andy smiled sympathetically.

"Just talk to her."

Malcolm had his back to the door, pulling a cup from the shelf, when he heard the familiar clunk of the latch followed by the scrape and rattle. In the moment before he turned he somehow knew it was Rachel. She looked briefly at him, then around the coffee shop. It was full. The November rains were keeping everyone inside. Malcolm had played this moment over dozens of times in his head and he was always confident and sure of himself, but now that it was actually happening he felt anxious and unprepared. A minute later, he handed the latte to the young man at the counter without remembering having made it.

"Hi, Rachel," he finally said. "It's great to see you."

"Hi, Malcolm."

"Can I get you something?"

Malcolm silently kicked himself for treating her like just another customer.

"Oh . . . sure," Rachel said, as if she were taken off guard. "Let me see . . ."

"A London fog?" Malcolm asked.

"No," Rachel said, scrunching up her forehead. "I haven't had one of those in ages."

Malcolm silently kicked himself again.

"I'll have a cappuccino."

"Right," Malcolm said. He couldn't remember her ever having a cappuccino. She always complained they had too much foam.

"And extra foam," Rachel said.

"With extra foam," Malcolm repeated. "Grab a seat and I'll bring it over."

Rachel looked around for an empty seat and found one in the corner beneath a framed tie-dyed T-shirt. After a minute, Malcolm appeared with her drink. He was still nervous, and as he placed it on the table he spilled some of the foam into the saucer.

"I'll get a cloth for that," he said.

"It's okay," Rachel said, but Malcolm insisted.

He returned with a cloth and carefully wiped the saucer and the bottom of the cup. Then he started to wipe the table. Rachel put her hand over his and stopped him.

"Malcolm, you said you wanted to talk," she said, leaving her hand on top of his.

He looked down at his hand, covered by hers, and took it as a positive sign. Rachel slowly removed her hand, as if worried he might start wiping the table again, but Malcolm sank into the empty wooden chair, clutching the damp dishcloth in his lap.

"How are you?" he asked.

"Fine."

The way she said it didn't seem like she was fine. It seemed like she was edgy.

"I hear you've got a new job."

"Dad told you."

Malcolm nodded. "He said it's with Covenant House."

"Working with homeless youth."

"Congratulations. I didn't know you were interested in working with youth."

"There's a lot you don't know about me."

He deserved that.

"When do you start?"

"The end of the month. It's coming up fast and I haven't even begun packing. But then I don't have a lot to move, as you know."

At first, he thought she was making a point, but her tone was different and she smiled.

"Andy's pretty excited that you're going to be back in Vancouver." He hesitated and said, "Where are you going to live?"

"I'm staying with Dad until I can find a place of my own."

Andy hadn't mentioned that part.

"That's good."

"We'll see. I haven't lived at home since university so it'll be a bit of an adjustment—for both of us."

She took a sip of her cappuccino.

"I was sorry to hear about your brother."

"He was lucky it was only a suspension. He could have been disbarred. My parents took it pretty hard. Harder than him."

Silence.

"Dad says you're writing a screenplay."

"Yeah."

"Based on your experiences in government."

"Yeah. I've written the first scene and the last scene. Now I just need to fill in the rest."

"Writing a screenplay and working as a barista . . ."

"Too cliché?"

"No, I just wouldn't have guessed it of you. You always hated the idea of working in a coffee shop."

"There's a lot you don't know about me."

She laughed.

"I guess I deserved that."

Silence.

Malcolm had planned to ask her if she would like to see a movie, but all the confidence he had when he practised it in the days and weeks leading up to this had deserted him.

"I'm sorry," he said. "For what I did; for hurting you. It was wrong. I was wrong."

He waited for Rachel to say something. She stared at the wall behind his head. It reminded him of the day she'd moved out. When she sat in the front seat of the car and wouldn't look at him.

Finally she turned to him and said, "Dad thinks I should get back together with you."

Malcolm squeezed the dishcloth so tightly that drops fell onto his pants.

"He says if I don't I'll regret it like he does."

She took a sip of her cappuccino. Her hands were steady. Malcolm silently urged her to continue. She placed the cup back in the saucer.

"But that's not how I feel."

Malcolm's stomach bounced up and down. It was his worst fear: over before it even started.

"I loved you, Malcolm."

Loved. Past tense.

She picked up her cappuccino, this time her hands were shaking so that some of the foam slipped over the rim and ran down the side. Malcolm wanted to reach over and catch the foam with his cloth but the way she gripped the cup, like a shield in front of her, made him think better of it.

"I'm not sure I can love you again. I'm not sure I even want to."

Malcolm thought of asking why she'd come if she didn't want to; instead he said: "You wouldn't be here if you didn't want to."

Silence.

"All I'm asking is that you give me a chance," he said. "Give us a chance."

"Why should I?"

Rachel's voice was firmer, defiant. Malcolm sat there for some time, letting the question hang in the air.

Finally he said, "I made a mistake. I'm sorry. I am. I really am. I promise you it'll be different. I'll be different."

"Why should I believe you?"

"I'll show you. Every hour. Every day. Every week. Every month. Every year."

Silence. Eventually Rachel put her cappuccino down.

"Malcolm, you think it will be like it was before, but it won't. We'll never get that back. It's like breaking this cup. You can glue the pieces together, but the cup is never the same."

"Like slouching towards innocence."

"What?"

"Slouching towards innocence. Getting back to the garden. It may not be the same, but maybe it's the best we can do."

Silence.

"How will we know unless we try?" Malcolm asked.

Rachel sighed and fiddled with the handle of her cappuccino.

He said, "We could start by going to a movie? See what happens. Take it from there."

It was a feeble attempt and he knew it. Over before it even started. Just as he'd feared.

"Hey," Andy said, approaching their table. He gave Rachel a hug and kiss on the cheek. "So . . ."

"So what?" Rachel asked teasingly.

"So . . . are you two . . . ?"

Malcolm wiped a spot on the table where Rachel's foam had fallen and left a thin white crust.

"Well, Malcolm's invited me to a movie."

"Oh yeah," Andy said hopefully. "What are you going to see?"

"We haven't decided."

Malcolm looked at Rachel. She was smiling. She was beautiful.

"Got any suggestions?"

"There's a documentary about the Grateful Dead on at the Rio. That's Jerry Garcia's T-shirt behind you. Did I tell you the story about how I got that shirt?"

Malcolm was about to say, "Too many times to count," but caught himself. Andy pulled up a chair from a nearby table and sat down.

"I was sixteen and it was the summer of 1966 and we were partying in a motel on Kingsway when Jerry and Pigpen decided we were running a little low . . ."

Malcolm heard Andy but the words all ran together as he stared across the table at Rachel.

EPILOGUE

EXT.—STREET—NIGHT

A bearded panhandler in his 30s is sitting on the sidewalk in front of an upscale men's clothing store. In the window behind the panhandler is a male mannequin dressed in a suit, white shirt and tie. It contrasts with the dirty and torn clothes of the panhandler. In front of the panhandler is a dingy baseball cap with a few coins in the bottom.

STEVEN DAVIS comes out of the clothing store carrying several bags.

                    PANHANDLER
          Spare any change, sir?

                    DAVIS
     What?

                    PANHANDLER
          Spare any change?

                    DAVIS
     What do you need it for?

                    PANHANDLER
          To do my laundry.

DAVIS looks at the man's dirty clothes.

                    DAVIS
          Why don't you get a job?

PANHANDLER
I have a job.

DAVIS
Then pay for your own laundry.

PANHANDLER
After I pay my rent I hardly have
enough for food.

DAVIS
What's your job?

PANHANDLER
Pumping gas.

DAVIS
What do they pay you?

PANHANDLER
$10 an hour.

DAVIS shifts the bags into his right hand and reaches into his left
pocket, then drops some coins in the hat. The panhandler peers
into the hat.

PANHANDLER
Fourteen cents?

THE panhandler takes the coins from the hat, two nickels and
four pennies. He holds out his hand.

DAVIS
Those aren't just any coins.

PANHANDLER
Keep your money.

                    DAVIS
Those coins were good to me. They
can be good to you.

                  PANHANDLER
No thanks.

DAVIS tries to push the man's hand away and an awkward struggle ensues.

EXT.—STREET—NIGHT

A flashing light from a police car reflects in the plate glass window of the upscale clothing store, bathing the mannequin in
blue. The camera pans to show a policewoman with her notebook out speaking to DAVIS.

                  POLICEWOMAN
Sir, can I have your name?

                    DAVIS
Everything is connected.

                  POLICEWOMAN
                (leaning forward)
Sir, have you been drinking?

                    DAVIS
He didn't know.

                  POLICEWOMAN
Sir, did you have something to drink
tonight?

                    DAVIS
Every choice we make.

SOUND OF POLICE RADIO

POLICEWOMAN
Sir?

DAVIS
We all make choices.

POLICEWOMAN
Sir?

DAVIS
He made his choice.

POLICEWOMAN
Sir, you're going to have to come
down to the station with me. Is there
anyone I can contact for you? To meet
you at the station?

DAVIS
What do you mean?

POLICEWOMAN
A relative?

DAVIS
No.

POLICEWOMAN
Then a friend perhaps?

DAVIS
No.

POLICEWOMAN

No one?

DAVIS

No one.

—END—

Acknowledgements

Adrian Chamberlain and Darwin Sauer for their careful reading and helpful suggestions; Devin Clarke for his thoughts on the prologue; José Millán for his support; Joan Young, Lauren Norman and Julia Norman for their encouragement and advice; the Normans; the Youngs; and Chris Needham at Now Or Never.